About the Author

Mary Davies has had a long and varied career, starting as an art teacher. After the Second World War she abandoned teaching, to study art history at the Courtauld Institute. Four years as research assistant to Nikolaus Pevsner on his 'Buildings of England' series was followed by twenty years as a professional civil servant, being a senior investigator of historic buildings. Retirement brought changes – the learning of Esperanto, the discovery of a gift for healing, and a career as a regression and past life therapist. Born in Hull in 1918, she lived for sixty years in Morecambe Bay through marriage and widowhood. She now lives on the Isle of Arran where, in her eighties, she has discovered the joys of writing.

By the same author

Spiritual Autobiography
The Journey: An Autobiography
Spanning Two Thousand Years

Arran Novels
Quiet Waters
Shifting Sands

THE RESTLESS TIDE

Mary Davies

ARDGOWAN HOUSE PUBLISHING

First published in 2004 by Ardgowan House Publishing,
Ardgowan House, Shore Road, Brodick, Isle of Arran KA27 8AJ

2004 Mary Davies

ISBN 0 9536398 3 5

All rights reserved. No part of this publication may be reproduced,
stored in a retrieval system, or transmitted, in any way or form, or by
any means, electronic, mechanical, photocopying, or otherwise,
without the prior permission of the publisher and copyright holder.

British Library Cataloguing in Publication Data.
A catalogue record for this book is available from the British Library.

*All characters in this publication are fictitious
and any resemblance to real persons, living or dead,
is purely accidental.*

Cover illustration:
The Cornish Coast
(Dick Richardson)

Design and typesetting:
Country Books, Little Longstone, Derbyshire DE45 1NN

Printed and bound by:
Antony Rowe Ltd, Chippenham, Wiltshire SN14 6LH

To Ravey

1

It all seemed so strange. So much had happened in so short a time. No wonder I didn't know whether I was on my head or my heels. To think that I could uproot myself after so long! Me, the demure wallflower, who couldn't say boo to a goose. Well, I'd done it, and who cares about mixing metaphors! I'd left my home, left my husband of nearly forty years. And here I was, transported as if by magic to a fairy-tale island. I couldn't help smiling to myself, as if the cat had got the cream. But if only the move hadn't been so sudden I could have got more used to the new situation. Goodness knows, the decision to leave George had been simmering for long enough before coming to the boil. Everybody who knew me would say I've never been one to make hasty decisions, not about important things like marriage anyway. And I had needed time to summon up the courage. In fact it had meant transforming myself, my whole character. Or was it perhaps that I had had to discover myself? Such was the modern jargon. But it was true. I felt I really had discovered myself at last. Or at least I had made a beginning. I was no longer the 'daddy's girl' who had been passed on like a package to be George's slave. Perhaps it was the spirit of the age that had got into me at last. It wouldn't have happened without prodding, I realised. And by my own children too! For years I'd felt obliged to remonstrate at John's constant succession of girl-friends, but I had to admit that 'playing the field' was more likely to lead to a permanent and happy relationship in the end, when he had become more mature. And it was true. It had led to his long-term commitment to Iolanthe and a modern, free sort of relationship that seemed to be working happily. And as for Sandra, she had decided a year ago to leave an unsatisfactory marriage, preferring that the children should have no father rather than a bad one. My son and daughter were wise; they had learnt early in their lives to benefit from their experience. I, stupid Muriel, had needed the further push from my new friend Veronica. She had shown me what freedom could mean. Freedom in the abstract had its attractions if course, but I would never have taken the plunge, I'm sure, if I hadn't been made aware of an incentive. After all, what is freedom worth if you have no use for it?

Veronica had introduced me to a new world, a new interest, even perhaps a new career. Our visit together to the Burrell art gallery in Glasgow had opened my eyes and understanding, to the realisation that I, Muriel Munro, can aspire to be a painter. A heady thought. My stomach muscles tightened. Was I really ready for such a plunge into the unknown? How far could I cast off the guiding reins, the restricting chains, imposed by George? Did I have enough courage? Could I even find enough courage? Surely there was nothing to stop me. I was a free agent. I had nobody breathing down my neck. I was mistress of my own destiny. I was at last here in my newly acquired Beach Villa at Lochranza, the sole proud owner of the ground floor flat and garden. What a wonderful life I could enjoy! So much happiness could lie ahead, I felt sure.

I still had mixed moods when I doubted my own shadow, but the newer, more positive mood started at Christmas, when even George's presence couldn't dampen the joy of seeing Sandra's happiness with her new friend Berry and the prospect of a successful marriage to a caring, thoughtful man whom the children already adored. There was no need to worry about Sandra any more. She would be happy there in Pitlochry and would find a useful niche for herself in the hotel Berry owned. And now, the New Year was bringing new life and happiness to me in my turn. Again, I positively sizzled in anticipation of the new adventures ahead of me.

Resting my hands on the polished oak window ledge that was still bare of any ornaments I gazed at the view that had drawn me to buy the flat. The tide was high, filling the loch. There was little wind. Seaweed floated gently against the fringe of rough grasses that softened the edge of the narrow track along the shoreline. If there were a gale, I mused, I would be glad of the protection of the low wall that bordered the property. But today all was peaceful. Across the loch was a mirror image of the main part of the village, of similar white villas strung out along the shore like pearls on a necklace. Behind them rose high hills of green and brown, dotted with stunted trees, gorse and bracken. Where the hills tapered down to the right was the ferry slipway, where I had landed last night in the dark after the Christmas break in Pitlochry. Who would have thought that Sandra would find such a rich fiancé – and such a kind man! She deserved some happiness, poor girl, and the children needed a decent father.

I sighed with satisfaction, turning my eyes past the grey ruins of the castle on its spit of land to the left, and moved away from the window. There were things to be done. I mustn't daydream any longer. The sitting room, like the rest of the flat, had been offered for sale fully furnished, and I had welcomed that. The previous owner, Mrs Fletcher, had decided to emigrate to her daughter in South Africa and had been happy to leave with nothing but her personal possessions. As a result, I was spared the expense of moving my furniture from Heysham and wondering whether everything would fit comfortably. And even more important, it avoided the possible – even probable – quarrels with George over the equitable division of the furniture. Both of us were now starting afresh, on a more satisfactory footing.

My eyes scanned the room again. In spite of the furniture it had an empty feel to it. It was telling me it had been abandoned and needed the tender loving care of another human being. It was waiting for me to make it my own. Its general appearance was of a style I approved of, new and modern. A square room with a bay window facing south, and a simple tiled fireplace on the opposite wall, where a coal fire added to the general warmth supplied by the storage heater. A three-piece suite of soft cream leather. A glass-topped coffee table. A glass-fronted oak bookcase and a plant-stand completed the furnishings. The only thing obviously missing was a TV set but there was no urgency; I could buy one later, after I was fully settled in. The overall impression was pleasing and the restful colour scheme of dove grey carpet and apricot walls and curtains was not one I would want to change in a hurry.

But the room would be made my own, with my own personality. It would look so much better with a few of my personal things around – some family photographs and plants. I had still to unpack the boxes that stood around on the floor. The essentials – kitchen things, overnight things, I had already unpacked and used on my overnight stay en route to Pitlochry. If only I had had more time! It was crazy to move house one day and go away the next, on Christmas Eve too! But this New Year would soon see me settled in my new life. I was quite determined on that.

My thought turned to George. Was he also feeling strange and disoriented in his new home? I smiled as I remembered my son's forthright comments when we announced our decision to separate.

"You two are crazy! Quite mad! You've been together so long, like the Rock of Gibraltar. At a pinch I can understand you separating. You've always been a bully, you know, Dad, and I'm not surprised Mum's got fed up, though it's taken her forty years to do something about it. I knew you were both unhappy, of course, but I thought you were probably staying together out of habit, like lots of other couples. So you're separating – OK. But to separate and then move to go and live under the same roof? Mad, quite mad! Even if they are separate flats. How are you going to explain to your new neighbours – still married and sort of together but sort of separate and with different addresses? What are they, Flat A and Flat B?" And he shook his head, laughing at our idiocy.

But, mad or not, I was confident George would be happier on his own; both of us would be liberated from the strain of trying to reconcile incompatible personalities. It must be the right thing to do. And, in spite of their filial disrespect, both John and Sandra supported our decision. After all, in forty years people change. It wasn't surprising that our paths, parallel perhaps at the beginning, had now diverged.

And now, having moved house, the next task was to integrate with the local community. That, I said to myself, I would start to do immediately, before I lost courage. And it would need courage, to face strangers and introduce myself. But I needed to do some shopping and the village store-cum-post-office was waiting to be explored across the other side of the loch. Though the shop and the main part of the village was visible and not far for a crow to fly, it was too far to walk round the head of the loch, so I was glad I had my own trusty car to rely on. Although Arran is a small island, distances between settlements could be daunting for sixty-year-old legs.

The little shop was only distinguishable from the adjoining cottages by the red post office sign, the official notices and local announcements in the window and the glass panel of the door. The loud ping of the old-fashioned doorbell could have summoned an assistant from a hundred yards away. But there she was, waiting and smiling behind the counter that extended across the whole of one side of the little shop. There was nothing impressive about the shop. It was only about fifteen feet square; Asda or Safeways it was not, but my first impression was that it was so crammed with goods that I would be able to buy anything I wanted there. But for now I gave my attention to the woman who greeted me.

"Good morning. You brought the sunshine with you; I think the rain will hold off, don't you?"

Her smile was open and friendly, in a round dimpled face of high colour, as if she spent a good deal of her time out of doors. Her hands, too, were broad and stubby-fingered. She was obviously a practical woman, no nonsense and down to earth. I immediately felt at ease with her and agreed about the weather.

"I like this crisp, bright winter weather," I said. "But they say it rains a lot here. I don't think I mind that. It means everything stays green, doesn't it." We batted remarks about the weather back and forth until the woman got down to serious business.

"I haven't seen you here before," she said. "Are you here for the New Year holiday?"

This was it! I had to explain. I took a deep breath and summoned up all my courage. "No, I've just bought Beach Villa, over the way there. I moved in just before Christmas and then went away for the holiday. I just got back yesterday and am beginning to sort myself out."

"Well, well! I heard it had been sold, and Graham told me he'd seen cars there before Christmas and then they disappeared, so we wondered what was going on, didn't we, Graham?"

Graham, presumably her husband, had appeared in the doorway at the rear of the shop – a portly square figure with a shock of white hair. "Oh, aye, we wondered who was coming. Pleased to meet you."

I introduced myself. "I'm Mrs Munro – well, that is, er, perhaps – er – Muriel," I ventured.

"And I'm Gladys. I'm the postmistress here but we run the shop together, don't we, love?"

She seemed to need confirmation of all her statements, but I suspected it was more a habit of speech than a sign of insecurity. Or perhaps she wanted to boost Graham's self-esteem?

"I shall want my pension transferring here, of course. Can you do that for me?"

"Well, of course, and glad to help. But I wouldn't have thought you were sixty. She doesn't look it, does she, Graham?" Graham shook his head. "No, no, you certainly don't," she went on. "And what about your husband? Or are you alone?"

"Well . . yes . . no . . that is. . " I took a deep breath. It had to be said and there was no point in putting off the ordeal. "My husband and I are separated." There, it was out now! I'd said it! However embarrassing, I would have to get used to explaining my status, until people got used to it.

"Oh, sorry to hear that. But you'll soon make friends here, you know. Won't she, Graham?"

Graham's main function seemed to be a smiling nod at intervals, which sufficed to include him in the conversation.

"There's the Rural," Gladys went on. "That's a good way to get to know everybody. They're a friendly crowd. You'd enjoy it."

"Well, yes, thank you. But I was hoping to contact an art class, perhaps. Is there anything like that?"

"Oh, you're an artist! Another one!" Gladys laughed. "The island's full of artists and craftspeople. You'll soon feel at home here. But I haven't heard of a class, not with a teacher and that, you know. But a bunch of them meet here in the village hall and just paint together, I believe. If you go along on a Friday afternoon I'm sure they'll make you welcome."

"Hmmm, well, yes, but I was thinking more of painting out of doors. Though it's not very sensible in the winter. I'll think about it on Friday."

I turned away to inspect the shelves behind me. Piled from floor to ceiling the stock was astonishing. Colourful tins and packets of every kind of food from baked beans to pumpernickel, spaghetti to poppadums, rows of tinned soups and breakfast cereals in bewildering array. I wouldn't have to drive over the mountain pass to Brodick, the main village, for my everyday shopping, that was clear. Even a few household goods were on display – light bulbs, batteries, toilet rolls and aspirins were amongst the emergency supplies. I looked down my list and turned back to Gladys behind the counter.

"When does the fresh bread come in? And what about newspapers?"

"Bread and rolls are fresh every day, Mrs Munro . . er. . Muriel. They're all made just along the road in the bakery. Couldn't be fresher. The newspapers come in about midday in the winter. The ferry, you know." And she explained the timetable, how delivery of goods from the mainland depended on the ferry, which made fewer crossings in the winter. "And of course it depends on the weather too. Ardrossan on the other side is a difficult harbour in bad weather, so occasionally the ferry doesn't sail or it goes to Gourock instead. But it doesn't happen often; it's pretty good on the whole, isn't it, Graham?"

"Oh, yes." Graham actually opened his mouth and spoke. "And the mail comes in by fishing boat in the winter, so that's all right."

They both smiled with contentment as I assembled my purchases on the counter – bread, butter, local cheese, pasta, eggs (local and free range, I noticed) and a few tins of vegetables as a standby. An exploratory trip round the island would reveal sources of fresh organic vegetables, meat and fish, I felt sure. On my previous visit I had noticed two cheese factories and several farms that sold their produce. No doubt there would be a butcher somewhere; I would enjoy exploring and asking around. Everything was going to be all right. I smiled at Gladys as I counted out the money for my purchases and prepared to gather up my things and return home.

Gladys had other ideas. It wasn't often a new resident settled in the village and, as postmistress, she was expected to know everything that was going on.

"It's quiet this morning, until the papers come in. I'm just going to have a cup of tea. Why don't you join me? Graham always has the kettle on at this time, before the customers start coming. It's the best cup of the day. So let's go through to the back room and sit down." And she emerged from behind the counter, to reveal a plump figure in a brown woollen dress, with a white apron tied round her ample waist.

I hesitated. Such spontaneous friendliness was a bit staggering; I felt as if I were being swept off my feet and needed to catch my breath. But . . Oh, what the hell! I thought. They're being friendly and I want friends, don't I? Don't be such a wallflower, Muriel. So I upbraided myself for hesitating, smiled my thanks and followed Gladys into a small room whose single window was darkened by a steep hillside rising a few feet from the house and blocking any view of the sky. Looking more closely I realised that Graham, or perhaps Gladys, had attempted to make a garden there in steeply stepped terraces. But today it all looked dark and dismal; the low sun was behind the hill, casting shade over the loch-side village. The sunlight was confined to the open view at the front where, as an added bonus, it was reflected back from the waters of the loch.

"Take a wee seat," Gladys invited, as she handed me a cup of ultra-strong tea, ready sugared, in a blue Denby mug. It was not my normal tipple; I preferred china tea, weak, unsweetened and fragrant, but I composed my features to hide my distaste and took the first sip.

"Now, did you say you were in the lower flat?" Gladys pursued her interrogation. "I was in there once. Mrs Fletcher had it beautiful. Such a nice lady. And her husband, God rest his soul. You remember him, Graham – he always came to carry her heavy bags for her." Graham smiled and nodded, speechless. "I was surprised when she turned it into two flats – such a lovely house. But of course it was too big for her. After he died, I mean."

Gladys drank her tea with gusto and wiped her mouth on her apron. "There were two cars there again last night, weren't there, Graham?" Her eyes brightened in anticipation of fresh news. She prided herself in knowing all the latest. After all, she felt it was her duty, part of her commitment to the community. "Does it mean that the other flat is sold as well, Mrs . . Muriel? Is someone living there now?"

"Oh, yes, it's sold." I hesitated. It was going to be difficult to explain, but I would have to get it over with.

"Well, have you heard who it is? Are they from the mainland? Have you met them? Do you know their name?" She was persistent.

"Well, yes, of course. It's my husband."

A stunned silence followed this statement. There was a tangible atmosphere of incomprehension. The air in the room ceased to circulate while mental processes grappled to absorb and process this information. I waited. What could I say? I couldn't explain. Why should I explain anyway? People had to know sooner or later, and I would have to put up with whatever they thought of such an odd sort of arrangement. But I certainly wasn't going to go into details. I tried to avoid looking at Gladys and Graham, but knew that they were looking at one another with raised eyebrows. Their thoughts were obvious and didn't need to be expressed. I could imagine the gossiping tongues that would wag later on among the customers and villagers. Well, so be it! There was nothing I could do to prevent it.

"Our son's here, you see," I said brightly, lifting my eyes and staring boldly at Gladys, defying her to make any derogatory remark. "He's a teacher at the High School."

"Oh, yes." Gladys straightened and pulled herself together, and achieved a smile of relief. "I heard he's just moved as well. They say he's bought the cottage where our famous painter was born. Peggy Paine. You must have heard of her. It's not long since she died. She was very famous. I didn't know her myself but it was a big funeral, I believe. People came up from London and all over. And now you have to be a millionaire to afford one of her pictures."

"Well, I didn't know that, .er. .Gladys. John has never said anything about who had lived there before. Actually he only just moved a month or so ago." But the news had already reached Lochranza twenty miles away. The bush telegraph was obviously very efficient, I realised. It wouldn't be long before everybody on the island would know about me and George and our unconventional arrangement. And it was obvious that I would have to be careful in future about what I said about anybody. It was like living in a goldfish bowl. But why should I mind what people said or thought about me? I had nothing to hide. Life was certainly going to be different from living in a suburb, I realised

"Are there any of her paintings on the island – that I can look at, I mean?"

"Hmmm, well, I don't know." Gladys raised her eyebrows at Graham.

To my amazement Graham became quite animated. "Yes, you know, at the Hydro there, they have one – a whacking big one at the top of the stairs. You see it as you go in." He waved his arms vaguely as if pointing them to the picture in his mind. "It was when I went for massage for my back I noticed it. You can't miss it really." He dropped his voice and confided to me, "It's quite nice I suppose. They say it's very good. But I can't see what all the fuss is about, myself."

I smiled. Beauty was in the eye of the beholder after all. I would go and see it for myself, and perhaps it would give me a benchmark to measure my own work by, or even to inspire me.

2

January 20
I think it is important that I keep a journal. The events, particularly the recent and future events in my life should be recorded so that my grandchildren understand what my life is like at the beginning of the twenty-first century. Sandra's two children, Peter and Lucy, are still at Primary School and John has no children as yet, but by the time they are adults the world will have changed a great deal and my life will be part of their history. Or OUR life, I should say, Muriel's and mine, though I can only record my own viewpoint here.

We had a conventional marriage. We met at college. Muriel was a sweet biddable girl, not pretty but appealing, needing the protection I was willing to offer her. We married young, perhaps too young. I pursued my career as an accountant in Morecambe while Muriel cared for our home in Heysham and, in due course, our two children. Accountancy was not the career I would have chosen. As a schoolboy I always dreamed of being a historian and even at college my leisure reading was always of historical novels and biographies of past heroes. But I could not withstand family pressure. If my mother had still been alive it might have been different, but my father was a very forceful character. He determined that I would enter the family firm and continue the tradition for the third generation. He dominated the firm and my own life until he was in his eighties, and died only months before my own retirement last year. I realise now that I should have rebelled when I was still young, and it has been painful for me to admit that my life has been unhappy. Unfortunately Muriel was unable or unwilling to understand what I was suffering at the office, where my father never allowed me to have the authority that was due to me. I should have been able to depend on the support of my wife, but Muriel failed in this respect, being wrapped up in her own thoughts. She has stated recently that she had been unhappy for most of our married life, but she never complained. I still don't know why she should complain. I was a good husband. I provided her with everything needful – a good home in a respectable neighbourhood in the best part of Morecambe, and she always had sufficient housekeeping money, though we were not extravagant. In spite of my doing my best for the family, Muriel became more and more discontented after the children left home, and recently she has become increasingly petulant and defiant.

My impending retirement was the catalyst that made us consider our future very seriously; it also forced us in the end to discuss it together. Particularly during the last year there was an increasing distance between us, with constant bickering and lack of any sympathetic understanding, to the extent that we agreed on separate bedrooms. We both at last had to admit we had grown apart over the years; in fact our children were the only factor we had in common, and their increasing maturity and independence left Muriel and me as isolated individuals trying to live in a marriage that had become a travesty. It could have led to acrimonious, long-drawn-out and expensive divorce proceedings, but I am thankful to record that we discussed the problem calmly, and after long and careful consideration we decided that separation was more advisable than divorce as neither had any extra-marital attachment. As a matter of record, our house in the Heysham suburb was sold and the assets divided equally between us; with the help of my father's bequests to us both we each had the means to buy our own home. By a strange coincidence and perhaps unfortunately we each, independently, chose the same property here on the Isle of Arran. This might have caused additional tension but it was already divided into two flats, so we agreed to buy a flat each and live experimentally under the same roof but in separate households. As Muriel wished to care for the garden I allowed her to take possession of the ground floor.

We removed here just before Christmas and left again immediately to spend the festive season with Sandra in her new home in Pitlochry. Following her divorce from a worthless philanderer she had taken up with a wealthy hotel owner, and announced her engagement to him at Christmas. While I deplored her previous marriage I fully endorse the wisdom of this one. She will be well provided for, the children are happy in Pitlochry and the future of the family seems assured. I have no need to worry about her any longer. Now I must think of myself. I am attempting to settle into my new surroundings and new way of life. It is as if the mould is broken. The pattern of my days – hours at the office, evenings at home, weekends catching up with repairs, bills, and household responsibilities – is not valid here. It will take time to adapt and to establish a new routine, where every minute is of my own choosing. I look forward to being able to pursue my own interests without being dragged down by an incompatible partner, but I have to admit it is not easy. I was unprepared for the day-to-day running of a home and had not realised how time-consuming it can be. Fortunately I have always had definite ideas about how things should be run and early in our marriage I instructed Muriel in an orderly routine and correct diet. I am benefiting now from the cookery course I undertook last year and look forward to experimenting with new recipes. As for the household tasks, I have made a list and a timetable, so that all the tasks are achieved in an orderly fashion.

The flat is not large – two bedrooms and a sitting room. As I have now registered to work for an Open University degree in history I shall use the spare bedroom as my study. I have already installed the TV, video, radio, computer and printer there but I need to build some shelves to hold all my books, both the ones which are still unpacked and the ones I shall acquire as needed. I shall also need to buy another TV for the sitting room, for my leisure hours. Otherwise the flat is fully furnished and newly decorated, though in a rather feminine taste. I shall change things gradually, but my main priority is to establish a harmonious setting for my work and a routine for my daily life.

First, I needed to acquaint myself with my surroundings and the places that would be useful to me. Having called at the village shop for my pension and my copy of the Guardian I paid my first visit to the public library in Brodick, some fifteen miles away over the mountain road. I had not yet got a list of required readings but I wanted to gain some insight into the history of Arran, as background to my more serious study.

It was a wet morning with poor visibility, and there was practically no traffic on the way. It was a very dreary road and there was nothing of interest to be seen. I believe this 'Scotch mist' is typical of winter weather here; it is not pleasant but I am thankful for the absence of snow and ice. No doubt this is due to the presence of the Gulf Stream; it had the same effect in Morecambe Bay, making for mild but wet winters. I was glad to descend into Brodick and drive at sea level again. The library seemed to be an extension of the village hall; it was not at all pretentious and I feared it was going to be a disappointment. However, the light and relatively spacious interior redeemed it, I thought, with its inviting chairs for browsers and a separate reference room.

"Good morning!" The middle-aged librarian greeted me. I had expected to walk in anonymously to browse among the shelves, and she must have noticed my surprise as she went on, "We don't see many strangers in January, so I assume you're a new resident on the island. Am I right? But in any case, of course, you're welcome to use the library whether you're resident or not. My name is Rosemary and I'm here to help. If you'd just fill in this form with your name and address, then you can borrow six books at a time."

She had a pleasing manner and I approved of the impression she gave of neatness and efficiency. She was a large woman, not fat but big-boned, grey-haired and with glasses. I don't normally notice details of people's appearance, men or women, but she struck me as being so different from Muriel. She had an air of self-assurance that Muriel lacked.

She interrupted my thoughts as I handed her the completed form. "So you live on the Newton shore," she said as she transferred my application to her computer. "I live along there too, at Deerholme. You will pass it as you drive around the loch to the village."

So we're neighbours, but it seems that everybody here is neighbourly. I had the same sort of response in the village post office. It is gratifying to be welcomed like this, though I expect the other side of the coin is an excess of gossip and the impossibility of keeping one's actions away from public view. With this in mind I explained, "I shall be using the library quite a lot as I'm hoping to start work on an Open University course on history."

Her eyes actually lit up and she smiled. "Oh, I'm pleased to hear that. We're always glad to see a scholar. I'm interested in history and biography myself. If you'd like some background reading on Arran's history I can recommend Robert McLelland's 'Isle of Arran' and John Prebble's 'Highland Clearances'. They'll help you to get a flavour of the island's history. You can order any other books that your course recommends – any we haven't got, that is – and we'll do our best to get them for you."

She was a handsome woman and her reaction pleased me. It was a good beginning, I felt, to my attempt to integrate into island life. The library and bookshop were obviously going to be my most frequent haunts. I browsed for a while along the shelves of non-fiction works, noting the variety of titles available, and the computers for public use. Then, well-satisfied with my morning's visit to Brodick I turned the Volvo towards home again, with copies of the books Rosemary had recommended carefully wrapped in a plastic bag to protect them from the rain. It was no longer a damp mist; the wind had risen, clouds had massed from the west and were now throwing horizontal rain across the mountains' flanks. It would be a suitable afternoon for reading, with the further anticipation of preparing my own dinner of local venison. With these thoughts I ventured up the twisting hills, my headlights achieving little against the rain thrusting against the windscreen. I was thankful that the road was empty of traffic, as there was no protection from the open moorland and often a steep drop at either side; there would be no need for any overtaking. My snail's progress round the hairpin bends became ever slower, as the Volvo seemed to be dragged inexorably over to the left, to tip me over into the frothing burn at the foot of the glen. Was it the camber of the road, I wondered? The road was clearly in bad condition, with crumbling verges. But the sensation of a giant hand pulling me into the void wouldn't leave me. I had to stop. I got out to investigate. With my back hunched to the rain I explored around. The front nearside tyre was flat. My heart sank. I felt as flat as the tyre. To be stranded, helpless, in such a godforsaken spot! I had no jack, so there was no point in trying to change the wheel. I would have to stay there until someone came along to convey a message to a garage. I scanned the landscape, as far as it was possible to see, but there was nothing but grey sheets of rain. "Damn and blast!" I said to myself, though I am not given to swearing. But I was furious with myself, impotent, feeling the rain dribbling down my neck, dripping off my gabardine and wetting my knees. I thumped my fists on the car roof in frustration, "Fool, fool! No jack, no warning cones, no mobile telephone! How could I be such an idiot?"

"Got a problem, then?" A welcome voice came from a craggy white head at an open window of a Landrover. The man had driven up behind me, and I had been so involved in cursing myself that I hadn't heard him. I turned to look at him, raised my arms in a helpless gesture and he drew up a few yards beyond me, heaved his bulky body out of the car and came

over to me. "Hah, so it's a puncture!"

"I'm afraid I can't do anything about it. I can't change the wheel because I haven't got a jack and I haven't got a mobile phone to call a garage. Even it I had I wouldn't know the number. I'm new here," I explained.

"I tell you what. There's no point in you hanging about waiting. The garage may be busy. We'll leave your car here. It'll be all right. Just lock it. Then I'll run you down to Lochranza and you can phone from there. That OK?"

My Good Samaritan bundled me into his Landrover, an old and battered model but practical for Arran's rough roads and many cart tracks. Though by now very wet I was not afraid of damaging his well worn upholstery, and I settled in to the unaccustomed luxury of riding high above the landscape. It was warm and comfortable inside his car, and gradually my agitation and annoyance abated. I began to realise I was lucky to have been rescued. There was no one else on the road and it would have been unpleasant to be stranded alone with a useless car in the middle of nowhere. I expressed these sentiments to the man at my side, who had his eyes firmly fixed on the road. He grunted a dismissal of my thanks, and then became quite chatty as we began to descend towards the west coast. "I'm Graham, by the way. My wife runs the post office. Everybody knows us. You've probably met her already."

I had indeed. A village gossip. She had surely told him all about my arrival and probably he knew all about Muriel and me. But to avoid any possible false rumours I gave him the minimum facts about myself. It was wise to stop any gossip at the source. I didn't know what Muriel might have said but I told him we were not divorced but had simply decided to live apart. He was easy to talk to and accepted my remarks without comment. His eyes kept firmly on the road, his face expressionless, he in turn seemed eager to talk to me. Maybe his wife – he called her Gladys – is such a chatterbox he never gets a word in edgeways at home.

I found him knowledgeable about the island and interesting to listen to. He had lived here most of his life and was obviously intelligent. "I was born here, on a farm up by the Cock, but had to go away to school, so I can't say I've been here all my life. But long enough. My wife is local too, from Thundergay along the coast there. She likes meeting people and enjoys being postmistress. Her income from the shop and my savings keep us going until I get my pension. And that won't be long now." His voice purred with either satisfaction or anticipation, I couldn't decide which. "I enjoy helping at the Museum on my free day." He turned his head briefly to look at me. "If you're studying Scottish history I expect you've already been to our little Heritage Museum. It's been highly praised by professionals, you know, though it's run by volunteers. But we're all very keen and some of the committee have become experts in a particular field. A bunch of us volunteers meets there every Wednesday to work at whatever is needed. There's always something to be done – repairs to the building or the artefacts, cleaning, cataloguing, what have you. And then of course now we've got the computer there's work to be done on that, researching Arran family trees etc. Do you think you might be interested to join us? There's no pressure – we just do what we're capable of. A great bunch, good to work with. Perhaps you'd let me know if you'd like me to introduce you one Wednesday?"

He again turned and looked at me with raised bristly eyebrows. I said I'd think about it. It certainly sounded interesting. I had visited the museum on my previous short visit to Arran and had been impressed by it. A more intimate acquaintance would be worthwhile and I would meet people of similar interests. It could also be helpful in my studies. I would certainly think about it and see if I could arrange my timetable to fit.

"When I've settled in and got my activities planned in some sort of order I'll see how I'm fixed," I said. We left it at that, with the understanding that I would contact him if I decided to go, and I would pick him up as the post office was on my way. But, although I was reluctant to make rash promises I felt sure I could make time to be free on Wednesdays.

One of the Arran McMillans had started the idea and had persuaded the Tourist Board to form a committee, which eventually created a non-profit Trust in 1976. The Trust then started acquiring properties in the old part of Brodick, at the foot of the Castle. One by one they bought a cluster of old buildings of whitewashed stone, the nucleus of which had been a school in the eighteenth century, with schoolmaster's house. Incredibly the school had taught navigation as well as the normal curriculum. The smiddy, barn and stables and a couple of small cottages comprise the present museum, round a cobbled courtyard and, of course, under a spreading chestnut tree. Now, as a tourist attraction, it looks homely and picturesque where once it was severely practical.

I was remembering these details from my previous visit as we began to drop down the hill into Lochranza. It was still not possible to see far into the distance. I peered out to the right past Graham's head but even the Glen Farm was not visible down in the hollow. Graham was a good driver and I would have been content to be driven in silence, but unfortunately he started to question me about Muriel. Not blatantly; it was done quite delicately but I knew what he was about. He assumed a casual tone and merely asked if I thought my wife would be interested in the museum, as he knew the women volunteers were also very keen and enjoyed working there as much as the men did. He studiously kept his face looking at the road as he questioned me, but I felt his tension. He was curious about our unusual marriage and wanted to know more details – so that he could pass them on to his wife, no doubt. But I soon knocked his idea on the head; I explained that Muriel's interests had been confined to flower arranging and, more recently, painting. She wouldn't be helping at the museum, I told him. I didn't mention her part-time volunteer job at the Heritage Centre in Heysham. It was part of her past, anyway, and it wouldn't do for us both to be working in the same place. We had both come here to start a new life with new interests, and we shouldn't expect to continue as we had done at Heysham. My history studies are my new life. What Muriel chooses to do on Arran is her own affair. She complained that I dominated her so I've decided to stay aloof from her life. I am not responsible for what she does in the future. I have other things to think about. The car particularly at that moment.

Mr Moody – Graham – drove me to my door and handed my package of books out to me on my doorstep. His hands were large and strong, I noticed, like a building worker's hands. Before his Landrover had disappeared round the bend to the opposite shore I was on the phone to the garage, explaining the problem. A pleasant Highland accent assured me that they would attend to my Volvo, repair the puncture and deliver it to me tomorrow. They would also supply me with necessary tools in case a similar accident happens in the future; it would give me some peace of mind. Of course all this will have to be paid for, but I can't complain about the service.

3

"You didn't tell me this house is where a famous painter was born, John," I protested. It was my first visit to his new home in Lamlash and I looked around with some curiosity. The titbit of news I had picked up about it added a touch of glamour and it intrigued me. I wanted to know more about this painter.

"Hmm, well, I didn't tell you because I didn't know myself until last week. The English teacher mentioned it; she seemed to think it was common knowledge, but the estate agent never said anything when we came to look around and said we were interested in buying. The truth is Peggy Paine wasn't born here, actually. It was her mother's place really, but I suppose she started painting here before she acquired her own studio."

We were standing in the little sitting room as we spoke. I had refused my son's invitation to sit down, as I wanted a conducted tour of the cottage first. It was small and compact, one of a row, with a public green in front instead of a private garden. And beyond the green was the road and the stone pier piled with ropes, creels and fishing gear, though empty of people. Otherwise there was only the sea, with Holy Island floating in the wide bay. An ideal position, I agreed, and congratulated John for finding it. The view was the main attraction of the little house and I was tempted to linger at the sash window.

John had joined me there, his arm thrown casually across my shoulder. "It's irresistible to a painter I suppose; I'm no painter but I like to watch the clouds come and go over Holy Island. Some days the clouds are so low it's not even visible. But come and let me show you round my baronial castle."

So I turned my attention once more to the room, which I noticed was furnished with John's old black leather armchairs, relics of his student days. He had bought them second hand in the first place and though old and sagging they were comfortable enough for him, he said. Iolanthe's hand was evident in the bright cushions, the pale primrose walls and the marigold-patterned curtains. A very pleasant room, I thought, and said so "And where did this painter, Peggy Paine, do her work, then? Do you know?" I asked as we proceeded to the kitchen at the back. John switched on the kettle.

"The studio where she lived and did most of her work – all the famous work, that is – is a former farm-house and barn out towards Whiting Bay. If there are ever going to be blue plaques scattered about, there'll be one there. Not here." John grinned as he took my arm and led me up the steep and narrow stairs to show me the two small bedrooms above. "There's nothing much to see," he explained. "The place is small but adequate for the two of us and we don't want to clutter it up with too much furniture. We've got the basics for ourselves, and the spare room is just for storage at the moment."

He flung open the brown-painted door at the back of the house and revealed a small room, scarcely big enough ever to have held a double bed, I thought, now filled with boxes and piles of books spilling out over the dusty floorboards. There was no furniture and a grimy window looked out on to a hillside of bare trees and dead bracken. "We just dumped everything here. We'll sort it all out in time and clean it up, perhaps make it our study. But there was so much to do all at once, moving from Ayr in the autumn, starting the new term in the new school and then going off almost immediately to Pitlochry. We didn't know whether we were on our head or our heels. But it'll get sorted, you'll see."

John smiled his confidence and propelled me to the front bedroom, which, in contrast, shone clean and bright. It was simply furnished, as befitted a young couple of modest means, I thought. I approved of the double bed, chest of drawers and wardrobe all of pine. Everything was practical, simple and in good taste. An enlarged and framed family photograph hung on the wall, I noticed, and a framed print of Iolanthe in a revealing evening gown hung behind the bed. John saw me notice it. "I wanted that where I could see it but she banished it back there," he smiled ruefully. I said nothing but thought she was wise. There's a lot more to Iolanthe than physical beauty. She was no narcissus. I suspected she had more intelligence.

"She is obviously very fond of yellow," I remarked, as I drew aside the curtains of printed yellow roses, which matched the duvet cover. "I like the colour scheme. It brightens the whole room, though I think you face south, too. And to wake up to see the sea, like me! Wonderful, isn't it!" And we smiled at one another. The lines are fallen to us in pleasant places, I probably misquoted to myself.

"So, I expect the kettle's boiled. We'll have a cup of tea." John interrupted my thoughts and led me downstairs to the kitchen again. Together we collected our mugs, added milk and sugar and took the drinks back to the sitting room, where we relaxed into the old black chairs. John's dark eyes twinkled as he stretched out his long legs across the front of the log fire, a picture of easy contentment. I smiled fondly as I savoured the Typhoo tea (weakened to my taste) in the thick mug decorated with a cartoon of Pooh, which Sandra had given him as a joke many years ago.

"I like your new home, John. And I'm not surprised that you do. Perhaps it's all the better for not being modern; it's probably well built and it's adequate for the two of you. I think you've been lucky to find it. And you won't miss having a garden, having all this green space in front." I moved from my seat by the fire, avoiding John's feet, and turned towards the tiny four-light sash window again. "And you couldn't have a better view, of course. Just look at that light on Holy Island across there, and the little ferryboat bobbing up and down by the pier. You know, it's only about ten miles as the crow flies between your home and mine, but it's incredible how the opposite sides of Arran are so different – it's all so interesting. As I drove round I noticed how every mile brought something different. One could never be bored." I turned my head apologetically. "I feel I'm probably gushing. All this beauty is new to me; it's no wonder I'm enthusiastic. I need to start painting, to work off some of this enthusiasm." I laughed and I'm afraid I felt myself blushing. It wasn't like me to go over-the-top like this. "I can understand that a girl brought up here, as they say Peggy Paine was, could hardly help being inspired to paint. I must find out more about her and study her pictures. And while we're on the subject, John, you can perhaps tell me where I can get some painting lessons."

I turned back and sat down again in front of John. "You have contacts through the school. You've been here a little longer than I have and you must have got to know a few people. I told you I joined a class in Morecambe just a few months ago, before I decided to move to Arran; I learnt a lot there and enjoyed it, so now I want to go on and learn more." I hesitated, pursing my lips. John's eyes swivelled to my face and he raised his eyebrows. "You look as if you don't believe me, John. I suppose you think it isn't like your old moth-eaten waif of a mother to branch out on her own and do something different. And it isn't. I want to be different, John, not just a tame housewife any more. I'm quite determined, but scared at the same time. It's hard to change one's spots. I'm terrified of meeting new people and launching myself in public and I know I shall be all of a dither to start with but I must do it. You do understand, don't you, John? I want you to understand."

"Oh, Mum, bless you. Of course." John hoisted his legs up and sat upright, leaning forward to pat my knees. "I think you're great. For a long time I've wanted you to break free from Dad. You know that. He was always too strong for you, too powerful, too much of a bully. You had your chance and should have rebelled years ago when Sandra and I got away, but better late than never." He smiled. "You'll be happier. And I expect he's happier too, doing his own thing at last. He always hated the office and his horrible old father. He told me he would enjoy his OU work. Last time I saw him he was expecting to hear from them about his course. Iolanthe got him on to that, didn't she? She's a great one for education, making up for lack of schooling I suppose. She's really thrown herself into this writing degree course. Goodness knows where it will lead. I can't see her getting a job as a writer, not on Arran. But I do support her. I'm a modern man, you see!"

I laughed and shared his light-hearted optimism.

Thank heaven my precious son had settled down at last!

"I'll find out about painting classes at the High School, Mum. They have various evening classes on offer – languages, computers and such like, and there may be one on painting. I'll enquire tomorrow and let you know. Then you can pluck up courage and just go, Mum. Nobody will bite you. You'll see!"

It was as if our roles had been reversed. He's counselling me, I thought. But I didn't mind. I deserved it and even welcomed it. I realised I needed help. And I certainly needed support. Iolanthe had taught me to think more about my appearance, to be more adventurous and less dowdy. And Veronica had opened my eyes that day in Glasgow. I would never forget that visit to the Burrell collection, those works of art of all cultures and all periods. And the Boudin paintings, which had been the catalyst of my own ambition. That day, important as it was for my artistic awakening, was even more important for me as a human being. I had at last begun to question what I was doing with my life, where was I going, what was the purpose – such fundamental questions I should have asked and answered years ago.

"So where is Iolanthe? I was hoping to see her. I expected you'd both be at home after school hours."

"Actually, I didn't hurry home today. I did my marking in the classroom after the kids had gone, so I'd just got in when you arrived. Iolanthe has a date with an aromatherapist on Thursdays at the Hydro and she often goes for a swim as well. Thursday's her day off, she says. She likes to have a session in the gym sometimes, too. A great girl for keeping herself in trim." He stood up and stretched his arms above his head, yawning. "And I forgot to post some letters on the way home, so I'd better go now if I'm to catch the late collection. I'll be back in a tick, so don't run away."

I looked up at my son. He was so like his father in looks – a slim athletic figure (though neither took any sort of physical exercise or indulged in sporting activities), taller than average, towering over me. And both my men had the dark brooding looks, heavy black eyebrows over dark eyes and, their most distinguishing feature, their black crinkly hair. Surprisingly, George's hair had not receded with age but had merely acquired speckles of grey among the black. I told him it looked distinguished, but George hated his hair, which no amount of fussing with cream would straighten. To his profound mortification his attempts at tracing his family tree had uncovered the existence of a black ancestor. Poor George! He had been so ashamed, as if it was his fault, for heaven's sake! and he couldn't bear anyone to know. Of course no one else was interested in his ancestors and he shouldn't be such a racist anyway. It had shattered his dreams and perhaps it had taught him to be more open-minded. One could only hope so. Thankfully, John rejected his father's racism; he was indifferent to his ancestors and felt no shame. His nature was more like my own family – my gentle mother and hard-working father.

I smiled at him with affection. "And while you're doing that, I'll make myself at home in the kitchen and wash up for you."

"Good. You do that, Mum. You'll soon find where everything goes. It's small enough. I shan't be long."

The kitchen was indeed small. I stood in the middle of the quarry-tiled floor and revolved slowly. The cooker, fridge, washing machine and worktops were all at arm's length against the four walls. It was like being a battery hen. But really, when I came to think of it, why should a kitchen be large? If one only stayed there long enough to prepare a meal, and if most of those meals were cooked in a microwave anyway this sized kitchen was more than adequate. And it was at least cheerful. The butter muslin curtains at the little window above the sink were rainbow-hued and the worktops were primrose yellow, so that the whole effect was sunny although the kitchen faced north. Iolanthe obviously had taste; although I had met the girl I had no idea what sort of domestic skills she had. I doubted whether Iolanthe could cook. She had left school at sixteen to become a fashion model; surrounded by glossy superficiality, she had married in haste and divorced at twenty. From childhood she had been adored and flattered, courted for her beauty and elegance. One wouldn't expect such a beautiful girl earning a living by showing off beautiful clothes to be too concerned about cooking for a hungry man. I hoped John wasn't suffering from deprivation. I was sure he was very much in love and so far looked fit and healthy. I sighed as I dried the mugs. It would be nice if they married. I really liked the girl and I knew John wanted to marry her but Iolanthe was hesitant for some reason. I wondered why? Perhaps she preferred the modern way of live-in partnership, but John was old-fashioned like his mother. Or like his mother used to be, I corrected myself. I had changed, so why shouldn't John and Iolanthe change too?

I shrugged off my introspection and got on with preparing a cup of tea for Iolanthe. There was the kettle standing waiting – a new stainless steel one, gleaming in the light filtering through the curtains over the small sink, with its little pot of snowdrops on the window ledge. Having switched it on I looked around for a tray. I guessed that Iolanthe would want to have her tea elegantly set out in delicate cups, not in vulgar mugs and found, as I had expected, a sunburst-patterned tray propped behind the microwave. The china was easy to find, in the wall cupboard to the right of the sink. A plain white service of fine porcelain, I took out three cups and saucers, hesitated, and then added a plate. Perhaps there were some biscuits somewhere. And paper napkins of course. It wouldn't do for Iolanthe to be ashamed of her sort-of mother-in-law.

4

Nobody warned me it was like this. A swimming pool and a couple of therapy rooms – that's all I expected. Something modern and functional like municipal baths, not this. I stopped the car, to readjust my thoughts and take it all in. I was on a long winding drive through a park of mature trees. The waxy cups of a huge magnolia gleamed out of the shadow cast by a copper beech and I thought I saw a rhododendron in bloom away to the left, half veiled by massive oaks. Surely rhododendrons don't flower so early? I wondered to what extent this park was open to the public. Would I be allowed to come and make studies of these trees, or even set up my easel and paint here? I unwound the car window and sniffed the dark earth and subtle aromas of new growth. Mmm! A beautiful spot! I sent up a little prayer of thanks to whoever planted these trees long ago, and started the car again, wondering what lay ahead. I was happy that day. I'd settled into my flat and made it comfortably my own with my personal treasures and a pot of white clematis on the window ledge of the living room. I'd joined the Rural and begun to respond to their overtures of friendship. I was a butterfly struggling to escape its chrysalis, but still half believing that the chrysalis was the safer place to be. I gave myself a shake. Don't think like that, Muriel. I told myself. Be positive. You're going to see this Peggy Paine picture. You were invited. It's a building open to the public and you've every right to be there. Nobody is going to throw you out or be rude to you. You're just as good as anybody else. I turned my thoughts resolutely back to the swimming pool, which reminded me fleetingly of Iolanthe and how relieved I was that she was such a good partner for John. I would have no worries over those two, I felt sure. Bringing my mind back to my present purpose I continued along the rising curves of the long drive. It was difficult to imagine a swimming pool in the middle of all this vegetation and I hoped the building, when I eventually reached it, would not be an anticlimax. An occasional glimpse of red stonework through the veil of green tantalised me as the drive twisted still further up the gentle rise. But at last the building revealed itself in all its glory. I was staggered. So this is where Iolanthe comes to swim, and where Graham comes with his backache? But this is a mansion, almost a castle, I gasped. Sandstone walls reared up before me, corner turrets, gables, arrow slits, traceried windows – a fairy tale concoction of elements that some Victorian architect had put together with humour and enjoyment, I decided.

I felt very grand as I swept up to the front area, where I could imagine horse-drawn carriages delivering ladies in silks and furs to county balls. But realistically I parked my little Golf inconspicuously in a corner under a large elm and turned to face the entrance. It was a bit intimidating, now that I looked at it closely. The red sandstone, obviously soft and now eroded in places, had tempted a sculptor into an exuberance of carving, though it was difficult to make out exactly what the carvings represented. To crown the entrance he had carved the family crest, so that nobody could mistake whose home this was and how proud they were that they could afford it. And today it was a Hydro, a commercial enterprise of complementary therapies. I wondered what the original owners would have thought of the general public being so freely admitted into their hallowed premises. The exterior at least made me feel their displeasure, as if they were muttering in their graves about desecration. But I shook off my old timidity. "Muriel," I said to myself, "Pull yourself together. You're a free woman. You're sixty years old and must have confidence. You've started a new life. You have no worries. The children are doing well and George is happy to be free. At least I hope he is. I hope he's settling in on his own. He's never been used to look after himself. Those cookery classes last year got him interested in making his own meals, but I wonder how he'll cope with cleaning and all the other household chores?"

But I shook away all my worry and doubts and stepped through the entrance into the large reception area and halted to get my bearings. Graham Moody said there was a Peggy Paine picture on the staircase, and I could see the curve of a staircase beginning in the middle of the ground floor area. Really, this part seemed more like a vast sitting room. It was thickly carpeted and dotted with sofas and easy chairs, tempting one to relax and leaf through the glossy magazines on the dark wood coffee tables. But to confirm that it was actually a reception area, I noticed there was a small desk in a corner to the right, behind me. I supposed I should announce my presence there and ask about the painting, but there was nobody behind the desk. I couldn't see any bell to ring and I stood there, hesitating and wondering what to do but fascinated by the colourful fish drifting across the computer screen on the end of the desk.

"Hello. Can I help you?" A smiling voice behind me made me jump.

"Oh, well, yes, I suppose. That is, I'm not here for therapy, I'm afraid. I'm sorry to be a nuisance, but I just wanted to look at a Peggy Paine painting. I hope you don't mind. I was told there was one here and I was interested." I began to turn to the woman with the warm voice, ready with more apologies, but at the same moment a pretty blonde in a black tailored suit appeared from behind the desk and smiled her willingness to be of service. I hesitated between the two women, but decided that the one to whom I had replied was the senior of the two. She was a commanding figure, standing at the foot of the stairs with one hand on the carved newel. She reminded me of an old-style actress, posed on a staircase, dominating the assembled company by her beauty and magnetic presence. She was taller than me – most people are taller than me – and was slim and straight in spite of being older, probably in her seventies. Her green eyes shone with intelligence in a wrinkled face liberally freckled. Her hair of pale ginger flecked with white must once have been spectacularly auburn. I liked what I saw. She had an air of dependability and compassion, as if one could trust her to be a loyal friend and confidante. I don't know why I felt like this on such a brief acquaintance, but so it was. Even her clothes gave one confidence. A casual but expensively simple green trouser suit with an amethyst brooch at the throat of a white silk blouse made her whole appearance impressive but appealing; she obviously had authority but without any show of superiority. At the mention of Peggy Paine her whole face lit up and I relaxed. I need not have been so scared about coming here after all.

"There are two in fact," she said, coming towards

me and nodding dismissal at the receptionist. "And you're very welcome to come and look. This one . . ." Turning, she beckoned me towards the foot of the staircase. . . ."is the last painting she did. She was going blind, you know. Or perhaps you didn't know. But she had to give up painting. It was a great tragedy, but fortunately it didn't happen until she was nearly seventy. She already had a lifetime of achievement, of wonderful work."

"I'm afraid I hadn't heard of her until I came to Arran. You see, I've just started to paint. I'm very much an amateur but I'm very keen to learn. I got interested when I went to the Burrell in Glasgow and saw the Boudin paintings there. I would love to paint like that." I babbled as I followed her. "It's the light and the air that fascinate me, the weather and cloud and . . .OH!"

I stopped dead, my mouth still open in mid-sentence. There, at the top of the stairs, was a painting. One could say it was no more and no less than a painting, simply some coloured oil paints disposed on a piece of canvas but it hit me in the solar plexus and brought tears to my eyes. I gasped and hung on to the newel post as I stared. Strange, really, if you come to think about it. If I had to describe it there was actually nothing remarkable about it. A large oil painting of a cloudy sky, a bit of beach with some rocks and a pool. But the power! No wonder I was silent before it. What could I say? To my relief the older woman also said nothing. I couldn't have offered any polite idiocies just then but I felt her eyes on me. I also felt a sort of sympathy emanating from her, as if she shared and understood what was happening to me.

So there we stood like human newel posts, one on either side of the bottom step. But at length she spoke.

Her voice was soft and became almost a whisper of remembrance. "It is very powerful, isn't it. I think it sums up her whole career, her whole life in fact. We were friends, you know, from primary school days. Three of us. We were so close." Shrugging off her nostalgic mood, she turned to me and held out her hand. "I'm sorry. I should have introduced myself. My name is Melanie. Of course you wouldn't know but it's common knowledge here that because of our lifetime's friendship, when I had the opportunity I bought this painting so that I could always enjoy it. It's on permanent loan to the Hydro because I want others – people like you – " and I felt the warmth of her smile – "to be able to appreciate it."

"It's wonderful. I can't say what it means to me, or what it's done to me. There's so much meaning in it. I'm so glad you've allowed me to see it. I shall go on thinking about it and finding more inspiration in it as time goes on."

"Yes, it has that effect. That is, on people who have eyes to see. If you like we can sit down here for a while and enjoy it. Nobody will disturb you." And she led me back to a deeply cushioned dark leather chair facing the staircase. "And of course you can come in again whenever you please. You may like to see the other painting of Peggy's that we have. It's a portrait of her husband Christopher. That's also very inspiring, but it may be because I knew him. Everybody loved him and he was quite a saintly character; Peggy has captured his spiritual qualities beautifully, I think. But the portrait is in the other wing, the hospice wing for long-stay patients. If you wish to see the other painting it would be best if you were to make an appointment with the sister in charge."

While she had been speaking my eyes were still focussed on the canvas on the stairs above me. It dominated the space around it. One couldn't ignore it. The power it exuded was an enabling power, a generous power. I breathed it in and wished I could analyse just what constituted that power. But I would come again and again, I knew, there was so much I could learn here. I sat transfixed, weaving dreams about the painting for I don't know how long. Time stood still while I was in another world. Melanie didn't exist for me any more and all was quiet. I was unaware even of the gentle clicking of the computer keys at the reception desk, or the presence of the blonde behind it over to my right.

I jumped when Melanie's voice called me back into my present surroundings, "I've been thinking," she said. "And I hope you don't think me impertinent or forcing you in any way. But I believe you're new to the island. Didn't you say?" I nodded. "I thought so. And with your interest in art I would like to introduce you to Sarah. She is the other survivor of our trio of friends. She is also starting to paint and she has Peggy's first painting, which will interest you and give you an idea how Peggy's style developed. I think you'll like Sarah, you have quite a lot in common."

What an amazing day! There I was, a timid little thing, approaching this awe-inspiring mansion and accosting strangers, thinking how brave I was, and now I seem to have had a life-enhancing experience and am being handed new friends on a plate! Incredible! I blinked away my hesitation and followed Melanie's straight back.

She led me out of the Hydro, back through the main entrance and round through the gardens at the back of the building. I was curious about this woman, Melanie, who had taken me under her wing. She walked firmly in front of me with an air almost of ownership. What was her role in this place? She was well past retirement age, yet obviously had authority.

As if she had sensed something of my thoughts she said over her shoulder, "Sarah and I are retired now, but we both were involved in the setting up of the Hydro from the start and we still have an interest in it and live here in the grounds."

These were extensive enough to sustain a sizeable hamlet, but the sense of space pervaded in spite of the towering bulk of mature trees – I noticed a good many oaks and beeches as well as Scots pines and rowans as we wound round the path away from the rear wings of the Hydro. Summer was still on the horizon. It had not yet crept in to blend the various spring greens of the trees to uniformity and soon I glimpsed the white walls of two cottages, separated or joined by a shrubbery.

"They were built for estate workers originally," Melanie explained. "But they serve us well, Sarah and me. They are spacious enough for our needs, now that our families have moved away, and we're near to the Hydro where we still have various commitments."

"And near to my son Ian, who is the clinical administrator," said Sarah, after the introductions and small talk on her doorstep. I was getting used to what seemed to be an Arran custom of introducing people by their given names and decided I liked it. It was more friendly than the formal Mr or Mrs or the awful Ms. I would hate to be a Ms. But who cared about one's marital status anyway? I liked the look of Sarah. Whereas Melanie was tall, slim and elegant, Sarah was short, plump and motherly in appearance, with wrinkled apple cheeks and kind eyes behind tinted glasses. She also must be in her early seventies, judging by her crumpled neck and brown-spotted hands, but both of them were obviously very alive and enjoying their third age. I apologised for intruding, as

Melanie left us, and explained about my interest in Peggy Paine's work.

"Oh, yes, of course, come in. I'll be delighted to show you the painting I have." Shutting the front door behind us she turned and led me through a narrow hall into the living room on the right. My immediate impression was of welcoming comfort, but my eyes were drawn inevitably to the painting over the fireplace. The rest of the room – furniture, colour scheme, curtains, ornaments – were unimportant. The picture, a simple composition of oranges and apples against a red cloth shone with a quality that was unmistakeable.

"It was her first important painting," Sarah said, standing beside me, like two devotees before an altar. "She was still a student at the Glasgow School of Art at the time but it gained an award and encouraged her to launch out as a professional painter." Her voice was soft with fond memories of her friend.

To have been close friends for sixty-five years, yet clearly quite different personalities, was something to be marvelled at. It was a great achievement and must have taken great strength of character to be sensitive to the changes in each other as they grew older, to adapt and tolerate the differences. I expressed something of this to Sarah, though I found it difficult to put into words. And I thought with shame of George and me, who had been unable to work such a miracle of understanding. Perhaps it needed a special gift of empathy?

But Sarah was going on to tell me more about Peggy Paine's development. The vibrant colours of the fruit painting were characteristic, she said. In fact, she had become internationally known as a colourist. "You know, the critics always try to put labels on artists; some compared her with Braque, others said she was in the tradition of Matisse, but she was just herself and she didn't model her work on anybody else's. She studied nature and went her own way. Of course she developed. The very glowing colours of her early work became later more subdued but with increasing power and greater depth, until the last painting you just saw in the Hydro. She could have gone on but she knew she was going blind and didn't want the quality of her work to deteriorate. She preferred to give up while she could still see clearly. I think she summarised the whole philosophy of her life in that final painting."

Sarah had given me a great deal to think about, and I told her so. I also told her, hesitantly, about my own desire to paint landscapes on Arran. "Of course, I'm only a beginner and ashamed of my attempts when I see pictures like these, but I enjoy painting and want to improve. Water-colours, not oils. I haven't been on the island very long, only a few months in fact, but artists like her are an inspiration for amateurs like me, aren't they?"

"Yes, very much so. I've also been inspired by Peggy to start painting. I never thought about it while she was alive, oddly enough, and of course there was the family to take up my time in those days. But after she died last year I got some paints and things and started. I find water-colours are easier to manage out of doors, as they don't take up so much room. I haven't a studio, nothing grand, just a small box of colours, a few brushes and a sketch pad."

It was amazing how much we agreed, as we chatted about our ambitions over a cup of tea in Sarah's comfortable living room. She had spent her whole life on Arran and I was a newcomer but we shared a love of the changing colours of the landscape, the cloud formations and the special light. Sarah's face became animated as we talked, and after a while she suddenly jumped up and went to a cupboard beside the fireplace. I thought perhaps she had remembered some more biscuits or something, but she produced a large portfolio and brought it back to rest at her feet against her chair. As she showed me some of her paintings I recognised how she was striving for these qualities; although amateur, I could see we had the same aims. Time flew by as we sat discussing her work and our ambitions.

"And are you involved in the Hydro, with your friend Melanie?" I asked as I put down my empty cup and brushed the biscuit crumbs from my lips. I don't know what made me ask such a personal question. It was unlike me to be so impertinent, but I liked Sarah and felt comfortable with her.

She must have noticed my flushed embarrassment as she answered. "Not so much as Melanie. She used to be the clinical director – she was a GP before she started up the Hydro – but my son Ian has now taken over. She and I are still part of the management team, however. I have a financial interest too, but I'm not a practising therapist."

So we both have a son and we both paint. So much in common. I felt I had begun to make a new friend and I hoped I would get to know her better. I ventured to say as much as I picked up my handbag and prepared to leave.

Sarah must have had the same thoughts. She smiled at me as she held the door open for my departure. "Perhaps we might go out painting together some time. Would you like that? It would be more fun to go together, wouldn't it? We might even get more work done and we could encourage one another. What do you think?"

I agreed with enthusiasm. We made a date there and then, and decided on a place for meeting. Her eyes twinkled among the wrinkles and I left with a light step.

5

"I'll meet you at Corrie. Ten-ish." It was Sarah's choice of venue as she knew the island so intimately and I was content to be led in this matter. I had been led by others all my life. But this was different, I told myself. I actually wanted Sarah's advice; I was new to the island and didn't know the terrain well enough to choose places for painting. It was true I had passed through Corrie several times and admired its picturesque cottages, but had never stopped my car to have a closer look. In fact it was difficult to look at the cottages while driving because the road was particularly narrow and twisting as it wound through the village. Any inattention would land one over the edge and into the sea or, heaven forbid, knock down a hapless pedestrian or cyclist. But today Sarah and I would be stationary, once we had found a patch of ground where we could park off the road and set up our stools. It was still early spring. The gorse was not yet fully ablaze on the mountain slopes; the day was dry and clear, no sun but light enough by ten o'clock for us to make a start on a sketch. We were both dressed for the purpose in woolly caps, warm coats over woolly jumpers, and trousers. We were there for the purpose of creating a picture, not to provide a fashion show for passers-by. Today each of us had come in her own car, though we agreed it would be more responsible and 'green' to share a car in the future, whenever practicable. In the event we needn't have worried about parking. There was plenty of room in front of the inn, as it was still too early in the season for many tourists to be about.

Humping our painting tackle – rucksacks and a folding stool – we dawdled round the bend behind the inn towards the row of cottages, seeking the viewpoint which appealed to us to paint. I was intrigued by their unusual arrangement. Their front doors led directly on to the narrow road, on the other side of which was their little gardens on the edge of the sea. The cottages were obviously old. I wondered how could a public right of way, even a footpath, have ever been allowed to bisect people's private properties? But so it was, and both cottages and gardens were well cared for and colourful with bulbs and spring flowers. Or at least the gardens were colourful.

I remarked to Sarah, "I like the contrast between the stark whiteness of that cottage wall over there and the fuss of colour over the road." We lingered for a while, moving slowly up and down the road, trying to decide on our viewpoint. I didn't want to tackle anything too complicated and abandoned the thought of including any of the gardens. I didn't think I could cope with so much colour and detail. "What appeals to me," I said, "is the white shape of that cottage against the dark mass of the trees on the hill behind. The colours are subtle and the shapes are almost abstract. It reminds me a bit of Cezanne."

Sarah agreed, though she moved her stool to an angle where she could include a bit of garden in the foreground. So we settled down to work, trying to get the composition right to start with. In my case it meant a lot of rubbing out and redrawing before I was satisfied with the way the shapes looked on paper.

Sarah was more confident and started painting while I was still worrying over the size of the hill and whether to include more sky.

"And how does your son like teaching in Lamlash?" Sarah asked as she unscrewed her bottle of water and started to mix her colours for the sky. "Is it much different from where he was before, on the mainland? Troon, wasn't it?"

"No. That is, he lived in Troon but he taught in Ayr at the Academy. He enjoys living in Lamlash, so near to the school, even being able to walk there. And I think he likes the school itself. He's not said otherwise anyway. He seems happy."

I sat back and held my drawing at arm's length. Yes, perhaps it would do. Now for some colour. But I wanted the colours to be muted and flat. I was aiming, perhaps too ambitiously, for a mosaic kind of pattern, not too realistic. I certainly couldn't cope with all that mass of trees in the background. They would have to be just a blur of different greens. It would mean washes of subtly blended tints, with no harsh outlines. My little patch of sky was best left plain blue, I decided, without clouds, and I got to work mixing up some cerulean in my palette, remarking to Sarah, "Your son has done very well, hasn't he, to be head of such a fine place. You must be proud of him."

Sarah paused to let her sky dry and rinsed her brush in the water bottle. "Yes, I'm happy for him. He's settled down and is doing a good job, I think. His wife Susie is partly responsible for that. I like Susie. In fact everybody likes her. She keeps his feet on the ground. There was a time when I was worried about him." Her face clouded over and I wondered at the cause but said nothing. I didn't want to pry. But she seemed to want to talk. "You see, he left home at sixteen. A wild teenager." Her voice held a note of bitterness, I thought, but apparently I was wrong as she went on, "He always knew what he wanted – to be a doctor like my friend Melanie. You've met her of course. He really worshipped her, I think, in those days. Anyway, he had the good sense to run away to Ayr, where Melanie had a practice. She gave him a room in her house and kept an eye on him while he completed his secondary education. More than that, she guided him in his career. He was so restless and adventurous – into everything, greedy for knowledge. I'm afraid he dabbled in drugs too – he said they were medical, scientific experiments, but I was terribly worried at the time. Especially when he refused a place at University. Instead he took off at eighteen and started wandering round the world, seeking for knowledge of all sorts of healing methods, witch doctors, gurus, what have you. But wherever he was, in whatever country he kept in touch with Melanie, I'll say that for him. And he was always willing to accept her advice. It wasn't until he was working in a big hospital in New York and met Susie that he began to think about a more settled life. And I'm thankful that he decided to come home. It was providential that Melanie was just getting the Hydro project off the ground and needed help at that time."

Sarah's long speech ended with her dipping her brush in water and beginning to mix her yellows and blues for the trees. She was intent on trying to show the different shapes of trees as well as the different shades of green while I, being less confident, mixed a splodge of greens on my paper, letting the colours run into each other. It required all my concentration for a while, but when I was satisfied I had to leave it. I couldn't paint anything else until it was dry, so I stood up and stretched my legs and arms and continued the conversation.

"Yes, it's an awful worry when they're growing up and you wonder if they'll ever settle down after their rebellious stage. We were very worried about John when he was younger. He was bright and had no difficulty with his schoolwork, when he deigned to attend. He often played truant but passed his exams easily. And at university he didn't seem to do any work, drank too much and was too attractive to the girls. If it weren't for the fact that he was set on being a teacher we would have despaired. I lost count of the girls he went out with and I was doubtful about Iolanthe at first. I think my husband George still has doubts about her, but I've grown to like her. She's a steadying influence on him, which is what he needs. And although she is younger she is more mature – unusually so, considering."

"We do worry about them, don't we? We can't help being mothers even when they're grown up. We can be glad they've developed into respectable and conventional citizens, but I expect we shall always cluck over them like a mother hen, until it becomes their turn to worry about us when we become old and decrepit." And she laughed as merrily as a teenager.

It would be many years before she needed looking after, I thought, and admired her attitude. I remembered reading somewhere about a scientific enquiry (in the U.S. of course) and it said that people with a positive outlook on life lived seven and a half years longer than more negative people. And Sarah and Melanie are among the most positive people I have met, and look as though they would live for ever. So perhaps there's something in it. I must try and live more positively. But, come to think of it, that's what I am doing now that I've left George.

These thoughts cheered me as I turned my attention to the little house and began to sketch in details of windows. I noticed Sarah was happily stippling bright colours on the window boxes and tubs in the foreground of her painting, but I decided to keep my cottage a pristine white and unadorned, simple and stark with only a grey strip of road in front. It didn't reflect the reality in front of me, but who cares? I wasn't intending to make a photographic record. I smiled to myself and remembered Turner's painting of Morecambe Bay. I had stood on the spot where he must have set up his easel, with a reproduction of his picture in my hand and realised that he had moved a mountain further to the south, presumably to improve the composition. So why shouldn't I omit window boxes? The finished result looked almost abstract, with the geometrical shape of the cottage and the flat background. I wasn't sure whether I approved, but it was the best I could do. Better next time!

We laughed at our efforts when we compared them afterwards, but it was happy laughter. We had had a good day and could go home with something to show for our endeavour. At least we had got away from household chores and done something more creative.

"What about finishing off our day with tea and cakes somewhere?" Sarah suggested and led me to her favourite café. She was very fond – too fond – of cream cakes, she explained, as she took a meringue from the plate the waitress had set before us. "It's no use, of course. I have to limit myself, though it takes a lot of will power. I'm really quite ashamed. I used to be far too plump and hated myself for years. But I've learnt a little bit of sense and the children keep tabs on me to make sure I'm not carrying excess weight. They want to keep me healthy, they say. They're very keen on people being healthy, of course. That's their business." Then she bit into her meringue with evident enjoyment. No doubt it tasted all the better for being forbidden.

I was thankful I didn't have such worries. I had always been skinny and frail looking and would probably remain so, whatever I chose to eat. But in fact I don't care for very sweet things. George was the one with the sweet tooth. I wondered how he was getting on, now that he was on his own. Was he managing as well as I was? How was he coping with the housework? Was he enjoying his freedom? I really hoped so and tried to shrug off these thoughts of George. We were on our own now and I mustn't worry about him any more. We separated in order to be free – so, then be free, Muriel. I shook myself and returned my attention to my new friend. "You're not a therapist yourself, Sarah?" I enquired as I added milk to my second cup of tea.

"No, I've never been anything but a housewife and mother. But I go for regular treatment, different therapies, to help my arthritis. I have massage and aromatherapy, and sometimes reflexology. I do believe they keep me mobile, you know. It's much better than having to walk with a stick, and much pleasanter than a lot of pills. My doctor agrees, fortunately." She smiled like a satisfied cat as she licked the cream off her fingers. "I know you don't have arthritis. Actually, you don't have to have anything wrong with you to benefit from a visit to the Hydro. I think you would enjoy aromatherapy. It's so relaxing and you smell nice afterwards, with the soothing oils. But when you go for the first time there's a consultation, to decide what is the best treatment for you. That is, what would be the most helpful."

I told her about Iolanthe going to the Hydro on a regular basis for therapy and swimming, and agreed I would give it a try. Since separating from George my adventurous spirit was coming out of retirement. And why not? I had nothing to lose and there might be some gain.

But Sarah interrupted my thoughts. "We've talked about our sons. And they're both here on Arran with their partners. What if they were to meet? I think it might be a good idea. Your son John hasn't been here long enough to make many friends and he and his partner might welcome the opportunity to meet a couple their own age who are outside the school environment. What do you think? Shall I get Susie and Ian to invite them?"

I didn't answer for a while. I stirred my tea and nibbled at a slice of fruitcake while I thought. Iolanthe may already know Susie but she hadn't met Ian as far as I knew. And John knew nobody at the Hydro. In fact I had received the impression that he had few friends apart from the other teachers at the school. They had been on Arran only for a few months and he had no interests outside his work. It would be good to introduce him to a different set of people and widen his interests. He seemed to be in a rut, I thought. He used to be so flighty, too flighty and superficial, and now he was in danger of becoming too staid, boring in fact, too like his father, I feared. And I wouldn't want that to happen.

"Well, yes, that's a good idea," I agreed. "I'm sure John and Iolanthe will be pleased to meet them and I feel confident they'll get on well together. They all have different interests and experiences and will have plenty to talk about. It would be good if they eventually become friends."

"Good. I'll get Susie to organise something. Leave it to me to set the wheels in motion. Susie will do the rest. She likes meeting people, but it will have to be some time when Ian is on the island. He travels quite a lot at the moment. And now, if we don't want another cup of tea, what about organising ourselves to meet again for another painting day? We have enjoyed today, haven't we? I know I have. And we've produced paintings, not masterpieces but worth looking at, I think. I like the simplicity of yours, and you've got the balance right." She frowned. "When I look at yours I see now that mine is too fussy, too chocolate-boxy and pretty. I was led astray by the flowers."

"Oh, no, your work is too honest to be chocolate-boxy. It's got the light in it. You caught that gleam of sun that lit up the cottage. I missed it and that's why your painting looks so lively. Anyway, whatever their faults, they're both worthwhile efforts and we've learnt something from the exercise. And yes, let's have another day out together. Where shall we go? Have you any ideas?"

Sarah puckered her brow and traced her finger across the tablecloth as if she were following a road map. Moving the teapot to the centre of the table she looked at me and smiled. "What about going to Lamlash and painting the view of Holy Island from the shore there?"

I also smiled, as I guessed the teapot represented the island in her imagination. "That's fine by me. It will be a change from painting buildings. And it will be more practice in painting trees in the mass. I find it very difficult. Either I produce a green fuzz or try to show every single tree. I can never get it right. And as for rocks – there are some rocks there, I believe – well, I tried painting some rocks at Lochranza and they turned out to look like balls of wool."

Sarah laughed at my description but had to agree she had the same difficulties. We would be a society for mutual support, we decided. Practice makes perfect, they say, but there is never any perfection in creative work. There is only development and change. And constant striving for the perfection we know we can never achieve. I don't know how we got on to such a philosophical discussion, but the tea had gone cold and the waitress was eyeing our table.

"We'd better go," Sarah said. "It's been a great day. I've enjoyed it so much."

"I'm so glad you suggested it," I agreed. "And I look forward to our next painting day."

6

March 10
I regret that I have not been able to keep up this diary. I intended it to be a day-by-day record of my life but I am not comfortable with words. My life has been spent with figures and I find it difficult to express not only my feelings but also even events in writing. But I owe it to my grandchildren to persevere, so that they will know what my life is like at this juncture.

It has not been easy to adapt to living alone and being responsible for everything in my life. It is what I wanted, and fortunately it is what Muriel wanted too, but until I had had some experience of being alone I had no idea what it would really involve. I will not mention the strange feeling of having nobody in the house with whom to exchange a word about one's daily affairs. The other things are more practical. Some things I can manage easily enough; for instance, buying food and making my own meals is not difficult. I enjoy being able to eat what I like, cooked the way I like it. But that is not the only part of the household chores. I had not realised how dusty things become, even though the atmosphere here is relatively clean compared with a city. But there is salt and sand in the air, windows become cloudy and the dust on the furniture is gritty. I am ashamed to say I have had to learn how to clean windows and polish furniture, and now realise how much time these tasks consume. I have always insisted on everything being clean and tidy, and Muriel learned how to keep the house as I wished, while I could devote myself to more important things. Now, to preserve my standards I have to rob my time spent on study. In addition to the cleaning there is also the washing and ironing. I had some difficulty at first, as the washing machine in the kitchen has no instruction book and it took me some time to master it. It grieves me to admit to all this ignorance, but I feel obliged to write it down for the sake of truth. Living alone involves adopting both male and female roles, I find, and it is not easy.

However, I think I have now evolved a routine that will give me regular hours for my study and a modicum of free time for relaxation. I shall endeavour to live a balanced life and remain healthy and fit into my old age. I have registered with the medical centre and had a check-up; all is well, apparently. So it should be, as I neither smoke nor drink and have always been careful of my health. My mental health is also adequate, I believe, to accomplish the degree course I have undertaken. I am enjoying the work, which has just begun. There is a great deal of reading involved and I settle down to the books in the evenings in my most comfortable chair in the lounge. So far I have had no difficulty in acquiring the necessary books. The librarian, Rosemary, is very helpful. She orders the books I need and delivers them to me in the evening when she returns home from work. I am not sure how one should repay her kindness but I feel obliged to invite her in for a drink; I bought a bottle of sherry for the purpose. She stays only for a short while as she says she has to prepare a meal. I hesitate to ask and I have not discovered whether she is or has been married. It is of course no business of mine, but if she is alone perhaps I should offer to make her a meal one day. I am not sure whether I could bring myself to do that, and face the embarrassment if she refused. I would like to invite her, however, and will continue to think about it. As well as borrowing books from the library I also buy the titles I wish to keep. The bookshop staff are very helpful and the books usually arrive within a week so my studies are not held up. The essays I have to write cause me some problems, I admit. I have not written any essays since my schooldays and it will take me a while to get used to organising my thoughts in the way that is required. It is so long since I was at school I had not realised educational methods had changed so much. It seems that, to gain a degree in history I must start by studying the humanities in general. I expected there would be a concentration on political history but it is now much wider and embraces art, music, philosophy, religion, science and literature. Having thought it over I agree it seems sensible. It is, or promises to be more enjoyable. If only I had done this earlier. But I am making the most of the course, listening to the tapes and watching the special TV programmes. As I am so new to studying I run through them many times to be sure I have grasped their content. I am determined to complete this first course within the year and then move on to a more specific historical period. Although I am finding it a little difficult in these early stages, no doubt I shall improve on my timing as well as the quality of my work as the course proceeds. My tutor is helpful and encouraging, I am pleased to say.

I have organised my life satisfactorily, I think. The mornings are devoted to household affairs – shopping, cleaning, paying bills, collecting my pension etc. The afternoons are for the OU assignments and the evenings for reading or watching videos. But I normally keep Wednesdays free. It is important to have some relaxation and a change of occupation. Mr Moody, or Graham (I must get used to this local habit of calling everybody by their given name) suggested an activity that appealed to me and in future I shall go along to the museum on a regular basis. Today I picked him up, as arranged, at his post office across the loch and he was kind enough to introduce me to the other volunteers who were already working at the museum when we arrived. I was unable to memorise all their names, there were too many. But I made a point of remembering the secretary, a woman called Esther, no longer young though younger than I, grey-haired and very active. She was never still, running about all over, supervising, organising and doing half a dozen things at once. The treasurer, called Simon, was the opposite; he was older, had little to say, scarcely looked up from his ledgers and merely grunted at me. The others, whose names I forget, were all busy at various tasks but all looked up and smiled a greeting as Graham led me from one to the other. He said he wanted to show me the choice of tasks so that I could decide what appealed to me to offer. Some of the men were shovelling fresh gravel on to the car park, others cleaning rust off the old farm implements or painting new direction signs. There were women volunteers too, washing smaller artefacts and doing general cleaning. Others were cataloguing and labelling. It was obvious that the museum needed plenty of volunteer labour to keep it in the condition that had earned it accolades in the past.

Graham had come prepared for heavier dirty work. I think he felt at home in his patched and paint-splattered dungarees and an old faded sweater, getting his hands dirty and wielding a hammer or shovel. That did not appeal to me. In any case I did not possess any such working clothes and I told him so. "I have never had to do any manual work and have no aptitude for it. I have always been a professional, an accountant, all my life."

I might have offered to do some cataloguing but that room was full of women and I would not wish to work with women. It was difficult to make a choice and I stood undecided in the courtyard, looking to Graham for suggestions.

He frowned at me and was quite gruff in fact. "Practically all of them are graduates of one sort or another, professionals and so on, but they all muck in to do what's necessary to help the museum and incidentally to enjoy one another's company. Nobody is snobby and stuck-up." He gave me a severe and calculating sort of look. "Perhaps working on the computer would suit you. All the hand-written records have to be transferred and stored on disks. Millie will show you how it's done, if you can bear to work with a woman."

Really, I found his last remark quite offensive, though he must have sensed my antipathy. I am not actually anti-female; the fact is I have never mixed with women in a normal way. My mother died when I was still very young, I had no sisters or aunts and Muriel was my first and only girl friend. So I just do not understand women and therefore feel somewhat afraid of them. This is a terrible thing to admit for a man of sixty, but I must try to overcome this prejudice (I realise now that it is a prejudice, and unjustified). Rosemary the librarian and Gladys the postmistress are friendly and helpful and I would have to trust that Millie would be helpful too. In the event she did so prove to be, though my first impression of her was alarming. She was so round and bulging – round face, red and smiling, heavy body and a bust that she carried in front of her like a proud trophy. But once I had got over my initial alarm I found her friendly and very patient as she showed me the piles of box files full of loose papers, all of which had to be computerised. It would be a task that would occupy us for many weeks, I realised. And it was a task that appealed to my sense of order. I would actually enjoy it, I thought. As we worked side by side, I reading the documents while she typed them into the computer, we chatted at intervals and she revealed that she had been a top-ranking civil servant in London at the Foreign Office and spoke three languages.

"They got me to work on the computer here," she said. "And I come practically every Wednesday now. There's no real urgency for this work to be done, it just has to be done eventually. But soon it will be all hands on deck to do the final cleaning and polishing, to make sure the museum is ready for opening to the public at Easter. I usually offer to do all the brasses then. It's a dirty job but I like to se them all shining afterwards. It gives me a sense of achievement."

She was so cheerful about it and I marvelled that she could be so adaptable. I felt quite humbled, which is an unusual feeling for me. It seems that Arran is a sort of melting pot where people mix together simply as people. Can this be? I am not used to this. I have always been accustomed to the convention of thinking of people in categories. People wearing labels. It is a tidy and comfortable way of thinking, which appeals to me. I wonder now if that was one of the differences between Muriel and me? I remember she made friends with that lower-class woman from the church and that coloured woman in the village. I refused to acknowledge them, but could I have been wrong? I am still not convinced that everybody is worth cultivating as a friend. One has to choose one's friends, male or female. Rosemary is becoming a friend, but I doubt if Millie will ever become a friend; I am too much in awe of her intelligence. I am certainly more comfortable in the company of men, if I can overcome my hesitation about manual work. As I am unskilled there is little I can offer, but I must correct the impression Graham has of me. Next Wednesday I will wear my oldest clothes and boots and offer to do anything they need to prepare for the opening. If the men do not require my services I will carry on with the computer work, now that I understand the system. I could even work on it alone, if Millie is doing the brasses.

I indicated this intelligence to Graham as I drove him home at the end of the afternoon. He smiled and said nothing, and I hope our relationship is once more on an even keel. Being near neighbours and seeing him so frequently at the shop it is important to retain good relations.

Having dropped him at his door I decided to turn round again and visit John to complete my day of leisure, away from my studies.

Iolanthe was also at home. I am still not sure about her. She is supposed to be working for an English degree. So she says, anyway. But I cannot believe that anyone who looks like she does can be a bluestocking – an ex-model, always immaculate and fond of clothes, and with little schooling. Moreover, how can someone who has been spoilt and courted by wealthy men-about-town since her teens say she is in love with John and chooses to live with him? Muriel seems to like her and says she trusts her, but I have my doubts. I do not think the relationship has any hope of permanence. John is obviously besotted with her, but his taste in women has always been volatile. I took the opportunity today to have a serious talk with him while Iolanthe was in the kitchen preparing a meal. He says he is happy with the school and also with his home situation. His house is modest, and if Iolanthe is responsible for the state in which I saw it today, she shows some talent for organisation. Everything looked clean and tidy. There was nothing I could fault. They had not expected my visit, so presumably this was its normal state. If so, they were to be congratulated, I said.

"Iolanthe does all that," John told me. "I have the excuse that I'm out all day and have homework to do in the evening. She's a great lass – gets complimented on her degree work and she's a wonderful housekeeper to boot. Except that she can't cook!"

"Then who does the cooking?"

"Oh, we manage between us. It's easy enough with package meals and a microwave; sometimes we get a takeaway or occasionally have a meal out. I have school dinners anyway during the week and Iolanthe says she doesn't eat lunch. She likes to keep her figure, you know, and of course I approve of that. Have you ever seen such a figure, Dad? Aren't I lucky?"

By implication, though I would not expect him to spell it out, she was also wonderful in bed. We had always been reticent about such private matters, believing that what went on in the bedroom was of no concern to anybody else. We had brought up our children in that way, contrary to the modern trend. I do not approve of every detail being paraded for public consumption, and I deplore the brutal frankness of modern novels and television programmes. I was glad to see that John was what I had brought him up to be – the breadwinner and head of the household. He will need to be firm with Iolanthe if the partnership is to develop into marriage, as John says he would like. I approve of him wanting marriage but would prefer a more suitable wife, one who would become a fitting mother to his children, and certainly someone less glamorous and more biddable. But time will tell, as they say. I keep my own counsel and do not criticise openly, though John knows my opinions.

While we had been talking Iolanthe had prepared – if prepared is the right word for something defrosted in the microwave – a meal of steak pie and chips.

"It's from Marks and Spencer's," she said. "I stocked up with some ready meals last time I was in Glasgow. They're quite good and they save time."

Actually, I would not have known if she had not told me. It was a good meal and she served it on china plates with silver cutlery and linen napkins, and she even lighted a candle on the table. She obviously thinks appearance is important. I appreciated it and perhaps it is important up to a point. But is there anything of substance beneath the appearance? That is what I doubt.

"Would you like a piece of Dundee cake, George? I made it myself," she surprised me by asking. There was no surprise in her calling me George as she has always done so. She can hardly call me father-in-law as she is not married and she declared that Mr Munro is too formal, which I had to accept. But I was surprised at her offer of cake made by herself. And I was further surprised at how good it was. She must have seen my reaction in my face as she remarked, "We students must take time off to do something practical now and again, to keep a balance, mustn't we, George? How is your OU work going anyway? Are you still enjoying it?"

I assured her I was, though it had its difficulties. Returning to academic studies after so long away from school and college meant a lot of self-discipline.

"I know what you mean. I have the same difficulty. But it's fun, isn't it?"

I really do not know what to make of the girl. To study for an English degree for fun! And what does she think she wants with a degree anyway? In one breath she says she wants a degree and in the next breath she says she wants to stay permanently as John's partner. But she refuses to marry him. It makes no sense. I finished drinking my tea and brushed off the cake crumbs from my lap. I excused myself then, as there seemed to be nothing else to say, and returned home to my evening study session.

It has been a difficult day to sum up but worthwhile on the whole. I shall be better prepared for the museum in future, and perhaps better able to deal with Iolanthe. At least I have no worries about John. He has settled down and seems to be a model citizen of whom I can be proud.

7

"What is the weather going to do today? What should I wear? These were burning questions as I opened my eyes at 7 a.m. I got up to look at the sky and guess the strength of the wind. A few clouds were massed over in the west, the seagulls floating on the loch were all facing west, which meant that the wind would bring the clouds across to the island. And no doubt when they touched the hilltops they would drop their rain. But would it rain in Glasgow? That was the question. To leave here at breakfast time and not return until evening required careful thought. It was still only April. It was not likely to be a heat wave sort of day. And tramping around city streets would be tiring, especially now that I had grown soft among the laid-back country customs of Arran. So, comfortable shoes were essential – the black brogues that I hadn't worn since Christmas in Pitlochry. As I picked them up from the floor of my wardrobe and blew the dust off them I wondered how Sandra and the children were settling down in their big hotel, which was their new home. It would soon be Easter and the beginning of their busiest season. I would send her a card from Glasgow, I thought, and cast my eyes along the clothes hanging above the shoes. My grey skirt and red jumper? Or perhaps the Aran sweater? Oh dear, Muriel, don't be such a ditherer. Be decisive, I told myself, and snatched up the red botany wool jumper that I'd bought in the sale at the sheepskin shop before I could change my mind. As all my coats and jackets were shower proof if not completely waterproof – essential cover for Arran – the choice was less difficult and I settled for my grey jacket, which had a hood.

I was much too early for the ferry. At that time in the morning I had the road to myself and it took me barely half an hour to reach the terminal and park the car. Like a dowager duchess the ferry approached, sliding gently and with dignity into her allotted berth, calculated without fuss to the nearest millimetre. Few people hurried down the gangway from this first crossing from the mainland; they were mostly men in suits with briefcases, coming for a day's business meeting, or perhaps salesmen; and one or two golfers, trundling their heavy trolleys completed the complement. As for the departing Arran people waiting in the queue to board, I thought a few faces looked familiar though I couldn't give them names. We smiled and nodded as we showed our tickets to the yellow-coated seaman and climbed on board.

"Why, hello, Muriel, good to see you!" And there was Iolanthe, bright eyed and bushy tailed, looking smart in a very brief black skirt that barely covered her bottom (her bottom was covered by black tights, I was thankful to see) and a very long ethnic sort of tunic in bright colours and sunburst design. The whole outfit was stunning but not outrageous; it emphasised her height and the length of her elegant legs. I smiled a greeting that I hoped would cover up my embarrassment at being seen in my relatively dowdy old state beside this young glowing vision. What must she think of me?

"I only just made it," she said, seating herself

beside me in the lounge. "I overslept and John didn't wake me. Thankfully I caught the bus. It was good that I had only three miles to come, but you must have had to make a much earlier start. Did you have any time for breakfast? Can I get you something?"

"Well, yes, that's very kind. It was too early to eat anything and I wasn't hungry then. But I think I'd like a bacon butty. And coffee of course."

"OK I'll go and get it. Milk and no sugar, isn't it?"

Such a kind girl, and so thoughtful. Not at all stuck up. She doesn't mind being seen with an old frump like me. How can George think she is superficial and not to be trusted? I thought she was perfectly genuine and welcomed the opportunity for an hour's chat. A bacon butty was not my normal fare for breakfast or any other meal but it tasted good and I munched happily while Iolanthe sipped abstemiously at her black coffee.

"Are you going away?" I enquired, indicating her briefcase and matching small suitcase at her feet.

"Not exactly. But I have to stay over in Glasgow once or twice a week. It depends on the lectures and tutorials. I think I shall have to stay more days next term, to get through the work. There's so much to do, and it's fascinating."

"Of course. I'd forgotten for the moment. You're at the University. I don't know why but I'd got it into my head that you were doing your degree by correspondence. I'm probably mixing it up with George's Open University."

"Well, quite a lot of the work is done at home, thank God – the reading and essays. But I have to attend lectures and it's good to have face-to-face advice from the tutors. They really keep me on my toes. I don't think I'd have the self-discipline to work entirely on my own like George. I think he's wonderful – at his age, too!"

Hmm. She had a point there. She was large-hearted where I had been sceptical. It was a brave undertaking and I shouldn't have been so mean-spirited to doubt his ability and dedication. I was glad that he had been very keen to start and now appeared to be enjoying it. I hoped he would persevere and eventually get the degree he had set his heart on.

"Isn't it very expensive to stay overnight in Glasgow?" I asked, wondering how she could afford all this on John's salary, and forgetting that she had received an unexpected bequest from George's father specifically for her own independent development.

"Oh, I'm lucky. One of my friends – that is, she's really only an acquaintance, a model from my catwalk days, but she has a flat with a spare bedroom, and it's near the University. So I stay with her and it's no problem. And in case you're wondering. . ." She laughed but I sensed the firmness behind the words. ". . .John is quite capable of looking after himself. He likes to tease his father and pretend neither of us can cook but both of us take a turn in the kitchen, you know. John likes to experiment and I find new recipes for him in Glasgow, though when it's my turn to cook I stick to the old traditional British."

This was a further revelation. Really, this girl never ceased to surprise me. It's true, one should never judge by appearance, I thought.

"And I suppose you're off for a day's shopping?" she asked.

"Yes, sort of. There are some paints I want, and another brush, and perhaps some better quality paper. But mainly I want to spend time in the gallery of modern art in Queen Street. I don't know anything about modern art and I'm not in the same league as those in a gallery of course, but I'm told the exhibitions are always interesting. It might even be exciting." I had no illusions about my painting. It was an absorbing hobby, no more, but that didn't mean I was prohibited from learning and trying to improve.

Iolanthe understood. She felt the same about her writing, she said. She had always been interested and had written a few articles for fashion magazines. Published, too! But she felt handicapped by having left school so early. If only she had gone to college straight after school she would have felt more confident. "As it is, I'm finding it difficult to concentrate on study. There's so much to get through. But I enjoy every minute of it too."

"And what sort of writing do you do now, or hope to do?"

"Well, during the course we work in all genres – poetry, journalism, short stories, fantasy, what have you. And we practise the different styles of famous literary figures. That's great fun. But as for my ambition for the future, I'll let you into a secret. You mustn't tell John, Muriel. Please." Her fine eyes were serious. "I don't want him to know just yet in case it doesn't work out, but I've started to write a novel. There! I knew that would shake you!" She sat up, smoothed away her frown of concentration, and grinned.

While she took the remains of our breakfast back to the cafeteria I tried to absorb this further revelation. Whatever would she come up with next?

"You see, I don't want to tell John until it's finished," she explained as she returned to her seat. "He'd only laugh at my efforts. He still doesn't take me seriously, you know." She paused and a frown puckered her brow again briefly. "But of course you know what he's like. He still thinks of me as a beautiful object that he's acquired – a pretty face but a bimbo, something he can be proud of possessing. I love him to bits but I won't marry him until he grows up," she finished with a toss of her head.

I did indeed know what John was like and marvelled that he had settled down so well with her and not strayed to new pastures. He was maturing and changing, I could see, and I felt confident that Iolanthe would in time achieve a transformation. I too loved him 'to bits' but neither of us had any illusions. He had his father's genes after all, and that stolid unimaginative character would emerge in due course. The combination of his earlier volatility and his father's stolidity would make a man of him. I was touched that Iolanthe could trust me enough to confide in me like this, and wished her success with her novel and assured her of my discretion.

The train link to Glasgow was too clattery for conversation and we parted with a wave at Central Station, she to dash for the Underground to the University, I to stroll along Union Street window gazing. I needed time to orientate myself and adapt to the culture shock. To be plunged from the peace of Lochranza, where the only sound is of lapping ripples and seagulls' cries, and the only sign of humanity is the occasional delivery van or a neighbour in his garden, and then to be catapulted in a couple of hours into the hurly-burly of a city centre, jostling crowds, shrieking brakes, clouds of dust and strident advertisements – well, I had to take it gradually. And I decided a small dose of this would be enough. I'd been in Glasgow only half an hour and already I was pining for Arran. But I pulled myself together. I mustn't be insular. At that I smiled. How could I help being insular, living on an island? But the physical fact didn't necessarily signify an insular state of mind. A large population needed all these amenities – even the fast-food restaurants at the corner. And only a large population could sustain art galleries and concert halls, not to mention noble buildings, both commercial and public.

Somewhat mollified by my philosophising I turned with thankfulness up the pedestrianised Buchanan Street and dawdled among the throng of shoppers enjoying the relative silence. I noticed that faces were less strained, feet less hurried, in this traffic-free street. It was possible to talk to a friend in a normal voice, or even to stop and listen to a busker. I decided I liked this aspect of city life. But I remembered the other side, the side that George uncovered on that last decisive trip to Glasgow. I found a new friend on that trip, Veronica, and through her encouragement and the inspiration of the Burrell gallery I had turned my life around. But George, in tracing his ancestry, had revealed unexpected and disreputable forebears who lived in overcrowded slums. Those slums have now been demolished and replaced with – what? New slums with bathrooms? I didn't know and had no inclination to find out. George was wise to abandon his investigation into his past. It was more sensible to study the past in the abstract, objectively. In that way he would satisfy his curiosity without his emotions being hurt. He too had turned his life around and I sincerely believed it was for the better.

Almost without being aware of my surroundings I had arrived at a triumphal arch leading across the back of the gallery. I wondered, why a triumphal arch? And as if one wasn't enough there were even two of them, flanking the rear of the gallery, which used to be the Royal Exchange. Perhaps there were ancillary buildings or even a stable block here once, where now are continental style pavement cafes. It was good to approach the gallery from the rear, letting the anticipation build up as I admired the ornate cast iron railings over the basement and the long row of fluted stone columns – sturdy columns, necessary to support the heavy cornice. The front did not disappoint me. Its Corinthian temple style had a grandeur that, while emphasising its dignity and importance, did nothing to intimidate the visitor. Students drinking cans of cola were lolling on the steps and the big glass doors were wide open in welcome. But once inside my boldness deserted me for a moment. I was confronted with a large atrium and an indication of four storeys of galleries. Where should I start? I felt bewildered with such a multiple choice but was determined it shouldn't overwhelm me; after pausing to give it some thought I decided the logical thing to do was to start at the top and work down. By the time I reached the basement I would be ready for something to eat in the tearoom there. Sensible Muriel! The lift was easy, only one button to press and the doors were automatic. I hadn't worked out what I expected from my visit. I was conscious of my lack of knowledge and ability. I had never tried to portray people in my paintings and I was not very good on trees; like Iolanthe I think I needed to study other artists, experts and their techniques so that I might find my own style. So I assumed there would be lots of landscapes and portraits, perhaps figure paintings or even abstracts in oils as well as watercolours. I thought there might even be attractive paintings of a size that one could visualise on one's walls at home.

But the paintings here were huge. I was thankful that there were seats around the perimeter of the gallery, as it was necessary to sit at a distance and contemplate the pictures at length. Their modern style confused me. They were not naturalistic, as I in my ignorance had expected. And most of them couldn't be called abstract, but I supposed they were symbolic of something, or at least expressed the artist's feelings about the subject. I did find a few purely abstract works and admired the colours, but I spent a long time just looking and pondering on the meaning behind the painted images. Some were sad and quite depressing. I felt sorry for those artists who needed cheering up. But one or two other paintings were obviously intended to poke fun at the spectator; I enjoyed their humour and sat for a while smiling at the almost caricatured figures. It was all a revelation to me. I had not realised that one could express personal emotions and even philosophy in paint. I didn't ask myself whether I liked these huge works. I suspected that liking or not liking was irrelevant. They had made me think. Perhaps this was what modern art was all about?

It was in a very pensive mood that I sat down to my tuna sandwich and coffee in the tearoom. It was a very splendid tearoom that was part of a library of pale gold and grey with a panelled and vaulted ceiling. It inspired hushed respect and radiated an atmosphere where one could read a learned journal while partaking of a dainty repast.

Stimulated and refreshed, my shopping expedition was easily accomplished, though I was tempted to buy more than I had on my list. There was such a bewildering display of everything an artist could desire in every medium, being picked over, even fought over by the young and bright-eyed. I wondered, were they already visualising finished works similar to what I had just seen? Or would they lead a counter-movement of some sort when they were older? Everything was changing so rapidly, why not art?

The clouds that had threatened earlier in the day

had moved away and I decided it was warm enough and I was tired enough to sit on one of the benches thoughtfully provided by the city fathers in the pedestrianised street. I could enjoy the passing scene of busy shoppers, serious businessmen, happy lovers and weary mothers while I wrote my card to Sandra before catching my train connection to the ferry. But I underestimated the variety of human beings who frequented Buchanan Street. I smelt before I saw the two elderly drunks. I assumed they were elderly as my first impression was that they must be in their seventies. They were both gaunt, bent, haggard of face and in ragged old clothes, but looking closer, they were probably no older than John. And I was forced to look more closely, whether I wanted to or not, because they chose to sit beside me in their filthy tatters and with their plastic shopping bags clanking with bottles. The bench was made to accommodate three people and I was there first, so why should I move? I didn't like their appearance or their smell but they were neither rowdy nor violent; I couldn't object, it was a public place and my own appearance was nothing to write home about anyway. It was just another experience in this day of revelations.

"Where's our Tom?" one derelict asked the other as he passed his bottle over; I couldn't decide whether it was vodka or methylated spirits that they were drinking. The more whiskery man took a deep swig of the liquid, belched and added his complaint about the absence of Tom. Fascinated and unashamed I listened to their conversation. The thick accent and slurred speech made it difficult but I understood that they were a trio of close friends with a common and absorbing interest in alcohol, who met on the same bench every day to share their booze and give one another support. They ignored me, but my heart warmed to them as I saw something of their pain and understood their attempt to deal with it. How human! I thought of my own pain and how by separating from George I was trying to deal with it; something that was not needing any great heroic determination or fortitude. And I thought of Nelson Mandela, one of Glasgow's heroes, who had not eradicated his pain but had transmuted it to enrich life instead of destroying it. How different we all are, and how many different ways we find to ameliorate our pain! What a day to remember!

8

"So that's the story of my day in Glasgow," and I sat back and took a deep breath and smiled at John. It was rather an apologetic smile, for such a long account of a short days' expedition, when nothing very exciting happened.

But John was in a playful mood. "A mad day of wild excess in the wicked city," he taunted me.

"Don't laugh at me," I chided. "Make me a cup of tea and the tell me about your get-together with the Hydro people. Sarah said she was going to suggest it to Susie and hoped it could be arranged when Ian was at home. I've only just heard that it actually happened. They mentioned it in the village shop. You know how it is. Graham (the husband, that is) had seen you and Iolanthe there and heard Susie welcome you. So of course he wanted to know what was going on. He goes for treatment for his back and that's how he came to be there. There's no way of keeping any secrets on this island, you know."

"Typical! Of course! Not that there was anything to be secret about." He returned from the kitchen, balancing a tray on which he had placed a teapot (bless him, he had actually made a pot and even added a jug of hot water), milk, sugar, cups and a plate of digestive biscuits. It was all in my honour, I was sure; he was trying to impress me with his domestic skills.

I knew that normally he just put a teabag into a mug. He set the tray down gently on the coffee table between us and I started to pour out.

"It was my first visit to the Hydro," he said. "I'd taken it for granted that it was all a bit of nonsense, harmless amusement, nothing serious. A bit left over from the Sixties you know – flower power, positive thinking and all that." He smiled. He was exhibiting some of his father's prejudices. "But it's not at all like that. They're very serious about it all, have loads of certificates and testimonials from doctors and grateful clients. Or maybe they call them patients. I didn't mind Iolanthe going. She's into all these modern things, though I didn't think it was anything more than a harmless hobby. But maybe she's got something. Maybe it's worthwhile. I think I might be tempted to expose myself to some pretty therapist for a massage." He grinned.

"Now sit down and be serious, John. Tell me about Sarah's family, Ian and Susie. What are they like? How did you get on with them?" As Sarah and I have become such good friends I was hoping our respective children might become friends too. Irrational of course, but there's no harm in hoping.

"We got on fine. No problem. If you insist on details, well – they're our sort of age, I suppose, though Ian looks older. He's beginning to have middle-aged spread and his hair's thin on top." He smirked and patted his own flat stomach. He may be proud of his figure, I thought, but it probably owes more to his genes than to his health awareness.

"Well, go on. What else?" I prompted.

"He's a very serious person, very conscious of his position as head of the Hydro and proud of its pioneering work. Apparently it was the first of its kind in the country. He explained what they do and it was quite an eye-opener. They work in cooperation with the NHS, but specialise in all sorts of other therapies, no pills, potions or injections, unless it's acupuncture. It all used to be amateur, you know, just as I thought it still is, but now it's mainstream and Melanie, Ian's mother, was the pioneer, they said. Ian gets invited to speak about it all over the world, he told us, and we were lucky to find him at home." He poured another cup of tea for us both and nibbled at his biscuit before continuing. "I think I may be giving you the impression that he's pompous and self-important. That's my fault for expressing it badly. He's actually not like that at all. In spite of his responsible position he can lighten up when required. And he did, over lunch. Susie got him to tell us some hair-raising and hilarious stories of his earlier travels in the Far East and Africa; he was foot-loose and fancy free in those days and spent his time and energy in studying ethnic healing methods – you know, witch doctors, gurus, dervishes and such like. Fascinating. Even drugs! That was years ago and he only experimented, never got hooked. It was all done in a laboratory, scientifically, he said. He was years wandering about, apparently. That's why he's such an authority on all these different complementary therapies. He practised them on himself, too, and kept us amused with stories of some of his experiences. He had to learn how he could walk barefoot over hot coals – that meant having to control his mind, he said. And another time he was immured in a dark cave for days, to commune with his inner self. And he learnt a lot about herbs and exotic plants that could cure sickness. 'Eye of newt, toe of frog' and all that. And he even learnt how to control other people's minds, get them into a state of altered consciousness, you know. Corrupt governments and advertisers do it all the time," he said, suddenly bitter.

"But Ian and the people he trains help patients to heal themselves; by controlling their own minds they can control their body, or so he says. Anyway, I think it's great!"

I had heard something of this story from Sarah and was pleased to hear more details. By controlling the state of consciousness I supposed he was referring to the use of hypnotic techniques. I'd read about this method being used to uncover the origin of stubborn problems, by regression to very early memories or even to a past life. I was not sure about this idea of reincarnation. It seemed very far-fetched, but they say a large part of the human race believe in it. I must try not to be prejudiced. I should keep an open mind and go along some day for a consultation. Maybe they could cure me of still feeling so guilty at failing my marriage.

While I was turning all this over in my mind John was continuing. "He finished up in Canada and North and South America, studying native Indian remedies. And then, as a complete contrast, to bring his mind back to present-day allopathic medicine he worked in a big hospital in New York. That was a big shock. I can just imagine it, with all the drug addicts, stabbings and shootings."

"I can understand that. It must have been dreadful and I'm sure he was glad to come back here, to his old home after all those experiences. But what about his wife, Susie? You haven't once mentioned her. He met her in New York, I understand, and they say she is very attractive. Sarah says everybody loves her. She's Chinese American, isn't she? That's what I heard, anyway." I wondered why he was so bashful at bringing her name into the conversation. It was unlike him to avoid talking about a good-looking girl. I put down my cup and pushed the tray away, to look him straight in the eye. "Actually, I've heard a rumour that you're seeing her for therapy."

A shame-faced half-laugh and he avoided my eyes. "Well, yes, I thought I'd see what it was all about. She offered. Aromatherapy. She's good at her job. It was very relaxing after all this marking I have to do," and he waved his arm at a stack of books on the table under the window, where pale sunlight exposed the stained and dog-eared pages. "I went swimming as well," he said defiantly.

He looked just as he did when, as a small boy he had stolen a biscuit or slice of cake from my kitchen. Guilt and self-justification. I knew him so well and still had fears for him. Was his apparent sense of responsibility, his new respectability and his attachment to Iolanthe ephemeral? All through his teens and student years I was plagued with trying to remember the name of each succeeding girl friend. There was Mavis, a dark bossy type, Alison the blonde bimbo, Karen who was no better than she should be, Maureen the gold-digger (she didn't last long). And so many others who didn't last long enough even to have names. Not that I ever met any of them. They were never important enough for that. I only heard his verdict later, as one after the other was abandoned and a new one enthused over. But Iolanthe was different; even her name set her apart, being the offspring of Gilbert and Sullivan addicts, and John seemed genuinely to be in love. Their partnership had lasted two years so far and I had hopes that it would be permanent. That is, if anything is permanent these days. And I thought of my own broken marriage. It felt as if I was holding my breath for John's relationship to succeed. I did so want him to be happy and felt sure that Iolanthe was right for him. Please God don't let him go wandering again, I prayed.

"I'm glad you're looking after yourself, John. Teaching nowadays must be very stressful, with all the changing regulations and the paperwork. I think some relaxation therapy is a good idea. There are other therapists as well as Susie, I suppose? I understood that new patients were assessed during the first appointment and allocated to the most suitable practitioner and treatment." I was hoping, of course, that John would have been assigned to someone older, or ugly, or preferably male.

"Yes, that is so, normally. But I skipped the preliminary interview because Susie offered. Naturally I accepted." He grinned

"Does Iolanthe go to Susie too? I've forgotten but I know you said she went to the Hydro."

"Yes, or at least she did go to Susie for aromatherapy and came home smelling like a flower garden every week. But she hasn't time now. She's off in Glasgow half the week. I hardly see her nowadays." He picked up the tray and carried it through to the kitchen, as if the subject was closed. As if he didn't want to talk about Iolanthe.

There was something troubling him. First his reluctance to mention Susie and now his avoidance of Iolanthe's name. What was going on? Probably nothing. Probably I was fussing too much and imagining things and it was just the general stress of his job and he was feeling sorry for himself. But I wanted to be sure. I didn't want my son to be unhappy. Perhaps I should try to get him to talk about whatever was troubling him. I eased myself up from the sagging old chair – it had been second-hand when he bought it years ago and now was too soft and low for older bones – and followed him into the kitchen.

"I'll dry for you," I said as I took out a clean tea towel from the drawer below the microwave. He already had his hands in the sink, splashing hot water into the cups and slapping a dishcloth about. He should have emptied the teapot first but he had left that on the draining board. I said nothing but quietly removed it and went to empty the slops into the toilet and the teabag into the waste bin. Giving it over to him to wash I said, as casually as I could, "You must be proud of Iolanthe, being so clever and working so hard to achieve her ambition. She said it was hard work but she seemed to be enjoying it. She was quite enthusiastic when she was telling me about it all." I turned my back and stacked the cups and saucers in the wall cupboard to the right of the sink. John grunted behind me and drew in his breath. "Yes, of course I'm proud of her. None of the other teachers has a wife as clever as mine. I even encouraged her to go for it, remember? Like I encouraged Dad." He banged the teaspoons on to the draining board with an unnecessary clatter. "But I never expected she'd be away like this. I thought it was a correspondence course that she could do at home. It started that way and it was fine. She was at home all day then and we could both be free in the evenings."

He turned an unhappy face to me as he dried his hands on the striped towel hanging beside the sink. His mouth, so often turned up in an impish grin, was drooped at the corners in a despondent curve. This was not like my light-hearted son. He was obviously more upset that I had previously suspected. And I had a feeling that he was not revealing his real problem. There was something deeper going on. I draped the tea towel over the oven door to dry and looked at my watch.

"I'm not meeting Sarah until six thirty. We're going out to dinner at the Imperial. She knows the chef; she says he has a good reputation." I led back into the living room. "So, come on, John. Sit down and tell me all about it. There's something troubling you, more than you've said. I can tell. You and Iolanthe are so right for each other. At least I've always thought so. I can't bear to see you so unhappy. What's wrong, really?"

We sat down as before, on either side of the fireplace though, as the April weather was unseasonably warm the room was heated only by the night storage radiator under the window. In an attempt to clarify the situation I went on, "Iolanthe told me a lot about her course. We had a long chat on the ferry. She was very fortunate that the University offered her a place on the strength of her work in the correspondence course. And they've been very good in arranging her studies to fit in with her living on the island. So her lectures and tutorials are organised so that she has to stay away as few nights as possible. And not every week, of course. There are the long vacations when she works at home." I raised an eyebrow, as if challenging him to contradict me, but went on, "There are people from the island, you know, who have to commute weekly to a job on the mainland. The postmistress was telling me about someone in Lochranza who has to do that because there are so few jobs available here. But he thinks that's preferable to living in the city. At least his family has the benefit of living here, it's so good for the children and they make the most of their weekends. I even heard of a woman whose husband is in the merchant navy and he's away for months at a time. Every homecoming is like a second honeymoon, she says. So cheer up, John. It's not really so bad, is it? Or is there something else you're not telling me about?"

"No, no, of course not. It's just that I miss her. I'd come home in the evening after school and she'd be here with a drink waiting for me. And we'd relax, telling each other about our day, before she set about preparing the evening meal and I did my marking. When she's away there's no point in coming home. I stay at school to do my marking and then haven't the heart to make a meal for myself. I can't be bothered. It's not worth it, just for me."

Oh dear, I thought, he does feel sorry for himself. What happened to that confident insouciance he once had? How did he come to be so self-centred that he can't see Iolanthe's life except as an adjunct to his own? He was in danger of repeating George's mistake. Were all men the same, I wondered? Did they all expect the woman in their life to be subservient to their whims? How could I help John to avoid making a mess of what seemed so promising? I sighed and uncrossed my ankles and shuffled my bottom. This sagging chair was no longer comfortable. Perhaps I'd said enough for today. I could think of nothing else that could help at this juncture, so was glad when John decided to change the subject.

"Do you see much of Dad?" He looked up at me, his eyes pleading to leave painful subjects alone. "He pops in to see me sometimes when he's on this side of the island, like you do. But he doesn't often mention you and I wondered if you had any contact." He burrowed even more deeply into the sagging leather upholstery of the chair opposite mine and smiled.

"I'm glad he keeps in touch with you. In spite of being so near I don't actually see him very often. Not to speak to, that is. I see him coming and going, of course, and I hear his car. He seems to be quite active, especially in the mornings. I hear him moving about quite early. Then he fetches his papers and does his local shopping. And I hear him hoovering, so I'm not worried about him. He appears to be looking after himself. Apart from the mornings he's very quiet, studying, I suppose."

"And he says you're very quiet, though that's about as much as he does say about you."

"Has he mentioned any friends or people he's met? Any social life?"

"Oh, yes. He's well in with the Heritage Museum lot, I think. He goes there every Wednesday, he says, so it keeps him out of mischief. It was the fellow at your post office who got him involved apparently."

"Graham? Oh, I am surprised. I can never get a word out of that man, though he's not often in the shop. His wife does enough talking for the two of them." I smiled, remembering the long monologues that always accompanied my shopping forays. "So George has been working at the museum? Well, well! I'm glad he's found a friend and something to do that he's interested in. I was afraid he would bury himself in his books and become a recluse. I wonder, John . . . " I hesitated. I wasn't used to asking my son's advice. "Do you think he'd welcome it if I suggested we meet some time? Just to exchange news, you know. Nothing serious. I'm not proposing that we live together again. Nothing like that. I enjoy my freedom too much and it looks as if he does too. But we could be friends, now that the animosity has died down. As I think it has. On my side at least."

"Oh, I'm sure you're right, Mum. Dad's not so bad now he's got nobody to bully; he's mellowed, becoming more human in fact. So go for it. Make up and be friends!" And his brow cleared and his old grin reappeared.

9

April 20
Muriel and I met last week. I state this as a bald fact, but I must try to explain the emotional nuances within the fact. As we live literally under same roof we naturally see one another occasionally by accident, when going out or coming in and in pursuit of our individual lives. But beyond normal civil pleasantries about the weather and polite enquiries about the other's health we have had little contact since we moved into our separate accommodation last Christmas and started to live our independent lives. While the decision was mutual, the parting after so many years of marriage was painful, though in the event it proved to be less painful than the years of bickering and resentment that led up to it. Adapting to a single life was also painful, for me and probably also for Muriel. I had not realised it would mean double the responsibilities, that one has to set aside time for things like shopping, cleaning and cooking. I am aware that many single individuals neglect these things and live happily in a state of squalor. But even in my student days I was very organised and kept my living conditions to a high standard. And I retained these high standards during my marriage. Having instructed Muriel in my requirements I had been able to devote my time to my career. Foolishly, as I now see

and am not ashamed to admit, I had forgotten how much time these housekeeping activities demand. And I now appreciate the time and energy that Muriel had to devote to running the three bedroomed house and garden in addition to bringing up our children. However, now that I have organised my time more adequately I find my academic work does not suffer. Indeed it may even benefit from the admixture of physical activity.

Because of this orderly arrangement of my life I was able to spare time for Muriel's suggested luncheon date. And, as it was a Wednesday I could make it fit in with my customary visit to the museum where, as I had explained to Graham on the phone, I would not be able to pick him up as usual, but would see him later. I would not have agreed to take time away from my studies, so I was glad she suggested Wednesday. That she made any suggestion at all astonished me, as it was so out of character. She never previously showed any initiative and always looked to me to organise anything. But I was glad that she had at least chosen a neutral venue. It would not have been appropriate to meet in her flat; I would have felt very uncomfortable, as if under some obligation. I acknowledge that the Seacrest Café was a suitable choice. It is a modern building, which I had passed quite frequently but never entered, not being a devotee of café society. It reminded me of the Pompidou Centre in Paris, having all its structural struts and stanchions indecently exposed, though of course the Seacrest Café is but a distant echo by a local builder. I was pleased that it was big enough to prevent overcrowding; our conversation would not be overheard. There were people at tables on the ground floor but Muriel led me upstairs, which, she explained, was a non-smoking area. "Unless you've taken up smoking in your retirement?" she asked. I think she was trying to be flippant, which I did not appreciate. I did not reply but followed her up the open staircase.

The upper room seemed even more spacious and airy than below. "It's a place where people come who wish to be undisturbed, business people, or lovers. The waitresses are discreet and one can stay half a day over a cup of cappuccino. I've been here several times," she said. With a lover, I wondered? But no, not Muriel, it was unthinkable. I shook off that suspicion as I looked at her more closely. She was still the frail-looking woman I had married. She never had much figure, though she is stronger than she looks. She has always been healthy, but I realise now that her attraction in the beginning was in her air of helplessness. It appealed to my sense of chivalry, which I now regret. It was not a good basis for marriage and that clinging helplessness soon began to irritate me and I had to look elsewhere for physical satisfaction. I am satisfied that Muriel never knew, as I have always been very careful and discreet. And now, looking at her afresh, I saw there was something new in her demeanour. She seemed brisk and lively, more so than I ever remember. She was certainly different from the last time we had met face to face.

That had been at Christmas, when Sandra had invited us to Pitlochry. It was good to see Sandra so happy with her new husband-to-be, but Muriel and I were not at our best, being tired from our removal, on edge and worn out by our years of unhappiness. And since then, while seeing her coming and going to the car, there had been no opportunity to speak. Now she smiled and suggested we choose a table at the rear, where we were not so likely to be interrupted by friends or acquaintances wanting to chat.

"And we can admire the paintings from here," she

said, waving her arms at the long side wall, which was covered with two rows of watercolours of Arran landscapes. I was not interested in the paintings, though they looked very professional. I did not ask her the name of the artist but assumed that none was of her work. I know that she is very enthusiastic about her new hobby, but she would not be capable of producing anything but purely amateur efforts. I made polite acknowledgment of the paintings and glanced away round the rest of the room, which revealed only two other customers, a couple of elderly women with heads together over a catalogue.

"Well, it's good to see you looking so well," she said as we seated ourselves at a bright blue melamine table. I was pleased she had noticed my more relaxed state. "So," she went on, "Are you happy in your flat upstairs? Have you got everything to your satisfaction? What about furniture? Did you have to buy anything extra?" She was prattling, nervous, keyed-up.

It was not easy. Both of us were constrained, remembering our past lack of empathy. It would be wise to adhere to polite social remarks until we had at least softened the ice of our mutual hostility.

The blonde young waitress obviously knew Muriel; she greeted her with a warm smile as we asked for the menu. Muriel must have noticed my raised eyebrows, as she explained, "Sarah, my painting friend, and I have been here several times and the waitresses have got to know us."

I enquired about her friends and her activities in order to keep the conversation going. This Sarah she talks about appears to be one of the directors of the Hydro, a large commercial venture in complementary medicine which, by all accounts, is very successful. It is good that Muriel has become acquainted with a worthwhile set of people. Her friendship with Sarah will give her entrée to the other owners of the Hydro and their friends. She likes to socialise, meet people in cafes or invite one another to meals. She tried to do that in Heysham with disastrous results. Her choice of friends there was deplorable – a shopkeeper's wife and a coloured woman. Her new acquaintances are an improvement, which I can only approve. And her painting is a harmless pastime, which I encouraged her to pursue. She told me about painting out of doors, and her meetings at the Women's Institute, and a painting group she attends, all of which kept the conversation going. She was still edgy and maybe talked too much, but gradually the atmosphere between us became less constrained as we discussed the merits of prawn salad and mushroom omelette.

"So, we've talked about me for long enough. What about your OU course, George? How are you getting on with it? John said you were enjoying it. What are you studying at the moment?"

"I'm enjoying it very much. It's hard work of course, and deals with subjects I had no previous knowledge of."

"Oh? But you've always been interested in history. You must have considerable knowledge already. How could it be new to you?

"Oh, but to get a degree with the OU these days one has to have a wide background knowledge, so the first course is to build up a sort of general knowledge of the humanities. Things like the history of music, art, literature, philosophy and – oh – so many things. It's fascinating. I'm having to learn so much that was previously unknown to me. I might in time even be able to appreciate those works of art that got you so excited in Glasgow." Her eyes lit up as I mentioned that I had to look at paintings – Old Masters mainly,

of course, but some modern ones and not amateurs. She must have thought it would give us something in common, to bring us closer together. Perhaps it might, but our main point of contact is still our son John.

"It's good that we both keep in touch with him and Iolanthe. They always ask after you when I go to see them." And she went on to elaborate about Iolanthe's absences and John's worries.

I am not surprised that he is worried. I never trusted Iolanthe from the first moment I met her. I don't know what her game is, but she is much too beautiful to be a fit wife for John. Or 'partner' as they call themselves nowadays. It seems to me she is neither a wife nor a tart. I expressed something of these doubts to Muriel but she just laughed at me and went on picking at her prawns. She pointed out that they had been together now for two years and Iolanthe had not displayed any behaviour to cause suspicion in that time. But Muriel had her own doubts. Why would Iolanthe not agree to marry John, as he wished and repeatedly asked her to? We talked about this enigma at length. It seemed to us inexplicable. What had she against marriage? That being her attitude, why did she stay with him? Neither of us had an answer to these questions but the discussion was amicable; although we had not made a lasting success of our marriage we could at least claim to be caring parents. On that note we parted, agreeing that the brief meeting for lunch was a success and worth repeating from time to time. Although the invitation had been from Muriel, she allowed me to pay and I was glad she showed so much sensitivity to my feelings.

10

I'd been to Lamlash many times before but I had not been along this particular road. It didn't lead anywhere at the end except to a farm and footpaths over the hill and round the point. But Sarah had chosen it because she said it was quiet and would give us a good view of Holy Island. As Sarah instructed, I turned the car left off the main road, to where the old church spire beckoned, and wound along the edge of the shore towards the car park at the far end of the tarmac. It seemed a long way though it couldn't have been more than a mile; because of the increasing narrowness I had to slow down to a crawl and watch out for the passing places. I hoped not to meet any other cars or, heaven forbid, lorries. As it happened I met nothing, not even a pedestrian. Actually I was surprised; there could have been considerable traffic as the road led to the turning to the cottage hospital and was lined on the left with substantial villas. But all was quiet and I could relax and enjoy the meandering route lined on the right like my road in Lochranza with wild flowers and grasses only inches above the pebbly shore. Occasional rocky outcrops, I noticed, were strangely yellow. Whether a marine type of lichen or some limpet-like animal I didn't stop to explore. Ever narrowing, the road wound on, past the last of the villas and into a wilder margin on the left, of woodland and fields rising up away from the sea. There was nothing here but seabirds and wild nature. I was happy. The day was grey, the colours subtle with no sharp edges, no sun, I was here to paint and I was happy. I rounded a bend and there was the car park sign, a municipal interruption of a pastoral idyll. But that was the place where Sarah said I should stop. Indeed, it was the only place where one could stop without blocking the road. As a car park it was thankfully less suburban than the signpost suggested, being merely a flattened piece of sandy earth with an old bench perched precariously on the edge as if it were about to tumble into the sea. Sarah had not yet arrived, so I was glad to be able to look around on my own, to get my bearings. From here I could see the whole sweep of the bay, with Holy Island rising in the middle like a plug in a washbasin. There would be no point in trying to put all of that in a painting, there was far too much; even the farther shore of Ayrshire was visible. It was obvious I would have to be very selective, I thought as I moved around, making my fingers frame the views.

"Yes, I thought we could concentrate on Holy Island with a bit of this in the foreground," Sarah said, waving an arm at the tangle of undergrowth at our feet. She looked very workmanlike in her grey trousers, warm boots and thick Aran sweater, and her bright eyes shone with anticipation of a morning's dedication to painting.

I had not noted her arrival. I had been too absorbed in the view to hear her car draw up beside me. "I don't fancy sitting on that bench," I said. "I prefer my little stool and I'll find a level spot where there's an interesting plant in front of me. I'd like to do a close-up of something, with the island behind. It will give it distance."

Sarah laughed. "You sound like a professional," she said. "But you're right. I've seen too many amateur paintings with the same green throughout, regardless of distance; they take no account of the atmosphere."

"Yes. Before I came here I went to a class in Morecambe and the tutor used to call it aerial perspective. How one has to think of the sky and air between the foreground and the background. He was very strict about us getting it right."

It was just as well it was a dull day; when an occasional flash of sunlight appeared it silhouetted the island into a mere black shape and blinded us. Sarah apologised. She had forgotten that we would be facing south. "Late afternoon would have been better for painting. I'm sorry I misled you. We'll have to think about the position of the sun when we choose our next venue. At least it looks as if it will remain cloudy but won't actually rain, so we can get a painting completed. They're interesting clouds too."

There was little detail that needed sketching in; only the shape of the island and the line of the shore. I decided to balance the white farmhouse on the right hand side of the island with some wild bits of bracken and grasses and perhaps a rock on the left of the foreground. The sea was calm, with no waves to strain my talent, and its colour was a subtle blend of greens and blues and greys. But first I concentrated on the shape of the island. "It's an exercise in masses of trees again, but easier this time because they're further away and I shan't be tempted to put in any details," I told Sarah and added that this exercise included some treeless mountain and rocky screes, which I hadn't tackled before. Really, Arran was proving to be a most exciting place for painting; I was finding endless stimulation. I didn't know whether my work was improving, but I did know that I was increasingly confidant and becoming more interested in the abstract.

Sarah was already painting fronds of bracken in her foreground. She would soon have finished. That meant she was almost ready for lunch and a gossip. Our gossip was never malicious but our painting meetings were an opportunity to catch up with local news from opposite sides of the island. She had been here all her life and knew so many people; she kept me in touch with what was going on, particularly in Brodick.

"Now I've done it I don't like my bracken," she said. "But it'll have to stay now. I can't wash it out; it would spoil the sea," and she washed her brush, threw away the water and screwed the lid back on her jar. I hurriedly dashed in some rough grasses in my foreground, waved the paper about to dry it and packed up, so as not to keep her waiting. The clouds had thickened while we had been sitting there and rain looked imminent, so it was wise to repair to a café for some lunch. The one by the pier was handy; I'd been there before with Moira from Lochranza and knew that the food would be fresh made. Moira's cousin was the cook. It was a small café, with only four tables, but we were lucky. The table by the window was free and there was space on the floor in the corner for all our painting tackle. We draped our coats over the back of vacant chairs and settled down to study the menu on the table.

"I've been thinking, Sarah, about my painting. I seem to be getting more interested in less naturalistic work. I want to flatten things and make a pattern out of them. And I'm wondering whether to try oils. What do you think? Am I too ambitious?" But her reply had to wait. The waitress appeared at our side, notepad in hand. The girl was a school-leaver, filling in time before getting a 'proper job' she said. She was gawky, her features cut out with a sharp knife and her hair dark with unwashed grease. Her appearance was less appealing than the offerings on the menu, and I hoped she would soon grow out of her teenage spottiness. Her hands looked clean, at least.. In spite of Moira's cousin's assertion about the fresh made pizzas we both settled for baked potatoes, mine with Arran cheese, Sarah's with tuna. We asked the girl her name. "Really it's Annabel, but I prefer to be called Belle," she said, and she tapped away on her high heels to give our orders to the kitchen. Sarah and I smiled at one another, sharing the unspoken thought of the unbeautiful Belle.

But then we returned to our interrupted conversation. I continued, "I'd have to work at home if I used oils, wouldn't I? I can't see myself lugging a board and heavy oil paints around with me, and the painting would be all smeary, and it wouldn't dry in time to do anything else to it. It's a different technique and I'm not used to it. I'm not sure what to do, Sarah, but I'd like to try it. Have you any ideas?"

"Well, to go back to what you said before our bellissimo interrupted, I don't think you're too ambitious. I think it's good to experiment and I admire your courage. I think you should go for it. Why not? You've nothing to lose. And you've got a spare room if you need to work at home. I agree, oils are better dealt with indoors but you could use your watercolours as sketches for larger paintings in oils, perhaps. And – here's an idea! Why not go for acrylics? They can be used either way. You could then paint out of doors, using them thickly like oil paint, and they'd dry quickly. Or you could thin them down and use them like watercolours, though their quick drying can be a problem there. But at least they give you a choice. What do you think?"

Sarah paused while she rolled hot baked potato round her open mouth, gasping cold air on to it. It wasn't a pretty sight but I was having the same problem. How else could one cope with a hot potato? I swallowed mine, ignoring my burnt tongue, and continued the conversation.

"You're a genius! Why didn't I think of acrylics? I'll have another trip to Glasgow to that wonderful shop and get some acrylic paints and some more brushes. And of course I shall want boards though I can probably get them here. I wouldn't want to carry them from Glasgow and it's not worth taking the car. And I'll think about a bigger, stronger easel, to hold the boards at home. You're right about my spare room. It's asking to be turned into a studio. George has turned his into a study, he told me, so we shall both have a workroom, a creative den. I can't wait!"

Sarah smiled indulgently at my enthusiasm and paused as she aligned her knife and fork at the side of her plate, now beginning to be strewn with brown tatters of potato skins. "I hear your husband is making a name for himself," she remarked as we continued the meal more comfortably with our cooling potatoes.

She surprised me. George enjoyed his voluntary work at the Museum. He had told me about it when we met at the Seacrest. But as far as I knew he had not got involved in any other outside activities that could conceivably make him famous. What could Sarah mean? "He's surely not been here long enough to become well known," I said. "And, although he's not a blushing violet like I am, he's not one to push himself forward."

"No, of course not. I didn't mean that. It just happened, apparently. Providential you might say. One of the committee at the Museum resigned suddenly and there was your husband, ready-made so to speak. So naturally they appointed him forthwith."

She forked up the last of her tuna with a morsel of potato and caught the eye of an acquaintance at the table beside the pay desk. She nodded to whoever it was behind my back. I had chosen to sit facing the window where I could see, through the veil of flowering geraniums, the yachtsmen and robed Buddhist monks going to Holy Island. There wasn't a lot happening today but I never tired of looking at the sea. "That's Eleanor Ponsonby and her husband," she whispered, leaning over the table towards me. "They used to run the Mayfair Hotel but went bankrupt in the foot and mouth epidemic. So sad. It was a good hotel. If they'd only hung on for another year it might have come all right. The tourists started coming back just as they gave up"

I was still no wiser, being unable to see the couple, and was more interested to hear how she know about George. Could it be true?

"Oh, yes, it's true. My late husband's cousin Sybil is on the committee. She's keen on archaeology; quite knowledgeable though she's taught herself. She digs things up. Surprising what she finds. Anyway it was she who told me. It must be true."

I had to believe her, and of course George was capable of the job. He had always been interested in history and he was a meticulous organiser, although, strangely, he had never expressed any interest in my work at the Heritage Centre in Heysham. I was glad he had found a niche for himself with a mixed group of people. All the same, I was amazed, though I said nothing to Sarah about how prejudiced and class-conscious he had always been, making it so difficult for him to mix. My mind went back to when he refused to be introduced to my friends, Naomi because she was of mixed race and Elsie because she was working class. How mortified I was that day! He must be changing! Perhaps it was Arran that was changing him; he must surely have realised at last that people shouldn't be fixed in pigeon holes, people were just people. And no doubt the committee members were an ordinary mixture; he couldn't vet them beforehand. I ruminated over the remains of my potato while Sarah finished hers and laid down her knife and fork neatly on her plateful of skins, which she had scraped clean of the last fragment of food. I had to admit to myself that I too had changed or was changing in this different milieu. The population probably had the same admixture as on the mainland, but the fewer number meant that we were all mixed up closely together. I found that at the Rural meetings, where we were all equal as women. That must be what had happened to George! I smiled at Sarah, suddenly full of happiness. Our separation and removal to Arran was working out. A good future lay ahead!

"I think I'll do some drawings of yachts while I'm here, and watch the little ferry boat go across to Holy Island. I can easily spend an hour or so with my notebook and then go along to see John when he gets back from school. Are you going to stay after lunch? Would you like to meet my son?"

"Well, that's very kind of you but I've got to do some shopping, then I'm going to Melanie's for tea. She's been on a coach tour of Scandinavia, so I want to hear about it. And she'll want to hear all my news." She sighed. "You're lucky to have your son here. I wish I saw more of mine. He's away such a lot. It's perhaps a good thing that Susie is kept busy at the Hydro. She's too busy to be lonely, I hope."

11

May 15
The tourist season here, as at other resorts in Britain, starts in earnest at Easter and, as the weather was good, I noticed a good many visitors were already on the island. We volunteers at the museum had worked very hard to get everything ready; even I was persuaded to help clean the concrete floors in the stables and to reseal it. There is considerable satisfaction in physical work I discovered. And I am now more accustomed to the camaraderie, which I have never before experienced. In the office there could only be the boss and employees. And I was neither one nor the other so long as Father was alive and in charge of the firm. So friendship on an equal-footing is new to me. Graham and I have formed such a friendship, easy and casual; we don't intrude on one another's private life but we know we can rely on one another. I give him a lift every Wednesday and he regales me with tales of Arran's history. This week he told me of the mysterious death on Goat Fell in the nineteenth century, and the man's climbing companion who was hanged for the murder although there was no evidence that the death was anything but an accident. I have made a note to ask Rosemary for more details about this mystery. There may be a book about it. My friendship with her is a surprising

development in my life here. She actually seems to enjoy my company, as I enjoy hers. She gives me a special greeting and her eyes light up when I go to the library. And she always accepts a cup of tea when she brings me the books I have requested. I wonder if the time may be ripe to invite her to a meal without fear of refusal. I hesitate, as a rebuttal of my invitation would cause embarrassment between us. And in addition, I do not wish her to get false ideas about my intentions. I have learnt that she is a widow; her husband was drowned at sea on a fishing expedition off the coast of Northern Ireland. But I must be careful. Friendship is one thing, commitment is another. Having just won my freedom from Muriel I do not wish to enter into another relationship. I must make this clear. It must remain on the easy, casual terms that exist between Graham and me.

I had explained to him that other Wednesday why I could not offer him the usual lift into Brodick. He raised his eyebrows when I said I was meeting my wife for lunch, but he said nothing. And he still said nothing when I arrived at the museum much later. My late arrival was not important, as it happened. The museum had been open to visitors since Easter and there was less for us to do. Our valiant efforts during the winter would now, we hoped, bear fruit in attracting increasing numbers of tourists, week by week.

Malcolm was away on holiday – in Cyprus, they said – but the rest of us spread around the premises, the old smiddy, the cottage, barns and stables, and the gardens, to check that all was in order. Once or twice I was accosted by a visitor who wanted to reminisce about their grandfather using the same kind of old tools we exhibited. Other visitors were more interested in the prehistoric remains, which Sybil was more capable of explaining. But these activities were not our proper function. There had been the annual general meeting in March when the year's guides had been appointed. There was Dorothy and Maisie and two others whose names I did not know. They were paid a salary and arranged their own duty rota They were retired women, happy to work part-time in agreeable surroundings.

The committee is a different matter. The members are unpaid and are expected to be active the whole year. Graham told me about it, as he is a member. That was the system and everybody seemed content. My only purpose in describing it in detail is to introduce the meeting we had there this week. Esther had rung me to say, "There's an extra informal committee meeting and I'm keen to have everybody there. I'd like you to be there, too, if you can make it. Malcolm is back from Cyprus and nobody else is away so it should be a full house."

And it was. There were eight of us. I now knew all their names, of course, and I had worked beside most of them at different times. Apart from the computer work with Millie I had helped Tom to remove the old display cases in the archaeology room and install new ones. I had acted as mate to Graham when he updated the electric wiring in the stable. And I had taken a turn with Joyce at chipping off the rust from the old ploughs. By now I really felt part of the team and I was pleased to be invited to their committee meeting. The little archive room was barely large enough to accommodate us all. In fact the younger ones, Joyce and Malcolm, stood and propped themselves against the computer worktable, while the rest of us sat around the long table that was normally strewn with papers and photographs waiting to be mounted. I kept myself in the background. Although I now knew all these people I still felt an outsider. They had all been officially appointed at the AGM in March, whereas I had merely been invited to attend this particular meeting as an observer. I looked around the table. Esther looked very business-like. She was severely dressed in a very masculine kind of suit with a spotted tie, and sat foursquare on her chair, every inch in charge. She pushed aside all the papers in front of her to make room for her minute book. A folder dropped to the floor, spilling its contents. Tom collected up all the spilled papers and slid the folder across to Malcolm at the farther end.

With her minute book open Esther smiled, her wrinkles settling into a habitual good-humoured pattern. "There's not a lot of business, very little in fact but I think we should keep in touch with one another about what's happening We can congratulate ourselves on having everything ready for the opening at Easter, which, incidentally, saw a satisfying influx of visitors. We have an excellent team of guides and receptionists. And so far there's been no dearth of volunteers to take over during staff holidays, Sundays or emergencies. Millie has a copy of the list of people who will come in on Sundays and others who will make themselves available at a moment's notice. As for the teashop, that is becoming very popular; one thing we have to decide. Should we make the teashop available without the obligation of paying for admission to the museum? What do you all think?" She waited, pen poised over her minute book. The others looked round at one another with raised eyebrows, then gave nods and murmurs of assent. "Good. So that's agreed. I've mentioned it to the staff and they are willing to organise their duties to cover the extra hours. It will bring in additional income anyway, which is all to the good. And now, the next bit of news is to say farewell to Tom and find someone to replace him on the committee." She beamed an encouraging and warm smile at Tom, seated beside her, and patted his hand which lay on the table. "Our old friend Tom, who is leaving the island and who has given the museum so many years of faithful service in so many capacities."

The others were vociferous in acclamation. "Remember, Tom, when there was that flu epidemic when the rest of us were laid low and you were left to hold the fort when the inspectors came about our charity status? You did us proud then." That was Millie. She must have been associated with him for a long time.

"Aye, well," Tom responded. "It all turned out all right, didn't it? We've gone on a long way since then, expanded, got a lot of other projects under way. And there's still work to be done. Still need for expansion. But I'm past it. I have to acknowledge it. I'm not at home in this computer age; I've no heart to do anything any more. It's time to pack up and let somebody look after me. Barbara's a good girl. Girl, did I say? Her husband's just retired." He laughed and everybody smiled. We could all understand what it meant to have aging offspring "They've been begging me to go ever since . . well . . . this last year. They've a nice house and I expect I shall like living in Surrey. When I get used to it." He gave a twisted smile and Esther squeezed the hand she was still holding

There was something here that I was not aware of. I was acquainted with the old man, of course. He had given me a conducted tour of the exhibits on my first visit, but I did not know his background. He must be over eighty; he had lost weight recently and appeared frail, with a stooped figure but clear complexion. Graham informed me later, on our way home, that

Tom was a native of Arran, one of the old families, but he'd gone to pieces after his wife died of cancer last year. He had lost his will to live and ceased to care for himself, so that going to live with his daughter was the best solution. It is sad to let oneself go like that but, as I said to Graham, it is no good being sentimental about leaving the old home. But that was a later conversation. To return to the museum committee, the talk had turned to finding a replacement for Tom.

"We don't need to wait for the next AGM," Esther said. "We have the power to co-opt whoever we want, and our choice can be ratified next March Are you agreed?" They all nodded their assent as she continued, "We've all been aware of your contribution this winter, George, ever since you came to Arran, and we appreciate the way you've been willing to help in any capacity, wherever the need arose. Would you now be willing to serve on the committee?"

All eyes turned to me. I looked around the faces. All were smiling, encouraging I had had no inkling that this was on the agenda, but now I knew why they had invited me 'as an observer'. I was pleased they recognised and valued my efforts, though rather surprised that they should accept me so readily. After all, I was a newcomer to the island. It has always been said that it takes many years – if ever for a newcomer to integrate into a small close-knit community, but it's not true here, apparently. I acknowledge that I am fortunate and therefore was willing to accept their invitation graciously. All renewed their smiles and words of welcome. Except Simon, who looked down at the table and frowned, while Esther wrote up her minutes. I took no notice of Simon. He was always taciturn and surly and his conversation was usually limited to grunts. He was older than most of the others and I had noticed that his hands were very shaky. I suspected that he had Huntingdon's disease; my suspicion was strengthened when he fumbled with some papers in front of him and shakily handed them round the table.

"What's this, Simon? Not another balance sheet? We don't require one in May, you know. And you didn't ask for a discussion of the finances to be put on the agenda for today. Not that it matters," Esther added hastily, as his lips trembled and he became more agitated. "What did you want us to discuss, Simon?" Her tone was obviously meant to pacify the old man. "This was intended as an informal meeting, just to fill the vacancy caused by Tom's departure." She looked at the others. "But now, under 'any other business' Simon evidently has something he wishes to bring up."

The old man bent down, almost disappearing from view, and then straightened up with two plastic shopping bags, which he threw on to the table in front of the secretary. "Here you are," he said. "I've finished. All the books and papers are there. Do what you like with them. I'm moving tomorrow to the old people's home. One room, no space for anything I've had enough. Don't want the trouble any more." And he heaved himself painfully to his feet and began to stumble out.

There was an electric silence as the shock wave passed round the table. I was appalled. How could a treasurer behave so cavalierly? He was obviously in need of care. Perhaps it was Alzheimer's he was suffering from? No doubt the old people's home was the best place for him, but to be so abrupt, so stark? What would the committee do?

Esther coughed and half-stood, reaching out her hand. "Here, hang on, Simon. You can't leave us just like that. Sit down and let's discuss it." The others made soothing noises and he grudgingly resumed his seat. "This is all very sudden, Simon. You must forgive us if we can't take it in. We didn't know you were planning to move. And we thought you were contented enough as treasurer. You've done a good job and it will be difficult to replace you. Are you sure you want to give up?"

"Aye, I am. Positive. It's time I went. I've been on the waiting list for a room in that place for two years. I can't manage on my own any longer. My hip's got worse and I can't get about. I've been on the waiting list for that as well. And now everything happens at once. New hip next week, some mainland hospital, can't remember which. And moving into the Dukeries home here tomorrow. Somebody died suddenly so they've got a vacancy." On a bitter snap of his false teeth he sat back and glared at Esther as if defying her to offer sympathy.

I am not usually susceptible to emotional atmosphere, but I could sense that his self-control was very precarious. Any expression of sympathy would cause him to break down in tears, to everyone's embarrassment. I held my breath. Nobody wanted a scene. I looked at Esther. She appeared to me to be out of her depth. Her talent was for running around organising things and I could see she was conscious of the quicksands fronting her but did not know how to respond.

But Millie came to the rescue. Summoning up her remembered expertise from her Foreign Office past she said, "That's great good news for you, Simon. It's a pity it's all come at once, but they're both things that you wanted to happen, aren't they? And you'll soon settle down in your new home, where I think you already have some friends and you'll soon make new ones. They have a good time there, I'm told, with lots of excursions ad other goodies denied to us ordinary mortals." She smiled. "And with a new hip you'll be living the life of Riley."

Graham then chipped in. "And I'll help you move your stuff tomorrow, Simon. No problem, mate."

Esther sighed with relief and minuted their gratitude to Simon for the years of dedicated work he had given to the museum and in particular in his capacity as treasurer. As there was no further business I was thankful that the meeting was brought to a close and Graham and I were free to drive home.

"Obviously it wasn't the right time to discuss who should replace old Simon." Graham was pensive in the car. "Poor old sod. He's gone down hill very rapidly." He turned his face away from me and gazed unseeingly at the new bracken fronds greening the mountainside. "Its not up to me, but I think it's providential you getting elected on the committee just now. You being an accountant, I mean. Think about it, mate. I guess they'll be after you. I saw Esther looking your way and I knew what she was thinking." If Graham was right I would have to consider what answer I might give. Would I want to be treasurer? I will certainly think about it and be prepared if the committee ask me.

12

"Hello, John. I let myself in. You don't mind, do you?"

"Of course not. I gave you a key, didn't I?" He clattered the front door shut with his heel, stumped into the living room and dropped a heavy bulging briefcase and an armful of books on to the table beside me. My shopping in Lamlash had not taken as long as I expected and I thought John might have returned early. I had been standing at the window watching for him and now turned towards the kitchen.

"I've got the kettle on. I'll make us a cup of tea while you relax."

He puffed out a tired breath and sank into the saggy chair he loved. "Pfouff! Why did I choose this job? I'm knackered, pooped, kaput, exhausted in any language you like." His arms hung down over the sides of the chair, his legs stretched right across the fireplace, and his spine bowed in utter collapse.

"Come on, John, you know you love teaching. It's all you ever wanted to do, and you like the school," I called from the kitchen, where I was setting out some garibaldi biscuits on an old willow pattern plate that he must have picked up at a jumble sale but which looked attractive with the blue mugs. I had brought the biscuits with me from Lochranza as I knew he liked garibaldis but couldn't buy them in Lamlash.

"Thanks, Mum. Just what I need. A dose of caffeine to pep me up. It was bloody awful today. Tommy Ferguson was over on the mainland for some hospital treatment and I had to give up my free period to take his lot for Civic Studies. A lively discussion on the uses of the census degenerated into a noisy argument about immigration. It all got very heated. They didn't quite get to blows, thank God, and at the end they agreed it had stimulated thought. I'm stimulated to a frazzle after it all though. Why do I do it?" His hand made a bee-line for a biscuit, which he snapped in half. He had become serious; he frowned and his voice became more thoughtful as if he were thinking aloud. "You know, I really do love teaching, I have to admit. And I'm mad about history. I guess I've done what Dad always dreamed of doing I've achieved my boyhood ambition. But now I'm wondering about a change"

"Oh, no, surely, you'd never be happy doing anything else but teach, John."

"Well, nothing drastic, I assure you. No, I was just wondering about a college job. Teaching adults, I mean. It might be more difficult in some ways. I'd have to keep up with research and I'd probably be expected to write articles for learned magazines, or monographs and things.' He waved his hand to indicate unknown 'things'. "But at least I'd have students who were really serious about wanting to learn. And I'd have access to a university library and work with colleagues with the same interests. What do you think?"

"What? You surely can't mean it, John. You haven't been here long enough, barely a year – and you've only just moved house. Whatever are you thinking of? And what about Iolanthe? What would she do? Have you spoken to her about this? Does she agree with this crazy idea?"

"Well, no, that's just it. She's never here. Why should I consider her? We might just as well be living in Glasgow; she spends most of her time there these days." And he poured a second cup of tea to accompany his second biscuit.

Oh dear, he's in self-pity mode again, I thought. I'd better change the subject. There's no more I can add to what I said last time and I don't want him to think I'm nagging. That would only drive a wedge between us. He knows the score. I've said enough. "I heard your father has been elected to the committee of the museum," I said brightly, changing the subject to something more neutral. "Did he tell you?"

"No, I didn't know. I haven't seen him for a week or two." He sat up and his face cleared. "Good for him. It'll keep him out of mischief. That and his OU work will keep him fully occupied I should imagine. Incidentally, talking of mischief, I heard a rumour that the finances there are in a pretty rocky state. There's been some creative accounting, I believe. Or so I've heard. It may not be true of course. You know what it's like here for rumours. If you sneeze in Lochranza you'll have pneumonia when they hear the news in Kilmory. Anyway, if there's anything wrong they're sure to appoint Dad to look into things."

I laughed and agreed something like that would happen. "But the museum is a charity, surely. They must have an auditor. The accounts and books and things must have been all right at the end of the financial year, whenever that was." I was getting worried. I hoped George wouldn't get himself involved in any shady business. I knew how meticulous he had always been. Everything in his office and even everything at home had to be just right, according to his strict standards. If he finds any discrepancies or irregularities in the museum accounts there'll be the devil to pay. "But it's only five or six months since the audit, surely? I would imagine the financial year ends on December 31st. That's usual, anyway."

"I presume so. The AGM was early in March. Felicity, our PT mistress went. It was open to the public and they had a speaker, I believe. I should have been there but had too much to do. Felicity is a friend of Sybil the archaeologist there. They go digging together. And hill-walking sometimes. She said there was no mention of any funny business then. The accounts were passed as OK."

"So who is the treasurer? Perhaps there hasn't been one this year? Or has he or she suddenly gone dulally?"

"He. His name's Simon Something-or-other. He's a cousin or cousin-in-law of the Head. You know, one of those local families where everybody is related to everybody else. I've never met him but he must be quite old, I think. Though age doesn't matter these days, they say. Who knows what's being going on?"

"It will have to be hushed up and sorted out quickly. George will have his hands full, if he takes on the job. Everything will have to be shipshape and presentable. If the Charity Commission hears about any irregularity they'd be in trouble. They could lose their charity status, which would make a big difference to their income. I wonder if George is aware of these rumours?"

"I doubt it. Even if there was a suspicion that everything was not right, nobody could know anything for sure until the treasurer handed over all the books and papers and someone else started to look at them. I'll ask Dad about it when I see him again. But it's only rumour so far. We're talking about it as if it were a fact.

That's what happens, and where the damage is done."

His tone of voice expressed deep bitterness and he frowned down at his clasped hands, whose knuckles had whitened, I noticed. There was more to this conversation than gossip. There was something personal here. He was really upset. He seemed genuinely troubled.

"What is it, John? You're not involved in any of this, are you? I didn't think you had anything to do with the museum. Your father will sort things out if there's anything wrong. And it's all rumour anyway. There may be nothing in it after all."

"That's just it, Mum. People spread rumour and don't ask whether it's true. There's no smoke without fire, they say, and everybody believes it and the rumours grow into something diabolical." He beat his clenched fist on the arm of the chair, raising a shimmer of dust in the sun's rays. "Bugger it all, Mum, there are rumours about Iolanthe and me. People have said things. They look at me and I know what they're thinking, damn their eyes!" He looked up at me, his face dark and scowling.

He never used to swear at all in my presence and now, restrained as his language was, it indicated strong emotion scarcely controlled. "Rumours? About you and Iolanthe?" I tried to make light of it, to lift him out of his mood. "But you know they're not true, whatever they are. Some people have nasty minds and like to make mischief, but it's only because they're unhappy and can't bear to see someone else happy or successful. Why worry about what people say? Why not treat it as a joke? They'll soon realise it's false. Anyway, what are these rumours that you've heard?"

"It's all very well for you to talk, but I can't treat it as a joke, Mum. It's too serious for that. It's Iolanthe. I've heard . . .they say . . . she's been seen . . ." He broke off and looked so miserable I wanted to hug him better, as I used to do when he fell over and cried as a small child.

"What have you heard? She's been seen, you say? I don't understand. You know what she does here, you're together. And how could anybody know what Iolanthe is doing in Glasgow? Tell me about it, John. What exactly are these rumours? Precisely, I mean." I couldn't see that she could possibly have any time for anything suspect, what with her university work and her novel, that only I knew about. So presumably the rumour wasn't about her writing, and that wouldn't cause a scandal, surely – or would it? One never knows what other people think is scandalous. I awaited further enlightenment.

John pulled himself together, sat up straight, drew his legs up and leaned towards me. "It was at a parents' evening. We have to socialise from time to time with parents, to answer their questions and talk about their offsprings' behaviour and accomplishments, you know. Well, this father came up to me, all matey, nudging me in the ribs and winking. He said he'd been on business in Glasgow and stayed the night at the Rennie Mackintosh Hotel. But that's by the way. The point is, he was invited by his boss to a posh hotel for dinner and he saw Iolanthe there. But she wasn't alone. The bloody man's eyes bulged and he positively leered when he described the other girl with her. A high-class tart, he called her. Not only that, they were with two men, business types. My Iolanthe! With men – and you know what businessmen are like away from home! And with a tart! How could she! Oh, Mum, what am I going to do?"

"Phew! Well, that's quite a rumour. I don't know what you can do about it, John. But think about it first. It is only a rumour. The man may have been mistaken.

He's judging others by himself, I think. He obviously has a dirty mind and enjoys spreading salacious slander. But he may not know Iolanthe well enough to recognise her. And even if it's true, it may not mean what he intends you to think. You can't always judge people by appearances, you know. It could all be quite innocent. I think you should trust her, John, until at least there's proof of anything wrong. She'll probably tell you about it when she comes home, about meeting some friends. She has friends from the time before she knew you, so maybe that was it. In fact, she must know a lot of people from her modelling days. It's not wise to judge by appearances. Just trust her, John. She trusts you, doesn't she? Trust has to be mutual, you know, in a relationship that is aiming to last."

I felt it was useless to pursue the subject until we had more facts and I left him then, feeling sick at heart. What was happening to my family? Why, when we think we have achieved happiness, does it fly away from us?

13

"Good morning, Gladys. Has the bread come in yet? I'd like a small wholemeal if you have it, please. And what a wonderful morning it is!" Though I was now on the sunless side of the loch I had awakened to a golden sky spreading over from the hills in the east, and by the time I'd had my breakfast the sun had filled the room with light and warmth. It was a glorious time of year, fresh green of young growth, bluebells, campion and violets competing in the hedgerows with the lingering gold of the gorse. Even the air smelt newly created. The tide was out as I drove round the loch; I opened my window to breathe in the scent of the seaweed that covered the floor of the loch. A pair of swans paddled and poked among it, and rowing boats slouched on their sides. All was peaceful and beautiful, and I was happy!

Gladys too was in good spirits. It was early, the papers had not yet been delivered and the morning rush had not yet begun. She had time to be expansive. It reminded me of that morning when I first arrived, when she invited me into the back room for a cup of tea and I met her taciturn husband. Today there was no cup of tea and Graham had found his tongue in the meantime. I had discovered, over the months that I had known them, that he must be shy, but only with women. George had mentioned how they had become good friends, and George didn't make friends easily. I couldn't think that I was particularly intimidating and so Graham was probably shy with all women.

Today he was relatively garrulous. "You're here early, Muriel," he said. "It's too nice a morning to be lying in bed. It's my day off. And the forecast's good. You see me all togged up for the garden. I want to get some late potatoes in." He looked down at his boots, just discernibly black between flaky patches of dried mud, threadbare cord trousers of brown gone to rust, a navy Aran sweater with a sagging neckline but shrunk and matted across his chest. It was his usual workday attire, which he seemed to be comfortable with. There was no point in wearing decent clothes for cleaning the streets and tending municipal flowerbeds, after all. He nodded a farewell and disappeared through the door leading to the back room and the garden.

"So what can I do for you, Muriel?" Gladys tied her habitual apron round her ample waist as if she had only just opened the shop but was now ready for action.

"I just wanted some fresh bread before you sold out. Just a small wholemeal will do fine. I'm catching the next ferry and may not be back in time before you close. And the wholemeal sells out so quickly."

Gladys kept the bread and rolls on the shelf behind her at the post office end of the shop. I sniffed – mmm! Why do fresh baking, coffee, toast and fried bacon smell so much more appetising than the taste, I wondered? She turned to the shelf, selected a small loaf and wrapped it in tissue paper before popping it into a plain plastic shopping bag. "Will that be all, then?" I smiled and nodded as I took the bag from her and paid.

"Off to do some shopping in Tarbert or Campbeltown, perhaps?"

But before I could reply the doorbell jangled and a breathless young woman burst in. Or rather, half of her burst in. She had one foot inside the shop and held on to the open door with one hand, the other extended towards Gladys, holding out some coins. "Milk, please, Gladys. Quick! I've left the kids alone. I've run out of milk and they're yelling for their breakfast. It's blue murder, it is!"

I stood aside. This seemed to be a real emergency. I wondered who the girl was. She looked very young, perhaps only about twenty, too young to be talking about 'kids'. Perhaps she was an au pair. I hadn't seen her before, though by now I knew most of the faces of Lochranza people even if I didn't know their names. I watched the little tableau with interest. Gladys seized the largest carton of milk from the fridge in the corner, smiled but said only, "Mind how you go now, and bring the kids round later." And the girl was gone, with a loud clang of the door.

I felt in need of an explanation. I moved back to Gladys – I had modestly retired to the back of the shop during this episode – and raised my eyebrows in invitation.

Her smile softened as she watched the door slam with a bang and she turned to me, leaning over the counter conspiratorially. "Poor soul! Jacqueline, she's called, but she likes to be known as Jackie. She looks ordinary enough, wouldn't you say?"

"Well, yes, I suppose so." It was a strange question, but the girl was ordinary in a young-mum sort of way; harassed, nondescript face with no makeup, long brown hair to her shoulders, slim figure in jeans and blue tee-shirt. Like any young mother might look early in the morning, preparing children's breakfast.

"I'm not telling any tales," Gladys began to elucidate. "It's common knowledge that Jacky's our local lady of the night. You know what I mean. She's a lovely girl, really; perhaps that's the trouble. She's too kind, wants to please everybody, can't say no. She's intelligent, did well at school I believe, but there's something lacking in her moral makeup – some genes missing or something. Her two 'kids' as she calls them are two and three years old by different fathers, and rumour has it that she's pregnant again. She loves children, fortunately, and looks after them beautifully, as well as she can, poor little things. There's no money to spare for spoiling them with luxuries, that's for sure!"

By this time I was hovering by the door, looking at my watch and waiting to make my escape to the ferry. But this was intriguing. I had to know more. "You can't help liking her," Gladys went on. "And you can't help feeling sorry for her. A single mother on the Welfare." She chuckled. "I suppose you could call her occupation moonlighting. But she doesn't leave the children – oh, no, it's all very discreet, just the occasional visitor to her little cottage after the children are in bed and none the wiser. At least they don't have to get used to 'uncles' in the family."

"I see. But hasn't she any other family – a mother – who could help?"

"No, that's the sad part. She doesn't know anything about her family. She arrived here as a runaway from a children's home in Glasgow, and as she was sixteen she was allowed to stay. But the neighbours help. We all help in different ways. She means well, poor lass, and does her best for those children. It's just that she's too easygoing where men are concerned. Though they say she's choosy and all her men are regulars." Gladys chuckled at the absurdities of human nature.

With this information ringing in my ears I made my escape. There was no time to take the bread home and set out again, so I covered it with another plastic bag and stowed it in the glove box and drove through the village past the villas, the little white church, the nature study centre and the youth hostel, then round the corner to the ferry. There was nobody to be seen on the way, but there was a queue of four cars waiting for the boat, their drivers and passengers standing chatting, probably exchanging news of their holiday on Arran and giving advice on where to go on Kintyre. And there was Maggie, waiting for me on the slipway.

"I can see the boat," she said as she got into the front passenger seat. "It will be here in ten minutes. You timed it well."

A black blob on a grey sea, gradually growing and revealing its white flanks and its master's cabin perched on top. It approached from the side, looking as if it would overshoot the end of the little pier. Which it did, and promptly made a smart right hand turn to come front-on to the slipway. Its black front, like a pursed mouth, only partially shielded the car deck as the ferry's hull scraped the concrete of the slipway. The mouth, now pouting, split its bottom lip to clank down metallically on dry land. We peered down into the now open mouth. The tide being low, the ascent up the slipway was steep, which caused a problem. Cars accelerated gingerly up the steep ramp and sped off to left or right at the top, on their way to holiday accommodation. And then the problem became more serious. A Spanish coach was too low in front and was unable to make the sharp transition to the climb. The tourist passengers gathered around, agog to see what was happening – another strange experience on their Scottish tour and something to write about on their postcards home. The problem was only solved when two seamen ran up with planks to put under the front wheels. With plenty of hand gestures and frantic activity in front of the coach, the seamen moving the planks as the coach progressed, the anxious driver at last reached level ground and the Spanish tourists could journey on to visit the Castle and enjoy their holiday. Hurriedly we and the rest of the little queue embarked, and with another loud clunk of metallic jaws we were off. Five minutes to turn around and thirty minutes across to the other side. The sea air was too cool for the upper deck; the inside cabin offered more cosy accommodation as well as the coffin-like box that served as a pay office. Oh, happy day! We pensioners paid nothing for our trip across!. Only the car had to be paid for, and Maggie insisted on paying her share.

She was a cheerful woman, my own age but very different in appearance. I told her I envied her her hair, which was thick and dark with a natural curl and stayed in place, though she kept it short. It suited her round ruddy face and round figure enclosed in a shapeless black woollen coat of calf length, below which were support stockings and black brogues. She was not fashion conscious any more that I was. I felt comfortable with her, though the only thing we had discovered we had in common was our interest in gardens. Specifically, our own gardens today. We had talked over cups of tea at the Women's Institute meetings. I had been wondering aloud about what to do in my garden, whether to wait a whole year to see what came up or whether to start planting and organising it to my own ideas. I'd left it rather late. If I were going to put in new plants it should have been done in the winter. But container plants should be all right, I argued.

That was when Maggie said she wanted to go over to Skipness, to a bigger nursery than Arran could offer. "I'm looking for a scented yellow rhododendron. They haven't any yellow ones in Brodick, and I have several of the other colours already – a white, two pinks and a purple. I might get a deep red one as well if I see any. They do so well in our soil. I love going to the Castle to see them. There are always some in flower at any time of year, whenever you go."

"They'll be in containers, of course, and probably in flower, so you'll know exactly what you're buying. I might be tempted too," I said. "My garden so far is just a narrow herbaceous border to the grass. I'd like to level it better and make a decent lawn, and gradually replace the annuals and perennials with shrubs, bulbs and ground cover plants, to make less work and yet look good all the year. A few bulbs came up this spring. There was a clump of snowdrops under the rowan tree, but I'll plant more this autumn. Meanwhile, today I would like to get something to form a windbreak at the back and along the west side. The prevailing wind comes sweeping down the hill and then turns up the loch and the glen, and in the process it blackens all the leaves or blows the tops off."

The nursery was only some three miles from the Claonaig slipway, along a level and narrow shore road cut through rocks which, millions of years ago, had suffered the indignity of being suddenly tilted at forty-five degrees and split into jagged layers. It was an eerie moon-like landscape, barren of human traces until we reached the small village at the end of the road, once protected by a castle, which was now a picturesque ruin on its spit of land. At the nursery rhododendrons and other shrubs of all colours in abundance made our choice difficult, but at last we were both satisfied. It had been difficult to resist so many temptations but I had to consider, not only my purse but also the car boot and back seat capacity. It took us both quite a while to pack everything carefully enough so that one plant propped up another and there was no slack space for any to fall over and spill. I didn't want to have to clean spilt soil out of the car afterwards. For my garden I'd fallen for some escallonias and fuchsias, both of which I knew were capable of growing really big on Arran. They would withstand the wind, I hoped, and also be decorative. I would probably need more, but it was a simple matter to pop across the Sound later. Maggie had got her wish; she had found a beautiful yellow rhododendron and also a deep red one, so we were both satisfied with our day's work as we relaxed in the little ferry on our way back.

It carried more cars this time, with families and piles of luggage; tourists who had come down the coast from somewhere like Oban or further north, or had hopped over from Gigha or even Islay. Most of the passengers climbed up to the upper deck to savour the air and admire the view, but Maggie and I settled ourselves in the lounge again. The weather had deteriorated; the sun had disappeared and a windy grey sky was beginning to produce white horses out on the horizon. We scanned the sea but there was no sign of dolphins today, and the seals would be in little bays nearer to the beach.

"It can get pretty rough here sometimes, but we shall be all right today," Maggie said. She had taken off her coat and was now rummaging in her capacious handbag – a brown plastic affair with lots of zipped compartments and a flap folding over the whole. Her hands displayed the brown patches of age, I noticed, and looked at my own hands – free of brown splotches and creamed every night to keep them soft. I was proud of my hands. Scrabbling around in the innards of the bag Maggie practically dismantled it, letting the items fall one by one on to her ample lap. A purse, diary, keys, a pair of stockings, two handkerchiefs, paper tissues from CalMac cafeterias, a tube of toothpaste in its carton – "I'd forgotten about that," she muttered – and a scattering of paper clips, hair slides, Polo mints, a Mills and Boon novel and a silk scarf. But eventually she produced a bar of chocolate. "There," she said, holding it aloft in triumph. "I knew it was somewhere," and she broke it in half and offered me the part with the wrapping still round it. "I know I shouldn't eat chocolate," she went on, snapping off a square and clamping her jaws over it. "I really shouldn't. Doctor Jackson says I should try to lose weight. And I do try. Most of the time." She smiled ruefully and I sympathised. "You're all right," she retorted. "I wish I could be as slim as you. But I've always been big, brought up on the Scottish diet of chips and fry-ups. But I do go to the Hydro every week now, ever since Easter in fact. I do aerobics and go swimming and I think it's helping." And she stroked her dress over her bulging stomach and smiled.

I assured her that all this exercise would strengthen her muscles and make her feel better in any case. " I keep meaning to go too. Not to lose weight but just for well-being. It's so easy to get into slipshod habits when you're retired. There's no compulsion any more, nobody dependent on you or expecting you to do anything. I don't want to let myself go and become depressed. I've seen it too often in other older people."

"No, of course. And there are so many different kinds of therapy there. I'm sure they'd help you to decide which would suit you best. The first consultation is free, you know, and you can accept their advice or not. It's up to you. You don't have to promise you'll attend ever week or commit yourself to a fixed number of sessions. But why not ask your son about it? He'll tell you. I see him there most weeks. He's usually coming out when I'm going in but I haven't actually spoken to him. We just say hello in passing. So I don't know what therapy he goes to, except that he always looks very relaxed and happy as he comes out. He's a fine young man and a son to be proud of." And she sucked noisily at another square of chocolate, her round face creased in satisfaction.

I forced a smile but my face felt frozen. I played with the chocolate wrapper, my fingers suddenly restless. John had said nothing about regular visits. I remembered very clearly that he'd mentioned – oh so casually – that he'd been there once, apart from the time when he went at Susie's invitation for aromatherapy. But he didn't say who it was with. He only mentioned a 'she' and I assumed it was Susie again. But who was this 'she'? I racked my brains, trying to remember exactly what he had said. My thoughts rose to panic level. Was it aromatherapy again? I couldn't remember. And didn't you have to take your clothes off for that? Of course you must. It was all-over massage with oils, wasn't it? Oh, horrors, was that why he daren't tell me about it? Was something going on between him and Susie, or some other woman? And to think he has suspicions of Iolanthe! What was happening to my family? Was their relationship breaking up? Or was it, please God, nothing but idle gossip and rumour? My mind was in turmoil and the chocolate started to melt in my hot hand, clenched tightly in my lap. I resolutely refused to entertain these disloyal thoughts. John and Iolanthe were a couple, well matched and happy, intelligent and sensible. Even if they decided not to marry, they would settle down soon when Iolanthe had finished her studies, and start a family. Wouldn't they?

14

"Do come in, Muriel, and take a seat." I ventured over the threshold and hesitated. Melanie indicated the bucket chair facing the window. It looked comfortable, even inviting. I was surprised. I had not pictured the consulting room like this. I had imagined something more austere, perhaps a little intimidating with a desk, office files, probably a computer. As I had driven up the drive to the Hydro for my initial interview these vague fears niggled at me and made me grip the wheel as if it were a drowning man's lifeline. Foolish, I know. But I couldn't help it. I tried to shake off my tremors by concentrating on the parkland through which I was driving. Since my first visit I had been again to look at the Peggy Paine painting, and now the tall trees wore their early summer foliage. Beneath them were the lower shrubs of evergreen rhododendrons, with undergrowth of lush grass and tender shoots of bracken. It was that magic time when all nature was fresh and bursting with new life, not yet full-blown and blowsy, inspiring only static boredom. I loved the spring. I loved autumn too. Both were seasons of change. That's why. Of course, things changed in summer and winter, but I liked to actually see the changes taking place. And in some mystical way, I feel I am changing with the season. Was George changing too, I wondered? And

John? But pull yourself together, Muriel, I said to myself. This daydreaming wouldn't do. I was here to ask for therapy and Melanie was here to assess what particular therapy would be most suitable for me.

The bucket chair, upholstered in dove grey velvet, was as comfortable as it looked and I began to relax. Melanie had seated herself in the matching chair with her back to the window. Over her shoulder I could see a gable end of another wing of the Hydro, perhaps the hospice wing for long-term patients. The sun was causing its pink stonework to glow in golden peach shades, against which Melanie's head appeared in silhouette. It gave her a halo, I thought with a sudden nervous giggle.

"I remember you, of course. You are the painter who came to look at our Peggy Paine on the staircase and appreciated it so much, aren't you?" She smiled and I felt the warmth of it. I also appreciated the informality of the greeting and of the room itself. It was not at all what I imagined a consulting room would be. And nothing like a doctor's surgery. Simplicity was the keynote. The room was not very big, the predominant colour was the dove grey of the carpet and chairs, enlivened by tangerine curtains at the sash window; apart from the chairs there was only a small table beside Melanie. A low bookcase to the left with some bright children's books and a few toys on the floor in the corner.

I shuffled my bottom deeper into the seat and tried to explain why I had come. "You see, really there's nothing wrong with me." I felt a fraud and somehow guilty as if I ought to have some complaint that needed curing or alleviating – arthritis or something.

"That's perfectly all right. 'I'm very glad you're so fit. You don't need to be ill to take advantage of our help, you know." Of course, I did know and murmured an apology. "Can I assume that you've registered with a medical practice on the island?"

"Oh, yes. And I've seen Dr Armitage and had a thorough check-up. He says everything is in order, but he'll check my blood pressure every few months. That's all."

"So, good. And how do you think I can help you? Have you thought about it? What are you hoping I can do for you?"

"Well . . . I don't know. Nothing in particular, really. I was hoping you would tell me what I need. I've heard that you do the initial assessment and advise what's best, the best therapy for the individual, I mean." I felt a bit at sea. I didn't know what to say. I'd expected Melanie to take charge and be more like an old-fashioned family doctor, with soothing words and a pat on the back. Metaphorically, of course. And I realised I was foolish to think so. But here she was, putting the onus on me. As if I could know what was needed!

I was sure she sensed what I was thinking (I was to experience her acute percipience very often in future sessions) because she smiled again and shifted her chair to one side so that I could see her face illuminated by the light from the window instead of blankly silhouetted. "You're quite right, Muriel. But we don't treat people here unless they have contact with a GP. We're not offering alternative treatments but complementary and additional treatments, with the doctors' agreement. I think you understand that." She turned to the side and picked up a small notebook and biro from the little table to her right. "So now we've got that out of the way, we'll talk about you, shall we? I'd like to get to know you better. All I know so far is that you're a painter and that you're John's mother. I met him briefly when he and Iolanthe came here to lunch with my family one day. Ian, my son, told me later how well they had all got on together. So, let's start with the painting, shall we? When did you begin to paint? What made you start? You mentioned something about it when you came before but I'd be interested to know more."

That set me off. I sat back, stretched out my legs and crossed my ankles, at the same time noticing with shame that my shoes were dirty and scuffed at the toes – I began to wonder how that had happened and remembered I'd been weeding in them, too lazy to change into my old gardening shoes. I tucked my feet under my chair, hoping they wouldn't be noticed, as I launched into an account of my visit to Glasgow. Every detail of that particular day was etched on my memory. It had been such a turning point in my life. How could I forget it? "Meeting Veronica was providential, really, though I didn't think so at the time. When I first saw her she was alone, propping up the bar in the hotel and looking so soignée. I was amazed when she approached me next morning at breakfast, after George had rushed off and left me for the day. I must admit I was somewhat suspicious, as I saw her coming toward me. If she'd been younger I might have thought she was selling something, but she was my age and looked respectable enough. I was alone and feeling miserable and lost. George had gone off and left me for the day in a strange city where I knew nobody. I was feeling neglected, abandoned and really sorry for myself. A long day lay ahead and what could I do, where should I go? I wasn't used to being alone and thrown on my own resources. I'd lost any initiative I'd had, and I never had much, ever."

I broke off. Listening to myself, it sounded so feeble – a grown woman unable to amuse herself in a strange city. So I started to explain how, during our married life we had scarcely been anywhere. Visits to the seaside were the rule when the children were small, but later we didn't have even that distraction. George was always too busy to get away and somehow there was never any money for holidays.

"So you see, being in Glasgow on my own was scary and I was in the right frame of mind to welcome Veronica's company. I think I might have welcomed any company, to tell you the truth. And when she took me to the Burrell – well, that day changed my life. The Boudin paintings captivated me; Veronica encouraged me to try to paint and even went with me to the art shop and helped me buy things to start me off. I owe her so much. And that's the story of how and why I started to paint." I looked across at Melanie, breathless at my courage in talking so freely to a comparative stranger, and wondering if that was what she wanted from me and if she was satisfied. I paused and waited for her comments.

"That's a great story," she assured me. "A case of serendipity, in fact. But I don't understand how you came to be in Glasgow. It obviously wasn't a family holiday." She raised her eyebrows and waited for my response.

"Ah, well, you see," I wriggled and crossed my legs, suddenly on the defensive and eager to justify myself. "It was George's idea. He thought he'd like to trace his ancestors – something to do in his retirement, you know. Well, he found out that in the nineteenth century and earlier they lived in Glasgow. So he had to plan a visit to look up the records." I decided to omit any mention of the slum conditions, the absconding thief and the black woman, all of which filled him with horror and shame and made him in the end abandon his quest.

"Tracing ones ancestors is a very popular hobby

nowadays," Melanie remarked, "And what does he think of your activity? I expect he's proud of you, branching out and being creative like this.

"Well, no, not exactly. At least he's never said anything. You know what men are like. He just thinks it's one of those harmless women's things – something to keep the little woman out of mischief." I laughed to hide the sudden bitterness that rose up in my throat and threatened to gag me.

Melanie shifted in her chair. "So he doesn't take you seriously. Is that it?"

I nodded and gulped. She was making me feel sorry for myself. I didn't want to look back and recall all the hurt. It was too painful.

But she went on with her questions. "Was there ever a time when he did take you seriously?" She smiled, as if to take away some of the sting from the question, and leaned a little towards me; her sympathy and support were almost tangible, encouraging me to recount the unhappiness in my life. I was beginning to realise that I had never talked seriously to anyone about how I was feeling. I had had no close friends to confide in. George had always discouraged my attempts to have contacts outside the home. My mind went back to the time when I first met him. I was shy, lacking in self-confidence, and was ready to welcome his confident superiority and – yes – his dominance. I was happy to have my life taken over in those days and allowed myself to become the conventional 'little woman', immersed in household duties and in time the conventional mother of two children, one boy and one girl. I fitted the stereotype, like a garment cut out precisely to the given pattern. And I had blamed George for it all. For all my hurt, resentment and anger.

As I poured all this out to Melanie, drip by painful

drip, I began to realise that it was I who was to blame. George had not forced me to become a prisoner in my own home, with no outside interests. I had allowed it to happen. I had asked for it, for heaven's sake! My life needn't have been like it was. I should have stood up for myself from the start. "It was all my fault. It didn't have to be like this. By giving in to George every time I was actually encouraging him to go on dominating me, until it became an unbreakable habit. What a fool I've been! Our marriage might have been happy if I hadn't been such a wimp. It's all my fault," I repeated and fumbled in my pocket for a hanky. My eyes were burning with the tears they had so long withheld.

Melanie waited until I had mopped up the worst of the flood. "Tears of regret, anger, remorse, guilt, blame – or what?" she asked.

I sniffed and tried to pull myself together. "Well, all of those, I suppose. But mainly anger. I'm angry at myself for being so weak, and angry with George for being such a bully. No wonder we couldn't stand one another in the end."

"I know you're separated. Sarah told me. I'm glad you and she are friends, by the way. She enjoys your company, I know. But how do you feel about yourself now that you're free? And how do you now feel about George? You're both independent, settled in new homes, with a new life before you. Are you still willing to be dominated? Do you still feel a need to be angry?"

"A need to be angry? How could I need to be angry?"

"Oh, yes. There was a need, surely, over the past thirty or forty years of your marriage. If you had acknowledged your anger at the beginning the problem would not have developed as it did. You would have done something about it, surely?"

"I see what you mean. I would have rebelled and forced myself to be more assertive, which would have helped to build up my self-confidence."

"Yes, the anger could have been used to give very positive results. As I think it is beginning to do at last, isn't it?"

I had to admit Melanie was right. I realised how different I had been since the catalyst of that day in Glasgow, but I had put it down to Veronica's influence – someone else's dominance again, though that time it was helpful – and then the physical separation of our lives on Arran. Melanie had prodded me, by her questions and her empathy, to dig deeper into my feelings and see that it was my bottled up anger that had finally exploded and liberated me. Phew! I felt exhausted by all this mental and emotional effort, and gave Melanie a rueful glance out of bleary eyes.

She smiled and said, "I think we could both do with a cup of tea, don't you?" And without waiting for an answer she disappeared into a tiny cupboard-like room behind me. I could hear the tap running, the kettle filling and the cups rattling as I wiped my eyes and blew my nose and tried to compose myself. I looked at my watch as she returned with a tray of tea and digestive biscuits. The fine porcelain, white with a simple gold rim was in keeping with the whole ambience of the place and of Melanie.

"You know," I said, "I thought this initial interview would be ten minutes or so, then you'd tell me which therapy I should make an appointment for. And here I am, still here after an hour. What must you think of me? I do apologise for taking up so much of your time."

"There's no need to apologise. I think you're a very courageous woman and I wanted to get to know you.

And everything you say here is confidential, of course. You understand that, I'm sure." Melanie handed me my tea and offered milk, sugar and biscuits. Seating herself with her own tea on the table beside her she went on, "I admire you and wanted to help. That's all. You see, I know what it's like to pluck up courage to free oneself from a restricting family background. But at some point eventually one has to learn to forgive oneself as well as others. It's not easy and it takes a lot of courage."

I raised my eyebrows but she didn't respond to my unspoken invitation. This self-possessed elegant woman, so cool and in control of her emotions and yet so sympathetic, like a universal guru or agony aunt, how could she have suffered and what sort of family background had she, I wondered? But she was not forthcoming with any more information. We drank our tea and munched biscuits in companionable silence.

Finishing, and flicking crumbs from her tailored skirt of herringbone tweed, she said, "While I've been drinking my tea I've given it some thought and I believe you would benefit from some healing." Seeing my look of astonishment – after all, I had told her there was nothing wrong with me – she explained with a smile, "I'm talking about spiritual healing or energy healing. There are various names for it but the word healing doesn't imply cure. It's more a matter of healing the whole person, the integration of body, mind and spirit. Though it does happen from time to time that a cure takes place, and that's a bonus. Nothing is ruled out. One never knows. Your body uses the energy where it's needed most. Quite simple, really! You'll see. If it appeals to you, why not make an appointment on your way out to see Susie? You'll like Susie and I'm sure you'll get on well together."

I stood up, gathered my things together – the coat I

had draped over the back of my chair and the handbag I'd dropped on the floor – and took my empty cup to join Melanie's on the little table. "Thank you for the tea and for your time, Melanie. I'm very grateful and I will come and see Susie and try this healing you talk about. Iolanthe has mentioned Susie, but I think Iolanthe goes to her for aromatherapy, not healing." I didn't add the thought uppermost in my mind. It would give me an opportunity to question Susie and find out more about her. I was intrigued. Was John seeing her or not? Was there any truth in Maggie's insinuation? Please God it was all just baseless rumour or idle tittle-tattle.

Melanie interrupted my pious prayer. "And please come and see me again. I'd like to keep in touch. You can always contact me through Reception. I don't work regular hours any more but I like to be available to my friends. No charge, of course. Or we may meet at Sarah's. The three of us have a lot in common, haven't we?"

I wondered about that as I went away. Sarah and I shared concerns over our sons. But Melanie? I certainly felt drawn towards her, but couldn't see that we had much in common. I would keep in touch and let the relationship develop as it may.

15

"It was Melanie who suggested I should come to you for healing." I had prepared my opening speech as I stood on the corridor outside the oak door with the simple plaque indicating Susie's name. The voice that replied to my timid tap had sounded pleasant and musical, a young voice, full of vigour and happiness, I thought. So, with increasing confidence I stepped into her consulting room to see a slight figure, even smaller than myself, who could have been mistaken for a schoolgirl. She greeted me with enormous black eyes set in a round smiling face framed by short black hair cut in a straight bob with a fringe. She exhibited her Chinese-American origins very clearly and seemed to have inherited the best features of both races. Her smile showed understanding, as if she knew how I had screwed myself up for this interview. I was still hesitant at meeting new people and starting new relationships. I was no longer the caged bird I had been but I was still not too sure that my wings would support me. But Melanie had gone more that half way to reassure me, and now Susie was doing her best to put me at ease. Her room, too, was conducive to relaxation; I looked around, appreciating its restful colours – it had the usual dove grey carpet that characterised the whole Hydro, but the walls were unusual. One, facing the window was a delicate primrose, the other three were of a pale bronze colour, and both were repeated in the subtle pattern of the curtains. The combination was unusual but pleasing and I made a mental note of it. If I ever wanted to redecorate my lounge I might use this same scheme. But I was less taken with the dominant feature of the room. This, on my right and lined up against the wall, appeared to be a divan upholstered in the same fabric as the curtains and with a pile of blankets on one end of it. It looked like a psychiatrist's couch. Not that I had any acquaintance with a psychiatrist's couch, but I had seen them on television programmes and imagined myself lying there and revealing all my secret thoughts. Horrors! I suppose I must have shuddered involuntarily as Susie welcomed me and offered me a chair (an ordinary dining chair, I was relieved to see).

She smiled and said, "I have a special couch for aromatherapy, – the oils, you know. It folds away when not in use. But sometimes my patients prefer to lie down for a healing session. It depends on whatever makes them feel more relaxed. I give them a choice. And I have an idea you would prefer to be seated. Am I right?"

So, she had read my aversion to the couch. I began to believe she could see into my head and know what I was thinking. Somebody (who was it? Somebody in Lochranza at the Rural, perhaps) had called her a witch. Stupid of me to think like that, but it was a persistent feeling. There was something in those eyes.

But she was speaking again while washing her hands at a tiny sink that I hadn't noticed in the corner by the window. "I understand you haven't had any healing before and don't know much about it. Is that so?"

"Oh, yes. I didn't really understand what Melanie

was trying to tell me. She said you would explain." I shuffled nervously in my chair.

"Yes, of course. I'll do my best." She dried her hands, disposed of the paper towel in a small metal bin and came to sit near me on the edge of the couch. In my hypersensitive state I thought it was a ruse, to put herself at a lower level so that I had to look down at her. Ruse or not, I smiled at her, already beginning to feel less tense.

Her musical voice went on, "You gave Melanie your medical details – I have them here – so we don't need to spend time going over those. But I want to make you more comfortable with the thought of spiritual healing before we begin the treatment. First of all, I must emphasise that 'spiritual' doesn't mean 'religious', nor does it refer to Spiritualism. Your personal beliefs or absence of belief have no bearing on the process. We call the healing spiritual because it's not solidly material. You see, we're dealing with the energy field. Do you know about that?"

I shook my head. Wasn't it something to do with flower power and all that business in the sixties? It was out of date, surely. I was not as blunt as that, but Susie knew what I meant.

She smiled at my ignorance. "When you're walking down the street or in a crowded room of strangers do you ever feel someone is staring at your back?"

"Oh, yes," I said. "It does happen sometimes. It's weird and uncomfortable."

"Well, we call that the magnetic or energy field that surrounds us all. It's always been known as a phenomenon but scientists are now taking it seriously and finding means to define it and even measure it. We talk nowadays of wanting our own space (oh, how true, I thought. I certainly wanted my own space), that is, keeping our energy field clear of other people's.

The energy can now even be photographed and assessed electronically. Some people can see it, too. Perhaps you can, Muriel. Would you like to try?"

Well! Susie was certainly taking my breath away. I tried to grasp what she was saying and decided to risk letting her do as she suggested. She asked me to just sit there and stare at her head with my eyes out of focus while she sat opposite me. It was fascinating and I was delighted that I could actually see a sort of halo round her head after she had directed me how to look.

"Not everybody can see it; it depends how sensitive you are. But we all have a halo. Artists through the ages have always given their saints a halo; they must have known instinctively about the energy field. But it's there round all of us; we don't need to be saints," she laughed and then was serious again. "The universal energy I allow to flow through my hands works in your energy field, your personal space, so I don't need to touch you," she explained. "Even if you can't see the energy you will probably feel it in some way. A pleasant sensation, at least."

Well, this was a staggering thought, but I was prepared to let her do whatever she proposed with her hands. It couldn't do any harm, surely, if she didn't even touch me. And it might do some good. I'd nothing to lose so I told her to go ahead and steeled myself for what might happen. But she said I must relax, take a few deep breaths and just let myself drift with my eyes closed. It was also important that I think positive thoughts during the session. She pointed out how important thoughts were; she would convey positive energy to me and I should be ready to accept it. The energy would be utilised by my energy field to the extent that it was needed. My body knew how to deal with it, she said. I tried to absorb all this information and obey her instructions, but was surprised when she said there would be no more conversation until she had finished.

Oh dear! This was a disappointment. I had hoped to introduce the subject of John and ask her, in a roundabout way, what he consulted her for and how often he came. I hadn't yet formulated my oblique approach. It would have to be subtle. I couldn't very well ask her 'Are you having an affair with my son?' But, subtle or blunt, I was to remain in ignorance, for now, anyway. Perhaps I could find another way. There was no point in pursuing that thought at the moment, and it probably wasn't positive enough.

So, I obediently closed my eyes and began to enjoy again in my mind's eye the afternoon drive over the hills. It was a fresh, sparkling day with bright sunlight and clouds chasing their shadows into patterns on the slopes. I looked for eagles and deer but saw only some sheep, white dots mingling with white rocks among the heather and bracken. The animals kept to strict territorial limits, apparently, the deer to the higher slopes except at dusk when they ventured lower down and explored farms and gardens. I had had to raise my fence at the back to keep them out, but they still came to nibble the juicy tops of my shrubs. I didn't mind too much, they neatened the hedge. I smiled to myself, thinking about my garden. It was looking good just now. The escallonias were in flower, both pink and red, making a flowering hedge at the back. The fuchsias were growing well and would flower later. Absorbed in these pleasant thoughts I gradually became aware of a tingling sensation in my spine, and a feeling of warmth and well-being was spreading over me. I was really enjoying it and mentally curled up like a cat purring with contentment. This could go on forever, I thought. No problem!

I nearly jumped out of my skin when Susie said, "If you'd like to move over to the couch now I'll get you a glass of water while you come down to earth again." She smiled at me as if she knew I was in a dream. I felt 'floaty'.

"It's as if I were floating above ground, nothing is quite real." I tried to explain. "I suppose it's like being on a high. Weird, but very pleasant." I seated myself very comfortably on the couch, which no longer held any terrors, and sipped the ice-cold water, while Susie waited for me to come down to earth.

"I don't want you to go out in this dreamy state and certainly not to drive. I assure you there are no bad side effects, and you'll feel more of the benefits later. The energy you have received will go on working in you and will have results. What those results will be we can't predict, but you'll certainly feel better in some way."

"Oh, I'm sure. Goodness, that was amazing. I feel wonderful. And you didn't even touch me! I can't believe it!"

Susie laughed. "I'm not a magician. The energy is there all the time, like electricity or radio waves. It's just a matter of utilising it. That's all."

It all sounded so simple but I still didn't understand how it had happened. And I was no nearer understanding Susie and her relationship to John. In spite of her delicate fine-boned appearance she was a powerful woman. That energy she gave me was powerful stuff. It was all very well for her to say it wasn't her energy but something from outside herself. I didn't believe it. Was it something magnetic? Did she use it to attract people to her? I couldn't believe she would do that. Would she? She seemed such a likeable person. Melanie recommended her and Sarah thought highly of her. She had been married to her son for many years, apparently happily, and any faults would have already revealed themselves, so I must try to keep an open mind. But there was still the problem of the rumours about John. Or rather, insinuations. As far as I knew they had not yet developed into definite rumours. Oh dear, what a mess and a muddle! It was like trying to find your way in a fog, when nothing seemed tangible.

I was still metaphorically treading on air when I arrived at Sarah's, no longer on a high but definitely different and somehow stronger, more positive. She knew I had an appointment with Susie and had invited me to go on afterwards to her house for tea.

"I want to hear how you got on, and what you think of Susie," she said. "Not that you need any excuse to visit me, of course. We have plenty of other things to talk about as well."

And indeed we had. There was a new gallery opening next week in Whiting Bay. We had both been invited to the official opening and were looking forward to seeing what kind of paintings was to be exhibited. Would they be traditional landscapes, to appeal as souvenirs to tourists, or would they be modern avant-garde? And, as it was in a private house, a normal small family house, we were curious to see how they had managed to turn part of it into an art gallery.

"I've met the wife of the artist who's organising all this," Sarah told me. "She's part of the management staff at the distillery. It was Melanie who introduced me to her. She plays the violin."

I raised my eyebrows over my cup of tea, wondering what was the connection.

Sarah apologised. "I thought you knew. Melanie plays the flute, very well in fact. She started as a schoolgirl and has kept it up. Only as a hobby, but she's good. She and a few other instrumentalists get together sometimes and give a concert, usually for a charity, and often in the drawing room of the Castle. Genuine chamber music in fact. I usually try to go. They play all kinds of music, from classical to folk, jazz – anything."

"All these hidden talents," I marvelled. "It's amazing – so many brilliant people on such a small island!"

Sarah laughed. "I don't think they'd like to be thought of as brilliant. They just enjoy using what talent they've got, and others (such as me) enjoy what they can offer. But I'll let you know when they plan to have another concert, though it will be advertised, of course. We could arrange to go together if you like."

I said I would look forward to that and was thankful to have an increasing circle of talented friends. I hoped George was also finding congenial people he could make friends with. It would have been hard for him as it was for me at first, but it was becoming increasingly easier. Spontaneously I burst out "What a wonderful life I have nowadays, so rich, so fulfilling! I'd never have believed it!"

Sarah looked at me with surprise at my outburst and I laughed sheepishly. "Sorry! I don't usually go over the top like this. It must be the magic energy that Susie's put into me."

"Hmmm, so that's what it is? I'm glad you're feeling so well. I know Susie's good, but she doesn't deal in magic. She hasn't any special powers, you know. She's had training, that's all. Years of training in fact, though I suppose there might have been some original gift to start with. But the energy she talks about is the same energy in all forms of healing, they say, even in NHS pills and potions."

"Well, it's a mystery to me and I prefer to think of

it as magic. But I'll go again." I drained my cup and pushed it aside, declining the proffered refill. "I wasn't brave enough but I wanted to get to know Susie better. And I wanted to find out about her and John. If there is anything in the insinuations I heard about."

Sarah looked at me, surprised. "Insinuations?" she enquired. "What sort of insinuations? Susie and John? What do you mean?" Sarah was looking puzzled, a frown deepening the wrinkles round her eyes.

I didn't like the way she looked and I didn't like what I had to say. Please God she would tell me it was all a fairy tale, nothing but vindictive tittle-tattle and mischief-making by idle gossips. I took a deep breath. "There's probably nothing in it, and I hope to God there isn't, but I've heard that John is visiting Susie every week. He's said nothing to me and seems to avoid talking about it. I'm wondering why not. If it's all innocent and he goes simply for therapy why can't he tell me about it?" I paused and looked anxiously at Sarah. I didn't want Sarah to be hurt and I hated the way I'd blurted it out. Stupid me, I was so unused to handling the nuances of a developing relationship. What a lot I'd missed in my life! I was so naïve. What a wasted life I'd led, really I was just emerging like a teenager or awkward adolescent. Oh, Muriel, what a long way you have still to go! I chided myself. What would Sarah think of me? She must think I'm accusing her daughter-in-law of misconduct! I peered up at her eyes. They were dark with pain and something more. I sensed there was the beginning of anger so far firmly suppressed. Our friendship is so important to me, please God don't let me spoil it, I prayed and twisted my hands in anxious supplication.

Sarah shook the anger out of her head and smiled at me, though with difficulty, I thought. "Oh, I can't think Susie would do anything foolish. She and Ian have been together a good many years now, you know, and they're very fond of one another. I do know that. You haven't known them long; in fact I don't think you've met Ian, have you? He is away a lot, unfortunately. I wish he was at home more, but I can't think Susie would start looking elsewhere. Not that your son isn't attractive, of course," she added hurriedly.

Oh, thank you, Sarah, I breathed a heartfelt prayer. Aloud I said, "I'm sure you're right. You must be right. I'm afraid I can't guarantee that John would never be tempted to stray, with Iolanthe being away, but if we can rely on Susie, then that's all right, isn't it? It really always depends on the woman, after all."

"I would ask her, but I'm afraid she would only say that her clients' visits are confidential, which is true. And that's another reason why she shouldn't get emotionally involved – that is, if John visits her every week, which we haven't even verified. She wouldn't be allowed to practice if she acted so unethically. She'd be struck off."

I heaved a sigh of relief. It really sounded as though Sarah knew what she was talking about. And she wasn't blaming me for introducing the subject. But I would still like to know the facts, otherwise suspicion would still keep niggling away at me. Dared I ask John outright? Even if I were clever enough to introduce the subject in a roundabout way he would only laugh at me. I knew he wouldn't treat me seriously and I'd be no wiser. And I ought to tackle Maggie too, and nip these insinuations in the bud before they expanded and spread round the island. A confrontation? Oh, dear, I'd have to face her and tell her she was wrong, though she hadn't actually made any accusation and I couldn't categorically say there was no truth in it. I wished I had more courage. Susie's healing made me feel so wonderful, and I had found the courage to talk to Sarah without damaging the friendship. Perhaps I was learning to be more confident. Yes, I was sure I was. And I nodded, and smiled at Sarah as I took my leave of her.

"So we'll meet at Lochranza to paint the castle next week, shall we? And I'll let you know about the next concert," were Sarah's parting words. So it seemed that all was well between us. I had done no irreparable damage, after all.

16

June 20
Muriel is till nattering on about John's indiscretion with this Chinese woman. That is, if there has been any indiscretion. She has no proof and I am surprised she listens to what people say. And if the rumour comes from Gladys at the post office she should certainly take no notice of it, and I told her so. The woman is a gossip; she listens to her customers talking in the shop and then passes it on, no doubt embroidered with her own brand of insinuation. Though in the privacy of this diary I would not be surprised if John did turn his eyes elsewhere. Iolanthe, that dolly-bird with the impossible name, is away more often than she is at home. He still says he loves her and wants to marry her; why did she agree to live with him and not be here to look after him? I think she neglects him. It seemed all right for a year or two, but even then I had my doubts. John always declared he was happy but I can't see that he can be happy any longer. Who is there to cook his meals, look after the housekeeping – all the work that I myself have learned how to do. I do it by choice because I prefer to live alone, but John has a partner who should be doing all the things that Muriel used to do for me. That is why one marries, apart from the sex, of course. Perhaps John is being led astray because he is

missing the sex in his life. I can understand that. But to take up with a Chinese woman? That I cannot understand. No son of mine would dream of demeaning himself to that extent. And part-American too! As I said to Muriel, I cannot countenance such behaviour and simply refuse to believe it. Muriel worries too much. I was quite firm with her. We were having lunch at the Mayfair Hotel on this occasion, again at her suggestion. I noticed she is becoming more assertive. She would never, during our married life, have ventured to express any initiative of her own. She always waited for me to take the lead, but I find these changes are making her more attractive. I am seeing a more likeable person. She is not the same as when I married her, though she still worries too much. Of course, I too am not the same person I was forty years ago. I hope I have changed for the better, but I still have my standards. Faithfulness in marriage – even in a modern type of relationship – is one. Another is to stay loyal to one's own class and status in society. In writing this I am reminded of my, and John's, ancestors, one of whom was suspected as a thief and another was a black woman. Perhaps, after all, I should not quibble about a Chinese-American woman. At least she is white and of the professional classes. But it is absurd to be thinking like this. I am sure John will be faithful. He has had our strict upbringing and our example to guide him. If Muriel wants to cease worrying she must ask John outright and settle the rumour. I have enough worries of my own.

There has been another emergency meeting of the museum committee to appoint a new treasurer. Esther reported that Simon is now away on the mainland having a hip replacement, after Graham helped to remove him successfully to the Dukeries. She had a pile of exercise books, paper bags and loose papers kept together with elastic bands in front of her on the table as she called the committee to order.

"I have to apologise for asking you all to come, so soon after our other extraordinary meeting. We have only the one item on the agenda, which I think you know is to appoint a successor to Simon. And this can't be done without the full agreement of the committee, with a formal proposal and a vote. I am sure you expected this to happen much sooner. Simon left us many weeks ago but in the chaos of his removal he was unable to lay his hands on all the documents we require. That problem has now been solved and I am confident that I now have all the financial papers of the museum before me." She frowned, hesitated and coughed apologetically. "I'm no expert – it takes me all my time to keep my own finances in order but, looking at this lot, it seems to me that a new treasurer will have a lot of work to do. Poor Simon has been letting things slip. Even I can see that." Her voice dropped to confidential level. "I'm afraid his papers were all over the place; I had to help him find them, but I think I've got them all." She surveyed the group. We were all present, Malcolm looking bored, Sybil fingering the Archaeological Journal as if she were itching to open it, the others mildly interested. Esther went on, a more severe note entering her voice. "I'm just pointing that out. I don't want a new treasurer to be appointed under a false premise. It may not be as straightforward a task as anticipated, at least to begin with. So . . ." And she sat back, pen poised over her minute book. " . . . Have we any proposal for the post of treasurer?"

They all turned to look at me, as Graham had predicted. He now said, "I propose George. He's the obvious choice, if he's willing."

To a circle of raised eyebrows and hopeful faces I nodded and smiled assent, and an audible gasp of relief rippled round the table.

"And have we a seconder?"

Millie raised a languid hand. "So, I take it you're all agreed. We're very grateful, George, and we'll help all we can, I am sure. I hope there won't be too many problems." And Esther bundled all the books and carrier bags of papers over to me and the meeting was over.

I am now having to spend every morning of my precious free time in trying to sort out the finances of the museum. Or, to be accurate, to sort out the paperwork and the account books. Mr Oyston at the Bank was very helpful when I went to arrange the transfer of authority. In fact, he was quite welcoming in spite of a prepossessing appearance. I suspected him of being too fond of rich food and liquid lunches; his high colour and paunch were not those of a health-conscious man. As he rose from behind his large mahogany desk he appeared to carry his rotund protuberance before him with pride, as if to say 'I am a successful man. I can afford good living and I enjoy every minute of it'. When he puffed out his cheeks and said, "And how may we help you?" I found it difficult to explain. I had no wish to calumniate my predecessor, who was probably suffering from senility, but on the other hand there was the desperate need to put the finances on a straight course. In other words, had Simon embezzled or otherwise acted illegally with the money entrusted to him? It was a delicate situation, but Mr Oyston was unflappable. He immediately produced sheets of figures, recording every deposit and withdrawal for the last six months, that is, since the last and presumably correctly audited balance sheet. Thankfully there were no with-

drawals and apparently no embezzlement or illegal dealings with the bank. On the other hand, I had a plastic shopping bag full of unpaid bills and a fistful of cheques that had not been presented; the cheques, moreover, had got separated from their covering letters, so I had no idea which of the members had paid their subscriptions or who had made donations. Among the many loose papers were letters of complaint that I would have to reply to as diplomatically as possible, and I would check the membership list with Esther. It would mean a lot of work but I would make sure the books were in order before the end of another month. I phoned Esther to assure her that I had it all in hand and she need not worry. At least there is now enough money in the bank to pay the outstanding bills.

It is fortunate that I have now so arranged my OU work and am so at ease with it that I can give some time to other interests. I am becoming more proficient in writing essays and I am beginning to appreciate the cultural aspects of the course. I was listening to some Mozart the other evening, trying to relate the music to its historical setting. To what extent did it reflect the 'zeitgeist' of Europe? The study of history is much broader that I had previously imagined, and certainly more interesting than what was taught me at school. I enjoy discussing these ideas with Rosemary. She has had a wide education in the humanities and has travelled extensively. When she was a student she and a friend backpacked round Europe. I did not enquire whether the friend was male or female but assumed that, in the 1960's, it could have been either, or perhaps it was her future husband. I am always careful to preserve the decencies of behaviour and conversation and would not encroach on personal confidences. But her accounts of visits to places like

Florence, Venice and Paris make me regret even more than previously that my life has been so narrowly circumscribed. If only I had taken advantage of the holiday periods and the earlier college vacations I might have travelled and seen works of art that I can now only appreciate through reproductions. But early marriage, children and stultifying work prevented anything so adventurous. I therefore welcome my meetings with Rosemary, and our talk of European culture. She is supportive of my OU studies and helps me with the assignments.

One memorable occasion was the lunch we had together. I had at last ventured to invite her; it was a fine warm Sunday, the sort of day one expects in June. She looked very attractive as she approached the house; I was looking out for her from my front window and admired the simple well-tailored outfit she was wearing – a jacket and skirt (she never wore trousers, I was pleased to note) in pale blue of some light material. It suited her; the blue of her outfit brought out the blue in her eyes, which I knew were flecked with brown. I watched the easy way she moved. I had never seen her in motion before. She had always been behind the library counter or at ease in my living room over a cup of tea. But now I could admire the spring in her step and the lithe movement of her hips; I could congratulate myself on having acquired such a handsome friend. I was circumspect, however, and did not allow myself to show too much of my admiration. I abhor gush and endeavour to preserve a civilised restraint in our relationship. But I believe she knows how much I welcome her visits, not only for the wealth of her knowledge and experience of the world but also for her own sake.

That particular Sunday I prepared a simple lunch, suitable for a warm June day; large, free-range eggs, scrambled with strips of smoked salmon and served with watercress and garden peas. On this, our first lunch in my home, I did not want to spend my time in the kitchen preparing something elaborate. It was better to keep it simple, I thought, and I was glad that she remarked on its suitability. I think the Australian chardonnay wine was appreciated, too, though I am no connoisseur and ought to learn more about wines. Receiving her at the door, I was presented with a bottle of asti spumante, which confused me. It was kind of her and it made me realise how much my education has been neglected.

The sun streamed into my living room, where I had prepared the lunch table with my best china and a pot of flowers. As well as the wine Rosemary had brought a portfolio of prints of works of art that she particularly admired, and postcards of places she had visited. But first we had our lunch, laying aside the portfolio on one of the armchairs. There was much to talk about. She told me tales of her travels in France, back-packing and youth-hostelling from north to south. She talked of the chateaux of the Loire and the gorges of the Dordogne. "But at that stage of my life I was really passionate about Van Gogh and wanted to visit Arles and experience the scenes he was familiar with. I've got lots of prints and postcards to show you if you're interested." And I was interested; I also marvelled at her enterprise, as a young woman. I couldn't imagine any other woman of my acquaintance, least of all Muriel, doing anything so adventurous.

After the meal Rosemary insisted on helping me to clear the table, but we left the dishes in the sink for me to wash up later. I was keen to see her pictures and to turn the conversation to the Napoleonic era. I needed her help with my current essay. I have the knowledge of the political history of the time but she has so much deeper understanding of the cultural background, which is so new to me. I chose a CD of a Beethoven sonata and we made ourselves comfortable in the two armchairs before the window, where we could see the opposite shore and the village houses reflected in the waters of the loch. I asked her about the paintings of the Napoleonic period she might have seen in the Louvre. "It must have been a very unsettling time," I said. "In many ways it was the birth of the modern era."

"Yes. There was Neo-Classicism giving way to Romanticism, with an exotic strand of Eastern influence. An exciting, but dangerous, period." She dug into her portfolio and brought out reproductions of paintings by Ingres and David, around the turn of the century. And then she showed me Goya's 'The Third of May' and contrasted it with Gericault's 'Mounted Officer of the Guard' – realism versus romanticism. We wondered if any major artist today would paint an equivalent picture to illustrate the horror of the American September 11 massacre.

This led us to philosophy and a much more wide-ranging discussion until Rosemary suddenly exclaimed, "Goodness! It's already three o'clock and I promised to visit a friend in hospital. I must fly."

So she left, after what I considered a very satisfactory lunch date. I feel confident she will consent to come again and I look forward to further discussions and a developing friendship.

My friendship with Graham was also developing, though he has recently shocked me. I no longer feel so awkward in the company of the museum committee members and helpers and find that life in more enjoyable than it ever was. I am ashamed at having to confess this, but believe it is essential to state the truth here. Until now, friendship has been an alien skill which other people seemed to possess and of which I did not know the secret. It was Graham who broke that mould and showed me the way out of my self-imposed isolation.

When he asked me the other day to help him with the terracing of his garden I was happy to do so. The garden at the rear of the post office is on a very steep slope and receives little or no sun. He had already, years ago, stepped it into terraces but the winter rains had loosened the rocks above, which he needed help to reposition. It was not a difficult task, it just needed an extra pair of hands to move the rocks and enable him to put back the displaced soil. I told him he should get some tenacious ground-cover plants to strengthen the banks.

Once the work was done he invited me into the back kitchen, to a can of beer from the fridge. His wife was safely busy in the shop and we could have a male get-together over a drink, as he explained. This was a new experience for me. My alcoholic consumption had been limited to the odd glass of wine over a business lunch, and that not very often. The lunch with Rosemary was the first time I had actually bought a bottle of wine. There was a tradition of strict teetotalism in my family, which on the whole I approve of. Drunkenness is anti-social and has always been abhorrent to me. However, to cement our friendship I accepted a can. I noticed it was lager, not beer, and followed Graham's actions in opening and drinking directly from it. Surprisingly it was quite refreshing after the physical work and I gratefully accepted a second can. I made a note of the name, so that I could stock my own fridge and entertain Graham at some future date.

Graham grinned at me. "Cheers, mate. Drink up.

We're celebrating!"

I asked what we were celebrating. I couldn't think of anything.

"Oh, yes, it's a celebration. You see before you a free man. With a free pass on the ferry!" He laughed at my astonishment. "Yes, I've retired. Joined the happy throng. And Gladys'll have to pay me my pension every week," he chortled.

I shared his amusement and anticipatory pleasure in retirement, but it occurred to me that I had never enquired about his work. Somehow I had assumed he was a landowner or farmer, because he had said he was born on a moorland farm above the village, and farmers don't retire on a state pension. Or do they? I think the unaccustomed lager was having an effect on me, as I was emboldened to ask straight out, "What was your work?"

"Why, didn't you know? I worked for the Council, cleaning out ditches, digging graves, planting flowerbeds, whatever. Plenty of variety and all outdoors. It just suited me down to the ground." He laughed again and would have dug me in the ribs if he had been near enough. "Down to the ground it certainly was," he gurgled.

I was seated with my back to the window on the opposite side of the table, so it was fortunate that he could not see my face. He had given me a shock. He had talked so knowledgeably about Arran's history it was natural that I should think he was an old family landowner and middle class. But a council workman! A street sweeper! How had I allowed myself to become friends with a common workman? I stumbled to my feet with strangled thanks and left hurriedly, I'm afraid.

17

It was George's turn to choose a venue for our lunch, which seemed to be settling into a satisfying pattern. It satisfied me, at least. I hoped it wouldn't develop into invitations to one another's homes. At least as far as George was concerned. I was not ready to think of seeing him in my home. Sarah and other women friends were welcome. We visited each other from time to time and it was all very pleasant because there were no lingering bad memories of quarrels and misunderstandings. It was different with George. Our relationship was still too raw; there had been too much between us in the past; I didn't want to be close to him any more; a casual friendship was all I hoped for and I thought and hoped he felt the same.

His choice of venue was one of the bigger hotels on the west side of the island. When he phoned down to invite me he said the chef there had a reputation for steaks and he wanted to try it. I am not partial to steak unless it's with onions in a pie; I prefer a nice piece of fish, but I was happy to drive along the coast down to the south end and to the hotel. It was a brilliant day, with bright sun, very clear, no wind. The coast of Kintyre loomed in blues and greens across the Sound, cormorants spread their wings on spiky rocks on the beach, and the only sound was of screeching gulls squabbling over a mussel shell. We had agreed to go separately and I was driving my own little Golf, as I was going on later to do some shopping in Brodick. In spite of it now being the high season for visitors, this side of the island was very quiet. I had little fear of meeting any large vehicles but picked my way cautiously all the same, as the sun was in my eyes and I had to go carefully over the humps in the road. One of Arran's many cataclysms had thrown out huge rocks to splinter and tip over at forty-five degrees, causing modern road builders to switch-back a way over them. It was not a road to speed along.

The hotel was not one I had entered before. It was big, not beautiful and a little intimidating, being white and blocky in shape, square-cut and sharp in outline. But it had a good reputation, they said, and, as a bonus, it had a large car park so that I had no trouble in disposing of my Golf. I noticed that George's Volvo was already there, so, gathering up my handbag and seizing my courage I marched in through the swing doors as if I were a habitué, seeking the dining room. But I saw George before I got there. He was sitting in the lounge – a large room with huge windows looking out to the sea, and decorated strangely in dark red and purple, with comfortable-looking bucket seats and round tables. I saw him before he noticed me, and I remarked to myself how handsome he still was, so straight and slim, so distinguished with his black hair speckled with white. Were there a few more white hairs this time, I wondered? Then he turned and saw me in the doorway; like the gentleman he is he rose and came to greet me. I could always depend on his good manners, except on that occasion when he snubbed my friends, but I drew a veil over that.

"You're looking well, Muriel," he said, peering closely at me with a puzzled look on his face. I think he was probably noticing my hair. I had just been to have it styled by a different hairdresser. I wasn't sure whether I liked it but it was a softer, more wavy style and I would probably get used to it. "You're not so bad yourself," I retorted, and we smiled as we sat down beside a window and he called for a menu.

"They serve lunch in here and in the bar," he explained. "I thought it would be better here, but would you prefer the bar? Would you like a drink?"

I was a bit staggered. He had never offered me a drink before. He was always so dead set against any sort of alcohol. I remembered his condemnation of that clerk in his office (Vincent, was it?) who became an alcoholic. "I'm driving, remember?" I said, as if it were an everyday occurrence to refuse a drink.

"Yes, of course," he flustered. I suddenly felt sorry for him, and sympathised. I realised he was uncertain of himself, shy and as unaccustomed to big hotels as I was. We had both led such a sheltered life – almost like voluntary prisoners in our own home for so long, it was difficult to behave like normal people. We were both emerging from our respective chrysalises. I certainly didn't want to revive his bullying and bluster, but the poor dear did need a little encouragement.

"I would like a lime and lemon, please, George, and the salmon stuffed with sole and shrimps. It sounds good. You're having the grilled steak, I suppose."

The conversation was a little stilted and falsely polite for a while, as if we were on our best behaviour, but by the time the food arrived we had mellowed to a more relaxed mood. George wielded his saw-edged steak knife with evident enjoyment, and I was pleased that his choice of restaurant was justified. Once inside the hotel I found it was less intimidating, quite comfortable in fact, with a relaxed atmosphere. It was pleasant in the lounge, eating in comfort while gazing out to sea. I kept my eyes scanning the waves in case there were passing dolphins, but there was no sign of anything more exotic than cormorants.

I turned to George and asked him about his studies. How was he getting on? Did he still enjoy it? What was he working on at the moment?

"Well, it's going very well. I enjoy it, though of course it's quite hard work. You would enjoy part of it, I'm sure. I have to study the paintings of a particular period, in relation to other arts, philosophy, religion and so on. It's as if everything is involved in everything else to create the spirit of the age." He cut off another portion of steak and chewed thoughtfully for a moment. "My most recent assignment was about the Napoleonic age. It was fascinating to discover how different sections of society reacted to changes. It was as if there was something in the air, like a virus, that was catching." His dark eyes looked into mine, pleadingly, I thought. He actually wanted me to understand. He wanted to get on the same wavelength with me. This was a staggering thought but I tried to respond.

"Yes, I know what you mean," I said. "Though I'm not keen on that period myself. All that classicism seems cold and calculating to me. I prefer something with a bit more passion in it, the Baroque or the later Romanticism. Even in architecture, I prefer the Gothic to the classical." I had finished my fish and laid down my knife and fork neatly on the side of my plate and waited politely for George to finish his steak and suggest ordering a sweet course. It was unlike me but I was suddenly hungry for something sweet.

He was still chewing, but the large steak had all but been demolished; a few bits of carrot and chips remained. "That's understandable. I think it's probably a feminine trait, to prefer the Romantic.

What about poetry and literature? You enjoy Keats, Wordsworth and the Brontes, perhaps?" He waved his knife in the air in a graceful curve, as if describing a dying swan ballet, then placed it precisely on to his plate and leaned back. Would he call for the sweet menu, I wondered?

"Of course you enjoy the romantic writers. I remember you always having a novel in your hands in the evening." He smiled with satisfaction. He had solved that question. "And now, I expect you'd like a sweet?"

"Yes, please. Though, as you know, I haven't such a sweet tooth as you, but today I feel like something sweet, or perhaps creamy rather than sugary." Having both chosen fruit trifle, the conversation continued about his OU study. His enthusiasm was catching, and I was pleased to be able to contribute a little to the subject, as far as painting was concerned.

"I am having to learn so much about subjects I'd never thought about before. It's amazing how one thing fits with another. One can't really understand political movements without also understanding the arts and culture generally. Even fashions in clothes are affected, according to Rosemary."

"Rosemary?" My voice sharpened. I couldn't help it. Who was Rosemary? He'd never mentioned her before. "Who is Rosemary?" I asked, modifying my voice to sound casual.

He looked sheepish. I think the name had just slipped out inadvertently and he was now regretting it. "Rosemary? Well, she is the librarian in Brodick. She has been very helpful in getting the right books for me. You must have met her."

She was surely not the twenty-something girl with red hair. Heaven forbid! She must be the older one, the plain one, rather statuesque but very pleasant and helpful. Was that Rosemary?

"Yes, she's very knowledgeable. She had a classical education at Cambridge and has a wide knowledge. She's also travelled a lot. She's actually seen those paintings you are so keen about. She lives near us, actually. At Deerholme, that older house just before you turn round the end of the loch. That's why I've got acquainted with her. Sometimes she brings me a book that I've ordered from the library, on her way home. You've probably seen her car."

"No, I haven't actually. I'd no idea you had a lady friend. Are you getting romantic ideas, George?" I wondered, would I mind if he had? We were still married, but what the hell! If he was happy, why worry? But a little twinge of jealousy twisted my guts all the same.

"No, of course not. She's a good friend, but nothing more. We enjoy one another's company and have stimulating discussions. But that's all. I certainly don't want anything more, and I don't think she does." He was quite emphatic, almost snappy, and I decided to be satisfied.

"Anyway, let's talk about you. Have you made any new friends? What do you do with your time nowadays?" He obviously didn't want to pursue the subject of Rosemary, but I would watch out for her visits in the future.

"I've joined the WI, the Rural, you know, and meet some of the members from time to time. We go for a coffee or meet at the shops. But mainly I paint. Sarah and I go out together sketching, mostly every week, depending on the weather. She's my friend at the Hydro, you know. We both paint in watercolours, but I'm thinking of trying acrylics. I would like to paint with a thicker impasto, something more solid. Sarah thinks I'm improving, and I do feel more confident than I used to. But I'd like to experiment, try something different. Like those modern paintings in the gallery in Queen Street in Glasgow. Have you been there?"

"No. Should I? But I suppose they are all modern by living artists. I should really go to the other galleries that display older works. It's been so difficult up to now to find time to take a whole day away on the mainland, but I must make time. And of course I must go to Edinburgh as well, and even London, though both of those involve overnight stays." He sighed. Life was getting so crowded with things to do; there was never enough time. How I understood!

I too was finding that time flowed past more rapidly than I had expected. Having only a small flat instead of a three bedroomed house to look after should mean a lot of spare time. But cleaning and shopping was as much work for one as it was for two, and of course now there was my painting. I tried to spend a lot of my time painting, out of doors whenever the weather permitted, with Sarah or sometimes with Jane or Teresa from Lochranza. The local group preferred to paint indoors from photographs or imagination, but one or two could be persuaded to join me sometimes when I decided to paint something in the village. They didn't like to go further afield. But I had made some useful studies of boats, which I would use in a bigger composition when I had bought the acrylic paints. I was looking forward to experimenting with more oil-like techniques. But I would never, in my wildest dreams, have expected to talk about painting with George of all people. This OU course was certainly broadening his outlook. He even looked brighter. And he was wearing his best suit, with what looked like a new shirt and a new more colourful tie.

"There might be a package trip to London some

time. For pensioners, I mean. We could ask around. I'd like to go too, if it's possible. I'll ask Sarah if she's heard of anything like that."

He looked doubtful and frowned, as if he hadn't expected I would show an interest. Perhaps he didn't want to be seen with me? But we were together here, in a public place. I didn't understand him. I looked around the lounge as the waiter brought our coffee. A noisy group of six tourists with Yorkshire accents occupied the next table, but otherwise the diners were all middle-aged or elderly couples talking in low tones and being as discreet as George and I were. But I saw nobody I recognised. Perhaps George had chosen this hotel because he thought there wouldn't be any islanders here to see us? A ridiculous thought, but, knowing George, it was a possibility. I shook the thought away and changed the subject.

"Have you seen John? Is he any more reconciled to Iolanthe's absences? I haven't been for a week or two, I'm afraid. I've been so busy."

"Hrmph! That girl is still away. I told him, he should put his foot down. If he wants to marry her, then he's going the wrong way about it. This living together idea is neither one thing nor the other. Either insist on her being with him at home as his wife, or break it up and tell her to go. He's not happy. I had a straight talk with him, but he doesn't take any notice. I wouldn't be at all surprised if he didn't have an affair with that Chinese girl you mentioned. Or indeed, with anybody else. He's only human, and Iolanthe is treating him very badly."

"Oh, George. I think you're being too harsh. I know John is unhappy, but it's his own fault. He doesn't understand. Perhaps he doesn't want to understand."

"Understand? What is there to understand? A couple should be together." He smiled a little grimly.

"Or officially separated, like us."

"But we are living in the twenty-first century, George, and women have some rights nowadays, you know. Iolanthe has a right to educate herself and have a career, if she so wishes. Just as John has the same right. I happen to admire her for committing herself to all this work. It's not easy to go back to studying so long after leaving school. You know that."

"But she's only doing it because she enjoys it. There's no career at the end of it. She'll never earn her living at writing. And what does she want with a career anyway? John can support her if they marry."

"Oh, George!" I sighed. Sometimes I despaired of this man! "Are you saying she shouldn't enjoy her work? And are you saying she should be dependent on a husband – that he should pay for her – buy her, in other words?" I was sorry to be so blunt. But really! When would he learn?

"I think, George, that you have a wrong impression of Iolanthe. You see her still as a fashion model. In reality I believe she is a serious girl who wants to be accepted for her own sake, not for how she looks. And I have an idea that is why she won't marry John. He, like you, thinks of her as a beautiful object. That's being crude, I know, but there is some truth in it. Don't you see?" I was amazed that I could say all this so plainly, defying George and contradicting him. The old Muriel was at last disappearing into the mists of time; I could almost hear the saints rejoicing! Seriously, I thought I should be grateful to Susie for her healing hands. Her ministrations were having a remarkable effect, strengthening my will and giving me a more optimistic outlook. Melanie, too, with her empathetic listening. I owed my friends a great deal. Dared I suggest that George visits the Hydro for therapy? Perhaps the time was not ripe.

I was ruminating about this when George burst out, "I don't understand anything any more. The world has gone topsy-turvy. People are not what they seem. I think I've got to know someone and then they turn out to be completely different." His outburst was almost violent. He obviously felt very strongly about something. Could Iolanthe be the source of all this angst? I raised my eyebrows to encourage him to continue.

"What do you think of Graham?" he asked.

"Graham? Gladys's Graham? From the post office? Well, I don't know him very well. He doesn't have much to say when I see him. I think he's shy with women because I've noticed him sometimes chatting to men. But he's very kind and helpful. I've seen him carrying heavy bags out for old Mrs Tomlinson and he even offered to deliver things to her when she had flu and couldn't go out. Why? Why do you want to know about Graham? You've met him. You know him."

"Do I? I thought I did. But I don't know anything any more, Muriel. Let's leave it at that."

Something was brewing in that head of his, but I thought it prudent to bring our lunch date to a close. We both had plenty to think about.

18

I didn't like the look of the clouds as I set off to pick up Sarah. They were too low over the mountains and threatened to drop rain at any minute. There was little wind to blow them away and the water was calm at high tide, lapping placidly among the rank grasses below my flat. Even the seagulls were silent. Manoeuvring my way along the minor road across the loch, then weaving in between the dawdling tourists on the main road through the village I at length got into top gear to start up the lower slopes of the pass. In spite of it being now the high season there were few cars, though I expected to meet the bus conveying passengers from the ferry. I thought of Marjorie and Hannah, my two WI friends who would be waiting in their cottages to greet new bed and breakfast guests. There would have been frantic activity – changing beds, cleaning, re-stocking provisions, all in the space of the two hours between the departure of one ferry and arrival of the next. Many tourists, especially those from overseas, were thrilled at being able to stay in a cottage which was a genuine home, rather than in an impersonal hotel. But it was very hard work for relatively little financial reward. I admired Marjorie and Hannah for their enterprise but didn't envy them.

By this time I had breasted the hill and now, looking eastwards to the other side of the island my spirits lifted. The clouds were rolling away. Sunlight was glinting on the distant sea and brightening the greens of the forested slopes. It was going to be a good day for painting after all. I rolled happily down Glen Sannox, braking sharply at the bottom, then proceeded more sedately along the shore into Brodick, dodging the cyclists and pedestrians who were probably heading from the ferry to the campsite in Glen Rosa. It was a marvel how they could carry so much in their backpacks; they must have their entire possessions with them, I thought. I hoped they would not attempt to carry so much to the top of Goat Fell.

I looked forward to the day's painting. The colours were bright, the light was clear and sharp, and it was comfortably warm for sitting out of doors. It would be necessary to find a place off the main road, I decided. As I got into Brodick I realised it was too busy. I would never be able to park the car on the road, and the small lay-bys were already full. I crawled along past the Castle walls, just in time to see a tour coach from Basingstoke turn in to the Castle drive. They were probably on a day trip to the island as part of a Highlands and Islands tour. I enjoyed seeing the coaches and noting the places they came from; most of the passengers were pensioners, and it occurred to me it would be a good way of seeing the country. Perhaps I might indulge in a coach trip round England one day? It was something to think about. Meanwhile I had turned in to the drive to the Hydro and wound my way round to Sarah's. She would be waiting for me, as anxious as I to start painting.

She must have heard my car, or seen it arrive, and I expected her to rush out with her painting gear, ready for work. But her door was closed and there was no sign of life. I knocked, and as I waited for a response my eyes wandered idly round the side of the cottage where, surprisingly, was a hire car beside Sarah's Ford. What was going on? There was something here I didn't understand.

But just then the door opened and a dishevelled and harassed looking Sarah appeared. She had been running her hands through her hair, I could see, as she always did when faced with the unexpected. "I'm terribly sorry," she whispered. "I can't come with you."

"What's happened? Why can't you come? Why are you whispering?"

"Some people have turned up from Australia. My late husband's relatives. I scarcely know them, I've only met them once before, briefly, and they didn't tell me they were coming. But I can't send them away. You understand." She screwed up her kind face, torn between social obligation and personal desire. My heart sank. Without Sarah's company the day would lose its appeal, the fun would be lost. I knew she had looked forward to it as much as I had. How inconsiderate people are! Why couldn't these people have told her they were coming and arranged their visit in a civilised way? Poor Sarah! I commiserated on her doorstep, but she obviously noted my woebegone face as she said, "I'll try to get rid of them and join you later. Where will you be?"

Hurriedly I ran through possible locations in my mind. The greens were too heavy and dark at this time of year, so I would avoid the woodlands. The village street was thronged with pedestrians and traffic, so that was best avoided. Though some day I would like to tackle a painting, or perhaps only a drawing, of a group of people in a street. But not today. "What about the beach?" I suggested. "I'll be on the bit behind the car park, so you'll find me easily. I'll paint the view of the village from there. Is that OK?"

"Yes, fine. I hope I can manage it. But if not, come back here when you've finished. They will have gone by then." Her face took on a rueful pucker. "If not, your arrival will give them the hint. I shall want to see what you've done and we'll have a blether over our tea." She smiled and I shrugged and reluctantly agreed to a day's painting alone.

She closed the door and I heard the voices of her visitors in excited chatter as she returned to them. Poor Sarah! Poor me! The joy had gone out of the day, somehow. Although I had often enough spent a day painting alone out of doors, it was so much more fun with Sarah. We always enjoyed each other's company while struggling with our compositions. It was so helpful to have someone else to share the problems and exchange views about the solutions to the problems. Yes, and I had often gone out alone in Lochranza, to sketch the boats or the cottages. That was different. It was a matter of making notes for possible future paintings. I was building up a repertoire of sketches that some day might become a larger oil painting, I thought. I was being ambitious, of course, and probably way beyond my capability, but I'd like to try something more professional. It would have to wait until I had bought the acrylic and oil paints, but meanwhile, today, I wanted to search out a suitable subject. But alone? And in the main village among all these people? Had I the courage to sit by myself, in such an open position on a public beach at the height of the holiday season and exposed to possible, probable ribaldry and criticism from passersby? I had seen other artists being accosted by strangers and I cringed at the thought of such vulnerability. Slowly I drove in low gear to the car park by the beach. It was nearly full, of shoppers' as well as tourists' cars, and families spilled out on to the sandy foreshore. I sat for a moment in my car, watching the scene and gathering courage. Fathers rummaged in car boots, gathering up blankets, stools, push-chairs and a clutter of paraphernalia, mothers pulled small children out of the back seats, straightened their clothes and combed their hair, the small boys wriggling, the girls hopping their impatience and grabbing the buckets and spades as their dads handed out the tackle and the mums sorted out the food. It was a happy scene, but I determined I would plant myself as far away from the family groups as I could. I watched them amble away, the children racing on ahead, to the sandy beach and the irresistible attraction of the water. It was so like my own children when they were young. Sandra wanted to make mud pies and John always wanted to be off exploring. Those were the only holidays away we ever had, just going to Morecambe to visit the surly grandfather, as a break from our first little home in Manchester. There wasn't much excitement in our lives, but those days with the children on the beach were truly happy. But that's it! The families with children will stay near the sea and the sand, I should have realised that. So my place would be further away, on the grassy part, between the beach and the children's swings. It would surely be a bit quieter there. So that problem was solved, I thought.

It took me only a few seconds to collect my things from the car boot. By now I was organised for painting expeditions and it had become routine – stool, rug for warmth if needed, and my large canvas bag that I'd found in a jumble sale and that originally came from Peru. It was invaluable; it held absolutely everything I needed – paintbox, spare tubes, brushes, bottle of water, rags, tissues, sketchbook, jumbo paper clips, spare dish for water, a ham sandwich and a kitkat. So armed, I walked across the grass, turning frequently backwards to look at the village, judging the view. It was a very wide view; from that position I could see practically all of the village, spread out along the shore road and rising up behind into the hillside. Obviously I couldn't paint it all. Dropping my clobber at my feet I made a frame with my hands and peered at bits of the view. Which bit would make the best picture? Or rather, which bit was I capable of tackling? Which bit appealed to me?

It didn't take long. There was one portion that reminded me strongly of a picture of Cézanne's, that I had seen reproduced somewhere. It was of a small town somewhere in France – Argenteuil? – I forget the name, but the houses rose up the hillside just as they do here, and made a pattern of roofs. I would like to do something like that. Having settled on the spot, I looked around to make sure I had it to myself. I felt very self-conscious, but nobody was looking and I made myself comfortable. That took a bit of fiddling about, as the ground was bumpy and I had difficulty finding a level spot for the stool.

But at last the work could begin. My 2B pencil ready sharpened, I made a start on sketching in the broad composition – a horizontal foreground of roadway to give stability, then the buildings rising up in a rough sort of pyramid shape up the hill. There wouldn't be room for much sky, and I didn't think the picture needed sky, not more than a thin strip of blue anyway. The buildings were difficult. First the shops, all different shapes and sizes, fascinating, but I had to be careful to get the proportions right. And even more so when I began to draw the houses above; again, I had to remind myself of aerial perspective; the houses further away should be smaller, even if I knew they were bigger in reality. Quite a problem! Absorbed, I sketched away and rubbed out and redrew until I had the composition as I wanted it. I moved a few of the houses and left out others, to get it just right. I wasn't aiming at a photographic reproduction, after all. My picture would be my own creation, based on what I could see.

So, to paint! This was not going to be a splashy sort of subject, with lots of water and runny colours. It would have to be more precise than I was used to and I regretted that I had not already invested in paints with more body. I felt the subject needed a stronger and more solid treatment than watercolour. Of course, I could always do it again, in a different medium and different light. It would look interesting with snow on the roofs. I wondered if Arran ever got snow, except on the mountains? Today the colours were clear and the outlines sharp. All was bathed in full sunlight, so that there were no harsh shadows. It was like a patchwork of pastel shades – cream, white, pale chrome, pink and green, with a few stronger accents in the shop fronts, which gave strength to the foreground.

"I like that!" A voice behind me.

I jumped. My water pot went flying and my brush streaked across where I didn't want it. Pfouff! I craned my neck round, wanting to hide myself and cover up my painting. But it was too late. The voice belonged to a man, a tall man. I had to screw my head round to see his face. It was a middle-aged face, brown and leathery as if he spent a lot of time out of doors in a bracing climate. He was smiling, showing very white and even teeth. "I'm so sorry I startled you. I didn't mean to. I've been watching you for some time, admiring the way you've got the village there." He came round to the side, not obscuring my view but to stand where I could see him more comfortably. He didn't look threatening. In fact he looked rather cuddly. Although tall he was well rounded, grey haired, slightly stooped in a schoolmasterly sort of way. I could imagine he was an academic; there was a dry superiority in his expression, as if he knew exactly what was what.

"I'm not used to people watching me," I stammered. "I'm only an amateur."

"I'm sorry, but it was irresistible. You see, I come every year to Brodick. My ancestors were farmers where the village houses are now and I have a sentimental attachment to the place. And I admire the painting you've done. It doesn't look amateurish to me. Not at all. In fact I'd like to buy it. How much would you take for it?"

I stared. I was speechless. I was struck dumb. I couldn't even move. I stared at him, becoming conscious that my mouth was gaping open. I gulped and stammered, "But . . . " It wasn't quite finished. I still had to put in some of the details of the shop windows. As for selling it – WOW!

"I'll leave you in peace to finish it and come back in half an hour. Would you accept £50? I'd really like to buy it, you know. I'm quite serious. I'll take it back with me to Canada and frame it. Think about it. Half an hour!"

And finish it I did, though my hands trembled with excitement. To sell a painting! The first! It was like being a real artist! If I had not felt so stunned I would have been proud. It was strange to see him wrapping up my precious painting in the brown paper he had bought during the half hour. It was the last I would see of it – my work gone for good, to Canada. I felt a bit bereft, like when the children left home. But he assured me my work would be cared for and appreciated, and smiled at me. I think he knew what I was feeling, as he peeled out five ten-pound notes from his wallet and gave me his card. A professor, no less! I smiled and thanked him and started to breathe again.

"You'll never believe!" I said to Sarah, as she greeted me at her door. I stumbled in, dropping my clobber on the floor beside the chair.

"Why? What's the excitement?"

And I told her, at length, every detail of the encounter. And I showed her the card he'd given me. And pulled out the roll of notes to show her. Proof! Somebody liked my painting! We laughed together in sheer joy. It was all so unbelievable but true.

"But tell me about your day, Sarah. Who did you say those people were?"

And she explained over our cup of tea and almond slices. Her husband, Timothy, had a sister who emigrated to Australia and married out there before Sarah knew her. They had never visited, and even Ian had not visited them when he was in Australia. "I don't know why. Perhaps he wasn't interested in looking up an unknown aunt, and he was more interested in aborigines at that time," she said. "Anyway, in the course of time, Timothy's parents moved to Corrie and they got it into their head they would like to see their daughter again before they died. They were already about eighty by then, and Timothy decided it would be wise if he went with them – to look after them. So of course I went too. It took a lot of organising, for some reason, and we didn't actually get there till a couple of years ago. They had, have, a big bungalow that would accommodate us all; the old people were happy and we were enjoying the climate and Australian hospitality. Until that day." She halted and a stricken look flashed across her face. But she drew in her breath and continued. "We were having a barbecue, as they do in Australia, all of us stretched out in deckchairs enjoying the sunshine, without a care in the world. I was nodding and Timothy was asleep. But he never woke up! He simply died in his sleep, there, with all of us around, not knowing!"

"Oh, my God, how awful!" Poor Sarah, what a terrible shock it must have been. And so far away from home, too!

"Yes, we decided he should be buried there. There was no point in bringing him back here. And in the event his parents decided to stay out there. They have died since, and I have not been back. I have no desire to go again. Australia has only unhappy memories for me now, I'm afraid. I was there too short a time to get close to any of them. We simply exchange Christmas cards, no more."

"So was it this sister who came over today, so unexpectedly?" I was puzzled. It seemed such an odd thing to do.

"No, it was her daughter's young son and his girl friend, backpackers. They're touring Europe and thought they'd like to see where the family came from. Nice enough kids, but I would have preferred prior notice of their arrival. And I didn't enjoy being reminded of things I would rather forget. I prefer to let the past stay in the past."

"Of course. And you missed a day's painting," I commiserated. "And you might have sold your picture. I'm sure the professor would have preferred yours. But at least it's given me more confidence. I shan't mind quite so much if someone looks over my shoulder in future. And I've decided definitely that I'm going to experiment with acrylics or oils or both. I really enjoyed doing that painting today, but I want to do the same scene again in oils, and larger."

19

"Why, hello, Muriel! Here again!" Iolanthe's melodious voice lifted my spirits as well as pleased my ears. Truth to tell, I was feeling a little depressed. I should have picked up Maggie at the crossroad this morning; she had cornered me at the post office and begged a lift to the ferry. I was happy to oblige, of course, and it was important to her. Her son was getting married to a girl from a wealthy family in the south and Maggie was afraid to let him down; she wanted some posh designer clothes and a wedding hat from Glasgow, and a special hairdo perhaps. The wedding was in two months time – would she be able to lose a stone in that time, she asked me? As if I knew! I thought it very doubtful, knowing her fondness for food, but I kept quiet. I'd rather keep her friendship. But, having arranged all that, she phoned me late last night, just as I was going to bed, to say she had to cancel her trip. "I'm afraid it's Alan. You know what men are. He's got a pain in his chest and is convinced it's his heart. I tell him he shouldn't have eaten that pork pie, he's always ill after pork but he won't be told. Anyway he's made me promise to stay with him. I'm sure he'll be all right tomorrow, but too late to catch the ferry. I'm sorry, but I hope you have a good day and can get all you want."

It was disappointing not to have her company for

the drive across the island, but that was only part of my depression. I think it may have had something to do with the weather. The atmospheric pressure weighed down heavily on me. Even the summer warmth was oppressive, as if the heat had drawn out the air and caused a vacuum. The sea would provide more breathable air, I knew, but I was too lazy to climb up to the open deck. Or too tired, perhaps. I had had a short but vigorous session yesterday cleaning my flat. The poor thing tended to get neglected as I told myself a little dust didn't matter because there was nobody else to see it and criticize. And the garden was more important in the summer. My new shrubs had come on apace. There must be something special in the Arran soil, or perhaps it was the mild winter, but the escallonias, which were only small plants in containers when I bought them were now large bushes that would need pruning next year. Incredible! Maggie said the same; her rhododendrons were doing very well; she wanted me to go and see them but I've put it off until next spring when they will be in flower. Perhaps we shall have another trip across to Kintyre later this summer, before the ferry reduces its timetable for the winter.

Meantime I must concentrate on my trip to Glasgow. I was not interested in clothes, like Maggie, but I had brought my credit card with me and was determined to buy oil paints and brushes. Not acrylics. I've had no experience but in my ignorance I decided I would paint out of doors in watercolour and indoors in oils. I rejected the idea of a medium that can do both. It seemed dishonest, somehow. The arrogance of the ignorant amateur!

And here was Iolanthe to cheer me up. She was always so bright and full of life, and it was a tonic just to look at her, in her denim jacket and skirt decorated with sequined stars or daisies in bright colours. It was a simple outfit but eye-catching and when she sat down beside me she tossed off her jacket to reveal a bright pink sleeveless top. I was intrigued and gave the jacket a closer look; the sequins were of rainbow colours stitched into sunbursts – very effective. I gave her full marks for style! "So, how is the work progressing?" I asked.

"OK. No problems. It will soon be the summer vacation. John will be pleased, but of course there is still work to be done." She removed her bulging rucksack from the adjoining seat and dumped it on the floor beside her, as another passenger, an old lady with a stiff leg, claimed the seat.

"And what about your novel?" I asked. "How will you manage to work on that while you're at home, and without John knowing about it?"

"It might be difficult while he is on holiday too, but as long as he's at school I'll be free to work on it. Otherwise I can pretend I have essays to do for my tutor." She smiled tranquilly. I could quite imagine she would cope, and get her own way. "But what about you? Are you off to the art gallery again?"

"I hope so, but I'm really going to the art shop, that's my priority today. I'm going to buy oil paints, Iolanthe. I don't know whether I'll be any good at it, but I want to try. I shall still use watercolour as well, for outdoor pictures. Did you hear that I sold a painting?"

"No. Wow, a famous painter in the family! Good for you! John must be proud of having such a clever mother. And he never told me, sod him! But I think you're wonderful – how you've changed. So enterprising nowadays!"

I laughed and said the painting wasn't so important; it was only a simple watercolour and I'd only sold one, for heaven's sake, it wasn't a major event. But I lapped up her admiration and puffed out my chest as I started to gather my things together; my light blue jacket and roomy handbag, which I hoped would hold the paints and brushes I intended to buy. The harbour at Ardrossan was already in sight. The voyage was so much shorter when one had someone to talk to. There would soon be the announcement for the car drivers to go down to the car deck.

"We must apologise. Owing to a reported bomb at Ardrossan harbour we are proceeding to Gourock. We are very sorry for any inconvenience; enquiries may be made at the purser's office." And the tannoy did indeed sound sorry. I was sure the captain would be annoyed.

"Oh, NO" It was as if a concerted groan was felt throughout the ship. It meant another hour before landing, and at least an hour later for arriving in Glasgow. And it meant that the next sailing would have to be cancelled, in order to catch up with the timetable. Thank goodness it didn't affect my return. The ferry would be back on schedule by the afternoon, but several people were badly affected. There were some who had booked flights they could no longer catch, and others who would miss train connections or business appointments. But all took it good spirits. There were no complaints that I could hear; bomb scares are a modern phenomena and one has to be philosophical about it.

"If you don't mind, Muriel, I'll leave you. I'll go upstairs to the other lounge. It's quiet there as a rule and I can get some work done on my novel. This extra hour is a bonus for that. I've missed a lecture, but I've got a cast iron excuse for that, haven't I?"

There was consternation for about ten minutes then resignation, with a concerted shrug of understanding.

With a cup of coffee from the cafeteria I watched other passengers busy with their mobiles up to their ears. It looked as if everybody had earache, I thought with a giggle. I'd not thought it necessary to acquire one of these modern toys. Who would I ring, anyway? There was nothing so urgent in my life that required instant communication. Life was lived at an easy, slower pace than was many people's fate, though it was infinitely more varied and enjoyable than my previous life, thank God. There was a happy medium between stagnation and burnout and I considered I was in the running to achieve it.

It wasn't until my head jerked up that I realised I had nodded off. Fortunately I'd already put down my mug on the window ledge. What would the woman with the stick think of me, asleep in the middle of the morning? I looked round at her but she was away too, and probably dreaming. Her mouth was slackly open, her brown felt hat (which inexplicably she had kept firmly on) had slewed over her left eyebrow and her liver-spotted hands twitched in time with her snores. Well, it was as good a way as any of occupying enforced inactivity, I supposed. We were not all as enterprising as Iolanthe. The more I got to know the girl the more I admired her. I couldn't think she was two-timing John. It seemed so out of character. But some day I would have to pluck up courage and ask her about her friends and what they do in the evenings in Glasgow. Tactfully, of course, though I feared she was too intelligent to be deceived about my motive. But I didn't want to destroy our easy relationship. Perhaps it might be better to leave well alone and hope that the truth – whatever it might be – would reveal itself without any effort on my part. Perhaps I should worry more about John. I did so want their partnership to be happy. Why couldn't they marry like normal people and have children? It wouldn't prevent Iolanthe carrying on with her writing. I missed Sandra's two; Peter and Lucy were growing up and Pitlochry was too far away for a quick visit. I missed their babyhood too. I wanted John to hurry up and start a family – I would be so happy to baby-sit. So there, that was it! I admitted it; I was selfish, thinking only of myself. Perhaps John and Iolanthe didn't want children. There was no law that says they must. I should let them live their lives in their own way and not interfere. Interfering mothers are a pest.

Such pious, even sanctimonious thoughts brought us within sight of Gourock pier. And what a shock I got! It was nothing like Ardrossan though, to think about it, why should it be? Here, looking down from what seemed a great height on to the quayside was an air of political correctness, of aloof knowingness, of bureaucratic efficiency. It was abuzz with activity – mental in the office block in front of us, which someone said was the headquarters of CalMac, and physical activity on the ground; men wrestling with ropes, cars inching their way round bollards on the restricted roadway, and passengers queueing to take our places on board. We, the foot passengers, were all agog, peering down on the exodus of cars and lorries from the bowels of the ship, waiting our turn to disembark from the car ramp.

"You see, we're too high up, or the pier is too low for us, there's no gangway that can reach up to the passenger deck." Iolanthe had come down to join me just as I was helping the old lady next to me to get on her feet and to hobble to the lift. I was glad of Iolanthe's guidance. She had had the experience of sailing to Gourock once before, she said, because of a storm, she explained. "You see, the harbour entrance at Ardrossan is very narrow and the ferry has to make a sharp turn into it. And if there is a strong cross wind it's too dangerous. But it doesn't happen very often, thank God." So now we had to go down the steep stairway to the car deck and walk out from below; then turn back along the pier to the train station; the covered passage to the station was a very welcome improvement on the windy walk at Ardrossan. And I enjoyed the train trip to Glasgow too; it was another new experience for me to journey along the shores of the Clyde. I'd heard so much about the shipbuilders of the Clyde, and it was sad to see the idle cranes and empty docks. But what I didn't realise, and nobody had told me, it is a beautiful river with a fine shore line of cliffs, woods and parkland, interspersed with small towns and villas. Costa Clyde, I said to Iolanthe, but she was immersed in her work and only smiled.

It was lunchtime when I got to Glasgow, after this tour round the river estuary, so that was my first priority. A quick sandwich in the nearest tearoom had to suffice, as I wanted to leave myself plenty of time to browse in the art shop. My second visit was less bewildering, but there was still a great choice of colours among the oil paints, and it all needed a lot of hard decisions. Sarah had advised me to stick to earth colours to start with, as they were safe and permanent – ochres, siennas, cobalt, ultramarine, carmine – glorious colours! And brushes; I needed quite a lot of brushes, I thought, as it's not so easy to wash one out to apply another colour, as it is in watercolour painting. I would need a separate brush for each colour, perhaps. Anyway, it was best to be prepared. Armed with a basket full of my choice I waved my credit card at the assistant, feeling proud and so sophisticated. It was a red letter event, as there was no need for my credit card on Arran; most of my purchases were modest enough for cash and otherwise my cheque was accepted without question. What a different life one lives on the mainland!

And, just as I'd anticipated, I paid by cheque to Mr Woodhouse at the art shop in Brodick when I arrived back. I knew he stocked boards and canvases, so there was no need to carry any from Glasgow. He had a few colours, but not the vast selection I wanted to look at. Sarah had introduced me to him, so he was interested in my decision to start painting in oils and advised about the size and texture of boards to start with. "To practise and get used to handling oils," I told him "I shall start with a still life. Maybe I am thinking of that powerful picture of fruit that Peggy Paine painted in her youth. Have you seen it? I would love to do something like that."

He hadn't seen it, but agreed that it was wise to paint a still life. "Some artists paint nothing else, you know. Look at the Flemish masters – all those dead birds and such!"

I laughed. I had no intention of painting dead birds, but a bit of fruit on a table would satisfy me.

"And what about an easel?" he enquired. "I know you got that sketching easel from me, but is it going to be big enough and firm enough to support the board for oil painting?"

"Oh, heavens, no! I'd forgotten that." So he showed me what he had – not many to choose from but there was one reasonably priced that he assured me would be adequate. Well! It could have been Christmas! The car was piled up with all these goodies. I was so excited I drove home in a dream, thinking of all the paintings I was going to do – such masterpieces!

It wasn't sensible to start right away, of course. Be sensible, Muriel I chided myself. There had to be a space to work in, preferably a studio set apart for the purpose. So that meant reorganising my spare room. I remembered George saying that he used his spare room as a study, so mine will become a studio. I stood in the middle of the floor and surveyed the room. Obviously the bed would have to go. The grey carpet could be disastrous; I didn't feel like replacing it with something more practical; for one thing it was relatively new and it would be a shame to throw it away, and for another thing I was spent up. So I would just have to be careful. I could place newspaper under the easel when I was working. The bedside cabinet could be useful for storage and the dressing table would serve to hold my paints and things. Perhaps I could use the wardrobe to store the boards and completed pictures? If so, there was no great upheaval necessary. I would advertise the bed in the post office window and simply set up my new easel in the middle of the floor. And hey presto – a studio! Second thoughts – what about a table for my still lifes? I had to think seriously about this. I looked at the window. It faced south. Today was dull but when the sun shone it was quite blinding in these rooms at the front. These thick cotton curtains were unsuitable; they would cut out too much light. I needed something thinner that would veil the glare but admit light. And to have the light coming from my left, which is my preference, meant that I would be facing the door when standing at my easel. Standing, yes, I meant standing. I'd seen artists standing at easels and I would try it. The brushes are longer and one has to walk back and forwards to see the effect as one paints. Or so I believe. I walked round and imagined the bed removed and my easel in place and me in front of it. Hmm, yes, I needed the dressing table to hold all my paints and things at my left hand against the wall. So, dragging and shoving, and puffing like a grampus, I eventually got it removed and coaxed into place, though it would have been easier if the bed hadn't been there. It was very much in the way and I regretted there was no attic to hide it in. For the time being I pushed it up against the wall opposite the window, and tried to forget about it. The wardrobe could stay where it was, to the right of the window. The one chair, an upholstered nursing chair was enticing enough to stay and play a useful part; I might be glad sometimes just to relax and think about painting instead of actually working. Yes, Muriel, I said to myself as I sank into its comfort, this is going to be a very happy studio. Tomorrow I start!

20

July 10
Now that I am more used to putting words together, due to the obligatory essays for the OU, it ought to be easier for me to write this journal more frequently. Looking back, I have accomplished this task no more often than once a month. This I regret. However, perhaps there is enough information contained in it to suffice for the enlightenment of my grandchildren. If I were more technologically inclined I would write my journal on the computer and store it on disks, which can be easily copied and transported. But looking ahead and remembering how rapidly and drastically things have changed in the last fifty years, I can believe it possible that computers will be out of date and unusable after another generation. I cannot believe it possible, however, that handwriting will ever be redundant or unable to be read and therefore I will continue to use this sturdy notebook and permanent ink. Now that I am immersed in serious study I realise and am grateful for the great contribution past diarists and writers have made to our knowledge of history, and I am encouraged to believe that my own efforts will ultimately add to the sum total of historical evidence.

My activities during the last month have been confined as usual to the OU work, the museum, Muriel and John. Although we are such close neighbours I see little of Muriel and I am scarcely aware of her movements. That was the way we both wanted our lives to be lived, but I was embarrassed when I had to admit to Gladys at the post office that I did not know that Muriel had sold one of her paintings. It was a humiliating moment and I had difficulty in responding to her conversation. I am still amazed that Gladys should know things about Muriel of which I am ignorant. I wonder now how far her news is accurate. She seemed quite confident about it but, knowing her propensity for gossip, I will have to confirm it with Muriel herself. I cannot imagine that such an amateur painter like Muriel could produce anything saleable, though Gladys said she had heard that the buyer was somebody important from abroad. Perhaps English watercolours are valued abroad. I have always thought – when I gave the subject any thought at all – that they were meant as rough sketches for a more important oil painting. I will discuss this with Rosemary. We talked a little about what she called 'The English School' in relation to the Napoleonic period but I cannot understand Rosemary's admiration for those vague and smeary paintings of Turner in his later period. Some of the other artists' watercolours are quite pleasing but I cannot see that they are really important or that they are any better than a modern photograph. Rosemary talks about the disposition of shapes and the balance of colour, and perhaps there is something I should learn to appreciate. I could ask Rosemary if there is an exhibition we could both go to; I would welcome her comments; she is so good at explaining things, without making me conscious of my ignorance. I will mention to her that I would like a trip to London, to the galleries, but hesitate to go alone; I would certainly not wish to go in a coach party with Muriel in the group. And it could be a waste of time when I don't know what to look for in all those paintings; it would be so much more enjoyable and valuable if Rosemary and I were there together. I think our relationship has progressed sufficiently for this to be a viable proposition; I am sure she understands that it is merely friendship and that I have no intention of making emotional or sexual demands on her. We are both now of an age, I believe, to enjoy a platonic friendship. A weekend in London together, visiting galleries and perhaps a concert or a theatre would be very agreeable. It is a pity that Muriel and I never had this sort of relationship, or this sort of pleasant life. There is no point in trying to apportion blame; it is too late for that, but not too late to make amends, albeit with someone else.

I trust and hope that John is not making the same mistake. It would be very regrettable if he were to discover he had committed himself to the wrong woman, but because of his pride he could not free himself. He has been wise in not marrying Iolanthe; I cannot understand why he says he wishes to marry her. He made the mistake in buying the house in both their names. I understand that she contributed half the purchase price too. One wonders how she could have accumulated so much money while still so young. But if, as I hope, John decides he has made a mistake the joint ownership would add to the difficulties of separation. Would either of them have the means to buy the other out? It would be tragic if John were left homeless and without enough capital to buy elsewhere.

I put all this to him when I went last week to see him, when I knew Iolanthe would be away. She is always away in the middle of the week and I knew

John would be feeling depressed. He is always in low spirits these days, though he persists in saying he can cope. He is being very brave and pretending that he simply misses her presence, but I believe it is more than that which is troubling him. His unhappiness must not be allowed to continue unchecked; I owe it to him, my own son, to prevent the unhappiness festering like mine did for forty years. He is still barely forty and deserves a better life. At least he is doing the work he has always wanted to do, but I want to see him contented in his personal life. I am sure Muriel also shares my concern. But Muriel will say nothing against Iolanthe, for some reason. She says she likes the girl and trusts her, though I am amazed that she should take sides against her own son. It is up to me to protect John's interests and my visit last week was primarily for this purpose.

He had just got in from school and was looking tired, with a pile of papers in front of him on the table by the window. I thought he was paler than the last time I saw him and hoped he was looking after himself. "Do you make proper meals when you are on your own?" I asked him. "And do you get enough exercise? You mustn't get into the habit of walking only to the school and back. You need proper exercise. You're young. You used to enjoy going out, rambling with friends."

"Oh, Dad," he said. "Don't criticise. I'm all right. Don't fuss. You're as bad as Mum. Come and sit down and have a cup of tea. Or is it beer nowadays? I think you've changed your mind about beer, haven't you? I heard something to that effect. One of our staff – I think it was Joe – saw you in the Fleece with a bloke from Lochranza and I don't suppose you were drinking tea there, were you?"

I think he was laughing at me for having been so

stiff in my attitudes all my life. He knows perfectly well that it was the way I was brought up. My father never allowed a drop of alcohol to enter the house or pass his lips – or anyone else's lips, for that matter. So I grew up taking it for granted that one didn't drink. I see now that such an attitude inhibits social intercourse. "Yes," I acknowledged, "I was with Graham from the post office." I did not explain my shock and disappointment at discovering earlier that he was or had been a council workman. John would ridicule me, I know. He has always been slack about social niceties. For the sake of Graham's continuing friendship I am now trying to take a more tolerant attitude.

So he produced a couple of cans of beer from his fridge, with glasses, I was pleased to remark. Beer is all right, a refreshing drink, but I do not approve of drinking it out of the can. One must keep some standards.

"And when is Iolanthe coming back?" I enquired when we had settled down in his old chairs. He is so fond of these chairs, though they are really very uncomfortable now, being long past their usefulness. Black leather appealed to him as a student, but I would hope that his taste will improve and that he will replace the chairs with something more suitable. I would welcome Iolanthe's input there, I believe. Black leather is scarcely a young woman's choice, surely.

"On Friday, on the last ferry, she says." He was nonchalant but there was something I could not understand.

"I don't understand, John. It's July now. It's the school holiday. Why are you still marking papers? You were marking when I came in, weren't you?" I indicated the papers I could see on his table.

John sighed and smiled. "Yes, you're right. It's the school holiday. But there's a little group of students who want to prepare themselves for university in October. They asked me to give them extra help. I wouldn't normally want to be bothered, but as Iolanthe's away I've got the time and I might as well earn a little extra pocket money. That's all. It's not onerous and I wasn't planning to go away."

"So you're spending your summer holiday alone and working!" My son seemed to have taken leave of his senses.

"Come on, Dad. It's not like that. I'm not alone all the time. I see these students only once a week for a couple of hours, and Iolanthe comes home at the weekend. It's not so bad."

"Not so bad? It's not very good either. What do you do with the rest of your time? You've been here nearly a year now. Have you found friends with similar interests? You've never mentioned anyone, so I wondered."

"Oh, yes, of course. Not that it's anything to do with you, but to satisfy your curiosity, I go to the Hydro. I've good friends there." He glowered at me, then smiled. *"They'd be good for you too, Dad. Why don't you go? There's Melanie there, your age. You'd get on well together. And there's a super swimming pool. I'll introduce you if you like."*

"No thank you. It doesn't appeal to me." I was beginning to realise he was trying to change the subject, away from the thorny topic of his relationship with Iolanthe. I felt it was time we had some facts out in the open. There had been enough innuendo, could we perhaps find the truth?

"You've told me why you are working in the holiday, but what about Iolanthe? The university is also on holiday, and for longer. Why is she still going to Glasgow every week? There will be no lectures now, in July. You must realise that. She should be at

home with you, if you're a couple as you say you are. Or you should be away somewhere, perhaps abroad, enjoying a break like normal couples." I didn't want to antagonise him but I wanted an explanation. It was time everything was out in the open. "So what excuse does she give for still being tied to Glasgow?"

John frowned, crossed his legs and threw his empty beer can towards the waste bin and missed it. "It's not a matter of excuses. I can't pretend I like it but if she is serious about this writing lark she has to attend these lectures and things. And the summer vac is the time when eminent writers hold workshops, she says. Sometimes they're at the weekend; sometimes they go on for a whole week. So that's what she's doing. Once she's got her degree it'll be OK."

His tone was defiant. He was hiding something, more than his loneliness, I suspected. What about the rumours? "Your mother's worried about you, John. About you both in fact. She's heard nasty rumours about Iolanthe being seen in restaurants with men. I don't like this. You know I've never trusted her. Have you tackled her about these rumours? What does she say?"

"No, I have not tackled her." He spluttered his indignation. "And it's no business of yours to listen to rumours. So stop meddling. You're as bad as Mum. I can't take any more. Iolanthe and I will sort out our problems together and live our lives as we wish. We don't want interfering do-gooders."

"Well, you were always a cocky young puppy, wanting to make your own mistakes. But you're still my son and I don't like to see you making a mess of your life. Of course I realise you don't want to tell Iolanthe how she should live her life; you've learnt from my mistake with your mother, I hope, but don't complicate things by your own misconduct. I've been

hearing rumours about you, which I hope you'll say are not true. It's all very well going for a swim at the Hydro, but are you sure your visits there are completely innocent? Have you heard the rumours? Can you deny them?"

John buttoned his lips and glowered. His hands clenched and he looked as though he would like to hit me. But I ignored his attitude and persisted in trying to rescue his happiness. "You mustn't risk ruining your reputation here," I pointed out. "It is a small population and news soon circulates and becomes exaggerated. You have a public position to uphold and cannot afford scandal. I can sympathise with your problem. It is difficult for a man to be alone so much, missing his conjugal rights, but there are other remedies. A trip to the mainland would be more discreet. A man's needs can be met with discretion, you know."

"And that's what you did, I suppose? Well, I'm not your sort of fucking hypocrite and I don't want your advice. I think you'd better go. I can't take any more of this." And he stormed to the door and ushered me out without another word.

It was a most regrettable incident. I had no desire to antagonise my son; my only motive was to help him to overcome his present problem and achieve a happy life. One's motives are often misinterpreted I find. No doubt it is the lot of parents to be misunderstood. I have to believe that John will consider my remarks in tranquillity and find them helpful.

My Wednesday visit to the museum was more profitable. Esther supplied me with a list of members, as of last year, which I was able to check with the money paid into the bank. This was useful but caused another problem. Ten members had not yet paid, but which? I can find no receipts, no records. Esther was very helpful; she offered to appeal in the next newsletter and hope the late payers will respond. I still have to discover the source of a few larger sums of money deposited in the bank but not accounted for. Thankfully all debts have now been traced and paid. Esther was thankful to have my report in good time for the next committee meeting. I had made an excuse not to give Graham a lift on this occasion. I was still trying to reconcile his personality with his demeaning work, and was not sure of my attitude. However, over our picnic lunch in the archive room, squashed round the inadequate table, there was no avoiding him. Sybil was talking about her discoveries of ancient sites during her walks over the moors. She is hoping to plot them all on a new map; some have been known for a long time but there are many more to be discovered. She is even hoping to go up in a helicopter in the winter, when the bracken has died down, because she says ancient disturbance of the land should be more visible. I was amazed, not only at her dedication but also at her knowledge and understanding of these ancient inhabitants of the island, when so little remained above ground. Having said something to this effect, Graham turned to me, smiling over his thick sandwich of white bread, cheese and pickle. "Talking of plotting sites, what about a hike up North Sannox some fine day, George? There's not much left but there's more than they'll find from the helicopter. It's not so long since North Sannox was a settlement of crofters. That is, it's a historical site, not pre-historic."

"You'd be interested, George. Didn't you say your ancestors came from Arran? Perhaps they lived in the glen? Did you find out?" Malcolm said. "I remember you came and made some enquiries last year. But I don't remember you saying you'd found any details."

He spooned some yoghurt into his mouth, with a tissue in his other hand to wipe spills or smears. He was a dainty eater.

"Actually," I said, "I did find a reference to Sannox but there wasn't time then to pursue it as I was only over for the day. And since then I've neglected my family history in favour of a wider field of history." I would welcome a walk through the glen and I had to admit that Graham was the obvious guide. He was very knowledgeable about Arran history and was genuinely enthusiastic in studying old maps and documents to increase his knowledge. I could not do better than take advantage of his offer.

Millie added her persuasion, slicing an apple and removing the core of each quarter. "He knows exactly where the crofts were. I don't think you'd be able to find them by yourself."

"No," Graham agreed. "Some are only a few stones buried in the bracken, but they make sense if you know what you're looking for. Can you draw, George? We could take spades to beat the bracken down and I'll uncover the layout of the remaining stones while you draw the plan of the buildings. How about it?"

I was forced into an instant decision. I wanted to accept, but to spend the day with a street cleaner? It was so unlike me. How could I do it? Then I recollected that he had been born here, and in this island community it gave him an aristocratic status. In fact I had discovered that there were three levels of society here, regardless of an individual's personal achievements in life. First there were the natives like Graham and Gladys and Muriel's friend Sarah, then there were the incomers, settlers from the mainland like myself, and lastly there were the people with second homes here, who were scarcely distinguishable from the tourists.

"Yes, that would be fine. I'd like that." I managed to respond. "It will be interesting to trace the old crofts and draw a plan of the houses. Give me a ring when you think it's a suitable day." I straightened my shoulders. I had taken a big step forward, felt, and hoped it was in the right direction.

21

The Australian waiter swung open the door and bowed me ceremoniously into the restaurant. It was not part of his duty but he had simply gone to blu-tack a notice to the door announcing an Australian party night the following Saturday. He smiled apology for almost bumping into me and waved me to the dining tables on the left. "Or are you just wanting coffee or something light?" he asked. I assured him I was here for lunch with a friend, and I would await his arrival before ordering. And no, I wouldn't order a drink until my friend arrived.

While waiting – I was early and not impatient – I took note of my surroundings. One never knew what details might be incorporated some day in a painting, and I had got into the habit of always carrying a little sketchbook in my handbag. The colour scheme of the restaurant was subdued, cream, light brown and pale wood enlivened by the bright summer dresses and tee-shirts of the diners. I was glad I had decided to wear my yellow blouse and grey A-line skirt. It was an outfit suitable for the bright summer day and the ambience of the place. The sun was now exerting its power and I wondered if it might be too warm to eat outside on the curved balcony. It looked tempting out there, beyond the huge windows and the glazed door. I could see a few favoured tables there, at the moment vacant, with a clear view over the fields to the mountains beyond. Perhaps George would like to eat out there?

At the thought, as if my mind had summoned him, he arrived, looking smart in light blue trousers and a pale blue and white striped shirt. And yes, after the conventional greetings he agreed the balcony would be the best place for our lunch.

"I didn't offer you a lift," he apologised, as the waiter brought us a menu. It was the same Australian, his name was Roger and he was spending his gap year in Europe, he said. He would move on to Greece in the autumn, as he didn't want to experience a winter in Scotland.

After this interruption and our request for Roger to bring us prawn salad and a lasagne George continued his explanation. "I have things to do in Brodick this afternoon and can't take you back. You don't mind?"

Of course I didn't mind. I wanted to be free. I'd had enough of always being ferried around, never choosing my own time or destination. I was proud of my little car and jealous of my hard-won freedom. So I smiled sweetly and assured him I had things to do too while I was over on this side of the island. It was too bright a day to spend indoors and I planned to make some sketches up Glen Rosa, to use in an oil painting later. "So what are you doing nowadays, George? Are you still busy at the museum?" I was so glad he had got interested in the museum, actually working there and making friends. I'd heard that he was even willing to roll his sleeves up and do some practical work too. So different from his dull sedentary life of forty years. I would not have thought him capable of changing to this extent. He was always so set in his ways and so resistant of any hint of change. I welcomed this new George as I welcomed my own change of life-style. Who says we can't change our spots? George and I are living proof, I decided.

I beamed at him over my prawn salad as he told me that he had just about sorted out the books and the accounts. It had been a troublesome task and very complicated. He had never imagined that accounts could get into such a muddle in so short a time. There were still some membership subscriptions outstanding but he had hopes of them being settled before the next committee meeting. It was clear that he took his duties very seriously. There was nothing new there. He had always been serious about everything he undertook and meticulous in its performance. Unlike slapdash me. I don't like things being too cut and dried. I like the freedom to be spontaneous if the occasion offers itself. It was in a spontaneous mood that I agreed to become a supporting member of the museum, thanks to George's persuasive powers, and I handed over my subscription, placing my cheque beside his plate of lasagne.

"I've met Millie," I told him. "She and I were at a coffee morning for the Save the Children. She said she knew you. And of course I know Graham. I got the impression they are a good crowd, and friendly"

George agreed and told me of the walk up North Glen Sannox to trace the remains of a former settlement there. "There's a lot of discussion about the Clearances," he said. "Some say it was a good thing, to clear away the poverty and make way for more energetic entrepreneurs. Others say it was the wanton destruction of a traditional way of life."

"Your own ancestors suffered when they were driven out, didn't they? They drifted to Glasgow and their life there must have been as difficult as it was here, perhaps even worse."

"Yes, perhaps they might have done better if they'd gone to Canada as so many of them did"

"Oh, I don't know. The first generation of immigrants there must have had a very rough life in poverty. Those who survived the voyage, the upheaval and the backbreaking work made it easier for the following generations, that's for sure. As your father made good, and you did even better. And John perhaps better still?" It was a persuasive argument. I didn't want him to dwell any more on the young thieving clerk who was his ancestor in a Glasgow slum.

"You're probably right." He was surprisingly conciliatory and went on to talk about his exploratory hike up the glen.

"Gladys told me Graham had enjoyed his day out too, and he's going to suggest you might like to join a rambling club he belongs to." It was strange that George, in talking at length about his walk in the glen had never even mentioned Graham. But I know that they are friendly – buddies, according to the information from Gladys. Graham has few words for me. He is strictly a man's man. As is George, I believe, and I hope he joins the rambling group. I was invited too. Gladys mentioned it but rambling doesn't appeal to me. I would rather go alone or with a fellow artist, just to walk far enough to find a spot to sit and paint. I launched into an account of my last trip to Glasgow and my decision to paint in oils.

"Oh, yes? That's more advanced work, isn't it?" he said. I heard you'd sold one of your watercolours. You never told me. Are you going to make a career out of your painting? Do you think you're good enough? Doesn't it need special training?"

I bridled a little at this remark. "Of course I know I'm not good enough. I have no illusions about my ability. I'm only an amateur, but if somebody likes one of my paintings why shouldn't I sell it?"

"All right. All right. No need to be defensive. I didn't mean anything. Only I've been to the McMillan gallery in Glasgow since seeing you and seen the oil paintings there. I confess I don't understand them. They are very different from your style of painting and they are professional. At least I can understand yours and know what they're supposed to be."

Well, that's a change, I thought. Praise, even if faint, from George is rare and precious. I didn't comment on it but finished the last piece of tomato on my plate, carefully synchronised with George's last mouthful of pasta.

"Shall we go over into the lounge for our coffee," he suggested. It would be more comfortable in the deeply upholstered chairs and sofas of brown or red moquette, artfully arranged in intimate groups. George knows me well enough not to press me to have a sweet course. We are both trying to keep our weight down as we grow older, George being more fanatical about it than me. He can be quite finicky over his food and it's just as well that he now does his own catering and cooking.

As I looked around the coffee lounge I thought it was empty. It was discreetly lit and so quiet – that is, apart from the pop music (thankfully muted enough to hear oneself speak). But as my eyes got accustomed to the dim lighting, I could see, on closer investigation, that many of the cosy corners were already occupied. The only corner free was near the door to the toilets. I raised my eyebrows at being obliged to sit beside the route to the toilets but, hang it all, the coffee would taste the same, wouldn't it? In the event it was not as public as I had imagined, as anybody wishing to go to the toilets gave us a wide berth, and I was emboldened to broach a sensitive subject.

"I heard you've been to see John and he wasn't too pleased. Was there some sort of disagreement?"

"Heard? How did you hear? What did you hear? Who told you anything about it? Tittle tattle!"

"Well, no, nobody. It wasn't gossip. It was John, actually. I went to see him yesterday and he was still upset at the way you'd ploughed into him. It seems you went way over the top in accusations and condemnation – and with no evidence. That's what upset him. You could have been more tactful, I think." I saw George's face darken and feared a storm was about to break. "It's all right, though. Although he's upset he does understand how you feel. In fact he is still concerned about Iolanthe himself, I know he is, though he didn't say so and I didn't mention her. There was nothing positive that I could add and I think it's best to say nothing; until we know something to the contrary, don't you think we should give her the benefit of the doubt?"

"Maybe. But there's still plenty of doubt, it seems to me."

"I'm afraid you're right. I didn't want to mention it, but I've heard from two different sources that Iolanthe has been seen several times, not just once, with men in hotels."

"Who told you that? Who's been gossiping? Some Women's Institute crone with nothing else to think about but make mischief?"

If only! It could have been pigeonholed as fantasy if that had been the case but my informants, via Gladys of course, were two respectable pillars of society, Raymond Smith a Kirk elder and Jack Mulroy a prominent businessman. They were not given to fantasise, I was sure, and they were familiar with

Glasgow hotels as part of their work. "I don't think there's anything we can do, George." I said. I've come to that conclusion. We have to let the young people sort out their own problems."

"You say you see her sometimes on the ferry. Can you tell from her attitude whether she is being deceitful?"

"No, I must say she seems very open and honest, keen on her writing and wanting to succeed in her degree course. In fact I can't help liking her." I couldn't tell George but she had talked more about her novel and how it was progressing and how she was being helped by her tutor. Instead I changed the subject. "Has Sandra rung you? She said she was going to. It's good news, isn't it? I'm so pleased for her. For them both, of course, and for the children."

"Hmm, yes, but it's a great barn of a place and all that staff. There can't be much privacy. It's no place for small children. And how will she manage with a baby?"

I poured him another cup of coffee and pushed the sugar bowl towards him. He needed sweetening. "I think it's good for children. They learn to mix with others, acquire social graces and everything. And Sandra has plenty of help with all that staff. She's not responsible for the domestic arrangements, you know. They have a very competent housekeeper and the rest of the hotel staff have been there for ever. They're very reliable. And Berry is a really caring man. There'll be no problems about having a baby there I'm sure." I hope Sandra hadn't told George about the problem she did have. I didn't want to discuss it with him but hoped it would solve itself, given time. After all, Tony had long gone and it was all official water under the bridge.

But George did know. "Hrmph! That Tony won't

leave her alone. He has no business to demand access to the children now, so long after the divorce. He never took any interest in them when they were married and now, well, she didn't even know where he was."

Tony had disappeared after the divorce and we all thought that was the last we would hear of him, but now he had turned up out of the blue or, to be accurate, out of South America expressing a sudden fondness for Peter and Lucy, who had probably forgotten him by now. I didn't say so to George, but I suspect that Tony is now thinking the children could soon be a source of income for him. He knows they were intelligent even as infants, and now that they're growing up they will soon be at High School and he thinks he can exploit them. I remember him as a skilled exploiter of women. He was expert at buttering people up in order to wheedle something out of them. He never gave anything in return, though I suppose he thought it was enough to bestow his charm on them.

George frowned as he stirred another lump of sugar into his coffee. "It won't come to a court case. Even he wouldn't have the effrontery. No lawyer would advise it, I'm sure. It will be no more than a toe in the water, meant to cause Sandra to worry. A letter from Sandra's solicitor should put a stop to it. But of course she'll be worried."

I assured him Berry would look after her interests. He is a businessman and must know a competent lawyer. It was unthinkable that Tony, the philanderer who had no idea of what it meant to be a husband and father, should now profess an interest. He was just causing a nuisance. And I didn't want to hear about it. "I've had enough of my family," I burst out, causing George to splutter over his coffee. "I really can't worry about them any more. I'm fed up. Worrying doesn't help them, anyway. They're both adults. Why don't they run their own lives? Why make us miserable with their troubles? I've other things to think about. I want to live my own life. It's time they lived theirs."

George looked at me over his glasses, opened his mouth to speak and closed it again. We sat in silence, uncomfortably. Something had gone from our lunch date. The atmosphere was different. I looked at the nearest table of coffee drinkers. They had finished drinking and were now smoking – two young couples, English tourists by their accents and their clothes; one of the men – the taller fair one with a tiger on the front of his tee-shirt – rose and passed us on his way to the toilet. I wafted away his cigarette smoke and tried to simmer down. It was difficult. I'd got really wound up. The worries had gone on so many months, all the time we were on Arran in fact. I'd come here with such high hopes of a new life free of problems and worries, and it seemed I'd done nothing but worry ever since. Arran was supposed to be relaxing and therapeutic, wasn't it? They said so. But then, why do we always find something to worry about? Anybody would think we couldn't live without pain. If it isn't imposed from outside circumstances we have to create it for ourselves. Or, to put it another way, it's the pain that assures us that we are part of the human race. And that's all right as long as we realise it. It's no good suffering dumbly like an animal. To be truly human one has to see some purpose in it. I sighed and looked away from George again. The four at the next table were gathering their things together. It looked as though they were going for an afternoon swim in the pool. George was still silent, brooding. I think he was afraid to say anything in case he aroused a further outburst. I was acting out of character. Or was I? Do I really know myself? I'm so mixed up. I want to be free, and yet I love my children and want their happiness. I can't walk away from them. Nor can George. I looked at him again. He was too quick to judge and apportion blame, but I knew he cared about the children. We both cared. There was that bond between us. Now that we were no longer living together the bond was no longer stifling and, to my surprise, I found I was beginning to enjoy George's company. We could say whatever we wanted to each other, or be silent together. It was refreshing. At this thought I shook myself and perked up. "The baby's due at Christmas. Of course Sandra wants us there. All of us, as last Christmas. And I'll try and stay on for a while after it's born, as long as she needs me. Another grandchild, George! Perhaps it will be a girl, a sister for Berry's Jonathan."

George blinked and smiled. "It's something to look forward to. Does John know he's going to be an uncle again?" I shook my head. I didn't think so, but I would go and tell him and hope that he and Iolanthe would repair their differences in time for Christmas.

22

Fruit! That's the thing to start with, like that student painting by Peggy Paine. I got a fresh supply yesterday, of oranges, apples, bananas, green grapes and a big pineapple. Problem – should I put them in a bowl or just have the odd one or two scattered over a tablecloth? And what about the background? It all needed very careful thought. With a landscape it's all there and the problem is knowing what to leave out. With a still life everything is under my control, what to put in, where to place it. A totally different ball game, as they say. I was embarking on my first attempt at oil painting and was all of a jitter – couldn't be still, flitted from place to place, picking things up, putting them down. I put an apple and a banana on my blue gentian plate. It looked ridiculous. Start again. The white cloth was too insipid; I wanted something neutral but with a bit of colour. Perhaps that cream and brown shawl Veronica sent me for last Christmas would be a better foil? Yes, it looked better, it showed up the warmth of the fruit – I had now added two oranges and taken away the plate. And now, I decided, it needed a touch of blue, just a touch, and a bit of vertical accent. What about that blue candlestick that I never use? I had almost forgotten it and intended to throw it away when it turned up in packing to remove house. Where on earth did I put it?

If I'm going to do more still lifes I shall have to collect a few suitable objects, I realised. I scrabbled around in all the kitchen cupboards, finding other things I'd forgotten, but finally I found the blue candlestick under the sink. And I can't even remember where it came from or who might have given it to me, but it looked right with the fruit. The composition needed that vertical touch and the pale apricot of the wall behind made a good background. I fussed around for ages before I was satisfied with the way it looked. Perhaps by this excessive fussing I was putting off the moment when I had to start the painting? But now I had to find the courage to begin. In watercolours I always paint from light to dark, but Sarah told me it's the other way round with oils. Rule or no rule, I had to start with the fruit or it would have gone off and changed colour. The banana would go brown very quickly, so I started on that.

My thoughts were in turmoil and my hands were shaking as I squeezed out some yellow paint on to my shiny new palette of beech wood. It wasn't the right yellow; it needed something else, perhaps white or ochre. I dabbed colour on the canvas-textured board, drawing the shape with my brush. It was difficult. I kept thinking in terms of watercolour, using too much oil to make the colour runny. So runny in fact that I suddenly noticed it had run on to the carpet. Horrors! My beautiful grey carpet! I hadn't thought of protecting it and I hadn't even provided myself with a rag. Stupid me! I ought to have realised all artists use a rag. But I'd cleared out all old bits of worn sheets and anything else that could be called a rag when I moved house. I dropped my palette and yellowy brush – I had at least had the forethought to cover my table with old newspaper – and dashed into the kitchen, grabbed a new dry dishcloth, sank to my knees and scrubbed hard at the spots with white spirit. The room stank now of white spirit as well as linseed oil, a not unpleasant smell, I decided, though I hoped it didn't penetrate upwards into George's flat.

Once the oily yellow spots were cleaned away to my satisfaction I stood back and surveyed my work again. It wouldn't do. I needed a different technique. I picked up my brush again, took a deep breath and obeyed my instinct. There! That felt better! Thick blobs and dashes of colour, mixed or not mixed on the board instead of on the palette. And with bigger brushes! I didn't know whether I was doing it right or not, but it felt right for me. I was comfortable with the thick lumps of colour and positively wallowed in squeezing out fat globules of brilliant colours, letting them sing together. It felt wonderful. I abandoned myself to the sheer sensuous joy of it, dashing the paint on at great speed. The result was crude, of course. It was my first attempt and I made excuses for myself but I knew then that that was the way I wanted to work with thick impasto and simple shapes. When this painting was dry I would scrape it off and use the canvas board again. That would be the way to learn without wasting too much. Oils had this advantage over watercolour, but I would continue to use both. I enjoyed both techniques and Sarah and I would continue to go out painting together, I hoped. I valued her friendship and the outdoor painting too much to think of abandoning them.

* * *

"Hello, Susie. Here again!" I removed my raincoat as I spoke. It had been a fine bight morning, too bright to last as the old wives say, and now what started as a drizzle had become sudden and heavy showers. The weather is always changing here and if it is raining on one side of the island it may be fine on the other. But this afternoon it was wet all over.

Susie smiled warmth into the day as I assured her, "These weekly visits are doing me good, you know. I really do feel better – more confident, not so scared of my shadow like I used to be, and more aware of myself and my potential."

"I'm not surprised, and I'm glad," she said simply. Susie never wasted words and always preferred to work in silence. I thought again of that first session of spiritual healing when, although she didn't touch me and nothing seemed to be happening at the time, yet something did happen and the results are still continuing. Susie had once told me that she had helped one or two people to die, not actively of course, but her healing ministration had given the dying patient an inward peace and acceptance of death. I thought that was wonderful. It must be a great service to cancer patients and others with terminal illness in the hospice wing. The benefit I received though was an enhancement of life and I was very grateful.

I sank down on her chair and prepared my mind to be receptive of positive life-giving energy. The usual tingling along my spine confirmed that the energy was flowing, as Susie would express it, and I basked in happy thoughts of the paintings I was planning to do. My next attempt in oils would be an interpretation of that watercolour I did of Brodick, the one that the professor bought. I would have to do another sketch; perhaps a pencil sketch would be enough just to give me the composition. The subject lent itself to a technique of thick impasto in patches of colour, I thought.

In no time at all, or so it seemed, Susie had finished

and turned to switch on the kettle for our customary cup of tea. This was the only time we had to talk, though even then she was not very vocal.

"Do you do a lot of work in the hospice?" I asked her.

"Oh, yes. I'm there every morning. Just available for anybody who wants me. It's all optional, but several of the people are regulars. Like you." She smiled. And like John, I wondered? But I knew better than to ask and receive a rebuff. Confidentiality was sacred in this place.

"I've invited Sarah and Melanie to lunch next week," I said brightly. "I went to that concert at the Castle when Melanie was playing her flute with the orchestra. I was amazed at their skill – so professional. Melanie is very clever, isn't she – a GP, an administrator and pioneer at the Hydro, and finding time to learn to play the flute to such a standard!"

"Yes, she is good. She's been playing for a long time, of course. She started while she was still at school and, even more important, she's kept it up. I'm afraid I haven't kept up the piano playing I did as a schoolgirl and so I admire Melanie all the more."

"So you once played the piano! And what do you do now, as a hobby, I mean, or something apart from your therapy work?"

She laughed. "Something quite different. I belong to a ramblers' group. It's not a large group and we're very mixed. That's what makes it interesting. We plan walks of different lengths and different difficulties, so there is always a choice. Sometimes I feel like a stroll along the shore, sometimes I go climbing, but always with one or two others, whenever I can spare the time off. The group is flexible and fluctuating, and all are interesting people. Perhaps you'd like to join us? You're not forced to go every week of course, only when you feel like it."

"No, I don't think it appeals to me, but thanks all the same. It must be the same group that Graham belongs to – the Lochranza post office husband, you know. I wonder if George would like to join. He is more keen than I am on physical activity and he's determined to keep fit – looks after his diet and all that."

* * *

Melanie and Sarah arrived together, which was sensible, in Melanie's silver BMW. No doubt it was very comfortable. She could afford it. She was reputed to be a millionaire by inheritance but she didn't flaunt it and had no reason to invest in a Range Rover, as she didn't need to drive up the notorious cart tracks to remote houses. Sarah was her usual self, cheerful and plump and limping a little on her arthritic hip. Melanie was elegant in a tailored suit of some lightweight material that was crease-free and of a pale spring green. It looked well with her faded red hair and green eyes. I had never seen her looking less than elegant and she had the height to carry off the exquisite and expensive clothes she wore. I knew Sarah could also afford designer clothes, or so I'd heard, but she had more modest tastes and invariably dressed like any other elderly matron of the middle classes.

I welcomed them with chaste pecks and bade them be seated on my comfortable sofa, and offered them a glass of the Chardonnay I knew they both preferred. "I don't have a dining room any more as I've turned it into my studio and it's full of smelly paints, so I hope you don't mind eating in here. It's only a low coffee table but I've made a simple dish that's easy to manage, I hope."

"That's all right, Muriel. Don't apologise. I'm sure it'll be all right." Sarah turned to Melanie. "Muriel's a good cook. You'll see."

"It's only a baked dish of chicken and broccoli in pasta – something we can eat with a fork," I explained and went on to ask them what they had been doing recently. Had they been to the mobile cinema that came over at the weekend? I forgot what film they were showing but no doubt the cinema's visit was as popular as usual. "I didn't go, I'm afraid. I wanted to but nobody I knew was going and I chickened out of going by myself."

"No," Melanie said. "There was a concert by the Rowan Singers at Brodick Hall so Sarah and I went to that instead. Things always clash, don't they, but the singers are always good and they were giving the programme that they're going to perform on their tour of Italy in the autumn."

Melanie, being so musical, could appreciate the finer points of their performance, I was sure.

"I'm thinking of going with them," Sarah said. "Not to sing," she added hastily. "No, but they usually have a few spare seats in the coach and it would be an opportunity to see some Italian cities and some works of art, even if there's only enough time to look at the architecture in passing through. Would you be interested, Muriel?"

I marvelled at the activities I was invited to join. The weeks were surely not long enough. One could be out at some function every day, but I decided I must limit myself to the WI and individual friends, in order to allow plenty of time for my major interest, which is now painting. I explained all this to them and they understood. Sarah in particular understood my desire to work hard at my painting techniques. She had seen my first attempts in oils and encouraged me to persevere. She actually liked my thick impasto technique and said it was distinguished. Perhaps it's as well that no other artist paints like I do!

As we picked at the simple bake with salad I led the talk to Susie and the Hydro. I still did not know all the details of how the Hydro started its life, I told them. It was a fascinating subject and I was keen to hear about it.

"Melanie's the one to tell you all about it," Sarah said. "It's all due to her."

Melanie shrugged her modesty but complied with my request. "It had always been my dream," she said. "As a GP I realised the allopathic medication I was administering was not always suitable or effective, particularly in the very many cases of psychosomatic diseases, stress and emotional problems. In other words I wanted to treat the whole human being, not just the physical body. And . . ." turning to Sarah with a warm smile . . ."Ian's reports of his discoveries and experiments encouraged me to think those esoteric practices could have a part to play in more holistic healing. But of course there would never have been the money to set up such an ambitious enterprise. Or so I thought, until my parents died and their legacy made me begin to hope. It was then that I took the plunge and gambled all I had on a huge mortgage to buy the hotel. It happened to be for sale at the time, so it was a case of now or never."

Sarah chipped in her pennyworth. "I'll never forget the shock we had that day when you invited us to lunch there at the hotel; Peggy and I sat there like country bumpkins in that luxurious setting and you announced that you'd just bought the place. Just like that! We were gobsmacked."

"Yes. I can remember your faces – mouths open,

eyes popping out – but seriously, it was Peggy's generosity that made the project realistic, after she died so soon afterwards."

Sarah patted Melanie's knee. "And Andrew of course. Tell Muriel about Andrew."

A dreamy look came over Melanie's face. "Andrew, yes, dear Andrew. Yes, well, I'd never married, I'd never met anybody to attract me enough, but I met Andrew at various medical conferences when I was in my sixties and I suppose we fell in love."

"Of course you did. Both of you. Starry-eyed too!" Sarah chivvied.

"Yes, all right. We were in love, but we couldn't marry and couldn't even be seen together because he had a wife and, as we were both doctors we had to be careful to avoid scandal. Andrew's wife had a terminal illness and that was all the more reason why we couldn't hurt her. But when she eventually died Andrew and I fixed a date for our wedding soon afterwards, and it was then that he confessed he was a millionaire. The future then looked wonderful. Everything was going to be marvellous. And then, just before the wedding he was killed in a car crash."

"Oh, how terrible! I didn't know. What a blow. And just when everything was going so well and you were going to be so happy!" I was shocked. Poor Melanie!

"But the Hydro is his memorial and Peggy's," Melanie finished her story.

"A very fitting memorial to two very exceptional people," I echoed.

* * *

It was only midweek but the ferry was crowded with tourists. The peak of the season brought families with children, who chased one another all round the decks with shouts of joy and excitement. To be on a big ferry boat was a special event in a young life, and even to their elders, being ferried to and from an island is a thrilling part of the holiday. Today gave them all an extra thrill because there was a slight swell on the sea (the wind was from the south west, force four) and the children screamed with happiness as they lurched around. I sought the calmer atmosphere of the cafeteria and seated myself by the window to await an opportunity to collect a cup of coffee. The queue was always too long at the beginning of the voyage, but I suddenly noticed a familiar figure between two hulking youths in the queue. It was Iolanthe. It was strange how my infrequent trips to Glasgow coincided with Iolanthe's crossing. I waved and willed her to look at me. At last her eyes drifted away from the back of the youth in front of her, she looked around and spotted me. She pantomimed should she get a coffee for me, so I nodded and made way for her on the plastic seats around the circular table and we enjoyed one another's company once more. I really did feel that the enjoyment was mutual. If not, she was a first-rate actress. We sipped our scalding coffee, watched the clouds scudding past the window and talked of John.

Iolanthe was troubled, she said, because he was restless and wondered whether to apply for a different teaching job, perhaps in a Glasgow college teaching adults. "I don't mind where he chooses to go. I can fit in my own plans around his. It's something we have to discuss, though I think it's a pity to think of leaving Arran when we've hardly been there long enough to feel settled."

I asked about her degree course.

"I should finish it this year and of course, once I've

got my degree I shall be at home more, writing, and perhaps John will feel more settled then. I just wish he would adapt to my having a career." She sighed wistfully.

"Would it be easier if you were married?" I enquired. I had often wondered why she refused to marry him yet was apparently content to live with him permanently.

"Perhaps I'm being silly and stubborn," she said. "But I want a really adult relationship. When we first fell in love he looked on me as a prize that he'd won – I was his prized possession in fact. It was all very flattering but it's not a good basis for a lasting marriage. I want something more mature, more of an equal partnership, you know, trusting one another, with mutual respect. I suppose I'm waiting for him to grow up. Am I crying for the moon?" She laughed ruefully and added, "That's terribly patronising, isn't it. I don't mean to be, but I couldn't bear to be a pampered poppet of a wife. You do understand?"

Oh yes, I understood all right. I knew only too well about John's immaturity. He shared his father's attitude to marriage and I had suffered what Iolanthe was determined to avoid. I explained this to her so that she could understand John's background; we talked and finally agreed that he was lately rather less boyish and was working his way through to a more mature outlook. I wished Iolanthe well and said I hoped to see them married before long. I told her of Sandra's pregnancy and slyly insinuated that there might be a pregnancy in the Lamlash family before or after marriage. But she only smiled enigmatically and said nothing.

23

August 15
I was surprised how enjoyable the walk up North Glen Sannox turned out to be. In the event I had no reason to regret Graham's invitation. He is a mine of information about Arran families. In addition to the knowledge imbibed with his mother's milk he has studied old family records in the museum archives. It still amazes me that so many accepted the offer of a hundred acres in Canada and half the cost of the voyage, when there was a risk of dying during the two months of the Atlantic crossing and the land they were given was not farmland but scrub and forest. There are letters from those first pioneers – the McKelvies, the Curries, the McKenzies and others – describing the diseases, the deaths and the backbreaking work of establishing a home in an alien hostile land. It is difficult to imagine the hardship of having to clear part of a virgin forest, to build your home from the timber and plant your carefully transported seeds in the first ploughed field. And all had to be done as speedily as possible before the Canadian winter made life impossible without home or food. Seeing the pathetic remains of their former homes made me think of my own ancestors. Considering it now, against this background, I realise they chose the easier option by removing to Glasgow although their life must also

have been grim and hard. The influx of a peasant population into the city early in the nineteenth century was bound to cause bad overcrowding, insanitary conditions and stinking slums. It was no wonder that the first generation of my city ancestors turned to drink in those conditions, but credit is due to his son who, although he embezzled money to do so, had the courage and initiative to learn a trade and set up in business in a smaller town where he could make a fresh start and found a dynasty of accountants. I see now that my father was wrong to keep all this family history a secret from me. He and I owe our successful careers to that young man who was bold enough to force himself out of a miserable existence into a respectable career. Father should have been proud of him. Now that I understand the background of his life I can feel grateful for that young man's perseverance, and I can appreciate the shock of that family moving from this peaceful glen to the teeming slums of Glasgow.

The remaining fragments of foundations were sufficient in some cases for me to be able to draw a plan of the individual buildings – farmhouse, barns, stables and byres, though it was difficult to decide exactly what purpose each building served. What I did realise was that it was a very close-knit small community. There must have been considerable dependence on neighbours, working together like an extended family – a quality they would need even more so in Canada. I remarked about this to Graham and told him of my ancestors moving to Glasgow and then to Lancaster, without saying anything about the drunkenness and embezzlement of course.

"My people were lucky," he said. "We had such a remote and small place. Probably it wasn't worth much to the landlord and it was too small to support

many sheep. It was bare subsistence, really, and we were isolated, not in a clachan like this." And he waved his arm at the glen, which once must have been fertile but was now covered with whins and bracken, which we had had to beat down to reveal the stone foundations.

This pleasant excursion with Graham made me more inclined to accept when he again mentioned the ramblers' group. *"It's mixed,"* he said. *"Men and women, all ages, but not everybody comes every time. Those who feel like it meet at the big car park in Brodick every Thursday and share cars to wherever the starting point of the walk may be. We have a printed programme so we can choose which walks we want to do. I'll show you when we get back to the shop. There's no compulsion,"* he stressed again. *"If you don't fancy a particular walk you can give it a miss."*

I enquired about who else was a member of the group. I didn't say so but I was wondering if the others would be congenial companions.

"Well, I don't know how many people you've got to know while you've been here. There's Tommy the electrician from Shiskine, Harry the barber – you know, at Lamlash. Of course, they're not always free; it depends on their work. But there's Sandy and his wife; they're retired and sometimes they bring their grandson with them, a wee lad, but that's only on the shorter walks." He looked sideways at me with what I imagined was a leer. *"As for the other women, the youngest is Susie. She's something special, a great looker but doesn't talk much. She's from the Hydro. I know her because I've been going for therapy for my back."*

"Oh, yes? Does she massage your back?"

"No, not her," he said ungrammatically, *"It's*

Rowena I go to, but I see Susie in passing sometimes. She's often too busy to come on a Thursday, but there's Jean and Helen. They're our age. Sometimes one or two get together on other days besides Thursdays, when they're free, and do their own walk. It's all free and easy."

We were scraping the mud off our boots at the time, using a sharp-edged rock as a scraper. It occurred to me that same rock must have been used as a scratching post for sheep in the past, though no sheep were visible today; and the deer were out of sight over the crest of the hill. We had come in Graham's old Landrover, as it was a more suitable vehicle for the terrain than my Volvo.

"Don't worry about a bit of mud," he said as he saw me trying to wipe the uppers of my boots with bracken fronds. "The old tub's used to muck. So long as it's not smelly," he added with a grin.

The ramblers' programme did look interesting, I had to admit, when he showed it to me in the shop. I still had reservations, however, as I was not sure I had anything in common with tradesmen. I had got used to Graham but doubted whether an electrician and a barber could be congenial company. I did not express my doubts to Graham at the time; he would not have understood. Gladys was busy at the post office counter, attending to the social security payments to that ne'er-do-well of the village who calls herself Jackie. Her children, all of whom have different fathers, she had left outside. Thankfully. They are often a nuisance, running about under one's feet when one wants to make serious purchases in a hurry. So Graham and I stood in the corner by the packets of cereals while he let me look at his programme of walks. It was dog-eared and scribbled over, with some items crossed out and notes added in the margins, but it was sufficiently legible to give me an idea of where they planned to go.

"We take our lunch with us on the longer walks," he said. "And sometimes we finish the shorter walks in a pub or tearoom somewhere." He leaned back, dislodging a packet of Weetabix, and cocked his eyebrows to invite my response.

I did not want to commit myself. I was cautious. I would ask around, discreetly, about some of these other people. The thought of meeting Susie was attractive, however, not because of her intriguing appearance or youth but because, by getting to know her socially, I may learn something about her relationship, if any, with John. "Yes, thanks," I said, picking up the Weetabix and handing the programme back. "It does look interesting. I'll think about it and let you know quite soon. I have to see how it fits in with my studies. I am not sure that I can afford a Thursday off as well as Wednesday. It may mean a major reshuffle of my own programme, but I'll see." And we left it at that.

I nodded to Gladys and turned to leave the shop and return home; my car was parked in front, ready to take me around the loch. To my surprise and embarrassment – I had never spoken to the woman before – Jackie turned at the same time and accosted me. "The government looks after us both, doesn't it, love? The old'uns and the young'uns. We couldn't do without them, could we, George?" And she actually laughed in my face and patted my arm. Such familiarity, and from such a person! I didn't deign to reply but stalked out to my car and returned home to a hot bath and a change of clothes. I chose lighter trousers and slippers, as I didn't intend going out again in spite of the evening promising to be fine and balmy. There was work to be done. I did not want to get behind with my assignments. If that happened it would grow progressively more difficult and there was a danger that I would become discouraged. So far my work had received favourable comments from the tutors and I was keen to keep up the standard and earn the necessary points towards my degree. At the moment I am enjoying the period of Henry VIII in England. It must have been a very stimulating time, with traditional standards being undermined on all sides. People were forced to think of the meaning of marriage and the importance of the family; the great Tudor houses vied with one another in the magnificence of their architecture; the king wrote madrigals, and philosophers and clerics questioned the political and religious systems of the day. No doubt it was a very exciting time for the educated classes, though the lower orders would scarcely be aware of anything that did not impinge on their miserable existence. After all, even today, how much does a simple labourer know or care about the avant-garde movements in London or other capitals of the civilised world? The television pictures of society life do not seem real and are hardly believable to someone living by the sweat of his brow and still less to those who are out of work and struggling to survive. I ended that day listening to a record of madrigals, which I had managed to acquire through the Internet. It is a strange form of music, deceptive in its apparent simplicity. The first hearing jarred on me, but by repeating it several times I began to hear the mathematical perfection of its cadences.

I talked about this to Rosemary when she came to lunch; a light lunch as I promised, because she had to attend a formal dinner of Rotarians in the evening. So we lingered over the grilled goat's cheese and salad with Arran oatcakes, talking about sixteenth century culture and how, through looking at architecture one could trace the great differences between the north and the south, and understand the reason for the slow spread of ideas. Rosemary is remarkably erudite and of course she has access to all the relevant books and knows which titles are most useful. She brings a lifetime's interest to our conversations whereas I can only contribute remarks from my newly acquired and limited knowledge. I was particularly grateful when she promised to find a video of the film of Henry Vlll. As she said, the dancing and the costumes are also part of the cultural scene. It made me think of modern culture – the cacophony of the music, the casual dress, no definitive style of painting or architecture, and a period of behaviour when anything is permitted. Or so it seems to me. A graceless period which has only technological advance to commend it. Rosemary disagreed. She sees the present century as a watershed, a transition and she thinks it is exciting. There is certainly a great choice of lifestyles. Convention is thrown to the winds. The corollary, as I pointed out, is anarchy and amorality.

It was a most interesting discussion, which I shall incorporate in my written work for the OU. Rosemary became quite animated; her eyes lit up and her cheeks took on a deeper flush as she talked. She is a handsome woman whom any man would be proud to escort in public. We had met a few times in restaurants but this was the first time she had come to my home for a meal.

It had been in my mind for some time that I would like her to accompany me to London for a weekend, to visit galleries, a concert, perhaps a theatre. She would know what to choose and I would be led by her. Today I found the courage to ask her. It needed to be done with finesse, as I didn't wish to alarm her or give her the wrong impression. I led into it quite gradually, mentioning that I had never been to the National Gallery or the Tate and how I would so much like to go. And how much more enjoyable it would be with an agreeable companion. Her first response was to wonder why I didn't ask my wife, as Muriel was such a keen artist.

"Oh, no, I think not." I said. "We do meet, but we have not got over our differences. We are such different people, you know. Perhaps we shall never come together again; I don't want to stir up any of the past; we have to accept that our personalities are incompatible and it's best that we stay apart as much as possible. But I was wondering . . . Would you be free? Would you be interested?"

Her eyes gave a start of alarm and I added hastily, "Strictly as friends of course. Single rooms. That is, if you agree. I would leave the hotel booking to you, though you'd book it in my name of course."

She smiled, obviously relieved. "I think that's a good idea I'll check on my computer what's on during my next free weekend, shall I?"

So that was arranged. I allowed her to aspire to a three-star central hotel and I booked two good seats at a symphony concert and a theatre for the two evenings, after days in the galleries. I am sure the visit will be a success. Rosemary will be a very suitable and elegant escort, able to sustain intelligent conversation. She reminded me, however, that London would be very busy with tourists at this time of year, especially foreigners. And although the Scottish schools have just gone back, there would still be plenty of English families on holiday there too. No doubt we would find it tiring after our quiet life here but the change would at the same time be a tonic, we hoped.

Her mention of school holidays made me think of visiting John again. I couldn't allow our last encounter to rankle. He is my only son and I want him to be happy. If that involves me turning a blind eye to his problems and standing aside to let him make a mess of his life I shall just have to grit my teeth and keep silent.

On the day I went, however, he seemed brighter. He greeted me cheerfully as though he had forgotten our former confrontation. Perhaps he was physically less tired now, after the summer break, even though he had not been away.

"Yes, Dad," *he agreed.* "I didn't particularly want to go away anywhere. After all, we've only been here a year and I haven't yet explored the island properly. So I did some walking and climbing. The geography bloke is a keen fell-walker." *He laughed ruefully.* "I had to slow him down. He's used to running races over these mountains and just galloped up Goat Fell, and there was I puffing like an old man. It made me decide to do something to get fit. I've got too used to sitting around with my work and my books. How about you, Dad? How do you keep fit?"

I explained about my winter work at the museum, that it was mostly physical and not sedentary. And now, in the summer, I sometimes walked to the village shop around the loch and I was wondering about joining a ramblers' group. Had he heard of them?

"Oh yes. I know one or two of them. They seem to have a good time together, though I suspect a few of the old stagers meet mainly to drink coffee together in bad weather. And why shouldn't the old dears enjoy themselves in their own way? They say it's the sort of group where you can be as active or inactive as you want. So if you join, Dad, perhaps I'll join too. It will get me out of the house at least at half term and at *holiday times. I'm not free on a Thursday otherwise. What about it?"*

I wondered if he knew that the Susie woman was a member. If I encouraged him to join the ramblers would I be encouraging an illicit liaison? "You go swimming at the Hydro, I believe?" I ventured, hoping he would elaborate about his visits there and create an opportunity to mention Susie. But he merely nodded and fetched two more cans of beer from the fridge.

"It's a pity you never learnt to swim, Dad. It's a super pool and they have lessons for older people if you're interested. There's an extra-keen group who do exercises, dancing and what not – you know, acrobatics as a group performance in the water. But I just paddle up and down. If you don't want to swim, though, there are plenty of other things to do at the Hydro. Mum goes, you know. She says it's helping her a lot. Why not ask her about it? You do meet her, don't you? To talk to, I mean, not just in passing?"

I told him of our recent luncheon together and the news about Sandra's pregnancy. "So you'll probably have another niece or nephew as a Christmas present," I joked. "Another one to buy a present for when we go up to Pitlochry." More seriously I added, "This year it will be a happier Christmas, I think. I feel sure."

"Mum and you are more comfortable with each other now, aren't you? There were some sticky moments last year at Pitlochry. I felt sorry for poor Berry, trying to be host to prospective parents-in-law whom he hadn't met before and who were scarcely on speaking terms. I was really sorry for him, trying to make everybody happy. At least the kids were happy. His Jonathan could hardly believe his luck when he was presented with an instant brother and sister. They

all get on so well and I'm not surprised that Sandra's so happy. She's fallen on her feet, to be chatelaine of that huge hotel. Good for her! She deserves a break!"

This time, we parted in complete agreement, both of us to return to our books.

24

I was too ashamed to admit to George that I had never visited the museum, so I went an hour earlier than our agreed meeting in order to have a good look round. It was a beautiful morning, the sun high and brilliant but with a mountain crispness in the air. I think we have the advantage here on Arran of gaining benefit from both sea and mountain air. Today, with clear views and a high tide the drive over from Lochranza to Brodick was sheer joy, and as the local schools had gone back there was less traffic on the road. Not that there is ever enough to be a nuisance. If I were to meet three vehicles going over the Boguille pass I would think it was busy! Today I met only one car, going slowly so that the four passengers could keep a lookout for eagles and deer, and a McKinnon butcher's van on his weekly round. It reminded me I needed to buy one of his free-range chickens for the weekend. I like a fresh roast for Sunday, then freeze the rest in small portions and make soup from the carcase. Cooking for one is a totally different skill from family catering, I had discovered, though I am enjoying the challenge. George, I think, will be better equipped, as he attended those cookery classes in Morecambe for single men. But today we were both eating out at the museum at George's suggestion.

I was amazed at the museum itself. I think I expected something like the old-style museums with dusty exhibits in rows of glass cases, with stuffed birds and butterflies on pins. I should have known better. It is a heritage museum and hadn't I been one of the helpers at the Heritage Centre in Heysham only last year? The reception and shop area here set the tone of the place with its low beams, thick stone walls, little iron fire grate and tiny window. The elderly lady behind the desk – her name was Molly according to the label pinned on her fairisle jumper – said part of the group of buildings was once a school and schoolmaster's house, and on the wall was an old photograph of local children, cheeky faces, caps, bare feet and scruffy clothes. I could just imagine them splashing about and muddying themselves with joyful abandon in the burn behind the school. Now the area is tamed and offers a lawn, flowerbeds and picnic tables for outside dining. Children and adults now come to watch horses being shod by the local blacksmith, or perhaps to see how sheep are sheared.

I didn't stay very long in the geology room. The rocks were so old they were bewildering. I couldn't grasp so many zeros in the dates, though the skull that was exhibited in the archaeology room was fascinating – fancy a sculptor being able to build a face on to an ancient skull! According to the sculptor, he was a handsome man, this prehistoric fellow, dug up somewhere on the moors here. I wondered if he had chicken for his dinner? If he did, it would certainly be free-range! Did he have children? What did he teach them? Today's children here learn about their forebears and the history of their own villages, apparently, and they record old folks' stories on tape. I was very impressed. I did nothing like that when I was at school and I don't think Heysham children are taught that way, but I suppose in England the population would be less stable. An island has neat edges to its population, which gives them an advantage.

The old cottage promised to be even more interesting, but the old pendulum clock on the mantelpiece told me I had only twenty minutes to absorb the details of the huge fireplace with its great stone lintel, blackened iron grate and ovens, the salt cupboard and old cooking things that I remember my mother and grandmother using. It was always a hard life for women in the home – no indoor sanitation, no water on tap, and no central heating. Now, in spite of modern technology, it is still a hard life for a woman who has to cope with a home, husband, children and a full-time job outside. I was thankful to be able to enjoy the modern gadgets without the other responsibilities. Life is easier at least for older people nowadays, I thought.

George was waiting for me at one of the outdoor tables. "A good idea," I said. "It would be a pity to sit inside on a day like this." He adjusted the striped umbrella so that the sun was not directly in my eyes as I seated myself opposite him. It was a pleasant spot, very peaceful with only the sound of the babbling brook at the foot of the lawn and a gentle movement of leaves among the beech trees flanking it. "I hope those ducks aren't on the menu!" I said.

George frowned. "They know where they get spoilt, but we ought to shoo them back to the burn. They shouldn't become accustomed to being fed or what will they do in the winter when nobody is here?"

The mallards and golden-eyes would not be shooed, however, and quacked around our feet clearing up the crumbs from our baked potatoes and later, our cheesecakes. They then waddled on to the next table of chattering tee-shirt clad tourists, as if they had been officially appointed to be the museum's efficient scavengers.

George was looking very fit. His face had lost the pallor that had been normal last year and he looked less careworn, though his brow retained its permanent furrows.

"How are your studies going, George? Are you still enjoying it all, delving into bits of the humanities? It sounds a fascinating way to start studying history. When does this course finish? To what extent is it part of your degree?"

George perked up. He loves talking about history and I think he appreciated that I was taking an interest. He told me, emphasising points by stabbing the air with his fork, that he was aiming to complete this particular course in the nine months the OU recommend, which will give him sixty points towards his degree. "I'll have a break over Christmas," he said, "I want to be free to enjoy our trip to Pitlochry and then start a course in the New Year called Princes and Peoples in France and the British Isles from 1620 to 1714. It's a mouthful of a title but I shall look forward to it and meantime I want to see that fine hotel that Berry is running and how Sandra and the children are adapting to living in such a big place – such a public place too! I hope there won't be any problems in her new marriage. Berry is a very different man from that other fellow Tony. She's grown up a lot since the divorce and I think she's made the right choice this time. Financially she's done very well, I think; she got nothing out of the divorce and now she's got everything she could wish for!"

I agreed but pointed out that it was a true love match, a really romantic boy-meets-girl affair, when Berry and his motherless little boy were stranded in a storm and begged bed and breakfast at Sandra's little establishment. What could be more romantic? Sandra's present happiness was something George and I could agree about. If only we could agree about John and Iolanthe! It was too pleasant a day and too peaceful a setting to bring up any contentious issue so I brought the talk back to the museum and congratulated him on its immaculate displays.

"I don't do quite so much of the maintenance work since taking on the financial responsibilities," he said. "That has meant spending a lot of time sorting out the muddle but it's all straightforward now and I shall be able to present a normal report to the auditors at the end of the year." He positively oozed with satisfaction. I was pleased to see this, as he had hated his accountancy job all through his working life, though I knew that that had more to do with his father breathing down his neck than with the job itself.

Our lunch had fed the ducks as well as ourselves very satisfactorily, and Donna had cleared the plates away. We sat back enjoying the sunshine and watched the ducks waddle over to a third table, where a young couple were locked into one another's eyes with a neglected teapot between them. The ducks quacked contempt and waddled over to a newly arrived party of Japanese, who were festooned with cameras and in a happy mood. They would willingly allow the ducks to exploit their generosity, I felt sure.

"Are you still painting?" George enquired. "Have you sold any more?"

I laughed at the idea. I'd made no attempt to sell my work and had no intention of doing so. "No," I said. "And I've started painting in oils. It's very different, but I shall do both. I sometimes use my watercolours as sketches for an oil painting. I enjoy using two such different techniques. I don't know whether I'm doing it right but it's interesting."

"Hmph. Yes, well, I'm sure it must be an absorbing hobby. I can't understand it myself. I've looked at quite a few paintings now, mostly in reproduction, but of all periods, and the styles are all so different. How can anybody say what is good or bad? It seems to me there is no standard to measure a painting by. I mean, there's Giotto, then Titian – how do you compare them? I can understand the Flemish painters – all that fruit and dead birds. I can at least see what the paintings represent. But when it comes to more modern painters like Braque or Klee – well! And the latest Turner prize-winners disgust me. I don't understand and I think I don't want to understand this modern stuff."

I didn't understand how these things – one couldn't call them paintings – got prizes, but it didn't stop me experimenting and enjoying my excursions into different styles. George could think of it as dabbling, but so what! He dabbles in history, I dabble in paint. So there!

To get on to safer ground I told him of the Women's Institute (that is, the Scottish Women's Institute I must remember) proposed trip to the Falkirk Wheel next spring. If he would be interested I'd let him know the date as soon as it was known, as there was sure to be spare seats in the coach. He looked doubtful. He is still very shy with women and has to pretend to be superior in order to cover it up. He can even be rude at times, in his avoidance of social contact. I still cringe at the memory of the way he treated Elsie, my Heysham friend, last year. The two of us were peacefully enjoying a cup of tea together when George came in unexpectedly and refused to speak to her because she was working class; that was George's judgment on her because her husband ran a shop. I was so ashamed, and daren't invite any of my friends after that. But now, things are changing. I know that George is friendly with Graham, who is very definitely working class, and perhaps in time he will feel easier with women.

"Maggie and I had another trip over to Skipness the other day. You know Maggie, don't you? She lives a few doors away from the shop in Lochranza and is fond of gardening. We went for some more plants. It's a pleasant trip out anyway. I enjoy going over on that ferry. I don't have to set out so early and it's only half an hour across from Lochranza. Some day soon, before this summer's over, I'm going to go over that way and up the west coast to Oban to visit Veronica. You remember Veronica in that hotel in Glasgow last year?"

He nodded. He didn't have much of an opinion of Veronica at the time, thought she was 'worming her way' into my affections. That was how he put it. In fact she opened my eyes to the possibility of a new life for myself, and I shall be eternally grateful.

"I invited Sarah and Melanie one day. You haven't met them but they're quite famous here, natives in fact, and well known because of their contacts with the Hydro. You know I go regularly for healing from Susie, don't you? I find it so helpful. You would benefit too, I am sure. You don't have to be ill, you know, or have backache like Graham. There are different therapies and Melanie advises which is best for you. You'd like Melanie, I think. She's older than us and very wise but has no side on her. She's very down to earth." I was pushing it a bit and hoped he wouldn't be offended. I did seriously think he could be helped to loosen up and get more out of life.

"Huh! Everybody's wanting me to join this and that. I seem to be popular all of a sudden. Graham wants me to join a rambling club. John wants me to go swimming. I really haven't the time to do all these things. I've said I will think about it, but my OU work comes first. I mustn't waste my time running about all over the place; I have better things to do."

"Well, I don't think anybody would suggest you neglect your OU work. We all know how important that is to you. But at the same time you need some relaxation. It doesn't do to get into a rut. We need to get out and meet people. As you do at the museum." I added hastily. I didn't want him to think I was criticising him. "We both visit John anyway. It's good to keep in touch with him. I think he's a bit lonely from time to time. What is your opinion, George?"

"Well he wouldn't be lonely if that so-called partner of his stayed at home more." He frowned and shooed away a duck that had mistakenly thought George was offering a crumb when he was merely brushing his hand across the table as if to wipe away Iolanthe. "I've no patience with that woman. She has been seen again, by a very respectable Rotarian this time, cavorting with men in a restaurant. Goodness knows what she gets up to in Glasgow. John should put his foot down. I told him so."

"Yes, and you nearly caused a rift between you. You mustn't do this, George. You can't tell other people how to run their lives. That's what caused us to split up, remember? I couldn't stand for it any longer. And John won't stand for being told what to do either. He's an adult, even though he behaves like a teenager sometimes, and Iolanthe and he have to choose their own way of living."

I feel like a record that's got stuck on the turntable, always reiterating the same message. George can't seem to get it into his head that human beings like their independence and do not like to be told how to behave, not after their infancy anyway. I marvel now how I ever put up with it for so long. I suppose I was brainwashed from an early age, as so many women of my generation were. We had to give way to our lord and master, do as we were told and shut up. The present generation were different, thank God.

"I was talking to Jackie the other day." I said, trying to change the subject. "You know, the young woman with the small children who lives near the shop. She was telling me her baby is due in December. She's very happy about it; I think she's a wonderful mother; she really enjoys her children and they all look so happy."

"That woman?" George's face took on the colour of last night's sunset but was not nearly such a pleasing sight. He thumped the table and made the ducks quack in alarm. "I don't want you talking to that woman," he pontificated. "That is, I'd rather you didn't." I was glad he had modified his edict somewhat. He must have remarked my raised eyebrows. "You'll get us both a bad name if you consort with tarts. And that's all she is, you know. She may pretend to be normal when you see her out shopping, but everybody knows what she is – a dirty prostitute." His voice was thick with loathing – and fear, I wondered? "So you understand why I don't want our name to be associated with her in any way."

"I understand that you're a bloody snob, George. And I think you're afraid of women. I even think you fancy her yourself but you're afraid to admit it. As for your precious name, what's so wonderful about it? I wish I'd changed it when I left you but it's too late now, unfortunately. Everybody here knows me now as your wife. And they know I'm not ashamed of mixing with other human beings – people who are kind, good hearted and pleasant to be with. There are plenty of people like that, and I don't ask what they do in their own home in private. I'll associate with Jackie and anybody else I want to. In fact I shall probably offer to baby-sit sometimes while she goes shopping. And why not? I've no patience with people who think they're better than anybody else."

George was speechless. He had never known me to be so outspoken and blunt. And, to be honest, I was amazed at myself. I had actually contradicted George! What is the world coming to? But I was proud of myself and smiled as I bade him goodbye and thanked him for the meal.

25

That blank sheet of paper! The whiteness of it accuses me, threatens me. I am about to violate it, destroy its purity. But I must; an inner compulsion drives me and challenges me to pick up my pencil and make those first vital strokes which commit me. Sarah says she feels the same before she starts a painting, so perhaps every artist has the same experience. It's very nerve-racking but exhilarating at the same time and I wouldn't have it otherwise, when I come to think about it. It was something about the paper today that was so intimidating. A blank canvas awaiting oil paints was less so, as I could hurriedly cover it with a thin wash of warm ochre and build up other colours on top afterwards – just to destroy that whiteness, that was the aim. Watercolour painting had to start with a drawing, or it had to today at least. I was sitting on the road above Balmichael, considering where to start putting the first mark on the paper and had been overcome with the enormity of the task.

It was late August and there was already an autumn touch in the air, a cool breath beneath the sun's rays. Those rays, too, had acquired their autumn cloak of mellow gold. As I left home the sun was still low on the horizon and clouds were massed over the hills, but I was confident it would be a fine day for our painting; the clouds were high and the westerly breeze from the

Kilbrannan Sound was moving them over to Brodick. It might rain in Brodick, as it often does, when the clouds reach Goat Fell but I didn't think Sarah and I had anything to worry about. I packed my gear in the boot and set off down the west coast road to our agreed meeting place. It was not often I drove down this side of the island, as there were few villages and fewer shops to make a journey necessary. It was an enjoyable route all the same, and quite exciting in a way, with its narrow switchback road and strange shaped rocks. The road compelled one to drive slowly, which made it all the more enjoyable and I was able to notice the seabirds; varieties of gulls, oyster catchers, a heron on a rock and a congregation of cormorants on another rock with their wings spread, looking like a conference of solemn undertakers. I didn't see any seals today; they were probably still on the north west of the island or in one of their favourite sheltered bays somewhere else on the island. There had been a full moon last night, a clear round orb in an empty sky, which meant that the tide today was high and almost overreaching the road in Lochranza. It lapped at the very edge of my garden and I was lucky and thankful that at each high tide since I had lived here the wind had never been strong enough to drive the water over the low wall that protected me. Spray thrown up from the rocks below me splattered the side window of my car as I drove down the coast but when I saw the tall standing stone of Auchencar I knew I should soon turn left to have my back to the wind. And there it was! The moorland road seemed to stretch into an empty distance, narrow, only wide enough for a single car, and twisting along most of its length. In contrast to the restive rocky shore, here was a flat emptiness, eerie even on a sunny day; it was difficult to imagine that once it was inhabited by ancient peoples who had the wisdom, knowledge and energy to erect the numerous standing stones, circles and cairns that are scattered over the now featureless and uninhabited moor. It was a short minor road and I met no other vehicle until I joined the main road again at Shiskine village and began to look out for Sarah who would approach from the opposite direction.

We had agreed to paint at Balmichael farm because it was a picturesque collection of buildings, of differing shapes and sizes grouped around a courtyard. Not only that, it had the advantage of being in the valley with a backcloth of hills and mountains. So there was plenty of choice of subject to paint, we thought. When I saw it and really looked at it I thought with dismay that there was too much choice. What on earth could I leave out?

"What shall we do, Sarah?" I cried in despair. "I can't cope with all this!"

We had parked in the car park behind the big barn and here, before us, were four groups of buildings around a cobbled yard, with huge old beech and oak trees bending protective branches over them.

"We have a choice," Sarah said. "We could do an impression of the whole, from the road above, or we could limit ourselves to a study of a portion in detail. What do you think?"

The various farm buildings had recently been converted into a community of craft shops, studios, craft workshops and a café; there were attractive small sculptures scattered around the cobbled yard and tubs of bright geraniums framed the entrance to the café. There was a particularly handsome oak tree overhanging the car park that caught my eye, too. What should we choose? I sensed that Sarah was inclined to go for a detail in the farmyard. She liked flower subjects and was good on detail. But I was wrong.

"I think it might be too chocolate boxy if I were to attempt anything in here," she said. "You could manage to make a decent picture of it, but I'm afraid I'd be too finicky and get too involved in details. The result would be pretty and meretricious."

"That's a good word," I laughed. "But maybe you're right. Let's go up to the road. It's further away and higher up. We can look down and see the whole complex as a complete picture, with the mountains as a background. And the trees would be less difficult to paint from that distance, too."

That was the first time I had had the temerity to suggest the subject; I had always left it to Sarah's superior experience before, but now she agreed with me and my self-confidence grew another notch.

So there we were, and I had at last conquered the blank whiteness of the paper and sketched in the disposition of the buildings and their relationship to the mountains and was ready to paint. My intention, in doing this watercolour, was to use it as a sketch for a subsequent oil painting if it turned out as I hoped. I was interested in the masses and shapes as well as the colours. My painting should be like a mosaic, I decided – flat shapes in a pattern of colour. And the colours were amazingly brilliant but subtle. Gold and silver predominated among the buildings – golden sunlight on weathered pale limestone, sandstone and slate, with sharp accents of black painted windows and doors. And all of this was mounted, as it were, in the green of the towering mature trees, which in turn was framed in the purple heather-clad hills. I had chosen a formidable task and we both slaved away at it without a word, occasionally blowing away dust from a passing car. The passengers must have thought we were crazy to sit on the verge of a narrow road, but artists are crazy, aren't they?

Sarah was behind me, so I couldn't see how she was getting on, but I was just putting in the details of the chimneys on the old farmhouse when she said, "I think I felt a spot of rain. Look at that cloud."

I looked and frowned. It was a big one, and black, and it was coming this way. A spot dropped on me too and I hurriedly covered my painting. It didn't matter if I got wet, but my painting must stay dry or it would be ruined. It would be a pity to spoil work that had taken such dedicated labour to produce. We agreed it was time to pack up our things and repair to the café for some sustenance. We had deserved a break.

Other people, mainly tourists, were also repairing to the café but we were able to find a table in the far corner where we could spread out our paintings for mutual appraisal. Sarah's was inevitably more detailed. She had delineated the slates, the panes of the windows and even the notice boards, though I told her it was less detailed than other paintings she had done.

"Yes, I think it's a bit better," she agreed. "I'm trying to be broader and using bigger brushes. More like your style, really, though not so abstract. I don't see things as abstract shapes like you do, but I'd like to simplify my style. Next time will be better!"

Yes, we agreed to be optimistic. The next time we would try harder and improve. Looking back, we had improved, at least in our own estimation. So we put away our paintings in our portfolios and thought about something to eat and drink. The lentil soup and salad sandwiches were the best choice for a late summer's day, we thought, to be accompanied by a pot of Earl Grey tea. The sandwiches had to be freshly made, so we started on the soup and relaxed in the happy atmosphere of the café, where all was cheerful chatter among the holidaymakers.

"Where shall we go next? Have you any ideas?" I asked Sarah. I was wound up with enthusiasm and couldn't wait for another expedition. I had really got the bug. It was strange that I hadn't had any leanings towards painting earlier in my life. I wondered how such a thing could lie dormant for so long. The nearest I had come to any artistic effort was the flower arranging at the little church in Heysham. They said I was good at that. And I've always been very conscious of colour. But I wasn't much good at school; art lessons were boring; we had to draw boxes and bottles and such like – nothing imaginative. Perhaps that was why my work was running riot now; I was letting myself go at last and having a wonderful time – an orgy of creativity – marvellous!

Flushed with these wild thoughts I turned to Sarah half apologetically, as she started on her soup. "I'm sorry if I seem too keen. I don't want to press you. You have commitments and don't have the time to spare like I have, but I am keen. There's no denying it, you know that."

Sarah put down her spoon and smiled. "Of course. It's great. I'm happy too and always look forward to our trips. My painting has improved so much since we started going out together regularly. It gives me an incentive. I was too lazy before you came." She broke off a corner of her roll and started to butter it. "But if you don't mind, can we stay somewhere close to Brodick next time? You see, Ian is due back from South Africa and I want to be at home when he arrives. He's been away so long, touring the hospitals and medical centres there and meeting heads of medical services, giving lectures, advising governments and goodness knows what. He's become an important authority and I feel I hardly know him."

She sighed and looked sad for a moment as she chewed on her roll. "Of course, Susie has the prior claim to his time. She's planning to go to the airport to meet him when we know the date. But after that, when he's settled in again at home I want to spend time with him and hear about his travels. I believe he's thinking about staying at home more in future. Susie says he's getting tired of all this travelling and wants a more peaceful life with his own family."

I could sympathise. "Susie will be happy that he's coming home. It must have been a strain, having to run the Hydro on her own. It's a big responsibility on top of her own therapy work. She's helped me a lot and I'm very grateful to her, but I sensed that she was lonely and missing him a lot."

"Yes, I've worried about that. To tell you the truth I've worried about both of them."

There was a break in the conversation as Betty the waitress brought us our sandwiches – fresh wholemeal bread bursting with salad and with wisps of cress scattered on top. My mouth watered at the sight; I pushed away my empty soup plate and picked up a dainty quarter. The crusts had been trimmed away, I noticed with approbation.

"You know," she resumed. "It's a strain on the marriage when couples are parted for some time. It's bound to be. There's such a danger that they'll grow apart or, heaven forbid, find consolation with someone else." She frowned and looked at me with troubled eyes. "I hope I'm worrying about nothing and imagining things that aren't true. But we can't help worrying about them, can we? We can't stop being mothers. It's difficult to let them go and make their own mistakes. One wants to protect them." Raw appeal was visible in her face. She wanted my support. She was uncertain of her son's happiness and needed reassurance. I could see all this and I could certainly understand it and even share it, but I couldn't reassure her, not with any conviction anyway.

"I know what you mean," I said. "And I sympathise. I have the same worries with my own son and Iolanthe. She is away in Glasgow for most of the week and I hear rumours of her being seen with other men. I think I told you. It's very puzzling because when I talk to her I'm convinced she is honourable and genuinely cares for John. George has his doubts; he's always had doubts about her, but I think it's partly prejudice. He has little experience of women and doesn't understand modern women. But we're both worried about John. We know he visits the Hydro regularly, not only for swimming but also for therapy of some sort. I heard it as a rumour at first and when I asked him he admitted it but wouldn't say who he visits or what therapy he has. He shuts up like a clam when I try to talk about it. It worries me. Could he be visiting Susie? Could there be something between them? It's an awful thought, Sarah. It would be terrible if our two families got involved in this way. I wouldn't want that to happen. Can we do anything to prevent it? Have you talked to Susie?" It was strangely comforting that Sarah shared my worries, even though the danger of our friendship breaking up with our children's marriages loomed in the background. In spite of it all I had to be confident that Sarah and I would remain friends. I leaned towards her and raised my eyebrows in appeal.

"Yes, and she refuses to talk about John. She doesn't talk much in any case, as you know, and always insists that everything in the Hydro is confidential. It's very frustrating and annoying but there seems to be nothing we can do but hope and pray. Do you pray, incidentally?"

"Pray? Well, not in church. Not any more. But if loving someone and wanting the best for them is prayer, then I do pray." It was a strange question and I wondered at it, as I knew Sarah didn't go to church either. Family troubles lead one to think more deeply about things, I suppose.

Sarah finished her last quarter of sandwich, wiped her mouth with the paper tissue and smiled. "Let's talk of something more cheerful. Tell me about your trip to Oban and your friend – Veronica, wasn't it?"

I sighed with relief at the change of subject. "Yes, Veronica. She is the one who opened my eyes to paintings and gave me the incentive to start. I owe her a lot. She's a professional painter, you know. She invited me to stay with her and I took the car across from Lochranza and drove up the west coast – a beautiful run – and found her address easily. She has a small house but she has the luxury of a shed in the garden at the back that she's made into her studio. It's packed with paintings; she's been working practically all her life, she says; even as a child she was always drawing or painting. The reason why she invited me just then was because it was the opening of her one-man, or one-woman, exhibition in the town's main gallery. It was quite a posh affair, with a speech by some bigwig saying how good she was, and drinks and nibbles and such crowds that you couldn't see the paintings. But I had a private view the next morning, all to myself. She really is good. She has that confidence; you feel she knows what she's doing. If only I had that confidence!"

"It'll come!" Sarah said, to encourage me.

"I did have the courage to take one or two of my paintings with me and asked her to give an opinion. I was grateful, she didn't flatter me and say they were good, but she was critical in a helpful sort of way –

really positive."

"She seems to be the sort of friend one always hopes to find. You were lucky to meet her in Glasgow last year – an accidental meeting, wasn't it? But I wonder how far it was an accident. It was providential, as they say. But you have a gift for attracting people; you offer friendship without apparently being aware of it. So the luck, if that's what it is, comes from you." And she smiled warmly as we began to gather our things together.

"I wish I could be sure that George is as fortunate in his friendships. He had so few in the old days, but now I'm glad he's friendly with Graham and others at the museum. He's still shy with women and perhaps he always will be, but I've seen the librarian coming to the house a time or two, and once she stayed quite a while. I think she probably had a meal with him. If so, I'm glad. I've met her at the library of course, and she looks a sensible and attractive person, but I don't know anything about her. George is apparently attracted to her. Perhaps it's the start of a beautiful friendship – who knows?" Sarah joined me in girlish giggles as we departed to our cars and made our separate ways home.

26

It was the following week when I was able to make time to visit John. I had not seen him for some time, not since the new term had started, in fact, and I didn't want him to feel I was neglecting him. I hadn't been to Glasgow for a few weeks either, so had not bumped into Iolanthe though I knew her writing course was almost finished and she would be getting her degree and coming home before long. I was curious about the novel she said she was writing and frustrated that I couldn't talk about it with John. Of course I know nothing about such things, but it seemed to me strange that she could work for a degree – a time consuming occupation in itself – and also spend additional time in writing a novel. However did she find that much energy? I marvelled at her youth and enthusiasm, and her dedication. But of course there was a flip side. To achieve an ambition involves sacrifice. Iolanthe was sacrificing a comfortable life of home-making with John, creating a family together and enjoying local friendships. That was her choice. But we can't act in isolation. Her decision involved John. He in turn was forced to sacrifice the warmth and comfort of his partner's presence and endure the consequent loneliness. How far was he doing this willingly or how far had he adapted to the situation? I was not sure. I wanted to talk to him about it but so far the moment had never seemed opportune. Perhaps today?

I was feeling a bit down, dreamy, mooning about the flat and accomplishing nothing. I went into my spare room – my studio as I grandiloquently called it – and looked at the oil painting of Balmichael that I started two days ago. It didn't inspire me. I looked out of the window. That wasn't inspiring either. Everything was grey, like my mood. The sky was a flat wash of a grey only a shade paler than the flat grey of the loch. I could scarcely see the opposite shore; it was veiled in mist and the only discernable accent was the bright red of the post office sign. It reminded me that I needed some stamps; I owed Veronica a letter; I also needed some hand cream from the Aromatics shop. The shopping would be an excuse for a run over the hill to Brodick, and, while at that side of the island I would call on John. He would not be at home until after four, so I would have some lunch out for a change, perhaps at the museum. It wasn't Wednesday, so George wouldn't be there. It wasn't the weather to sit outside in the garden although it was still only the beginning of September, but the little room inside was cosy and quaint. I hoped it wouldn't be too packed with tourists seeking somewhere dry to spend the day. Although the rain was not sheeting down it was wet enough, being the typical mountain mist that is wetter than it looks.

I was lucky. By the time I had finished my bits of shopping in various shops around Brodick – some pan scrubs, shoelaces, large envelopes and turps as well as soap and hand cream – it was quite late when I got to the museum and most of the diners had departed. I had a small table near the counter and could chat to the waitress in between her trips to the kitchen. She was the young daughter of one of the SWI members in

Lochranza; her name was Megan and she was a student doing philosophy at Edinburgh University. She would finish working at the museum café at the end of this week, she said, so that she could have a couple of weeks holiday hiking round the Continent before her term started. I wished her a happy holiday and success with her studies, and privately wondered what sort of career does a degree in Philosophy lead to? I admire these young ones today; they are so enterprising and not afraid of change and uncertainty, as I was. Here was Megan, cheerfully serving my cream of broccoli soup with Arran cheddar this week, hitching lifts from strangers in a foreign country next week, and then deep in philosophical thought soon afterwards. Good luck to her, I thought, as I tucked into my soup and admired the blue and white cottage décor with bits of Delft, and the black and white photographs of old Arran life. I wondered if people of a hundred years hence would look at photographs of our life and think how primitive we were?

I tried to shake off this grey mood and drove to Lamlash along the shore for a walk before going to John's house. It didn't matter that I got wet; I didn't care; I needed the exercise to shake me into a more positive, less introspective frame of mind. I was annoyed at myself. Wake up, Muriel, I said to Holy Island when nobody was within hearing, take a grip on yourself and be more optimistic, for John's sake. The little island was hardly visible and didn't reply; I didn't expect it to, but I breathed in the salty fragrance of the sea between us and thought of the prayers of the good Buddhists there in retreat. That and a vigorous walk to the end of the shore road and back made me feel better and ready to pursue a normal conversation with my son. Whenever I had visited him before he had been in a low mood and I didn't want to add to it;

he needed support and encouragement. By the time I had reached the car again it was four o'clock and I felt more prepared to face John with a cheerful face and optimistic conversation.

He had just come in and although I had a key I rang the bell. I didn't want him to think I would just barge in at any time, and to let him know who was at the door I waved to him at the window. As usual his arms were cradling a pile of exercise books, which he dropped on to the table when he saw me, and smiled.

"Long time no see," he said cheerfully. "It must be three weeks since I've seen you. How are you getting on, stuck out there on the other side of civilisation? Does it rain over there?"

We laughed together at the joke about the ever-changing climate of the island and how it can vary from one mile to the next and one hour to the next. "Are you going to put the kettle on to give me a cup of tea or shall I do it?" I enquired. "Have you a lot of work to do this evening?"

"Yes, but no more than usual. I'll pile these up out of the way while you get the tea ready, and then we can have a blether. I never heard how you went on in Oban, and I want to hear the latest from Pitlochry."

"Yes, all right, I'll tell you all the news. But you seem to be out of milk. Your fridge is empty in fact. The kettle's boiling and I've made the tea, found the sugar but no milk."

"Oh, hell! I forgot! Hang on a second. I'll run and get some from the Co-op." He slammed the door as he went out, and I saw him sprinting along the few yards to the shop. It was fortunate that a food shop was so near and that the school provided his main meal during weekdays. He was not the world's best provider of meals for himself, though I think he tried harder when Iolanthe was at home. I had the impression that they shared the tasks of housekeeping.

I carried the tray of tea through to the coffee table and in no time he was back with the milk. The tea was strong, as I knew he liked it, but I added a lot of water and milk to mine to make it palatable as I told him of my trip up the west coast to Oban. "You never met Veronica, did you? I keep forgetting that she was only the one day on Arran; we had a quick trip over while George was tracing his ancestors in Glasgow. That was brief too, but it was packed with the sort of moments that have far-reaching consequences." I paused for breath. John knew about George's disappointment over his ancestors and I had told him something about the excitement and new beginnings that had started for me at the Burrell gallery, but I had never described Veronica.

"Veronica?" he repeated. "It's an unusual name. I imagine a prim maiden lady with a reticule," he teased me.

"Well, you'd be wrong," I chided. "She's not in the least like that. She's tall and elegant and great fun to be with. It was I who was like a prim maiden aunt before I met her; she put a squib under my bum and got me thinking differently about myself. That's what she did. And I owe her!"

"OK. I withdraw my allegation," he grinned. "But I bet you enjoyed your trip up the west coast. I've only been the once, and in winter, but it's really something!"

"Yes, it reminded me of our first trip over on the Lochranza ferry, last Christmas, when we stopped for lunch at Inveraray. You remember? I must say it was much pleasanter this time, being summer and not having the trauma of our separation hanging over George and me. I shall never forget that Christmas. I think it was the worst few days I've ever spent in my life. It was such a relief to come back. Unpacking and settling in to a new home in Lochranza. was far less traumatic." I grimaced over the bitter taste of the tea and went on, "This Christmas will be very different. Sandra says her baby is due Christmas week. She refused a scan as they don't want to know beforehand whether it's a boy or a girl; they will be happy with either. So I've sent her little first garments in primrose yellow; she's knitting some as well and the children are excited at having a baby for a Christmas present. I can't wait. I'm itching to get up there and help, but she says my help will be more needed afterwards so I shall stay on after Christmas. George can come back with you after the holiday."

"Yes, of course. What a difference from last year. I could have killed the old man. Even Dad looked murderous when his father behaved so foully. Grandfather was always rude and said exactly what he thought – we called him the curmudgeon, remember? – but he surpassed himself when he insulted Iolanthe. Telling her she was skinny and anorexic! But she gave as good as she got, didn't she! I was proud of her. She showed us all how to treat the old man."

"Yes, by answering him back she gained his respect. I wish George had stood up to him when he was younger; his life would have been very different. Ah, well!"

"It was after that that he made his will and left money to Iolanthe 'to further her ambitions'. So that's why she's in Glasgow learning how to write." John gave a deep sigh, put down his mug and crossed his legs. "I don't know how she thinks she'll make a success out of writing. Our English teacher has tried to get short stories published but she says it's hopeless – nothing but rejection time after time. I think it's a waste of time studying to write for the waste paper basket."

"Don't be so cynical, John. She's always been writing, you know, even when she was a fashion model she had articles published in magazines. Now she's learning the techniques, the craft, to be able to write professionally. Her tutors say she's good, so why not believe it and give her some encouragement?"

"Oh, I do. I don't let her know I'm sceptical. I let her do as she likes, don't I? And when she's finished in Glasgow she can write at home. I shan't stop her. Nobody can stop Iolanthe if she has a mind to do something!" He smiled, ruefully, I thought, but with affection.

I know how much he loves her and I have to trust that this present suspicion and lack of trust is just a temporary hiccup in their relationship. "She'll be free to be at home soon, John. Just a few weeks more. Meanwhile I hope you're looking after yourself. I think you're looking a bit peaky. Do you get any exercise – outdoors, I mean? And are you looking after your diet? You're not living on chips, I hope? Are you still going to the Hydro – working out, do they call it?"

"Now, now, Mum, don't fuss. Of course I'm looking after myself. And yes, I work out at the Hydro. Can we stop this third degree?"

He was still reluctant to talk about his visits to the Hydro and it still worries me. Sarah too! I wish I knew how to break through this wall of silence and get at the truth. I sighed and decided to change the subject. "Last time I was here you were talking about looking for a job in a college somewhere. Have you thought any more about it?"

He uncrossed his legs and sat up. "I've thought, yes. I've even looked at advertisements in the Times Ed but I'm having second thoughts."

"Times Ed? What's that?"

"A newspaper. Times Educational Supplement. All the adverts for teaching jobs are in there. I noticed one or two attractive-sounding jobs and considered applying. And then I thought again. I've only been here a year, and I was only three years in Ayr. It doesn't look too good on a CV if one moves too often. I like it here; I've nothing against the job or the place except the boredom of constant marking. And I had an idea that teaching adults would be more stimulating." He was serious and frowned in concentration, trying to make me understand. "I'll have to discuss it with Iolanthe of course, but while I've been so much on my own I've had time to think of what I want to do in the future, Mum. I'm a historian. I enjoy teaching. But I don't want to spend the rest of my life teaching in a high school. Another couple of years, and then it will be time to move into a college of further education or university in a bigger centre of population where I can use the libraries and do some research. That's what I would like to do. That's my ambition, Mum."

"Ah, I see." And I did see. It made sense. I was glad he had ambition and hoped he would be lucky enough to fulfil it. "And what about Iolanthe. Where does she come in all these plans?"

"That's easy. Her ambition is to write, she says. So, no problem. Writing can be done anywhere; she only needs a notebook and pen or a laptop; she doesn't need an audience and she'll send manuscripts by post to publishers. I don't se any difficulty. We shall be together, doing our own thing – and married, I hope!" He grinned.

It was part of his ambition, I knew, for Iolanthe to marry him. I hoped, too, that it was part of their ambition to produce a family in due course, but I didn't mention that. I wished him well and congratulated him on having such a worthwhile ambition. I felt sure he could achieve it; I agreed it was long-term but sensible. "So, you'll stay in Lamlash for another three years perhaps?" I said. "And then you could be anywhere?"

"That's right, Mum. But don't tell anybody, please. I don't want people to think I'm not satisfied here. I am, and I'm happy, but one has to have ambitions. One can't stay in the same rut for ever, even if it's such a pleasant rut."

"Of course I won't mention it to anyone. We'll live a day at a time. I wouldn't dream of starting any rumours about you." I thought about my conversation with Sarah; we discussed existing rumours; that's not so reprehensible I hope.

"Talking of rumour," John went on. "I heard that Dad is seeing the librarian rather a lot. Did you know?"

"I'm not sure what I know. I've seen her at the library of course, as you must have done. Her name is Rosemary, but I've only spoken to her in the course of borrowing books. She's always pleasant and polite, but she would be, of course. It's part of the job. I don't know anything more about her. It's only just recently I've discovered she has been visiting George. I'd seen a strange car there once or twice and wondered who was calling but had never seen the driver until a couple of weeks ago. And then I saw that it was the librarian; I saw her go up to George's flat and she was there quite a long time, so she must have stayed to lunch. It was a Sunday, so it would be her free day. That's all I know."

"Wow! Dad with a lady friend! What next! He has changed, hasn't he! Branching out with a vengeance; I must say I'm amazed. He never showed any interest in women before, and to be blunt, Mum, he didn't show much interest in you. He treated you like a hired housekeeper. Do you think he's looking for a new housekeeper? How would you feel if he wanted to divorce you and marry her, eh?" He gave me his usual grin but his eyes were darkly serious. He was concerned about me.

I had no wish to discuss marital affairs with John, but it was true that George had little interest in me as a woman. Our sex life had been decidedly tame; no ecstasy or excitement in it, only dutiful routine. In the beginning, when I was newly married and dewy-eyed with romantic love I simply followed his lead and was too ignorant to know that it wasn't all it should or could be. Now, I doubt whether he is capable of sexual love but I hope he can find happiness. That is, one part of me, the nobler part, hopes he will find happiness, but the other part of me quivers with revulsion at the thought of any other woman sharing his bed. Illogical, I know, but there it is. I would have to think more about it and sort out my feelings; meantime I would watch for any developments and hope that Gladys would keep her mouth shut. I had no doubt that she knew what was going on – she knew everything – but perhaps I could have a word in her ear and squash any gossip. The situation was delicate and I didn't want George to be hurt. "We are both of us free, John," I said, rather too primly. "I wish him well. We have a right to make our own friends. It's too soon to think about divorce, anyway. And I hope you won't go spreading tales, John." I added as I walked out stiffly, after sitting too long in that old sagging chair.

27

September 10
Since my last entry in this diary I have been much occupied. The summer season on Arran has been very busy, as I believe it has been in other resorts. The hoteliers and shopkeepers say they have now fully recovered from the foot and mouth epidemic and the September 11 disaster in the States. Tourists are now venturing to travel abroad again and this, thankfully, is reflected in the increasing numbers visiting our heritage museum. It is open seven days a week in the summer, which entails a lot of work and organisation. Esther has used her contacts to good effect and has been able to stage special events – not only sheep-shearing and horse-shoeing with local men but also she attracted a woman from Irvine to give a workshop weekend on spinning, weaving and dyeing; there was also a display of quilting and embroidery. The crafts are mainly women's work; Malcolm and Graham organised an exhibition of transport; they found old photographs and handbills of old ferryboats, early buses and even earlier carriers. Setting up and manning these events was the responsibility of various volunteers and committee members, but my responsibility was to supervise the increased flow of cash into the bank account. As it was all cash and in small amounts taken as entrance fees and postcard

sales it caused a problem; there was no safe in the museum, so it could not be left there overnight. Dolly, the most responsible of the receptionists, often took it home with her for overnight keeping, but I felt it wise to collect it as often as was practicable, to transfer it to the Bank. Thus, it was time-consuming, driving over the Boguille almost daily. My OU studies suffered to some extent because of this; I was writing my last essay on the philosophy of Marx into the early hours of the morning, which is not my usual habit. However, I have kept to the agreed timetable and expect to finish the course well before Christmas.

Giving priority to the OU course and disciplining my time very carefully I was able to allow myself the indulgence of the visit to London with Rosemary, and also the occasional visit to John and a lunch with Muriel. I believe my social life has been satisfactorily varied and I am content with my state of health. Muriel hints that I should take more physical exercise but I am sufficiently active and fit for my age; I am careful of my diet and I am not overweight. Rosemary at least appears to think I am still attractive.

Our relationship, since our weekend in London, has been more relaxed; the awkwardness of the first night dissipated in the enjoyment of the days. It was an enjoyable break from our normal routine; we have so many interests in common and never tire of one another's company. Aside from the visits to galleries and theatres we learnt more of each other's personality and discovered a deeper affinity. I feel I ought to record here that I discovered something about myself, too, which made me ashamed and embarrassed at the time. It is not appropriate to write about this in detail but I wish to record that Rosemary was very understanding and assured me she was not troubled by my inability to satisfy her. Her sympathy and thoughtfulness made me realise that sex is not necessarily important in a relationship. A burden has lifted from my shoulders and I feel less inhibited and freer. It would seem that Rosemary feels something of the same reaction. She is a very understanding woman with definite views. Sometimes she can be stubborn in holding to these views, but I enjoy our vigorous discussions. It was never possible to discuss anything with Muriel.

Last week Rosemary invited me to dinner. This was a watershed in our relationship. She had been to my flat several times and we had met for meals in various public places but this was the first time I had entered her home. It was with confident steps that I walked along the lochside track to Deerholme, breathing deeply of the tangy air of the high tide. The forecast was good and I did not expect rain today, so wore only my light jacket with open white shirt – sufficiently summery and informal, I hoped. I avoided the muddy ruts and puddles that the previous day's rain had left, so as not to dirty my shoes and Rosemary's carpets, and paused a moment at her gate. I had passed the house many times in the car, but now I observed it at leisure. Deerholme is much older than Beach Villa; it is a traditional Scottish cottage of a single storey built of stone, with two small dormers in the roof. There was a tidy garden of short cut grass all round it and the whole had been carved out of the native woodland, she had once told me. She had a man to cut the grass, as she had neither time not inclination for gardening and in any case she preferred the natural trees that remained, rather than create unsuitable flowerbeds.

I had scarcely stepped back from ringing the door-bell when she was there at the open door, with a welcome smile and outstretched hand in greeting. I noticed again what an attractive woman she was, with a comfortably curving figure and round face with rosy cheeks; there was nothing frail or delicate about her; she looked strong and healthy though completely feminine. I remarked that she looked well; I admired her dress of some soft material in a subtle colour I couldn't put a name to but which reflected the blue-grey of her eyes. It floated sinuously over her hips as she led me through the hall into the living room on the right.

"You're looking well, George. That jacket you bought in London looks just right for Arran – casual but smart. Not everybody can get it right. I see some strange get-ups sometimes walking into the library. But now, what would you like to drink?" She turned to the drinks table beside the fireplace, which I noticed was filled with an assortment of flowers in a big bowl; it was very colourful and reminded me of the sort of thing Muriel used to do at her church, but I was never able to give a name to the kinds of flowers she used. While Rosemary was busy with the drinks and had her back to me I was able to note her taste in furnishings. She apparently favoured practical furniture and sensible colours; the chairs were upholstered in a sort of red that Muriel might have described as cherry, while the carpet was patterned in deeper shades of red and brown. I liked the effect; it was cheerful and warm. The pale greys and apricots of my own flat seemed cold and I determined to make a change in the New Year.

"The dinner will be ready in half an hour," she said. "I've just put the vegetables on." And she seated herself in the matching chair opposite me.

There wasn't any need for chatter, we were easy together, but her mention of my jacket reminded me of the purchases she had made in London. "That material you bought – did you make that dress from it?"

"How clever of you to remember and notice. Yes, I enjoy making my own dresses when I have time. That Liberty's store was a revelation, wasn't it. Such a huge choice of lovely things. One only needed the money," she smiled.

We continued to reminisce about our visit to the National Gallery and the Tate while we drank our sherry and waited for the dinner to be ready. *"I love the early Italians,"* she said. *"So direct, so deceptively simple, and so innocent in a way."*

"I can appreciate those Old Masters a bit better now," I admitted. *"But I can better understand the English painters – Constable and the Norwich School as they call it. Muriel does paintings like that. Not as good of course and I can see the difference, but I can understand what they're meant to be. I still don't like Turner, though, with all those weird swirls of colour. Some of his early paintings aren't so bad, though."*

Rosemary laughed; we had had arguments before about Turner and she knew my opinions and prejudices. There was no need to continue this topic, as the dinner would now be ready, she said. We repaired to the dining room, a small room dedicated to nothing but a dining table and four chairs. Even here was severely practical, with no unnecessary frills. She disappeared into the kitchen, where I would have liked to follow her. I was curious to see what culinary skills she had and how she organised her kitchen. I felt sure she would be competent in everything she undertook, and I was not disappointed when she appeared again with two bowls of steaming Cullen skink and crispy rolls. The aroma of the smoked haddock set the taste buds tingling and it tasted as good as it smelt. Little was said as we gave it our full attention and the respect it deserved. Over the main course of local *lamb cutlets, local peas and roast potatoes we relaxed into further talk of our London trip.*

"I did so enjoy that weekend, George, and I think you did too. We had such fun. It even started in the station waiting room in Glasgow, between trains. You remember that little tableau of the two women, the man and the four cat baskets? How we wondered what was going on! And then the ceremony of exchanging the two cats from the man's baskets to the women's – one to each, as we decided the women weren't together. The cats were obviously pedigrees, both beautiful and both tranquillised. I liked the ginger one with the fluffy squirrel-like tail and I know you preferred the brown one with the long body that looked like a ferret. It was amusing to watch them, how careful they were and what ceremony was necessary over the paperwork. One would have thought they were signing away an inheritance. They all seemed pleased with the transaction, though. The two middle- aged women went separate ways and the thin man went looking for a taxi at the end. We enjoyed the entertainment and it made a good start to our holiday, didn't it? I was wondering –." She broke off and chewed another mouthful of potato, looking at me with some doubt in her eyes.

"Well? What are you wondering?"

"Hmm, well, I was wondering if you would be interested in a trip to France. Together, I mean. There are special organised trips to Paris and Versailles and the chateaux of the Loire, you know. I'm not pressing it; it's just a suggestion but I think you would enjoy it. You haven't been abroad, have you?" Her face was rosy from the dinner and her eyes were bright with persuasion and anticipation.

"I'm ashamed to admit it, but you're right. My misspent youth was wasted in dull routine and boring

work. It's time I made up for what I lost. But you don't mean this year, do you? I still have to finish my course and then there's Christmas. I wouldn't be free until early next year. That would be ideal, when I come to think about it as my next course is closely concerned with France and the royal court. Such a trip would be very helpful as well as enjoyable, I'm sure."

"Nearer to Christmas the tour companies will have their brochures available. If we both look out for suitable ones in the newspapers as well, then we can compare them and make up our minds. I can arrange my holiday entitlement with the other staff if I have sufficient notice."

So that was the arrangement. I would have a day on the mainland enquiring at travel agents' and Rosemary would trawl through the newspapers. It was a pleasure to look forward to. I was amazed at myself, at how I had so easily grown into this new kind of relationship with a woman. It was so unlike me. I had only ever had business acquaintances among men, and had always shied away from women. Except for Muriel, and my relationship with her was never of this kind. Since these meetings with Rosemary I have come to realise how much my marriage lacked. If only Muriel and I had been close friends, as Rosemary and I are now! I have not been given to introspection but I am coming to realise that I treated Muriel like my father treated his wife. I resented his dictatorial ways with her and with me, and yet I repeated his mistakes. In bullying Muriel I think I was trying to punish my father. But I wasn't the only one at fault. Muriel was also to blame. She should have stood up to me. It was as if I chose her as a wife because I saw myself in her – a timid submissive creature unable to stand up to a bully. If only we had seen this earlier! We were so immature and each saw the other as a continuation of past wrongs – Muriel wanted to replace her father's dominance and I needed to dominate someone else. What a waste of potential! At least we are both now trying to break the mould.

Rosemary interrupted my thoughts, tapping her plate with her fork. "Hello George! Are you still there? Would you like more vegetables? Or is the meal sending you to sleep?" She was laughing at me, and not for the first time, I'm afraid.

I had been unaware of my lapse of manners and apologised. "I'm sorry. Yes, I was miles away, thinking of my good fortune, but I would like some more of those roast potatoes, please."

"The good fortune is in two directions, George." She was serious suddenly. "And I suppose you realise there may be rumours and gossip about us? Are you prepared for that? I've lived on Arran a long time now and know what it's like. People here love to talk about one another. It's not malicious, you know. No. Not that. It's taken me a while to analyse what it is that drives people to gossip and I've come to the conclusion that it's simply an absorbing interest in other people. You see, we're a small population confined to an island, many related to each other for generations back, so it's natural that everybody should come to be regarded as part of the extended family, which includes us newcomers. That's how I see it anyway, and on that basis I can't resent it when other people take an interest in the intimate details of my life."

"Huh! I see what you mean. I'd begun to realise something of the sort. Gladys at the shop always wants to know what I'm doing. I tried to keep her at arm's length at first, but she worms things out of you and, as you say, she is not malicious. She spreads news about everybody as if she were in duty bound to

disseminate it. But she doesn't sit in judgment on people, I notice." I finished the last potato and Rosemary cleared the plates into the kitchen. She knows I don't indulge in sweets so she returned with the coffee, which we took into the lounge to drink at leisure. I was pleased to notice that the coffee was filtered and served in fine porcelain cups.

"Talking of gossip," I continued the conversation. "Have you heard any more about John and his partner? I'm still worried about him. I've tried to get the truth out of him but he clams up and it only results in him telling me to mind my own business. I don't think Muriel has any more success than I have, though she still trusts Iolanthe, on what evidence I don't know. I doubt that she has any real evidence. It's just women's intuition."

Rosemary smiled at that. "Women's intuition is very often to be trusted, you know. I've not met Iolanthe. She gets the books she needs from the University library I presume. But if she's a mature student, that is, not one of the school-leaver generation, she must take her work very seriously. She's what – in her thirty's?" I nodded. "Well, then, I doubt that she wants to jeopardise her relationship with John. You say they've been together for several years. As well as that, I don't think she would waste her energy and opportunities by indulging in a casual affair."

"Mmm, well, you may be right," I replied. "But I hope John isn't going astray in her absence. He used to be too inclined to chase a pretty face and I thought he'd settled down. It's all a great worry."

"Yes, I'm sure. You can't help worrying about your children even when they're grown up and supposedly independent." She put down her coffee cup and leaned forward in her chair. Her brow was creased in earnest entreaty and I detected a pleading look in her

eyes. "I've never told you much about myself, have I, George? You've been very patient and made no demands. I appreciate that, but I think it's time I was frank with you." She took a deep breath and clasped her hands, the fingers tense. "I did tell you that I was a widow, but what I didn't tell you was that I had an illegitimate child." She paused again, as if to allow that startling fact to sink in. "Yes," she went on. "It happened a long time ago, when I was a student. A youthful escapade, my first and only, as a gesture of independence which had consequences I was too stupid to have foreseen. I never saw the father again. He was another student and there was no point in burdening him as well as myself with a shotgun marriage that neither of us wanted. It would only have led to unhappiness. It was my last term at college so I simply disappeared from the scene. My parents were a wonderful support in every way, giving me and my son a secure and loving home. Mother looked after Alec while I was at work; they adored their only grandson and I was able to contribute to the family and save for an eventual home of my own. Alec was a happy little boy, bright and enjoying his first days at primary school." Another pause, this time to shake her head as if to expel a memory. "Then, suddenly, he wasn't there any more. Diphtheria. It was so sudden. There was nothing we could do. Nothing would save him." She brushed a hand across her eyes, then shrugged and went on, in a firmer voice. "It was later when I married – a good man twenty years older than me, and we were happy until he died of a heart attack after only two years together. I suppose that's why I've always been alone since then. I've never wanted to become involved with a man again. Perhaps I was too afraid of risking another child and another disaster. So you see, George, you and Muriel aren't the only ones to be starting a new life." And she smiled through the tears glistening on her eyelids.

28

"I don't mind coming to Brodick," I told Sarah when she rang. "I can do some shopping at the supermarket there afterwards." It suited me, actually. I had a list of things I needed, that I could only buy in Brodick – wine glasses, some underwear, knitting wool and some hand cream, apart from normal supermarket groceries. Gladys was very good and did her best to supply all my needs but of course it was impossible to stock everything and unreasonable to expect it. So occasionally I had a trip over the Boguille for shopping. Sometimes, if time allowed, I went on to Lamlash to see John but there wouldn't be time today. It was our painting day but Sarah had rung me very early – I didn't tell her but she had got me out of bed; I had slept badly in the night and then fell asleep when I should have been getting up. It had happened suddenly, she said. A call from South Africa. Ian was on his way home. He expected to arrive today but didn't know when. He'd first rung Susie of course and she had rung Sarah in a panic because she was tied up all day with a meeting she couldn't cancel. Some delegates from a mainland hospital had come over specially to meet with her; they were already on the island and there was nobody else at the Hydro who could take her place. Would Sarah meet him? He had been away so long, it would be dreadful if there was nobody at the ferry to welcome him back. He had promised to ring her mobile to say which ferry he was able to catch. So of course Sarah was delighted to agree. Her voice on the phone to me was spluttering with excitement. She had not seen her precious son for so many months and now, suddenly, he would be here today! Naturally I understood her excitement and told her I would be content to spend the day painting by myself; she obviously had other things to think about.

"No, no," she said. "I'd only wander from room to room, wasting time and getting fidgety. I'd be better occupied with something. I'll bring all my things, and try to concentrate on a painting or perhaps just a drawing. It will keep my mind busy and pass the time. He probably won't arrive until the last boat, anyway, and there's no point in wasting a whole day waiting and fidgeting. So long as I'm in Brodick and have my mobile phone with me I can be free at a moment's notice to collect him from the ferry."

She had agreed to my suggestion that we should meet at the museum; there were several possible viewpoints and there was also the tearoom for lunch. As often happens, because I was late getting up I was early at our appointment. I must have rushed through my breakfast and morning chores without being aware. I was aware of the autumn morning, however, as I drove over the hills. The air had a crispness in it and the light had that golden colour that is only seen in autumn. The gold of the sunlight enhanced the gold and rich browns of the dead bracken and beech trees; really, I thought, autumn and even winter here are as colourful and as golden as the spring with its gorse. My spirits sang as I steered happily round the bends and descended at length to sea level; it was going to be a good day.

The museum was not yet busy, so early in the day.

It had only just opened its doors and there was plenty of room in the car park. I left my painting gear in the boot until I'd decided where to set up my stool and easel. It was quite a difficult problem. The buildings were all attractive. I wandered around the complex. There were several bits that would make good detailed sketches, but I wanted a more comprehensive view, one that I could use as a semi-abstract pattern of flat planes. I was still fumbling with this new style and I wanted a suitable subject for an exercise; I needed lots of practice and I hoped the museum would provide something that would appeal to me. It did, but it meant that I had to sit in the roadway, to get far enough away to see the building as a whole. The road was narrow and there was still plenty of holiday traffic. Would I be in everybody's way, and, more important, would I be in danger? Had I even the courage to sit in such a very prominent position, visible to all the world? I stood there, on the grass verge, pondering. I could put my stool by the bus stop, where the road was slightly wider and the verge less muddy, and why shouldn't I sit there painting? There was no law against it and I wouldn't actually be obstructing anything. Only providing amusement and entertainment for passers-by. So what the hell!

"Sorry I'm late!" Sarah tottered over the road to me, weighed down by all her gear and limping a little on her arthritic hip. "I got held up. Melanie wanted to know about Ian and I had to explain. She'll see him tonight. Susie rang me late last night to say he would be on the six o'clock ferry, so she'll be able to meet him herself when it gets in at seven. She's organising a family get-together – just the two of them and Melanie and me for supper. He'll be tired with all his travelling but we want to welcome him and hear about his adventures, naturally. I'm glad that's all settled, so

I'm free to have a day's painting." She looked at my set-up then looked back at what I was attempting to draw, peering between the passing cars. "Huh! I don't think I want to tackle this. There's too much of it. And I don't like the idea of swallowing dust and car exhausts. I'll go inside the yard and paint a small portion, perhaps round the back, with a bit of the tearoom cottage and garden. It will be peaceful there."

"That's great. You'll make a good job of that, it's so attractive. We'll meet up there for lunch later, then? I'm so glad you're free for the day, and you've got a happy evening to look forward to."

Sarah disappeared behind the smiddy and I settled down again to arrange the elements of the view into an acceptable composition. It was not easy. The old cottage was still rather too close to me and I had to use a lot of ingenuity to make it fit into the canvas as I wanted. In order to include the trees in the background I would have to shrink the buildings a bit to provide a contrast between the graceful informality of the beeches and the static flatness of the whitewashed planes in the foreground. And the colours – stark white dappled with shadows and punctured by the blue of the door and window frames against the deep gold and bronze of the trees.

At last I was satisfied with the composition and started happily to squelch paint on to the canvas. Wonderful thick pigment! I loved it! I could have dabbled my fingers in it! Having a paintbrush loaded with oil pigment is such a sensuous feeling, much more so than watercolour. I had no idea that they required a different mental and emotional approach until I had tried both. How I loved painting – in any medium! Even when the result was not what I had aimed at.

But almost immediately, it seemed, it was time to

break for lunch, which was a nuisance as I couldn't leave all my tackle to languish by itself on the roadside; I had to lug it all back to the car boot, tacky painting and sticky palette, box of paints and stool. It needed two trips, but I was hungry and wanted to see what Sarah was doing and catch up with her news.

"You're lucky. You've got the full sun on your side," I remarked. "And it brings out the colours so well." She was good at detail and enjoyed painting masses of flowers.

We decided to sit indoors, to be more comfortable in the little blue and white cottage with its gingham, low deep-set windows and potted plants. Three of the five tables were already occupied by elderly tourists – it was the time of year when older people chose to travel – so we settled ourselves at the table beside the counter, where Angela was waiting to serve us. We ordered simple salads and coffee while we talked about our work. We talked about hers at least, and she explained that she was trying to show the contrast between the plain cottage and the fussy flowerbed at the foot of the wall. Similar aims to my own, in fact, but I couldn't show her mine until we were ready to go home. I wasn't prepared to carry it around in its present state.

She had some news. "Have you heard? There's to be an art exhibition at the Castle in November. Anybody can enter. There's even a special section for amateurs, with a prize for the best. I don't know who will be the judge. It all depends on the judge, doesn't it? It's all so subjective. But it would be good to exhibit something, wouldn't it? To get somebody else's opinion? What do you think?"

"Yes. If you think we're good enough. I'll see what I can produce. I've got one or two that might be worth looking at. They'll have to be framed of course, so that'll keep me busy for a while. Thanks for letting me know. I'll get the form to fill in and decide which paintings to send, and then get busy with the framing. Perhaps Graham knows somebody who can do it for me. Or I'll ask one of the Lochranza painting group." I pushed away my empty plate and stirred milk into my coffee. "Did I tell you that the SWI have asked me to give them a talk about colour? Maggie asked me, she has the job of finding speakers for the winter programme and thought I might agree. I laughed at her at first – me as a speaker! – but then I thought, why not? So there it is, booked for February. I'll get down to thinking about it after Christmas."

Sarah was goggle-eyed at my announcement. Fancy me doing something so out of character! She approved, of course. I cut her off when she started to comment on my courage. I wanted to hear more about Ian's arrival and what Susie was doing, why she couldn't go to meet him.

"But she can now that he's not coming until the late boat," she said. "She's been busy all weekend with this group of medical people from the Glasgow area. They've come for a workshop with her about the ways in which complementary therapies can be used in the NHS - or something like that. She couldn't cancel it of course, because they were already here, and she couldn't delegate because nobody else at the Hydro has the experience. But all is well. They are leaving at four o'clock, to catch the 4.40 boat out, and Ian will catch it coming back. No problem!"

So that was that. All panic over. Having finished our lunch and feeling refreshed we parted to our separate plots and set up our gear again. It was a nuisance that we couldn't leave things for an hour or so but it didn't take long to settle back to work. I was concerned about getting the right colours for the shadows on the white walls. Screwing up my eyes and pursing my lips I tried to analyse them. In one place the shadow would be bluish, in another place greenish. Nowhere did they seem to be plain grey. It made me think of the Impressionists, those painters who represented colours in spots and dabs. I thought perhaps it was a good idea and worth trying. I was still only experimenting and there was nothing to lose. If it didn't work I could always paint over it.

"Hello! You must be Muriel!" I jumped, startled out of my concentration. Above me towered a silhouette of a man, broad, bulky, impressive. I gaped, frozen into immobility, my brush suspended in mid-air and dripping white paint. Who was this and how did he know my name? His voice was deep and had a kindly ring, and now that I could focus on his face, dark against the sun, I could see that he was smiling. "I'm sorry if I startled you. I knew you must be mother's friend. She has told me about you and your painting trips together. I am Ian Fraser, just arrived. We were lucky and caught an earlier boat. I didn't want to phone. I thought I'd surprise them all. I hope it is a surprise and not a shock." He smiled broadly and shrugged. Looking more closely I could see a man in his late forties, about six feet tall and muscular, a man with a commanding presence and dressed in a light tweed suit of a lovat mixture. I struggled to stand up, to greet him properly, but he waved me down. "Don't bother," he said. "Your painting is important. I'll see lots of you later, I'm sure. But now I'll find Mother and give her a surprise. Where is she hiding herself?"

He had flummoxed me; there was no doubt about it. A lovely man, and a world authority and lecturer! Sarah's son! He positively oozed charisma. I could feel it wrapping me round – warm, caring and kind. I shivered with tingly trickles down my spine. If I'd been twenty years younger I could have fallen in love with this man. How could Sarah have a son like this? It wasn't fair! Sarah, my friend, but ordinary like me, nothing special to remark about. Neither she nor I would be noticed in a crowd. But this son of hers could never be ignored wherever he was. He would always attract, whatever company he was in. I sat there, my brush still suspended, thinking of the injustice of it all. Why was my son so immature? Why were there always problems with him? Why couldn't he be settled in his ambitions? Why didn't he have more determination to make his marriage a success? He was so ordinary! Like me, of course, lacking backbone. I had to acknowledge the truth of that. And I realised too that he had inherited his father's way of compensating for lack of confidence by trying to dominate his nearest and dearest. Poor John. He couldn't avoid his genes, but I hoped he would try to realise their influence needn't rule his life. I sighed. We are an ordinary family, after all. There's no point in wishing for genius. We just have to struggle to make the best of things and develop whatever gifts and abilities we have. I sighed again and blobbed a touch of white on the gable end. I ought not to be jealous of Sarah. It was reprehensible. I should be glad for her, that she has such a lovely son. I would really try to be generous. I don't want anything to spoil our friendship.

Thinking of her, she immediately appeared like a genie out of a bottle. "I've packed up," she said. "We're going home now." She was bursting with happiness. Her face was rosy and it seemed as if her whole body was smiling. "I'm so glad Ian has met you. There's no need to introduce him. But I don't think you met Sam." She turned to a youth who was hiding behind her and pushed him forward. "Sam

Shen. He's the son of Susie's cousin. From Africa. He's coming to study at Glasgow University, so they travelled together. It's his first time in Britain."

My mind was still full of the wonder of her Ian. I scarcely grasped what she was saying, but caught the mention of Africa. Africa? Shouldn't he be black? This youth was Chinese, or I was a Dutchman! I shook myself. Of course, Susie had Chinese blood and why shouldn't her relatives settle in Africa as she settled in America and now here? Stupid Muriel! I smiled at the boy. He looked like a schoolboy who had not yet stopped growing. Small, slight, with small bones, delicate features in a pale face framed by dark hair. His dark eyes looked at me with bright intelligence, as if he were assessing my character, but he gave me a shy smile and my heart melted towards him. He needed mothering, poor lad! It was understandable. He was a long way from home and even though he might be among family members they were still strangers. He would have to face more strangers and an unfamiliar milieu when he started his studies in Glasgow. His shy appeal would be irresistible to any woman, I thought, and hoped Susie would help him to acclimatise. I would ask about him next time I consulted her.

Sarah was speaking again. "Ian's come home for good now, he says," giving him a fond look. "It's wonderful, isn't it. I'm so proud of him. He's world famous now, you know. In future people will come here to learn about what they are doing at the Hydro, so he won't have to travel to publicise it. The mountain will be coming to Mahomet, in fact." She beamed around and pressed his arm until he was embarrassed. "I'm so glad they got the earlier boat. He hired a car, you know, and expected to find me at home, but Melanie knew where I was, fortunately.

He's dying to get home to Susie, but I'll take them both home with me for a couple of hours until she's free. Susie doesn't know about Sam, does she? She never mentioned that a relative was coming from Africa."

"No, she wouldn't because I was in South Africa and Sam is from Algeria – a continent apart. His family have a chain of restaurants and they asked me if he could accompany me, to ease the strain. He'll spend a few days with us before going on to Glasgow. It will be an opportunity to show him Arran and the countryside before he gets enmeshed in city life."

Sam smiled. He seemed to smile a lot but say very little. I had yet to hear his voice. I hoped he would settle in and be happy in this country, and then they left me.

Sarah said she would get in touch, to tell me more details about the art exhibition. I didn't feel like painting after they'd gone. Their absence left a sort of emptiness. I packed up. My painting was horribly gooey and I'd omitted to bring enough rags to clean my palette. And it all had to be carried back to the car. I stood and contemplated what order to do things in. First, the painting on to the back seat, out of the way. Then the bulky things – the easel and the stool and finally the palette on top of them. I hoped the bumpy road would not dislodge anything and smear the work I'd sweated over. So be it! Perhaps in future I should stick to watercolours out of doors. Oils were too messy to cope with. I would think about it, but I also now had to think about the exhibition that Sarah wanted us to submit work to. I suspected it was because she was keen to show her own work that she was trying to encourage me to enter as well. I would certainly think about it, and contact someone who would advise about frames. And I must look at my work and pick out one or two that might be worth showing.

29

October 30
At the time I did not object to Rosemary suggesting we arrange a holiday in France together, but now I must put it on record that I am having doubts about it. In the first place I am not accustomed to a woman taking the lead, though I enjoy her company and I am beginning to be accustomed to her contradicting my opinions. She is always polite and courteous but has definite opinions of her own. There are times when I welcome this, I must confess, as the discussions are enlivened by our differences of viewpoint. A more serious doubt is over her motives. Is she motivated simply by friendship or is there something ulterior in her mind? I do not want myself to be drawn into a position where I cannot withdraw. I have no desire to marry her. I wish to make that clear in this diary. I am still married to Muriel and, as long as she is content with our present arrangement there is no question of divorce. I must make it plain to Rosemary that, if I consent to go to France with her, it will be on a strictly friendly basis. There will be no attempt on my part, as unfortunately happened in London, to take the relationship into a sexual one, and I trust she would not expect it. I will allow her to collect some details of possible tours then, if we agree on a particular package, I will make the arrangements. I would feel

happier if I am in charge. It is important to confirm that the travel arrangements are well organised and that the hotels are suitably clean and comfortable. One used to hear derogatory stories about French hotels from colleagues at work, and I hope there has been some improvement in the last few years. If all seems satisfactory I shall welcome a visit to Paris and the chateaux, as it will be an introduction to the OU course I may undertake next year.

Now that I am near the end of this year's course, which I have enjoyed, I must begin to think seriously about what I should do next year. My tutor has made very encouraging remarks about this year's work and I feel competent at commencing further study. For the history degree there is a choice: either Britain and France from 1620 to 1714 or nineteenth century Europe. The latter deals more with the economic situation, which would appeal to me, but perhaps the former would be more interesting. It includes a study of the conditions of the ordinary people as well as the nobility and traces the reasons behind the fact of France becoming an absolute monarchy and Britain a constitutional one. I am drawn to embark on this, as it was such a crucial period of change, but I cannot defer my final decision until Christmas as I intended, as the application has to be sent in at the end of this month.

When this is done I have the task of sorting out all my papers and files and checking the computer disks. As far as I know everything is in order but I need to make sure before storing it all away. Then I must spend time on the finances of the museum. The auditor will want the books before the end of the year and I shall have to justify the fact of having no deposits for the first six months, before I took over. It will be embarrassing. I will try to be tactful, as I do not wish to incriminate Simon. He did nothing criminal; he was simply too old and senile to carry on the work. He should have given up much earlier and the museum committee were at fault in not realising what was happening to him. I believe he is now happy in his old people's home, though his mind is deteriorating, they say. Millie visits him occasionally, I believe. I have looked back over earlier books and realise that the museum has done well this year, more than making up for the two previous years.

The museum closed to the public this week and now is the time when the committee must review its progress and plan for the future. In addition, it is the time when the volunteers begin their work in earnest. Graham and I have enjoyed one or two more walks to explore old settlements this summer but now we revert to our winter custom of going together, either in my car or his, to the museum on Wednesdays.

This week was an important committee meeting. Esther insisted that we should all be present. "It's good to see you all, fit and eager for work," she beamed round the table. "It's an important agenda, as you see." It was not a long one and I hoped it would not be a protracted meeting, but I noticed there was at least one important item. Her secretary's report was soon dealt with. It was encouraging – several hundred more visitors than last year, a favourable report in the Saga magazine, and a good write-up in the local tourist brochure. "I believe people have commented favourably about our advertisements, too, and the remarks in the visitors' book are very flattering. But I'll skip now to Item Six if I may, as it is relevant to our next item. I have here an application form for a grant, which is offered for development work concerning educational projects. They would pay half the cost over two years. It's just so that you bear it in mind when we consider Item Five."

I had noticed she had included an item about possible development and I wondered where the money would come from. It seemed they were eager to discuss such a project and dismissed my financial report without comment except to congratulate me and remark that it was satisfactory. We were all anxious to talk about a possible extension of the premises. The increasing popularity of the museum had resulted in more people donating artefacts, which we had no possibility of displaying.

Malcolm said, "What about building a wing out into the garden from behind the toilet block?"

"Oh, no!" Several voices were raised in protest.

"The garden is a valuable asset," Millie pointed out. "We can't encroach on that. It's used a lot in summer. In fine weather, that is."

"That's just it," Malcolm stressed. "It's either too wet or too windy very often, and it's big enough to allow a bit to be built on at the right hand side."

Others were emphatic that it mustn't be touched. I could see Graham was keen to keep the garden too. He is an enthusiastic gardener. I said nothing. I felt I was too new to the island and the museum to have any strong opinion. So long as the finances were in order I would approve of any development. So I kept quiet and listened to the arguments going back and forth. It appeared to be a question of either or; nobody had any other constructive thought.

It was beginning to become rather heated and we weren't getting anywhere until Millie intervened. "I've been thinking," she said. "It's no good arguing to a stalemate. I've been considering this problem all summer as I've poked around the buildings. I really can't see that we have any space anywhere for an extension of the buildings. We have already built up to the boundary on both sides; on the front is the road and at the back is the garden, then the burn. So,. . ". She took a deep breath and looked round the table at each of us in turn. *"What do you think about inserting another floor in the stable block? It's high enough to allow an extra storey. It wouldn't involve any alteration to the exterior except for skylights. Although it's a listed building I think skylights would probably be allowed or perhaps traditional dormers."*

It was a radical idea and unexpected. We had to give it some thought and for a moment nobody said anything. I did not intend saying anything, anyway, but it did occur to me that such a solution could cost less that an extension on new foundations. This would have to be gone into and until then it was inappropriate for me to express an opinion.

But Malcolm had opinions, which he was not averse to expressing. "No," he said, and I noticed his fists were clenched. "You can't put dormers or skylights in that roof. And you can't lower the ceiling. It would ruin the whole stable. It would never be allowed. You mustn't think of it!" His face was becoming quite red and set in rigid lines and I looked at him in amazement.

Graham nudged me in the ribs. "Here we go again," he muttered under his breath. "Something's buggering him."

It was certainly unlike Malcolm to behave so irrationally. He was usually a very logical quiet man, good humoured and open to reason. What had got into him, I wondered? We were all looking at him and I expected a storm of conflicting opinions to break out, but Sybil, who was sitting next to him, patted his arm and said, "Don't worry, Malcolm. Nothing's been decided yet. We shan't make any decisions in a hurry. And none of us wants to spoil the place. You know that." Her little speech seemed to have the desired effect: he calmed down and looked at Esther. I expected him to apologise, but his look indicated something more, which I could not interpret. It was as if he were pleading for understanding. Whatever was the cause, the little volcanic eruption was over and the meeting resumed.

Esther wisely went on to other items. "We'll think about how to enlarge our premises and I hope you'll all come back with some positive ideas next time. I'll go into the logistics of Millie's idea and will let you know if it could be viable. Meanwhile we have to consider what we are going to do for our special theme next year. Any ideas?" There were plenty of ideas. They came thick and fast – Clyde ferries, the history of public transport on the island, costumes, education, and fishing. The discussion was lively. It seemed that there was no lack of possible subjects. I was in favour of education. I pointed out we could involve the schoolchildren in collecting artefacts and memories from their grandparents; no doubt many had early photographs and the children could be encouraged to paint pictures of the old schools. Joyce argued similarly for the history of domestic dwellings, but I was pleased when my idea was accepted. This time Malcolm merely nodded his consent. The main items of the agenda having been dealt with, we considered the rest without much discussion. Esther told us about some of the more interesting of the donated artefacts, and we agreed that a new storage heater should be provided for the old cottage. And that was it, until the next meeting.

It was raining as we came out to the car park. I wanted to ask Graham about what had caused Malcolm to act so out of character, but waited until we were on the road out of Brodick. There was a string of cyclists all the way along to Corrie, which meant slowing down, even stopping, at intervals on the narrow road. It was a frequent occurrence in summer but unexpected at this time of year. Concentration was needed in driving, so it was not until after Corrie, when we were beginning to climb the hill, that I broached the subject.

"Is Malcolm ill, Graham? Do you know why he acted so strangely? I don't know him very well, but you all were as surprised as I was when he burst out as he did."

"Huh! Yes, poor sod. If it was me I'd have thumped somebody and got it out of my system before now."

"Got what out of your system?"

"His wife's left. That's what!" Graham snorted with disgust. "I'd say, good riddance to bad rubbish, smash a few things, get drunk and then sue for divorce and start again. But not Malcolm. He has to bottle it up and tear himself apart."

I had noticed he was the quiet sort who kept things to himself. "But they had that holiday together in Cyprus only a few months ago. Surely she wasn't having an affair even then? Wouldn't he have known?"

"If she was having it off on the island here everybody would have known." I thought of Gladys and her propensity for knowing everything and reporting everything, not always accurately. "No, it was worse than that. It happened on the holiday. She got too friendly with the Greek waiter, apparently. They came back and I suppose they tried to patch things up, but she's now upped and gone to join the bugger in his little love nest in the sunshine." And Graham snorted in disgust and would have spat it out if I had not been there, I am convinced.

I had not met Malcolm's wife, and apparently,

according to Graham, she was about fifteen years younger than her husband and inclined to flirt.

"She's always been a flighty piece. Pretty, mind you. Might be all right for the odd fling, but not to marry. It lasted two years, mind you, and I expect he got his value out of her in bed, but I don't think she was good for anything else. He's well shut of her. Poor bugger."

The talk of Malcolm's troubles continued when we arrived back at Lochranza, as, inevitably, Gladys took up the story. She had known the wife, whose name was Anna, since her childhood. Her own parents were divorced while she was still at primary school and she had always been restless and frivolous. "She's still a child, looking for love, but not having the sense to know what it's really about. I always thought she saw Malcolm as a father figure, to give her love and support. It might have worked eventually, but she's been led astray by the glamour of this foreign fellow. It's sad, it really is, but what can you expect of human nature?"

She had been reorganising the leaflets behind the post office counter when we entered and now stopped to put away her spray polish and duster in the cupboard below. As she bobbed up again her plain face cracked into a smile. "It wouldn't happen to us, would it, love? No fancy foreigner for me. Anna's welcome to him. And to all that sunshine. Give me a bit of Arran air and clean rain for a clear complexion – eh, Graham? And whatever this husband of mine married me for it wasn't my pretty face. He's got more sense, haven't you, love?" She chuckled and gave the grinning Graham a playful nudge in the ribs, where he had moved to stand beside her on her side of the counter.

I was somewhat embarrassed by this public display

of affection but stood my ground, as I wanted to make some purchases before going home. I stood patiently and waited for her prattle to allow a gap for me to speak. But before I had time to enumerate my requirements she turned her conversation to Muriel and me.

"You were sensible," she pronounced. "I can admire that – parting and not sharing a bed any more but staying friends. That's sensible when you're older. You know what I mean." She gave Graham another nudge and a wink. "But these younger men, they're all at sea, aren't they. They don't know the first thing about women and think a pretty face will last them a lifetime. Some of them never grow up, and that's a fact." She pretended to straighten a poster behind the post office grille, her face partly hidden by the upright support while she continued her intimate interrogation. "I was thinking of your John the other day. Mrs Brown next door mentioned him. Her Daphne thinks he's wonderful. It's puppy love, of course, but it's made her do her history homework so Mrs Brown isn't complaining. He must be a fine teacher. Is he any more settled with his partner nowadays – that young woman who travels a lot? She's studying, they say."

Gladys knows perfectly well what the situation is. She knows Iolanthe is working for a university degree. There was no need for this innuendo, this assumption that something was wrong with the relationship. Not for the first time I resented her remarks and yet felt inhibited from a harsh rejoinder. She is a neighbour in our small village and I need to patronise her shop, which is the only one for miles. Muriel has assured me that Gladys means no harm; it is only her way of expressing herself and showing genuine friendly concern. And it's true that Muriel has had more dealings with Gladys than I have. Women don't appear to mind sharing their family secrets with relative strangers, but I felt at a loss, not knowing how to reply. I looked at Graham. When in Gladys's presence he is usually taciturn; there is no room for two talkative people in their household. No doubt he is thankful to spend some time with me, when he can talk freely about what is on his mind. Looking at him now for some male support he gave me only a shrug and a rueful smile. I forced a smile at Gladys, said something bland and turned to collect the groceries I needed from the shelves behind me. "I'm going to see him again tomorrow," I said. "I believe he's expecting Iolanthe home on Thursday." With that, I paid her and departed, glad to escape further interrogation.

I might have said more – that Iolanthe's course was almost finished and she would have no more need to go to Glasgow every week, but why should I publicise my family's affairs? The problems that John and Iolanthe are having in their relationship are purely their own private business, which naturally and inevitably Muriel and I share. Village gossips! They should keep their mouths shut! At least Gladys has not heard any rumours about John's thoughts of applying for college work on the mainland. Muriel has obviously said nothing. May it remain a secret until he has made up his mind. I hope he discusses it thoroughly with Iolanthe first; I must warn him not to make the same mistake that I did in making unilateral decisions.

30

I couldn't stop dithering. Which paintings should I submit to the exhibition? I looked at first one and then another. Would they like watercolours or would they prefer oils? The watercolours were on the table in the middle of the room, spread out in disarray while I was shuffling through them. I'd propped the oil paintings against the walls, all round the floor, so that I was alternately flicking through the work on the table and revolving to look down at the floor. No wonder I was dizzy and disorientated! And after all this effort I still hadn't decided. Pull your socks up, Muriel, I told myself. It's a long time since you were like this. You've gained self-confidence, remember? Be decisive!

But it was Sarah who came to the rescue and took me in hand. "Thank heaven you've come," I said as I dragged her into the room. "I'm going mad over this lot. I never realised I'd so many and now I can't make up my mind about any of them. Help!"

"Hey, let me let my breath first," she protested, and took off the deep hyacinth blue coat I so admired. It was of the softest and warmest cashmere, which she told me she had bought in a sale, though I know she could afford to buy as much cashmere as she wanted. I apologised for my abrupt rudeness and explained my dilemma. "I've had the same problem," she said. "But

I've now made my choice and I thought we might go together to get them framed. So let's have a look." She stepped further into the room, approached the table and started to riffle through the watercolours. "I didn't know you had so many. You must have been very busy on your own, as well as when we were together. I admire your industry. I'm afraid I'm lazy. I haven't got such a lot to choose from, but I've picked out three that might be acceptable."

"What do you think? Watercolours or oils? Or both? How many of each? Such problems! I can't decide."

While I was hopping about at her heels she had put aside three watercolours, I noticed. She looked up at me and smiled. "A short list, I think. And now let's look at the oils."

She revolved slowly, absorbing each oil painting in turn, pursing her lips in thought and cocking her head to one side in judgment. "Hmm. Yes, I think that one, perhaps. And that." She pointed and went to pick them up for a closer look. "Yes, why not these two oil paintings?" She raised her eyebrows for my agreement. "This one of the rocky shore shows your impasto technique. It's very effective, too. And this other one of the moorland is more traditional, with a nice wide landscape and distant hills. Then, what do you think about that watercolour of Brodick from the beach – the one you had to do again because that man bought the original? They make a good trio, I think. And we're limited to three. Perhaps it's just as well. It would be even more difficult to choose any more, unless one submitted the whole lot. Perhaps some day you'll have an exhibition of your own – a one-woman show?" She smiled but was obviously half-serious, as if it were a real possibility, but I shrugged away her flattery. She wasn't given to flattery and the thought would niggle at me in the future, I knew, though for now I ignored it and gathered up the three paintings she had pointed out.

"So what now?" I asked her. "What do we do about framing? Do you know anybody?

"Oh, yes. I know one or two, but the one near me is away and we can't wait for him to come back. He's a slow worker anyway. I think we'd best approach Alec Sinclair. He's a quick worker and good at advising on what frames would be suitable. If we explain the urgency and apologise for leaving it so late I think he'll oblige."

I don't know what I expected Alec Sinclair to look like, but I was surprised when I saw that he was not a joiner type of workingman. Definitely not! He could have been any age over seventy, a top-heavy but droopy figure with shoulders like a prizefighter under a heavy head with a brown bearded face full of well-established wrinkles. Old and wizened as he was, there was nothing wrong with his mind. His eyes peered up at us, bright as a button. He knew Sarah from many years back, he said, and would be pleased to help me for her sake. "She's a grand lass. You'll do well to take notice of her. I'll never forget how she helped me when my wife died and I was all at sea and didn't know what to do or where to turn. She straightened me out." He revealed gappy stained teeth in a wide smile as he took the paintings from us and caused Sarah to blush bright pink. I laughed and assured him I agreed Sarah was a good friend. And then, thankfully, we got down to business. He had a bewildering choice of frames from which to choose – gilt plain and simple or ornate, and wooden ones of every size and colour. And mounts for watercolours – really, how were we to choose among such a cornucopia? It took us the rest of the morning but at last we were all satisfied with the choices we had made, and Alec had carefully recorded our decisions. "Come back on the Thursday before the exhibition," he ordered. "They'll be ready then for you to pick up. Without fail."

As we turned away from his workshop behind the cottage that had once been a stable Sarah sensed my fears and doubts, but asserted firmly that we could trust him. She had never known him break a promise or not fulfil an order to time. We would have our paintings ready for the submission day, without fail. I had to believe her and stop worrying. It was the first time I had tried to exhibit anything and no wonder I was nervous. Perhaps, after the first time, one would become more blasé?

Sarah was anxious now to get home again. She was going to have lunch with Ian and Susie; there was some Hydro business that had to be discussed. I decided to have a quick bowl of soup at home and then go over to Lamlash. Iolanthe, I believed, was now home for good and it would be an opportunity to see them both together.

I'd been too busy all morning to notice the weather but now I could appreciate the late autumn mists as they formed and re-formed, now coyly veiling the mountainside like a temptress and now creeping along the valley bottom. I had to watch myself or I would have been absorbed in the changing views and fascinated by the tantalising glimpses of burnt umber landscape instead of attending to the road. But all was well. I met only an Arran Deliveries van and a bus going to Blackwaterfoot via the north end of the island.

Brodick was busy. It always is, or seems to be, though it is only relative to the absence of traffic, both human and vehicular, in Lochranza. I enjoy the contrast and wouldn't have it otherwise. John had chosen a compromise. Lamlash attracted business to its administrative and public offices rather than tourists, and was therefore more middle-class; I preferred the cosmopolitan mixture of Brodick, I decided as I drew up in the car park near John's row of cottages.

"Well! Muriel! How lovely to see you! Do come in, John's up in his study but we'll call him down for tea. I've just made some scones."

And indeed I could smell the aroma seeping from the kitchen and felt quite hungry. Iolanthe looked as I had never seen her before. When we had met by chance on the ferry she had been smartly but practically dressed, usually in trousers and tunics, but today she was covered up in an all-enveloping white cotton garment, a cross between a coat and an apron, or sleeveless overall, crisp and brilliant white as if she were about to perform an operation. Bless her, she was really taking the housewifely role very seriously now that she was home, and I smiled as she welcomed me. The old black leather armchairs awaited us by the blazing fire but I excused myself and chose a higher chair with padded seat and back, giving the excuse of my stiff knees. It was time the old sagging things were replaced with something more comfortable, I thought, and wondered if it would insult them if I offered to pay for some new ones, perhaps a suite? The black ones were John's choice from his student days and I hoped Iolanthe could persuade him to change.

"It's good to see you again, Iolanthe, and these scones are delicious. I won't have any jam, thanks; they're good enough as they are. You're a lucky man, John."

He had joined us by the fire and I was able to have a good look at him. He had been looking so careworn and unhappy for several months past, with the burden of loneliness, I knew. But now, he should be over the moon, with Iolanthe at home and her studies finished. He didn't reply to me but sat there looking morose and withdrawn. I turned to Iolanthe and raised my eyebrows in a mute request for enlightenment, but she shook her head and went on serving the tea.

"What's the matter, John?" I said, frustrated at finding him in such a mood. He had always had such an ebullient personality, even cheeky but certainly bright and cheerful. I'd seen him cast down recently and understood the reason but now? He should be bouncing back, full of life and joy at being reunited with his beloved partner. I couldn't understand but thought perhaps I had better keep quiet. Whatever was the matter was evidently a very sore point and he was not ready to share the problem with me. So there he sat in his corner, brooding, while I enjoyed the scones and talked to Iolanthe, feeling a little desperate for normal conversation. The atmosphere was so oppressive and strained it was a real effort to behave normally. Probably a stranger would not have noticed but I knew them both so well. Or thought I did!

"I've just come from Pirnmill," I said. "I met a funny little man. Sarah introduced me to him. He's going to frame our pictures for the exhibition. Sarah says he's very good, and he seemed to know what he was talking about. He'll have them ready at the end of next week. I told you I had decided to submit something, didn't I? Of course, they might not be accepted, but I thought I might as well try." I was babbling, trying to cover my embarrassment and pretend I had noticed nothing unusual. John raised his eyebrows politely but said nothing. Iolanthe expressed interest and wished me luck. She would go and see the exhibition, she said. "It's to be at the Castle, isn't it?

I've heard about it. They have one every year apparently and it's very popular. Perhaps you'll sell another one!"

The topic of painting was pursued for a while between Iolanthe and me, both of us trying to ignore John's dark brooding figure slumped in the chair opposite. "Tell me about your studies, Iolanthe. I expect you're glad it's all over. How did the examination go at the end? Have you had the results?"

"Oh, yes. Thank goodness it's all over. The results came through yesterday. I've got a First! I couldn't believe it!" Her dark eyes sparkled and her whole face took on a glow which lit up her natural beauty and almost took my breath away. She was an amazing woman, there was no mistake.

I turned to John. He had to be part of this joy, surely. "You've got a very clever partner, John. You must be proud of her! All that work she put in, all that dedication. And now success. Well earned. Congratulations, Iolanthe! It's great news, isn't it, John?" I was trying to get some response from him. What was the matter with him?

He looked up at me then, grunted, and said, "Yes, she's clever. I'll say that about her. She's clever!" And he thrust himself up from the low chair and left the room.

I was speechless. My son John, the extrovert, so proud of the beautiful model who had made her home with him and stayed so long, and whom he was always begging to marry him. There was something very much wrong here. I had felt from the beginning of their relationship, from the first time I met her at our momentous Christmas party, that she was the right partner for John. She has the strength he lacks. And now that she is successful he seems to be regretting his former approval of her studies. Did Iolanthe know what was going on in his mind, I asked?

She frowned. "I'm afraid there have been rumours about me. I didn't know about them, of course, not being here to listen to them. But John has listened. And unfortunately he's believed them – all the filthy lies." She pursed her lips tightly and her hand trembled as she put down her teacup. She was near to tears but trying not to give way. I had never seen her so dejected, sitting there suddenly like a rag doll – beautiful and tragic.

"I know about the rumours. Things get exaggerated out of all proportion. John's very emotional and tends to judge everything in terms of black and white, you know. You say it's all lies – have you explained to him? Something must have given rise to the rumours. There must be an explanation. Can you tell me?" I moved over and took John's vacated chair, carefully lowering myself into its depths. It sagged uncomfortably but I wanted to be near her, to show that I would listen. I also hoped she would realise I was offering sympathy and an open mind.

"They say I'm a prostitute! Oh, Muriel, how could they?" The tears were coming freely now and I passed her my hanky to augment her flimsy tissue. And waited. It was the first time I had seen her less than elegant and self-assured. Even that first time, when she burst upon us like a vision from a glosssy magazine and grandfather insulted her, she was magnificent in being mistress of the occasion. I was impressed then with her integrity and inner strength. She would ride out this storm, surely. But she needed John's support. I sighed.

She sniffed and wiped her face again, looking at me with a rueful smile. "I'm sorry to let go like this, but it is a relief to talk to someone who will listen." She sat up straight and resumed her usual elegant posture.

"I've tried to trace it back, and it must have started when my tutor and I met occasionally in a quiet pub for extra discussions about my work. He's a dear," she laughed. "At least sixty, and happily married. But he's been very generous with his time, helping me out of hours because he knew I couldn't be in Glasgow every day. That's all it was, really. Someone from Arran must have seen us and reported it."

"Yes, I can understand that. But other occasions were reported when you were seen with another young woman and two men at what was said to be an expensive restaurant. What was that about?" I didn't add that the other woman was assumed to be a tart.

"That would be Judy, my flat-mate. We were both photographic models with the same fashion agency until we were too old. She is still in the flat she had then, and offered me a room when she heard I had to be in Glasgow. It's near the university, so it was convenient. We were never close, only colleagues, but we didn't see much of one another as I was out all day and she was out most evenings. It suited me, as I could work at my novel in the evenings and was usually in bed before she returned." Iolanthe looked at me quizzically, as if she wondered how I was taking all this and how far I was prepared to go on listening. I nodded encouragement.

"She has an unusual job. It's easy to misunderstand," Iolanthe went on. "She's registered with an escort agency and has to entertain visiting business men. And before you say anything, it's not what you think. The agency is very respectable and insists on responsible behaviour. The women are mature, well educated and cultured – something like the Japanese geishas. They have to make intelligent conversation and – well – simply be an escort to the restaurant and theatre. And that's it! It's made plain from the beginning that there's no question of going to bed with the client. Judy has her own lover and she's fiercely keen on him. She quite enjoys her work – a free meal, usually stimulating talk and a cheque at the end. But once or twice – I think it was only twice – she was asked if she could entertain two men, foreign diplomats over for some political discussions, so she invited me to accompany the man's other colleague. I didn't mind. The man turned out to be interesting. He told me a lot about his country and the evening passed quite happily and I was even paid for my trouble! But that must have been where the rumours ran riot. Judy is not a prostitute and neither am I." She screwed her hands into tight balls and pressed them deep on to her thighs. "How can I get it across to John? He believes all these lies and says he doesn't want to have anything to do with me. He's moved into the spare room." And tears glistened again on her eyelids.

"Oh, Iolanthe. I'm so sorry. John's behaving very badly. But I can understand the rumours were a great blow. He loves you so much. Perhaps he's been too obsessive and possessive in his loving. I think that might be it." I sighed, remembering my own problems with George. Thankfully we seemed to have weathered our storms and come through them wiser and more compassionate of others' problems. Marriage is no good without mutual trust, I told her, and John would have to learn to trust her if he wanted the relationship to be permanent. How he was to achieve this trust I didn't know. I felt helpless.

"It was a shock. I was ready to tell him I would marry him. I had it all planned. I've had some articles and short stories published, and an agent says she is interested in my novel. I was going to be happy, writing and caring for John, making a home for us and perhaps making a child. And now – well, I'm devastated. And angry, too. He should trust me!"

I plunged in, perhaps making matters worse, but I had to know. "There have been rumours about John, too, you know. Or perhaps you don't know. That he visits the Hydro rather a lot. That he's been seeing Susie while Ian was away. There must be some explanation there. Have you spoken to him about it?"

"Yes. I heard the rumour and asked him to explain. It's all about nothing, of course. He wasn't seeing Susie, except occasionally. No, it was Melanie he was visiting so regularly, for counselling. He's been worried about his future, as I think you know. Whether to move to adult education and a bigger environment. I think he feels unsettled in some way. Perhaps it's because of me being away so much. He says he's decided to stay here. I think he realises he hasn't quite got what it takes to be a college lecturer, and he is happy here – in the school at least."

"Well," I breathed a sigh of relief. "I'm thankful that he's seeing Melanie. She is a very wise woman and has lots of experience. I'm sure she's helping him come to terms with life. In some ways he's still a boy, you know. He will grow up, I'm sure. But we have to give him time. I'll come some day when you're out and give him a good talking to. And I'll have a word with Melanie, to put her in the picture about his problem with you. Perhaps if you were both to go together to see her? She's a wonderful person. I'm sure you'd love her."

Iolanthe smiled through her tears and agreed some marriage counselling was called for. She would try to persuade John. And meantime? "I'll just hang on and try to be patient. I love him to bits and I'll marry him as soon as he decides he can trust me. It's no good being married otherwise. And I want our marriage to be successful."

I left her then, on this more positive note. She is a strong woman; she has made a success of her degree work, would be successful as a writer and would be successful in her marriage. Optimism tried to seize the ascendancy in my mind as I carefully drove home. George needed to know the situation. I must put him in the picture.

31

November 26
I have not been sleeping very well lately. Muriel brought me disturbing news. Her visit in itself was disturbing because unexpected. She and I had never entered each other's apartments since the day we moved in and then suddenly she was ringing my bell and wishing to speak to me. Although we had met socially in various tearooms and restaurants it had always been by prior arrangement and the conversation was kept at a superficial level. It was right that we should proceed slowly if any reconciliation were to take place. Now, however, she seemed to want to force the pace. At least, that was my first thought when seeing her at the door. She too must have been aware of the uniqueness of the occasion, as her face was drawn and anxious and her voice hesitant as she asked if she might come in for a talk.

"It's about John and Iolanthe," she said as I took her coat and invited her to sit in the dark blue easy chair by the fire. To ease the awkwardness we still feel in each other's presence I brought in a tray of coffee and seated myself opposite her, inviting her to take a home-made biscuit to eat with her coffee. "I made them yesterday," I said when she congratulated me. "You know how I got interested in cooking a year ago and now I'm experimenting with pastry and cakes. But

what is this about John? Is there anything new that I don't know about?"

"Well, you know of course that he has been worried about Iolanthe, lonely without her when she was away so much. And worried, of course, about these rumours that were floating about. I don't think you've seen them for a week or two, but I popped in yesterday because I'd heard that Iolanthe had come home for good. I wanted to hear about her final exam and her writing." She paused there and poured herself another cup of coffee and took another biscuit, nodding her approval of my baking. It was as if she were fortifying herself to tell me bad news. I wished she would get on with it but refrained from comment.

"It was lovely to see her home again, and she's got a First! Isn't that splendid? I knew she was clever. And she's had stories published too. And did you know she's written a novel? Some agent is already interested in it so she may get it published! Perhaps we shall have a best-selling author in the family!" She nibbled again at her biscuit and looked at me – pleadingly, I thought, though I couldn't imagine what she was getting at.

"Yes, yes. I always said she was clever. Too clever for her own good, or John's. But you didn't come to tell me how clever she is. What about the rumours? Has John tackled her, as I advised him to do?"

"Yes, apparently he did and they had a row. It's serious, George. Iolanthe explained everything. And he refuses to believe her. That's what the row was about." She paused, as if to let me absorb the news so far.

"Explained everything? I don't understand. How has she explained? What is there to explain? There must be some truth in the rumours. I don't trust that girl. You just said she's clever. Yes, and she's clever

enough to cover her tracks. But go on. What fairy tales did she come up with?"

Muriel looked at me rather sternly but her voice was mild enough when she spoke again. "It was all a misunderstanding. I can understand how it happened. It was perfectly innocent but got blown up out of all proportion. The first story we heard was that she was out with a man, you remember. Well, that was her tutor, helping her with advice about her writing – a happily married man and a purely academic relationship. So that mistake is easily explained. As for the other incident, with another girl and two men, that was a business arrangement. Two foreign diplomats had paid an agency to provide them with intelligent and cultured companions for an evening. It sounds very odd but apparently that's a service they provide. The agency is very reputable, she assured me, and the men were made to understand that there was no sex included in the deal. So that's all it was – a pleasant evening out as a change from her studies."

"Well! And you believe her? It sounds like poppycock to me."

"Yes, I do believe her. I've got to know her a lot better recently and I think she's honest. She told me she genuinely loves John; she had achieved her ambition to get a degree, given the relationship some breathing space to test it and had come home prepared to marry John, work at home on her writing – perhaps another novel – and become a wife and perhaps even a mother. I can imagine how she was brimming with these hopes and all excited about telling John her agreement to marry him. And then, to be met with accusations – ." Muriel broke off in some distress at that point.

We both stayed silent for some minutes. It was a lot for me to digest. Actually paying a strange woman to have dinner with one! Whatever next? Can it possibly be true? I tried to imagine myself in the position of the foreign diplomats, in a strange town and lonely. I had to admit, though I didn't say anything to Muriel, that if I were in that position and wanted sex I would go to an obvious prostitute in a back street. I wouldn't need an agency. But to be seen publicly in an expensive restaurant and at the theatre I would certainly want some intelligent conversation. I suddenly realised, isn't that what I get from Rosemary – the companionship of someone of similar background with whom to exchange ideas and opinions? Thankfully, I didn't have to pay Rosemary, to bribe her, but under the circumstances in Glasgow – well, perhaps? "It's difficult to believe, you must admit," I said. "Are you sure she's speaking the truth?"

"Yes, George. I trust her. She was very upset. I'd never seen her in tears before. It was a great shock, to come home with all these aspirations, thinking John would be overjoyed that she's agreed to marry him. And then to be called a liar and a tart!" *I could see Muriel was very upset but she went on stressing how she was convinced of Iolanthe's sincerity.*

Reluctantly, I said I would suspend judgment, and hoped that they would stay together. It had been in my mind that if they were to separate it would be best if it were done earlier in their relationship, before too much damage was done. But now, as they both declare that they love one another, it would seem wise to encourage them to stay together and talk over their problems. I would not like my son to suffer a lifetime of tacit unhappiness, once love has died, as happened in my case. I said as much to Muriel and she agreed.

"He's our son, George. Our marriage may be over, but we are still parents. How can we help him?"

We agreed – a rare event, but welcome – that there

was nothing that parents could do. He was an adult and must make his own decisions. We would not take sides in this quarrel but would assure them both of our support, and encourage them to persevere in talking through their problems. We might suggest a marriage counsellor if they were open to suggestions.

"And the other rumour, about John and Susie. Apparently that's false as well. He's been seeing Melanie; she's been helping him to deal with his depression and his uncertainty about his future. Iolanthe is going to suggest they go together, so I think there is hope that they might find a way out of their problems. I'm sure Melanie will give them wise advice. I felt I should come and tell you about all this myself, in case any other false rumours got around. You don't mind, do you?"

"Yes, of course you were right. And you didn't want me going to John and putting my big feet in it, did you?"

"Well, something like that," *she agreed with a friendly smile as I handed her her coat and saw her to the door. She knows me only too well, and I am beginning to know myself. I would have made the quarrel worse, I realise, by demanding behaviour that was impossible to achieve at the time. Freedom and living alone has been a time of recollection and discovery. I hope and trust it has been the same for Muriel. Our encounter was peaceful and cooperative, closer than it has been for some considerable time.*

"Congratulations on your success at the exhibition," *I called out as she turned to enter her own front door.* "Gladys told me there were red 'sold' spots on two of your paintings!"

There are times when one is grateful that Gladys passes on the news she hears, for instance when someone dies or is ill. The local grapevine then is invaluable. She is not selective enough in her choice of news, however, and I blame her for causing the trouble with John and Iolanthe. The men who saw Iolanthe in Glasgow should have kept it to themselves in the first place and not tried to make mischief, and Gladys should not have repeated it. I shall listen to her tales in future with a large pinch of salt, ready to refute them. It is not always tale-telling, though; she also provides a sort of amateur social service. For instance, this month – it followed on from thinking about prostitutes in Glasgow – I was in the shop intending to buy my weekly groceries when she emerged from the back room with Jackie, our notorious local tart. The girl was awash with tears and holding her hand to her chest. The hand was bandaged and red with fresh blood, I noticed.

"Oh, George, thank goodness you're here. You've got your car? The poor girl has cut her hand badly. It needs stitches and Graham has taken the car to the mainland. Could you run her to the hospital, George? Please?" Gladys was flustered. The girl had gone to her in distress, leaving her children with a neighbour. She has no telephone, apparently, and Gladys was her lifeline. "I've tried to stem the blood but straight to hospital, that's what's needed. You'll do it, George!"

This final request was more of an order, which I had to obey. I was reluctant to be seen with a prostitute in my car, but could hardly refuse. There were no other customers in sight at the time, who could have been asked to help. And the girl was in pain, that was clear, the blood still obviously oozing out from the bandage. It wasn't too easy, wedging her into my car, with her huge bulk and her damaged hand. But with some shoving and tucking we managed and settled down to our trip over the Boguille to Lamlash hospital. There was some snivelling to start with but after a while she calmed down and began to tell me what had happened. She was opening a tin and the tin-opener slipped and gashed a deep hole in her palm. "It's a bloody mess and it hurts," she said. "The kids went frantic. I dragged them round to Jessie next door, dripping blood over everything, and ran to Gladys's. What else could I do? Bloody hell, I could do without this. The baby's due any time and how can I cope with a bandaged hand?" She turned a pathetic face to me, soliciting sympathy, but I almost panicked and I'm afraid the car swerved out of control for a split second. The baby due! Oh my God! Let it not come now, I prayed. Whatever would I do if it did? I had never been present at the birth of my own children. It wasn't encouraged, it was even taboo in those days, and I'm sure Muriel would not have wanted it, so I had no idea what one should do.

"It's been a right shake-up," she sniffed and fumbled in a pocket for another hanky. "I don't feel very well. I think the baby's trying to get out. Can you hurry up?" She screwed up her face in pain – whether birth pains or the injured hand it was impossible for me to judge, but I flew the last four miles along the shore road, regardless of the speed limit. By the time we got to Brodick she was screaming, though there were intervals of quiet when I asked her how she was feeling. "Shut up! I'm breathing!" was the alarming response. My own breath was held tight in my chest until we got to the hospital, when I could let it out in relief. I hope I never have another journey like that. I felt ten years older and had to recuperate with a beer at the hotel in the village before I felt strong enough to drive home again. At least I was thankful the baby had waited until it could be cared for. It didn't arrive until a few hours later, as it happens. Gladys informed me – of course, she would know. It was a boy and she said

Jackie was going to call it George! I am not sure that I like the idea. It is meant to be an honour, they say, or gratitude in this case perhaps, but what if people think I am the father? Her other two children have different fathers and I've never enquired about them. They say the girl is not exactly promiscuous; she has a regular clientele. Really! It's a scandal in the village, though nobody seems to think so. She's popular with the women, it seems, and Gladys says Jackie has decided to give it up as soon as the children start nursery school next spring; she will be free then to get a normal job. So it appears that her unsavoury activities up to now have been of necessity, to support the family. Or so she says! Her devotion to her family is genuine, however. I see the children from time to time at the shop and they are well nourished, clean and appear to be happy, though somewhat noisy. I have not previously acknowledged the girl, but I am told she now regards me as a friend. It is an embarrassing development from a simple visit to buy vegetables. I shall be more circumspect in future.

The rest of my time this month has been spent mainly on museum business. The committee finally decided that the extension should be within the existing stable and barn. It means the insertion of another floor and staircase, and the skylights that we feared might be disputed by the planning authority. Fortunately they agreed, though not without considerable discussion. Esther was in constant correspondence with the planners about the details but at last we can go ahead with the work. I undertook to obtain three estimates – two from local builders and one from the mainland. These caused considerable discussion in the committee. Understandably, as some members knew the local builders personally, and Joyce was even related to one of them. A lengthy argument took place, from which I held myself aloof. All three were unknown to me and I had no wish to be drawn into the controversy. My task is to pay the bills and advise on the financial aspect. It was a difficult problem, as all three quotations were reasonably close. The arguments went back and forth. Joyce wanted us to employ her cousin, Sybil favoured the other local man; she said he had better tradesmen. Graham wavered between the two, as did the others until Graham said, "Why not choose the one that will promise to do the work soonest and quickest? I think the mainland firm would be best. They'll bring all the stuff ready prepared, and then the men will stay on the island with nothing else to do but get on with the job. With the locals, you never know when they're coming or when they'll finish. They start a job and then disappear for weeks. We want this extension to be open for next season, don't we?" Millie pointed out that we would have to pay for the men's accommodation, but she agreed that if they could start immediately she would be in favour. We had already spent over an hour on this discussion, but eventually it was decided that Esther should contact the Wilson firm in Saltcoats and confirm that they would do as we wished; if they agreed, they would be given the order to start. The next item to discuss was where the money was coming from. They already had my provisional balance sheet for the year-end and it was obvious that we need help. Esther had already been negotiating with various sources and was able to inform us that half the cost would be borne by charitable foundations. This was a considerable relief, as I was beginning to be afraid that we were over-reaching ourselves. I had warned them that we must be cautious. I know the need for development is great, but we have to consider our financial commitments. The ongoing costs must be taken into account and we must not spend to the limit. I think I impressed them with the need for caution and I hope all will be well on the financial front. I reported to them that I had paid all the outstanding accounts and made up the books to the end of the year. The books are now with the auditors. I did not report it to the committee, but I wrote privately to the auditor to explain why there were no entries in the books for the first six months, and then a plethora of entries for the last six months. I hope my explanation will be accepted. Simon, they say, is happy enough in the old people's home, but he is not well. I do not visit him. There is no point in asking him about the financial affairs and I only met him the once.

Now that I have decided on my next year's study, which will be about France and England in the seventeenth century, and sent off the relevant forms I feel free to tidy away my papers and begin to think about Christmas and the visit to Pitlochry. Presumably there will be some upheaval in the household there if Sandra's baby arrives on the date she has given us, but the atmosphere in the family should be much happier this year. It was difficult to bear the strain of last year's Christmas, with Muriel and I newly separated and still suffering and nursing our hurt. During the course of this year we have become more relaxed, which augurs well for Muriel and me. But I wonder what it will be like if John and Iolanthe are still at loggerheads? Shall we ever be a happy family?

32

What an extraordinary thing to do! Whatever has come over him? It's most unlike George. I was flabbergasted when he rang me. "Muriel," he said. "I'd like you to come to dinner with me, and meet my friend Rosemary. What about it?" Just like that! I was bowled over. My mind was in a whirl. In all these months that we've been living under the same roof and enjoying our separate freedom, we've only met occasionally in tearooms or once in a restaurant and just once in his flat. The animosity was gradually wearing away and I think we were both thankful for that. The next move, if I had thought about it, might have been an invitation to dinner in one or another's flat. There was a tacit agreement that the thawing of the relationship could only be undertaken gradually. But the thaw had definitely set in and we were learning to become friends. I had heard that he had become friendly with the librarian and wondered how serious it was. In fact, I had asked myself how much I cared. As I didn't want to live with him, did I mind if he wanted to live with somebody else? Was I jealous? We had achieved the freedom we both wanted, but how free was I really? Did I still want to hang on to him? Did I still want to feel married but have the freedom of single living? Was I being possessive? Such painful questions flashed through my mind at the speed of lightning when I heard his voice on the phone though they had been in my mind ever since I heard of his friendship with this woman. Now there was the more serious question – was this invitation an introduction to the possibility of divorce? It was very odd behaviour, anyway. To invite his wife and his mistress to meet under his roof! Is she his mistress? Do they sleep together? Oh, God, what a mess! What am I to do? I stammered and spluttered over the phone and finally, without fully thinking it out, I agreed to go. My knees were weak after that and I had to sit down with a cup of tea to recover.

By the time the kettle had boiled and I had made the tea I was beginning to think more rationally, however. How possessive was I? Did I really want to prevent him marrying someone else if he wishes it? Did I care so very much if he does sleep with someone else? He had never been very keen on the sexual side of marriage; I always felt he was merely fulfilling what he considered a duty, an obligation. Did it matter to me that he has a woman friend? After several cups of tea I decided that, although I still had niggles of doubt, I must try to be compassionate and realise that he needed a woman's influence and I should welcome the fact that he had found a suitable woman to be his friend. I assumed she was suitable; I had only met her over the counter at the library but she must be intelligent and sufficiently middle-class to satisfy George's exacting standards. I was going to meet her, anyway. The die was cast. I had accepted his invitation to dinner without thinking and in a daze of shock at his phone call but, now that I had had time to think sensibly, I would let the acceptance stand.

The next problem was what to wear. What impression did I want to make? I was beginning to feel angry by that time. Angry at George – how dare he think of replacing me? And angry with myself for being jealous. I didn't want to live with him, so why should I object to somebody else taking my place? At least he hadn't picked up a bimbo. A librarian should be easier to meet over a dinner table. I had seen her several times in the library van in Lochranza. I usually change my books there when it comes on alternate Monday afternoons to the Medical Centre car park. It's more convenient than going all the way to Brodick just to the library, if I need nothing else. Whether in Brodick or in the van, she is always very pleasant and business-like, not much younger than me. Unlike me she is quite big and plump, almost motherly and self-assured. Her working clothes seem to be quite ordinary skirts and jumpers, so perhaps I will wear the turquoise trouser suit with a heather-coloured blouse that I bought in Ayr. I have to do something to boost my confidence in place of this woman's air of brisk efficiency. Giving my hair a final brushing I surveyed myself in the mirror – still a mouse-like, frail-looking little person, but I tossed my head and determined not to be intimidated.

In this mood I faced George as he opened his door to me and led me into his sitting room. When he first saw me his eyes had opened wide in some astonishment and, I ventured to think, in admiration at my appearance. So fortified, I fixed a smile on my face and was prepared to greet his paramour.

"May I introduce Rosemary to you, Muriel? And this is my wife, Rosemary. You may have met one another at the library." We shook hands, mutually smiling the dutiful social smile and sizing one another up, but before we could speak George turned to the man in the room. "And this is Malcolm, Rosemary's cousin. I don't think you've met him. He's on the museum committee and lives in

Shiskine."

After that fraught moment it wasn't so bad. I found I liked Rosemary. I couldn't help it. As is the way with women, we did a lot of communicating without words and I realised she was as nervous as I was. She didn't want to give me the impression that she was usurping me; I was sure of that, and could breathe more easily. George was also a revelation. Gone was the gauche reluctance to be sociable, the shyness with women. He poured us all drinks – he had actually provided sherry! - and kept the conversation going until the ice was thoroughly broken, then departed to the kitchen, saying he would attend to the dinner. I was too overcome by George's transformation to say much but Malcolm was a younger man who chatted about himself to fill the gap. He explained that his wife had gone away – he didn't say where to and I noticed Rosemary gave me a warning look – and the children were out with friends at a disco, so he was glad when Rosemary asked him to escort her for the evening. He and George got on well together at the museum, he said – another revelation of George's metamorphosis! I needn't have worried about my clothes. Rosemary wore a plain tunic of rich red over a long black skirt, quite a sober ensemble, which went well with her rosy face and brown hair. I had no need to be ashamed of my appearance.

We had all remarked on the appetising aroma floating out from the kitchen and were only too eager to respond when George called us to the table. He had changed the dining room around, I noticed. Like me, he had turned it from its intended function into a study or workshop. But now, as he saw me looking around he explained. "Yes, Muriel. I've moved the computer out of the way and tidied up all my papers since finishing the OU course, and now I have a dining room again. "I hope you don't mind," he went on, seeing us all looking at the strawberry-decorated melon slices on our plates, "but I've prepared a simple meal that could be done mostly beforehand and left in the oven until ready."

"Of course," Rosemary said. "Muriel and I know how difficult it is to entertain one's friends and produce a meal at the same time." And she smiled warmly at me as if to a sister. We knew he must have prepared the melon earlier and kept it in the fridge, and I wondered how simple such a wonderful aroma would turn out to be. We were not sure what to talk about at that stage. We had exhausted the personal details that politeness demanded. Rosemary had long been a widow and had no children; she had been brought up on Arran and now lived a few yards along the coastal track. Malcolm was an electrician, had always lived on Arran but in different villages, and had married a Saltcoats girl.

We were glad when George appeared again, his hands swathed in cloth and carrying a large and obviously heavy casserole dish, which he deposited in the middle of the table between the two lighted red candles in silver candlesticks that I didn't remember seeing before. He must have bought them especially for today. With what I realised was an unaccustomed flourish he drew off its cover and announced, "It's lamb and fennel cassoulet. I hope you like it. It's traditional French, with a lot of herbs, but I've used Arran lamb of course. There are some mixed vegetables to go with it."

It tasted as good as it smelt and we congratulated him on his expertise. Rosemary asked him for the recipe but I wasn't interested. I prefer to cook things that are really simple, without all the herb flavours. I suppose I'm lazy, or just have more interesting things to do than cooking.

George had turned the conversation to holidays. Malcolm told us about his fortnight in Cyprus. It had been a special holiday to celebrate their wedding anniversary. "We booked a special package," he said. "We normally don't go very far – perhaps to the Highlands or to an English resort. But the children had been invited to some friends on a farm so we thought we would be more adventurous." I wanted to ask him about Cyprus, but he seemed reluctant to say any more about it.

"I once had a holiday in Morecambe," Rosemary said, turning to me. "George has told me you came from there. I don't remember much about the town. It was a long time ago. But I remember the view across the Bay and the huge flocks of oystercatchers. And the way the tide goes out so far and leaves a great expanse of mud."

That reminded the men about the latest discovery displayed in the museum. George started to tell us about it. "Arran museum has become world famous," he said. "It's a footprint of a creature that lived even thousands of years before the dinosaur. It's incredible that it hasn't been discovered before, but it was a stroke of luck really. A tourist was messing about on the shore, turned over a rock and there it was. Fortunately he was a geologist and realised its antiquity and its importance, otherwise nobody else would have recognised it for what it was. It's unique – the only footprint in the world of such an early date."

"We're very fortunate," Malcolm added. "We've now got a plaster cast of it in the museum, with a brief description. We're waiting for the geologist – a professor from Cambridge – to write a paper on it. Then we'll go ahead with more publicity. It should attract tourists from abroad, I think." It was a fascinating topic and one that we pursued for some time. I had not realised the museum could be such an exciting place. I raised my eyebrows at Rosemary. Had she seen these footprints? But she shook her head and said she would welcome any printed report for the library shelves in due course. She liked to keep the Arran material up to date as the news came in.

"Talking of news, " Malcolm said. "I hear you're quite a hero, George. A knight who rescues damsels in distress."

"What's this?" I queried. "What have you been up to, George?" I put down my knife and fork tidily on the side of my now empty plate and waited. Was this still another facet of George? I was learning so much today.

He had actually blushed! He wriggled in his chair and looked sideways at Malcolm. "It was nothing," he said sheepishly.

"Go on, tell us!" Rosemary urged. "This sounds intriguing."

"Oh, it was really nothing. But I'll tell you when I bring in the dessert. Have you all finished?"

He collected our dirty plates and the remains of the meal on a large tray and carried it all out to the kitchen, returning with a sherry trifle. "Something light to finish with," he said.

"Well, go on!" I was impatient to hear his story. He had served the trifle and was now hesitating again.

"Oh, well, it was Gladys," he began. Of course, we might have known Gladys would be involved. I was agog to know what happened. "I was in the shop when that Jackie girl was there. She'd gashed her hand rather badly and Gladys was trying to bandage it. There was blood everywhere and she couldn't stop it. Gladys said she ought to go to hospital to have it stitched. Gordon was away with the car on the mainland, and I was the only one available at the time with a car. So I had to take her, of course. That's all." He smiled modestly and started on his portion of trifle.

"Oh no. That isn't all." Malcolm intervened. "Did you know Jackie was nine months pregnant? The accident with the hand, the shock and all brought the baby on, and our Sir Galahad raced like a hero to deliver her to the hospital before he had to deliver the baby in his car. But he did it. He rescued them both in time. The baby is a boy and she's called him George. So that's our hero!"

Well, well! Wonders never cease! Fancy George acting the hero! Rosemary and I were loud in our amazement and congratulations. A true Good Samaritan, we said. I could just imagine George's panic and admired him all the more for his action. Truly, we don't ever know one another completely. There is always something more to discover. I was definitely discovering that I liked George. I thought I had loved him once, but I know now that it was my own image of George that I loved. Now I was seeing more of the real man and I liked what I saw. What a pity that the real man could not reveal itself until he had separated himself from me! Was I to blame? Did I stifle George to that extent?

My thoughts were interrupted by Rosemary. "Talking of babies, I believe your daughter's baby is due soon? Have you news of her?"

I shook myself free of more serious thoughts and turned to Rosemary with a smile. "Yes, Sandra says it's due on the 23rd, just in time for Christmas. But one never knows. Thinking of Jackie's coming early, we've decided to go over next Tuesday to be sure of being there in time. We wouldn't like Berry to be left to cope with the three children on his own as well as visiting Sandra in hospital. George and I are going then, anyway. John and Iolanthe can't get over until Christmas Eve because of the school holiday. They'll go on the last ferry on the day they break up; it will be late by the time they get to Pitlochry but it will give them the whole of the next day. I will probably stay on to help with the baby. George can come back with John and leave his car for me. He can use my car when he gets home. So you see, it's all arranged. Except for the baby. And babies have their own agenda, so we have to be flexible." I saw Malcolm nod his head as if he had experience of babies arriving inopportunely. Rosemary murmured sympathy and good wishes, then reverted to the subject of Jackie.

"Have you seen the baby, your namesake, George, since Jackie's been home?"

"Hmm, yes. I just happened to be passing and called one day – just to check that her hand had healed, you know. It was a nasty cut. Bled a lot. It's not healed up yet and some neighbours are having to help out with the baby, bathing it and so on, she said. The baby, George, looked all right, I suppose. That's all. The nurse will remove the stitches here at the Centre, so there'll be no need to drive her to the hospital again."

I smiled, almost laughed. I believed George had called on Jackie deliberately in the hope of renewing their acquaintance and taking her to Lamlash again. George, of all people, going soft in his old age, and over a tart! Though an about-to-be-reformed tart, according to rumour. Dear George! I could have kissed him! Why had he not shown such compassion when we were together? Was it the influence of Rosemary perhaps? I looked at her and she actually winked at me. She knew what I was thinking! So it was something to do with her influence! I realised she had stood up to him from the start and treated him as if they were both equals. That had never been possible for me. It had taken me until now to reach that stage. I should be grateful to her. I smiled and felt an affinity with her. I was glad George had found such a good friend and was sure she would be my friend too. There was no need to be jealous. I straightened my shoulders and looked proudly at George. He was still handsome in his dark brooding looks, though there was silver among the black hairs and his frown lines were more deeply embedded..

"How is your back, George?" Malcolm enquired. I raised my eyebrows, so he explained that George had complained of backache at the last committee meeting. He had said nothing to me when we met for lunch a few weeks ago.

"Oh, I went to the doctor at the end. Painkillers didn't do any good. There was a new doctor – a black man called Singh. All he did was refer me to the Hydro!" George frowned and looked disgusted. I'm afraid we all laughed. But it was Rosemary who gave voice to what we were thinking.

"Oh, George. You're not saying he's no good because he's got a darker skin than you have? And he probably gave you the best advice possible. You said yourself that painkillers didn't help, so the doctor was right in not prescribing any. You're much better to get advice from the medics at the Hydro."

"Yes, George. They assess what treatment is best for you. Didn't you tell me that Graham goes for his back? Well, then, talk it over with him. He'll tell you about it. I've met Melanie there – she's the older one – and the younger couple Susie and Ian. They are all charming and helpful. You'll see." I tried to reassure him.

He had hung his head at Rosemary's admonition, but I was glad that he was not going to argue about his racist ideas. I think she may tease him out of them. She has the right attitude – brisk, no-nonsense but with humour.

By this time Malcolm was getting restless. He said he wanted to be home before the children, so Rosemary gathered up her handbag and George brought their coats. As they snuggled into their fleece-lined winter coats and woollen scarves against the cold night air they both expressed their pleasure at spending such a delightful evening. Rosemary said they must meet again, at her place next time, and Malcolm said he'd like us to meet again at his place. So that was satisfactory! I was glad for George's sake that it had been successful.

I waited at the outer door for George to bring me my coat. As he held it over my shoulders he said, "Have you any more news of John and Iolanthe? It will be terrible if they are still quarrelling over Christmas. There was enough upset last year; I don't want to have another Christmas like that."

"I think it's just a question of time, George. I keep in touch with Iolanthe and she says he is beginning to think more rationally about the affair. He is trying to believe her, she says. But the belief and trust have to come from deep within him; it's not just a case of giving lip service to a belief. So time is needed. She told me that Melanie is helping him a lot. He talks it all out with her. She's a good listener and I think it's better for him to talk to someone who is not part of the family and not so involved as we are. So we'll have to hope that all will be well by Christmas. The new baby will help too, surely!"

"Well, we have to hope. Thank you for coming tonight. I wanted you to meet Rosemary. There's nothing going on, you know. We're just friends."

"Yes, George, just friends. I realise that. As you and

I are, at last, just friends. Something to be very thankful for!"